PLANETS
OF
ADVENTURE

MURRAY LEINSTER

**Edited and
compiled by
ERIC FLINT &
GUY GORDON**

Planets of Adventure

This is a work of fiction. All the characters and events portrayed in this book are fictional, and any resemblance to real people or incidents is purely coincidental.

The Forgotten Planet was Leinster's rewrite and novelization of three novellas published previously: "The Mad Planet" (*Argosy*, June 1920), "The Red Dust" (*Argosy*, April 1921), and "Nightmare Planet" (*Science Fiction Plus*, June 1953). In the original first two stories, the adventure was set on a far future Earth. The rewritten novel version was first published by Gnome Press in 1954. The stories collected as *The Planet Explorer* were originally published as four independent tales: "Sand Doom" (*Astounding*, December 1955), "Combat Team" (originally published as "Exploration Team," *Astounding*, March 1956), "Critical Difference"—later retitled "Solar Constant"—(*Astounding*, July 1956), "The Swamp Was Upside Down" (*Astounding*, September 1956). Leinster rewrote the four stories to give them all the same protagonist and reissued the stories under the title *Colonial Survey*, published by Gnome Press in 1956. The book was reissued in 1957 by Avon Press under the title *The Planet Explorer*. "Anthropological Note" was first published in *The Magazine of Fantasy and Science Fiction*, April 1957. "Scrimshaw" was first published in *Astounding*, September 1955. "Assignment on Pasik" was first published in *Thrilling Wonder Stories*, February 1949. The author was listed as "William Fitzgerald," one of Leinster's pseudonyms. "Regulations" was first published in *Thrilling Wonder Stories*, August 1948. "The Skit-Tree Planet" was first published in *Thrilling Wonder Stories*, April 1947.

A Baen Book

Baen Publishing Enterprises
P.O. Box 1403
Riverdale, NY 10471
www.baen.com

ISBN: 0-7434-7162-8

Cover art by Bob Eggleton

First printing, October 2003

Distributed by Simon & Schuster
1230 Avenue of the Americas
New York, NY 10020

Production by Windhaven Press, Auburn, NH
Printed in the United States of America

CONTENTS

THE
FORGOTTEN
PLANET

PROLOGUE

The Survey-Ship *Tethys* made the first landing on the planet, which had no name. It was an admirable planet in many ways. It had an ample atmosphere and many seas, which the nearby sun warmed so lavishly that a perpetual cloudbank hid them and most of the solid ground from view. It had mountains and continents and islands and high plateaus. It had day and night and wind and rain, and its mean temperature was within the range to which human beings could readily accommodate. It was rather on the tropic side, but not unpleasant.

But there was no life on it.

No animals roamed its continents. No vegetation grew from its rocks. Not even bacteria struggled with its stones to turn them into soil. So there was no soil. Rock and stones and gravel and even sand—yes. But no soil in which any vegetation could grow. No living thing, however small, swam in its oceans, so there was not even mud on its ocean bottoms. It was one of that disappointing vast majority of worlds which turned up

3

when the Galaxy was first explored. People couldn't live on it because nothing had lived there before.

Its water was fresh and its oceans were harmless. Its air was germ-free and breathable. But it was of no use whatever for men. The only possible purpose it could serve would have been as a biological laboratory for experiments involving things growing in a germ-free environment. But there were too many planets like that already. When men first traveled to the stars they made the journey because it was starkly necessary to find new worlds for men to live on. Earth was over-crowded—terribly so. So men looked for new worlds to move to. They found plenty of new worlds, but presently they were searching desperately for new worlds where life had preceded them. It didn't matter whether the life was meek and harmless, or ferocious and deadly. If life of any sort were present, human beings could move in. But highly organized beings like men could not live where there was no other life.

So the Survey-Ship *Tethys* made sure that the world had no life upon it. Then it made routine measurements of the gravitational constant and the magnetic field and the temperature gradient; it took samples of the air and water. But that was all. The rocks were familiar enough. No novelties there! But the planet was simply useless. The survey-ship recorded its findings and went hastily on in search of something better. The ship did not even open one of its ports while on the planet. There were no consequences of the *Tethys'* visit except that record. None whatever.

No other ship came near the planet for eight hundred years.

Nearly a millennium later, however, the Seed-Ship *Orana* arrived. By that time humanity had spread very widely and very far. There were colonies not less than a quarter of the way to the Galaxy's rim, and Earth was no longer overcrowded. There was still emigration, but it was now a trickle instead of the swarming flood of centuries before. Some of the first colonized worlds had emigrants now. Mankind did not want to crowd itself together again! Men now considered that there was no excuse for such monstrous slums as overcrowding produced.

Now, too, the star-ships were faster. A hundred light-years was a short journey. A thousand was not impractical. Explorers had gone many times farther, and reported worlds still waiting for mankind on beyond. But still the great majority of discovered planets did not contain life. Whole solar systems floated in space with no single living cell on any of their members.

So the Seed-Ships came into being. Theirs was not a glamorous service. They merely methodically contaminated the sterile worlds with life. The Seed-Ship *Orana* landed on this planet—which still had no name. It carefully infected it. It circled endlessly above the clouds, dribbling out a fine dust—the spores of every conceivable microorganism which could break down rock to powder, and turn that dust to soil. It was also a seeding of molds and fungi and lichens, and everything which could turn powdery primitive soil into stuff on which higher forms of life could grow. The *Orana* polluted the seas with plankton. Then it, too, went away.

More centuries passed. Human ships again improved. A thousand light-years became a short journey. Explorers reached the Galaxy's very edge, and looked estimatingly across the emptiness toward other island universes. There were colonies in the Milky Way. There were freight-lines between star-clusters, and the commercial center of human affairs shifted some hundreds of parsecs toward the Rim. There were many worlds where the schools painstakingly taught the children what Earth was, and where, and that all other worlds had been populated from it. And the schools repeated, too, the one lesson that humankind seemed genuinely to have learned. That the secret of peace is freedom, and the secret of freedom is to be able to move away from people with whom you do not agree. There were no crowded worlds any more. But human beings love children, and they have them. And children grow up and need room. So more worlds had to be looked out for. They weren't urgently needed yet, but they would be.

Therefore, nearly a thousand years after the *Orana*, the Ecology-Ship *Ludred* swam to the planet from space and landed on it. It was a gigantic ship of highly improbable purpose. First of all, it checked on the consequences of the *Orana*'s visit.

They were highly satisfactory, from a technical point of view. Now there was soil which swarmed with minute living things. There were fungi which throve monstrously. The seas stank of minuscule life-forms. There were even some novelties, developed by the strictly local conditions. There were, for example, paramecia as big as grapes, and yeasts had increased in size until they bore flowers visible to the naked eye. The life on the planet was not aboriginal, though. All of it was descended and adapted and modified from the microorganisms planted by the seed-ship whose hulk was long since rust, and whose crew were merely names in genealogies—if that.

The *Ludred* stayed on the planet a considerably longer time than either of the ships that had visited it before. It dropped the seeds of plants. It broadcast innumerable varieties of things which should take root and grow. In some places it deliberately seeded the stinking soil. It put marine plants in the oceans. It put alpine plants on the high ground. And when all its stable varieties were set out it added plants which were genetically unstable. For generations to come they would throw sports, some of which should be especially suited to this planetary environment.

Before it left, the *Ludred* dumped finny fish into the seas. At first they would live on the plankton which made the oceans almost broth. There were many varieties of fish. Some would multiply swiftly while small; others would grow and feed on the smaller varieties. And as a last activity, the *Ludred* set up refrigeration-units loaded with insect eggs. Some would release their contents as soon as plants had grown enough to furnish them with food. Others would allow their contents to hatch only after certain other varieties had multiplied to be their food-supply.

When the Ecology-Ship left, it had done a very painstaking job. It had treated the planet to a sort of Russell's Mixture of life-forms. The real Russell's Mixture is that blend of the simple elements in the proportions found in suns. This was a blend of life-forms in which some should survive by consuming the now-habituated flora, others by preying on the former. The planet was stocked, in effect, with everything that it could be hoped would live there.

But only certain things could have that hope. Nothing which needed parental care had any chance of survival. The creatures seeded at this time had to be those which could care for themselves from the instant they burst their eggs. So there were no birds or mammals. Trees and plants of many kinds, fish and crustaceans and tadpoles, and all kinds of insects could be planted. But nothing else.

The *Ludred* swam away through emptiness.

There should have been another planting centuries later. There should have been a ship from the Zoological Branch of the Ecological Service. It should have landed birds and beasts and reptiles. It should have added pelagic mammals to the seas. There should have been herbivorous animals to live on the grasses and plants which would have thriven, and carnivorous animals to live on them in turn. There should have been careful stocking of the planet with animal life, and repeated visits at intervals of a century or so to make sure that a true ecological balance had been established. And then when the balance was fixed men would come and destroy it for their own benefit.

But there was an accident.

Ships had improved again. Even small private space-craft now journeyed tens of light-years on holiday journeys. Personal cruisers traveled hundreds. Liners ran matter-of-factly on ship-lines tens of thousands of light-years long. An exploring-ship was on its way to a second island universe. (It did not come back.) The inhabited planets were all members of a tenuous organization which limited itself to affairs of space, without attempting to interfere in surface matters. That tenuous organization moved the Ecological Preparation Service to Algol IV as a matter of convenience. In the moving, one of the Ecological Service's records was destroyed.

So the planet which had no name was forgotten. No other ship came to prepare it for ultimate human occupancy. It circled its sun, unheeded and unthought-of. Cloudbanks covered it from pole to pole. There were hazy markings in some places, where high plateaus penetrated its clouds. But that was all. From space the planet was essentially featureless. Seen from afar it was merely a round white ball—white from its cloudbanks—and nothing else.

But on its surface, on its lowlands, it was pure nightmare. But this fact did not matter for a very long time.

Ultimately, it mattered a great deal—to the crew of the space-liner *Icarus*. The *Icarus* was a splendid ship of its time. It bore passengers headed for one of the Galaxy's spiral arms, and it cut across the normal lanes and headed through charted but unvisited parts of the Galaxy toward its destination. And it had one of the very, very, very few accidents known to happen to space-craft licensed for travel off the normal space-lanes. It suffered shipwreck in space, and its passengers and crew were forced to take to the lifecraft.

The lifeboats' range was limited. They landed on the planet that the *Tethys* had first examined, that the *Orana* and the *Ludred* had seeded, and of which there was no longer any record in the Ecological Service. Their fuel was exhausted. They could not leave. They could not signal for help. They had to stay there. And the planet was a place of nightmares.

After a time the few people—some few thousands— who knew that there was a space-liner named *Icarus*, gave it up for lost. They forgot about it. Everybody forgot. Even the passengers and crew of the ship forgot it. Not immediately, of course. For the first few generations their descendants cherished hopes of rescue. But the planet which had no name—the forgotten planet—did not encourage the cherishing of hope.

After forty-odd generations, nobody remembered the *Icarus* anywhere. The wreckage of the lifeboats was long since hidden under the seething, furiously striving fungi of the soil. The human beings had forgotten not only their ancestors' ship, but very nearly everything their ancestors had brought to this world: the use of metals, the existence of fire, and even the fact that there was such a thing as sunshine. They lived in the lowlands, deep under the cloudbank, amid surroundings which were riotous, swarming, frenzied horror. They had become savages.

They were less than savages, because they had forgotten their destiny as men.

1. MAD PLANET

In all his lifetime of perhaps twenty years, it had never occurred to Burl to wonder what his grandfather had thought about his surroundings. The grandfather had come to an untimely end—in a fashion which Burl remembered as a succession of screams coming more and more faintly to his ears, while he was being carried away at the topmost speed of which his mother was capable.

Burl had rarely or never thought of his grandfather since. Surely he had never wondered what his great-grandfather had thought, and most surely of all he never speculated upon what his many-times-removed great-grandfather had thought when his lifeboat landed from the *Icarus*. Burl had never heard of the *Icarus*. He had done very little thinking of any sort. When he did think, it was mostly agonized effort to contrive a way to escape some immediate and paralyzing danger. When horror did not press upon him, it was better not to think, because there wasn't much but horror to think about.

At the moment, he was treading cautiously over a brownish carpet of fungus, creeping furtively toward the stream which he knew only by the generic name of "water." It was the only water he knew. Towering far above his head, three man-heights high, great toadstools hid the gray sky from his sight. Clinging to the yard-thick stalks of the toadstools were still other fungi, parasites upon the growths that once had been parasites themselves.

Burl appeared a fairly representative specimen of the descendants of the long-forgotten *Icarus* crew. He wore a single garment twisted about his middle, made from the wing-fabric of a great moth which the members of his tribe had slain as it emerged from its cocoon. His skin was fair without a trace of sunburn. In all his lifetime he had never seen the sun, though he surely had seen the sky often enough. It was rarely hidden from him save by giant fungi, like those about him now, and sometimes by the gigantic cabbages which were nearly the only green growths he knew. To him normal landscape contained only fantastic pallid mosses, and misshapen fungus growths, and colossal molds and yeasts.

He moved onward. Despite his caution, his shoulder once touched a cream-colored toadstool stalk, giving the whole fungus a tiny shock. Instantly a fine and impalpable powder fell upon him from the umbrella-like top above. It was the season when the toadstools sent out their spores. He paused to brush them from his head and shoulders. They were, of course, deadly poison.

Burl knew such matters with an immediate and specific and detailed certainty. He knew practically nothing else. He was ignorant of the use of fire, of metals, and even of the uses of stone and wood. His language was a scanty group of a few hundred labial

sounds, conveying no abstractions and few concrete
ideas. He knew nothing of wood, because there was
no wood in the territory furtively inhabited by his tribe.
This was the lowlands. Trees did not thrive here. Not
even grasses and tree-ferns could compete with mushrooms and toadstools and their kin. Here was a soil
of rusts and yeasts. Here were toadstool forests and
fungus jungles. They grew with feverish intensity
beneath a cloud-hidden sky, while above them fluttered
butterflies no less enlarged than they, moths as much
magnified, and other creatures which could thrive on
their corruption.

The only creatures on the planet which crawled or
ran or flew—save only Burl's fugitive kind—were
insects. They had been here before men came, and they
had adapted to the planet's extraordinary ways. With
a world made ready before their first progenitors
arrived, insects had thriven incredibly. With unlimited
food-supplies, they had grown large. With increased size
had come increased opportunity for survival, and
enlargement became hereditary. Other than fungoid
growths, the solitary vegetables were the sports of
unstable varieties of the plants left behind by the
Ludred. There were enormous cabbages, with leaves
the size of ship-sails, on which stolid grubs and caterpillars ate themselves to maturity, and then swung
below in strong cocoons to sleep the sleep of metamorphosis. The tiniest butterflies of Earth had
increased their size here until their wings spread feet
across, and some—like the emperor moths—stretched
out purple wings which were yards in span. Burl himself would have been dwarfed beneath a great moth's
wing.

But he wore a gaudy fabric made of one. The moths
and giant butterflies were harmless to men. Burl's
fellow tribesmen sometimes came upon a cocoon when

it was just about to open, and if they dared they waited timorously beside it until the creature inside broke through its sleeping-shell and came out into the light.

Then, before it gathered energy from the air and before its wings swelled to strength and firmness, the tribesmen fell upon it. They tore the delicate wings from its body and the still-flaccid limbs from their places. And when it lay helpless before them they fled away to feast on its juicy meat-filled limbs.

They dared not linger, of course. They left their prey helpless—staring strangely at the world about it through its many-faceted eyes—before the scavengers came to contest its ownership. If nothing more deadly appeared, surely the ants would come. Some of them were only inches long, but others were the size of fox-terriers. All of them had to be avoided by men. They would carry the moth-carcass away to their underground cities, triumphantly, in shreds and morsels.

But most of the insect world was neither so helpless nor so unthreatening. Burl knew of wasps almost the length of his own body, with stings that were instantly fatal. To every species of wasp, however, some other insect is predestined prey. Wasps need not be dreaded too much. And bees were similarly aloof. They were hard put to it for existence, those bees. Since few flowers bloomed, they were reduced to expedients that once were considered signs of degeneracy in their race: bubbling yeasts and fouler things, or occasionally the nectarless blooms of the rank giant cabbages. Burl knew the bees. They droned overhead, nearly as large as he was, their bulging eyes gazing at him and everything else in abstracted preoccupation.

There were crickets, and beetles, and spiders. . . . Burl knew spiders! His grandfather had been the prey of a hunting tarantula which had leaped with incredible ferocity from its tunnel in the ground. A vertical pit, a yard in diameter, went down for twenty feet. At the bottom of the lair the monster waited for the tiny sounds that would warn him of prey approaching his hiding-place.

Burl's grandfather had been careless. The terrible shrieks he uttered as he was seized still lingered vaguely in Burl's mind. And he had seen, too, the webs of another species of spider—inch-thick cables of dirty silk—and watched from a safe distance as the misshapen monster sucked the juices from a three-foot cricket its trap had caught. He remembered the stripes of yellow and black and silver that crossed upon its abdomen. He had been fascinated and horrified by the blind struggling of the cricket, tangled in hopeless coils of gummy cord, before the spider began its feast.

Burl knew these dangers. They were part of his life. It was this knowledge that made life possible. He knew the ways to evade these dangers. But if he yielded to carelessness for one moment, or if he relaxed his caution for one instant, he would be one with his ancestors. They were the long-forgotten meals of inhuman monsters.

Now, to be sure, Burl moved upon an errand that probably no other of his tribe would have imagined. The day before, he had crouched behind a shapeless mound of inter-tangled growths and watched a duel between two huge horned beetles. Their bodies were feet long. Their carapaces were waist-high to Burl when they crawled. Their mandibles, gaping laterally, clicked and clashed upon each other's impenetrable armor. Their legs crashed like so many cymbals as they struck against each other. They fought over some particularly attractive bit of carrion.

Burl had watched with wide eyes until a gaping hole appeared in the armor of the smaller one. It uttered a grating outcry—or seemed to. The noise was actually the tearing of its shell between the mandibles of the victor.

The wounded creature struggled more and more feebly. When it ceased to offer battle, the conqueror placidly began to dine before its prey had ceased to live. But this was the custom of creatures on this planet.

Burl watched, timorous but hopeful. When the meal was finished, he darted in quickly as the diner lumbered away. He was almost too late, even then. An ant—the forerunner of many—already inspected the fragments with excitedly vibrating antennae.

Burl needed to move quickly and he did. Ants were stupid and short-sighted insects; few of them were hunters. Save when offered battle, most of them were scavengers only. They hunted the scenes of nightmare for the dead and dying only, but fought viciously if their prey were questioned. And always there were others on the way.

Some were arriving now. Hearing the tiny clickings of their approach, Burl was hasty. Over-hasty. He seized a loosened fragment and fled. It was merely the horn, the snout of the dead and eaten creature. But it was loose and easily carried. He ran.

Later he inspected his find with disappointment. There was little meat clinging to it. It was merely the horn of a Minotaur beetle, shaped like the horn of a rhinoceros. Plucking out the shreds left by its murderer, he pricked his hand. Pettishly, he flung it aside. The time of darkness was near, so he crept to the hiding place of his tribe to huddle with them until light came again.

There were only twenty of them; four or five men and six or seven women. The rest were girls or children. Burl had been wondering at the strange feelings that came over him when he looked at one of the girls. She was younger than Burl—perhaps eighteen—and fleeter of foot. They talked together sometimes and, once or twice, Burl shared an especially succulent find of foodstuffs with her.

He could share nothing with her now. She stared at him in the deepening night when he crept to the labyrinthine hiding place the tribe now used in a mushroom forest. He considered that she looked hungry and hoped that he would have food to share. And he was bitterly ashamed that he could offer nothing. He held himself a little apart from the rest, because of his shame. Since he too was hungry, it was some time before he slept. Then he dreamed.

Next morning he found the horn where he had thrown it disgustedly the day before. It was sticking in the flabby trunk of a toadstool. He pulled it out. In his dream he had used it.

Presently he tried to use it. Sometimes—not often— the men of the tribe used the saw-toothed edge of a cricket-leg, or the leg of a grasshopper, to sever tough portions of an edible mushroom. The horn had no cutting edge, but Burl had used it in his dream. He was not quite capable of distinguishing clearly between reality and dreams; so he tried to duplicate what happened in the dream. Remembering that it had stuck into the mushroom-stalk, he thrust it. It stabbed. He remembered distinctly how the larger beetle had used its horn as a weapon. It had stabbed, too.

He considered absorbedly. He could not imagine himself fighting one of the dangerous insects, of course. Men did not fight, on the forgotten planet. They ran away. They hid. But somehow Burl formed a fantastic picture of himself stabbing food with this horn, as he had stabbed a mushroom. It was longer than his arm and though naturally clumsy in his hand, it would have been a deadly weapon in the grip of a man prepared to do battle.

Battle did not occur to Burl. But the idea of stabbing food with it was clear. There could be food that would not fight back. Presently he had an inspiration. His face brightened. He began to make his way toward the tiny river that ran across the plain in which the tribe of humans lived by foraging in competition with the ants. Yellowbellied newts—big enough to be lusted for—swam in its waters. The swimming larvae of a thousand kinds of creatures floated on the sluggish surface or crawled over the bottom.

There were deadly things there, too. Giant crayfish snapped their claws at the unwary. One of them could sever Burl's arm with ease. Mosquitoes sometimes hummed high above the river. Mosquitoes had a four-inch wingspread, now, though they were dying out for lack of plant juices on which the males of their species fed. But they were formidable. Burl had learned to crush them between fragments of fungus.

He crept slowly through the forest of toadstools. What should have been grass underfoot was brownish rust. Orange and red and purple molds clustered about the bases of the creamy mushroom-trunks. Once, Burl paused to run his weapon through a fleshy column and reassure himself that what he planned was possible.

He made his way furtively through the bulbous growths. Once he heard clickings and froze to stillness. Four or five ants, minims only eight inches long, were returning by a habitual pathway to their city. They moved sturdily along, heavily laden, over the route marked by the scent of formic acid left by their fellow-townsmen. Burl waited until they had passed, then went on.

He came to the bank of the river. It flowed slowly, green scum covering a great deal of its surface in the backwaters, occasionally broken by a slowly enlarging bubble released from decomposing matter on the

bottom. In the center of the stream the current ran
a little more swiftly and the water itself seemed clear.
Over it ran many water-spiders. They had not shared
in the general increase of size in the insect world.
Depending as they did on the surface tension of the
water for support, to have grown larger and heavier
would have destroyed them.

Burl surveyed the scene. His search was four parts
for danger and only one part for a way to test his
brilliant notion, but that was natural. Where he stood,
the green scum covered the stream for many yards.
Down-river a little, though, the current came closer
to the bank. Here he could not see whatever swam or
crawled or wriggled underwater; there he might.

There was an outcropping rock forming a support
for crawling stuff, which in turn supported shelf-fungi
making wide steps almost down to the water's edge.
Burl was making his way cautiously toward them when
he saw one of the edible mushrooms which formed so
large a part of his diet. He paused to break off a flabby
white piece large enough to feed him for many days.
It was the custom of his people, when they found a
store of food, to hide with it and not venture out again
to danger until it was all eaten. Burl was tempted to
do just that with his booty. He could give Saya of this
food and they would eat together. They might hide
together until it was all consumed.

But there was a swirling in the water under the
descending platforms of shelf-fungi. A very remarkable
sensation came to Burl. He may have been the only
man in many generations to be aware of the high
ambition to stab something to eat. He may have been
a throw-back to ancestors who had known bravery,
which had no survival-value here. But Burl had imagined carrying Saya food which he had stabbed with
the spear of a Minotaur beetle. It was an extraordinary idea.

It was new, too. Not too long ago, when he was younger, Burl would have thought of the tribe instead. He'd have thought of old Jon, bald-headed and wheezing and timorous, and how that patriarch would pat his arm exuberantly when handed food; or old Tama, wrinkled and querulous, whose look of settled dissatisfaction would vanish at sight of a tidbit; of Dik and Tet, the tribe-members next younger, who would squabble zestfully over the fragments allotted them.

But now he imagined Saya looking astonished and glad when he grandly handed her more food than she could possibly eat. She would admire him enormously!

Of course he did not imagine himself fighting to get food for Saya. He meant only to stab something edible in the water. Things in the water did not fight things on land. Since he would not be in the water, he would not be in a fight. It was a completely delectable idea, which no man within memory had ever entertained before. If Burl accomplished it, his tribe would admire him. Saya would admire him. Everybody, observing that he had found a new source of food, would even envy him until he showed them how to do it too. Burl's fellow-humans were preoccupied with the filling of their stomachs. The preservation of their lives came second. The perpetuation of the race came a bad third in their consideration. They were herded together in a leaderless group, coming to the same hiding place nightly only that they might share the finds of the lucky and gather comfort from their numbers. They had no weapons. Even Burl did not consider his spear a weapon. It was a tool for stabbing something to eat only. Yet he did not think of it in that way exactly. His tribe did not even consciously use tools. Sometimes they used stones to crack open the limbs of great insects they found incompletely devoured. They did not even carry rocks about with them for that purpose.

Only Burl had a vague idea of taking something to some place to do something with it. It was unprecedented. Burl was at least an avatar. He may have been a genius.

But he was not a high-grade genius. Certainly not yet.

He reached a spot from which he could look down into the water. He looked behind and all about, listening, then lay down to stare into the shallow depths. Once, a huge crayfish, a good eight feet long, moved leisurely across his vision. Small fishes and even huge newts fled before it.

After a long time the normal course of underwater life resumed. The wriggling caddis-flies in their quaintly ambitious houses reappeared. Little flecks of silver swam into view—a school of tiny fish. Then a larger fish appeared, moving slowly in the stream.

Burl's eyes glistened; his mouth watered. He reached down with his long weapon. It barely broke through the still surface of the water below. Disappointment filled him, yet the nearness and apparent probability of success spurred him on.

He examined the shelf-fungi beneath him. Rising, he moved to a point above them and tested one with his spear. It resisted. Burl felt about tentatively with his foot, then dared to put his whole weight on the topmost. It held firmly. He clambered down upon the lower ones, then lay flat and peered over the edge.

The large fish, fully as long as Burl's arm, swam slowly to and fro beneath him. Burl had seen the former owner of this spear strive to thrust it into his adversary. The beetle had been killed by the more successful stab of a similar weapon. Burl had tried this upon toadstools, practicing with it. When the silver fish drifted close by again, he thrust sharply downward.

The spear seemed to bend when it entered the

water. It missed its mark by inches, much to Burl's astonishment. He tried again. Once more the spear seemed diverted by the water. He grew angry with the fish for eluding his efforts to kill it.

This anger was as much the reaction of a throw-back to a less fearful time as the idea of killing itself. But Burl scowled at the fish. Repeated strokes had left it untouched. It was unwary. It did not even swim away.

Then it came to rest directly beneath his hand. He thrust directly downward, with all his strength. This time the spear, entering vertically, did not appear to bend, but went straight down. Its point penetrated the scales of the swimming fish, transfixing the creature completely.

An uproar began with the fish wriggling desperately as Burl tried to draw it up to his perch. In his excitement he did not notice a tiny ripple a little distance away. The monster crayfish, attracted by the disturbance, was coming back.

The unequal combat continued. Burl hung on desperately to the end of his spear. Then there was a tremor in the shelf-fungus on which he lay. It yielded, collapsed, and fell into the stream with a mighty splash. Burl went under, his eyes wide open, facing death. As he sank he saw the gaping, horrible claws of the crustacean, huge enough to sever any of Burl's limbs with a single snap.

He opened his mouth to scream, but no sound came out. Only bubbles floated up to the surface. He beat the unresisting fluid in a frenzy of horror with his hands and feet as the colossal crayfish leisurely approached.

His arms struck a solid object. He clutched it convulsively. A second later he had swung it between himself and the crustacean. He felt the shock as the claws closed upon the cork-like fungus. Then he felt himself drawn upward as the crayfish disgustedly released its hold and the shelf-fungus floated slowly upward. Having given way beneath him, it had been pushed below when he fell, only to rise within his reach just when most needed.

Burl's head popped above water and he saw a larger bit of the fungus floating nearby. Even less securely anchored to the river-bank than the shelf to which he had trusted himself, it had broken away when he fell. It was larger and floated higher.

He seized it, crazily trying to climb up. It tilted under his weight and very nearly overturned. He paid no heed. With desperate haste he clawed and kicked until he could draw himself clear of the water.

As he pulled himself up on the furry, orange-brown surface, a sharp blow struck his foot. The crayfish, disappointed at finding nothing tasty in the shelf-fungus, had made a languid stroke at Burl's foot wriggling in the water. Failing to grasp the fleshy member, it went annoyedly away.

Burl floated downstream, perched weaponless and alone upon a flimsy raft of degenerate fungus; floated slowly down a stagnant river in which death swam, between banks of sheer peril, past long reaches above which death floated on golden wings.

It was a long while before he recovered his self-possession. Then—and this was an action unique to Burl: none of his tribesmen would have thought of it— he looked for his spear.

It was floating in the water, still transfixing the fish whose capture had brought him to this present predicament. That silvery shape, so violent before, now floated belly-up, all life gone.

Burl's mouth watered as he gazed at the fish. He kept it in view constantly while the unsteady craft spun slowly downstream in the current. Lying flat he tried to reach out and grasp the end of the spear when it circled toward him.

The raft tilted, nearly capsizing. A little later he discovered that it sank more readily on one side than the other. This was due, of course, to the greater thickness of one side. The part next to the river-bank had been thicker and was, therefore, more buoyant.

He lay with his head above that side of the raft. It did not sink into the water. Wriggling as far to the edge as he dared, he reached out and out. He waited impatiently for the slower rotation of his float to coincide with the faster motion of the speared fish. The spear-end came closer, and closer. . . . He reached out—and the raft dipped dangerously. But his fingers touched the spear-end. He got a precarious hold, pulled it toward him.

Seconds later he was tearing strips of scaly flesh from the side of the fish and cramming the greasy stuff into his mouth with vast enjoyment. He had lost the edible mushroom. It floated several yards away. He ate contentedly nonetheless.

He thought of the tribesfolk as he ate. This was more than he could finish alone. Old Tama would coax him avidly for more than her share. She had a few teeth left. She would remind him anxiously of her gifts of food to him when he was younger. Dik and Tet—being boys—would clamorously demand of him where he'd gotten it. How? He would give some to Cori, who had younger children, and she would give them most of the gift. And Saya—

Burl gloated especially over Saya's certain reaction.

Then he realized that with every second he was being carried further away from her. The nearer river-bank moved past him. He could tell by the motion of the vividly colored growths upon the shore.

Overhead, the sun was merely a brighter patch in the haze-filled sky. In the pinkish light all about, Burl looked for the familiar and did not find it, and dolefully knew that he was remote from Saya and going farther all the time.

There were a multitude of flying objects to be seen in the miasmatic air. In the daytime a thin mist always hung above the lowlands. Burl had never seen any object as much as three miles distant. The air was never clear enough to permit it. But there was much to be seen even within the limiting mist.

Now and then a cricket or a grasshopper made its bullet-like flight from one spot to another. Huge butterflies fluttered gaily above the silent, loathsome ground. Bees lumbered anxiously about, seeking the cross-shaped flowers of the giant cabbages which grew so rarely. Occasionally a slender-waisted, yellow-bellied wasp flashed swiftly by.

But Burl did not heed any of them. Sitting dismally upon his fungus raft, floating in midstream, an incongruous figure of pink skin and luridly-tinted loincloth, with a greasy dead fish beside him, he was filled with a panicky anguish because the river carried him away from the one girl of his tiny tribe whose glances roused a commotion in his breast.

The day wore on. Once, he saw a band of large amazon ants moving briskly over a carpet of blue-green mold to raid the city of a species of black ants. The eggs they would carry away from the city would hatch and the small black creatures would become the slaves of the brigands who had stolen them.

Later, strangely-shaped, swollen branches drifted slowly into view. They were outlined sharply against the steaming mist behind them. He knew what they were: a hard-rinded fungus growing upon itself in peculiar mockery of the trees which Burl had never seen because no trees could survive the conditions of the lowland.

Much later, as the day drew to an end, Burl ate again of the oily fish. The taste was pleasant compared to the insipid mushrooms he usually ate. Even though he stuffed himself, the fish was so large that the greater part remained still uneaten.

The spear was beside him. Although it had brought him trouble, he still associated it with the food it had secured rather than the difficulty into which it had led him. When he had eaten his fill, he picked it up to examine again. The oil-covered point remained as sharp as before.

Not daring to use it again from so unsteady a raft, he set it aside as he stripped a sinew from his loin-cloth to hang the fish around his neck. This would leave his arms free. Then he sat cross-legged, fumbling with the spear as he watched the shores go past.

2. A MAN ESCAPES

It was near to sunset. Burl had never seen the sun, so it did not occur to him to think of the coming of night as the setting of anything. To him it was the letting down of darkness from the sky.

The process was invariable. Overhead there was always a thick and unbroken bank of vapor which seemed featureless until sunset. Then, toward the west, the brightness overhead turned orange and then pink, while to the east it simply faded to a deeper gray. As nightfall progressed, the red colorings grew deeper, moving toward mid-sky. Ultimately, scattered blotches of darkness began to spot that reddening sky as it grew darker in tone, going down toward that impossible redness which is indistinguishable from black. It was slowly achieving that redness.

Today Burl watched as never before. On the oily surface of the river the colors and shadings of dusk were reflected with incredible faithfulness. The round tops of toadstools along the shore glowed pink. Drag-onflies glinted in swift and angular flight, the metallic sheen of their bodies flashing in the redness. Great, yellow butterflies sailed lightly above the stream. In every direction upon the water appeared the scrap-formed boats of a thousand caddis-flies, floating at the surface while they might. Burl could have thrust his hand down into their cavities to seize the white worms nesting there.

The bulk of a tardy bee droned heavily overhead. He saw the long proboscis and the hairy hind-legs with their scanty load of pollen. The great, multi-faceted eyes held an expression of stupid preoccupation.

The crimson radiance grew dim and the color over-head faded toward black. Now the stalks of ten thousand domed mushrooms lined the river-bank. Beneath them spread fungi of all colors, from the rawest red to palest blue, now all fading slowly to a monochromatic background as the darkness deepened.

The buzzing and fluttering and flapping of the insects of the day died down. From a million hiding places there crept out—into the night—the soft and furry bodies of great moths who preened themselves and smoothed their feathery antennae before taking to the air. The strong-limbed crickets set up their thunderous noise, grown gravelly bass with the increasing size of the noise-making organs. Then there began to gather on the water those slender spirals of deeper mist which would presently blanket the stream in fog.

Night arrived. The clouds above grew wholly black. Gradually the languid fall of large, warm raindrops—they would fall all through the night—began. The edge of the stream became a place where disks of cold blue flame appeared.

The mushrooms on the river-bank were faintly phosphorescent, shedding a ghostly light over the ground below them. Here and there, lambent chilly flames appeared in mid-air, drifting idly above the festering earth. On other planets men call them "Will-o'-the-wisps," but on this planet mankind had no name for them at all.

Then huge, pulsating glows appeared in the blackness: fireflies that Burl knew to be as long as his spear. They glided slowly through the darkness over the stream, shedding intermittent light over Burl crouched on his drifting raft. On the shore, too, tiny paired lights glowed eageriv upward as the wingless females of the species crawled to where their signals could be seen. And there were other glowing things. Fox-fire burned in the night, consuming nothing. Even the water of the river glowed with marine organisms—adapted to fresh water here—contributing their mites of brilliance.

The air was full of flying creatures. The beat of invisible wings came through the night. Above, about, on every side the swarming, feverish life of the insect world went on ceaselessly, while Burl rocked back and forth upon his unstable raft, wanting to weep because he was being carried farther away from Saya whom he could picture looking for him, now, among the hidden, furtive members of the tribe. About him sounded the discordant, machine-like mating cries of creatures trying to serve life in the midst of death and the horrible noises of those who met death and were devoured in the dark.

Burl was accustomed to such tumult. But he was not accustomed to such despair as he felt at being lost from Saya of the swift feet and white teeth and shy smile. He lay disconsolate on his bobbing craft for the greater part of the night. It was long past midnight when the raft struck gently, swung, and then remained grounded upon a shallow in the stream.

When light came back in the morning, Burl gazed about him fearfully. He was some twenty yards from the shore and thick greenish scum surrounded his disintegrating vessel. The river had widened greatly until the opposite bank was hidden in the morning mist, but the nearer shore seemed firm and no more full of dangers than the territory inhabited by Burl's tribe.

He tested the depth of the water with his spear, struck by the multiple usefulness of the weapon. The water was no more than ankle-deep.

Shivering a little, Burl stepped down into the green scum and made for the shore at top speed. He felt something soft clinging to his bare foot. With a frantic rush he ran even faster and stumbled upon the shore with horror not at his heels but on one. He stared down at his foot. A shapeless, flesh-colored pad clung to the skin. As he watched, it swelled visibly, the pink folds becoming a deeper shade.

It was no more than a leech, the size of his palm, sharing in the enlargement nearly all the insect and fungoid world had undergone, but Burl did not know that. He thrust at it with the edge of his spear, scraping it frantically away. As it fell off Burl stared in horror, first at the blotch of blood on his foot, then at the thing writhing and pulsating on the ground. He fled.

A short while later he stumbled into one of the familiar toadstool forests and paused, uncertainly. The towering toadstools were not strange to Burl. He fell to eating. The sight of food always produced hunger in him—a provision of nature to make up for the lack of any instinct to store food away. In human beings the storage of food has to be dictated by intellect. The lower orders of creatures are not required to think.

Even eating, though, Burl's heart was small within him. He was far from his tribe and Saya. By the measurements of his remotest ancestors, no more than forty miles separated them. But Burl did not think in such terms. He'd never had occasion to do so. He'd come down the river to a far land filled with unknown dangers. And he was alone.

All about him was food, an excellent reason for gladness. But being solitary was reason enough for distress. Although Burl was a creature to whom reflection was normally of no especial value and, therefore, not practiced in thought, this was a situation providing an emotional paradox. A good fourth of the mushrooms in this particular forest were edible. Burl should have gloated over this vast stock of food. But he was isolated, alone; in particular, he was far away from Saya, therefore, he should have wept. But he could not gloat because he was away from Saya and he could not mourn because he was surrounded by food.

He was subject to a stimulus to which apparently only humankind can respond: an emotional dilemma. Other creatures can respond to objective situations where there is the need to choose a course of action: flight or fighting, hiding or pursuit. But only man can be disturbed by not knowing which of two emotions to feel. Burl had reason to feel two entirely different emotional states at the same time. He had to resolve the paradox. The problem was inside him, not out. So he thought.

He would bring Saya here! He would bring her and the tribe to this place where there was food in vast quantity!

Instantly pictures flooded into his mind. He could actually see old Jon, his bald head naked as a mushroom itself, stuffing his belly with the food which was so plentiful here. He imagined Cori feeding her children. Tama's complaints stilled by mouthfuls of food. Tet and Dik, stuffed to repletion, throwing scraps of foodstuff at each other. He pictured the tribe zestfully feasting. And Saya would be very glad.

It was remarkable that Burl was able to think of his

feelings instead of his sensations. His tribesmen were closer to it than equally primitive folk had been back on Earth, but they did not often engage in thought. Their waking lives were filled with nerve-racked physical responses to physical phenomena. They were hungry and they saw or smelled food; they were alive and they perceived the presence of death. In the one case they moved toward the sensory stimulus of food; in the other they fled from the detected stimulus of danger. They responded immediately to the world about them. Burl, for the first significant time in his life, had responded to inner feelings. He had resolved conflicting emotions by devising a purpose that would end their conflict. He determined to do something because he wanted to and not because he had to.

It was the most important event upon the planet in generations.

With the directness of a child, or a savage, Burl moved to carry out his purpose. The fish still slung about his neck scraped against his chest. Fingering it tentatively, he got himself thoroughly greasy in the process, but could not eat. Although he was not hungry now, perhaps Saya was. He would give it to her. He imagined her eager delight, the image reinforcing his resolve. He had come to this far place down the river flowing sluggishly past this riotously-colored bank. To return to the tribe he would go back up that bank, staying close to the stream.

He was remarkably exultant as he forced a way through the awkward aisles of the mushroom-forest, but his eyes and ears were still open for any possible danger. Several times he heard the omnipresent clicking of ants scavenging in the mushroom-glades, but they could be ignored. At best they were short-sighted. If he dropped his fish, they would become absorbed in it. There was only one kind of ant he needed to fear—

the army ant, which sometimes traveled in hordes of millions, eating everything in their path.

But there was nothing of the sort here. The mushroom forest came to an end. A cheerful grasshopper munched delicately at some dainty it had found—the barrel-sized young shoot of a cabbage-plant. Its hind legs were bunched beneath it in perpetual readiness for flight. A monster wasp appeared a hundred feet overhead, checked in its flight, and plunged upon the luckless banqueter.

There was a struggle, but it was brief. The grasshopper strained terribly in the grip of the wasp's six barbed legs. The wasp's flexible abdomen curved delicately. Its sting entered the jointed armor of its prey just beneath the head with all the deliberate precision of a surgeon's scalpel. A ganglion lay there; the wasp-poison entered it. The grasshopper went limp. It was not dead, of course, simply paralyzed. Permanently paralyzed. The wasp preened itself, then matter-of-factly grasped its victim and flew away. The grasshopper would be incubator and food-supply for an egg to be laid. Presently, in a huge mud castle, a small white worm would feed upon the living, motionless victim of its mother—who would never see it, or care, or remember . . .

Burl went on.

The ground grew rougher; progress became painful. He clambered arduously up steep slopes—all of forty or fifty feet high—and made his way cautiously down to the farther sides. Once he climbed through a tangled mass of mushrooms so closely placed and so small that he had to break them apart with blows of his spear in order to pass. As they crumbled, torrents of a fiery-red liquid showered down upon him, rolling off his greasy breast and sinking into the ground.

A strange self-confidence now took possession of

Burl. He walked less cautiously and more boldly. He had thought and he had struck something, feeling the vainglorious self-satisfaction of a child. He pictured himself leading his tribe to this place of very much food—he had no real idea of the distance—and he strutted all alone amid the nightmare-growths of the planet that had been forgotten.

Presently he could see the river. He had climbed to the top of a red-clay mound perhaps a hundred feet high. One side was crumbled where the river over-flowed. At some past flood-time the water had lapped at the base of the cliff along which Burl was strutting. But now there was a quarter-mile of space between himself and the water. And there was something else in mid-air.

The cliff-side was thickly coated with fungi in a riotous confusion of white and yellow and orange and green. From a point halfway up the cliff the inch-thick cable of a spider-web stretched down to anchorage on the ground below. There were other cables beyond this one and circling about their radial pattern the snare-cords of the web formed a perfect logarithmic spiral.

Somewhere among the fungi of the cliffside the huge spider who had built this web awaited the entrapment of prey. When some unfortunate creature struggled frenziedly in its snare it would emerge. Until then it waited in a motionless, implacable patience; utterly certain of victims, utterly merciless to them.

Burl strutted on the edge of the cliff, a rather foolish pink-skinned creature with an oily fish slung about his neck and the draggled fragment of moth's wing drap-ing his middle. He waved the long shard of beetle armor exultantly above his head.

The activity was not very sensible. It served no purpose. But if Burl was a genius among his fellows, then he still had a great deal to learn before his genius would be effective. Now he looked down scornfully upon the shining white trap below. He had struck a fish, killing it. When he hit mushrooms they fell into pieces before him. Nothing could frighten him! He would go to Saya and bring her to this land where food grew in abundance.

Sixty paces away from Burl, near the edge of the cliff, a shaft sank vertically into the soil of the clay-mound. It was carefully rounded and lined with silk. Thirty feet down, it enlarged itself into a chamber where the engineer and proprietor of the shaft might rest. The top of the hole was closed by a trap-door, stained with mud and earth to imitate the surrounding soil. A sharp eye would have been needed to detect the opening. But a keener eye now peered out from the crack at its edge.

That eye belonged to the proprietor.

Eight hairy legs surrounded the body of the monster hanging motionless at the top of the silk-lined shaft. Its belly was a huge misshapen globe colored a dirty brown. Two pairs of mandibles stretched before its mouth-parts; eyes glittered in the semi-darkness of the burrow. Over the whole body spread a rough and mangy fur.

It was a thing of implacable malignancy, of incredible ferocity. It was the brown hunting spider, the American tarantula, enlarged here upon the forgotten planet so that its body was two feet and more in diameter. Its legs, outstretched, would cover a circle three yards across. The glittering eyes followed as Burl strutted forward on the edge of the cliff, puffed up with a sense of his own importance.

Spread out below, the white snare of the spinning-spider impressed Burl as amusing. He knew the spider wouldn't leave its web to attack him. Reaching down, he broke off a bit of fungus growing at his feet.

Where he broke it away oozed a soupy liquid full of tiny maggots in a delirium of feasting. Burl flung it down into the web, laughing as the black bulk of the watchful spider swung down from its hiding place to investigate.

The tarantula, peering from its burrow, quivered with impatience. Burl drew nearer, gleefully using his spear as a lever to pry off bits of trash to fall down the cliffside into the giant web. The spider below moved leisurely from one spot to another, investigating each new missile with its palpi and then ignoring it as lifeless and undesirable prey.

Burl leaped and laughed aloud as a particularly large lump of putrid fungus narrowly missed the black-and-silver shape below. Then—

The trapdoor fell into place with a faint sound. Burl whirled about, his laughter transformed instantly into a scream. Moving toward him furiously, its eight legs scrambling, was the monster tarantula. Its mandibles gaped wide; the poison fangs were unsheathed. It was thirty paces away—twenty paces—ten.

Eyes glittering, it leaped, all eight legs extended to seize the prey.

Burl screamed again and thrust out his arms to ward off the creature. It was pure blind horror. There was no genius in that gesture! Because of sheer terror his grip upon the spear had become agonized. The spear-point shot out and the tarantula fell upon it. Nearly a quarter of the spear entered the body of the ferocious thing.

Stuck upon the spear the spider writhed horribly, still striving to reach the paralytically frozen Burl. The great mandibles clashed. Furious bubbling noises came from it. The hairy legs clutched at his arm. He cried out hoarsely in ultimate fear and staggered backward— and the edge of the cliff gave way beneath him.

He hurtled downward, still clutching the spear, incapable of letting go. Even while falling the writhing thing still struggled maniacally to reach him. Down through emptiness they fell together, Burl glassy-eyed with panic. Then there was a strangely elastic crash and crackling. They had fallen into the web at which Burl had been laughing so scornfully only a little while before.

Burl couldn't think. He only struggled insanely in the gummy coils of the web. But the snare-cords were spiral threads, enormously elastic, exuding impossibly sticky stuff, like bird-lime, from between twisted constituent fibers. Near him—not two yards away—the creature he had wounded thrashed and fought to reach him, even while shuddering in anguish.

Burl had reached the absolute limit of panic. His arms and breast were greasy from the oily fish; the sticky web did not adhere to them. But his legs and body were inextricably tangled by his own frantic struggling in the gummy and adhesive elastic threads. They had been spread for prey. He was prey.

He paused in his blind struggle, gasping from pure exhaustion. Then he saw, not five yards away, the silvery and black monster he had mocked so recently now patiently waiting for him to cease his struggles. The tarantula and the man were one to its eyes—one struggling thing that had fallen opportunely into its trap. They were moving but feebly, now. The web-spider advanced delicately, swinging its huge bulk nimbly, paying out a silken cable behind it as it approached.

Burl's arms were free; he waved them wildly, shrieking at the monster. The spider paused. Burl's moving arms suggested mandibles that might wound.

Spiders take few chances. This one drew near cautiously, then stopped. Its spinnerets became busy and with one of its eight legs, used like an arm, it flung a

sheet of gummy silk impartially over the tarantula and
the man.

Burl fought against the descending shroud. He strove
to thrust it away, futilely. Within minutes he was completely covered in a coarse silken fabric that hid even
the light from his eyes. He and his enemy, the monstrous tarantula, were beneath the same covering. The
tarantula moved feebly.

The shower ceased. The web-spider had decided
they were helpless. Then Burl felt the cables of the
web give slightly as the spider approached to sting and
suck the juices from its prey.

The web yielded gently. Burl froze in an ecstasy of
horror. But the tarantula still writhed in agony upon
the spear piercing it. It clashed its jaws, shuddering
upon the horny shaft.

Burl waited for the poison-fangs to be thrust into
him. He knew the process. He had seen the leisurely fashion in which the web-spider delicately
stung its victim, then withdrew to wait with horrible
patience for the poison to take effect. When the
victim no longer struggled, it drew near again to
suck out the juices—first from one joint or limb and
then from another—leaving a creature once vibrant
with life a shrunken, withered-husk, to be flung from
the web at nightfall.

The bloated monstrosity now moved meditatively
about the double object swathed in silk. Only the
tarantula stirred. Its bulbous abdomen stirred the
concealing shroud. It throbbed faintly as it still
struggled with the spear in its vitals. The irregularly
rounded projection was an obvious target for the web-
spider. It moved quickly forward. With fine, merciless
precision, it stung.

The tarantula seemed to go mad with pain. Its legs
struck out purposelessly, in horrible gestures of delirious

suffering. Burl screamed as a leg touched him. He
struggled no less wildly.

His arms and head were enclosed by the folds of
silk, but not glued to it because of the grease. Clutching
at the cords he tried desperately to draw himself away
from his deadly neighbor. The threads wouldn't break,
but they did separate. A tiny opening appeared.

One of the tarantula's horribly writhing legs touched
him again. With a strength born of utter panic he
hauled himself away and the opening enlarged. Another
lunge and Burl's head emerged into the open air. He
was suspended twenty feet above the ground, which
was almost carpeted with the chitinous remains of past
victims of this same web.

Burl's head and breast and arms were free. The fish
slung over his shoulder had shed its oil upon him
impartially. But the lower part of his body was held
firm by the viscous gumminess of the web-spider's cord.
It was vastly more adhesive than any bird-lime ever
made by men.

He hung in the little window for a moment, despairing. Then he saw the bulk of his captor a little distance away, waiting patiently for its poison to work and
its prey to cease struggling. The tarantula was no more
than shuddering now. Soon it would be quite still and
the black-bellied creature would approach for its meal.

Burl withdrew his head and thrust desperately at the
sticky stuff about his loins and legs. The oil upon his
hands kept them free. The silk shroud gave a little. Burl
grasped at the thought as at a straw. He grasped the
fish and tore it, pushing frantically at his own body with
the now-rancid, scaly, odorous mass. He scraped gum
from his legs with the fish, smearing the rancid oils
all over them in the process.

He felt the web tremble again. To the spider Burl's
movements meant that its poison had not taken full

effect. Another sting seemed to be necessary. This time
it would not insert its sting into the quiescent tarantula, but where there was still life. It would send its
venom into Burl.

He gasped and drew himself toward his window as
if he would have pulled his legs from his body. His
head emerged. His shoulders—half his body was out
of the hole.

The great spider surveyed him and made ready to
cast more of its silken stuff upon him. The spinnerets
became active. A leg gathered it up.

The sticky stuff about Burl's feet gave way.

He shot out of the opening and fell heavily, sprawling upon the earth below and crashing into the
shrunken shell of a flying beetle that had blundered
into the snare and not escaped as he had done.

Burl rolled over and over and then sat up. An angry,
foot-long ant stood before him, its mandibles extended
threateningly, while a shrill stridulation filled the air.

In ages past, back on Earth—where most ants were
to be measured in fractions of an inch—the scientists
had debated gravely whether their tribe possessed a
cry. They believed that certain grooves upon the body
of the insect, like those upon the great legs of the
cricket, might be the means of making a sound too
shrill for human ears to catch. It was greatly debated,
but evidence was hard to obtain.

Burl did not need evidence. He knew that the
stridulation was caused by the insect before him,
though he had never wondered how it was produced.
The cry was emitted to summon other ants from its
city to help it in difficulty or good fortune.

Harsh clickings sounded fifty or sixty feet away;
comrades were coming. And while only army ants were
normally dangerous, any tribe of ants could be formidable when aroused. It was overwhelming enough to

pull down and tear a man to shreds as a pack of infuriated fox-terriers might do on Earth.

Burl fled without further delay, nearly colliding with
one of the web's anchor-cables. Then he heard the shrill
outcry subside. The ant, short-sighted as all its kind,
no longer felt threatened. It went peacefully about the
business Burl had interrupted. Presently it found some
edible carrion among the debris from the spider-web
and started triumphantly back to its city.

Burl sped on for a few hundred yards and then
stopped. He was shaken and dazed. For the moment,
he was as timid and fearful as any other man in his
tribe. Presently he would realize the full meaning of
the unparalleled feat he had performed in escaping
from the giant spider web while cloaked with folds of
gummy silk. It was not only unheard-of; it was unimaginable! But Burl was too shaken to think of it now.

Rather quaintly, the first sensation that forced itself
into his consciousness was that his feet hurt. The gluey
stuff from the web still stuck to his soles, picking up
small objects as he went along. Old, ant-gnawed fragments of insect armor pricked him so persistently, even
through his toughened foot-soles, that he paused to
scrape them away, staring fearfully about all the while.
After a dozen steps more he was forced to stop again.

It was this nagging discomfort, rather than vanity
or an emergency which caused Burl to discover-
imagine-blunder into a new activity as epoch-making
as anything else he had done. His brain had been
uncommonly stimulated in the past twenty-some hours.
It had plunged him into at least one predicament
because of his conceiving the idea of stabbing something, but it had also allowed him escape from another
even more terrifying one just now. In between it had
led to the devising of a purpose—the bringing of Saya
here—though that decision was not so firmly fixed as

it had been before the encounter with the web-spider. Still, it had surely been reasoning of a sort that told him to grease his body with the fish. Otherwise he would now be following the tarantula as a second course for the occupant of the web.

Burl looked cautiously all about him. It seemed to be quite safe. Then, quite deliberately, he sat down to think. It was the first time in his life that he had ever deliberately contemplated a problem with the idea of finding an answer to it. And the notion of doing such a thing was epoch-making—on this planet!

He examined his foot. The sharp edges of pebbles and the remnants of insect-armor hurt his feet when he walked. They had done so ever since he had been born, but never before had his feet been sticky, so that the irritation from one object persisted for more than a step. He carefully picked away each sharp-pointed fragment, one by one. Partly coated with the half-liquid gum, they even tended to cling to his fingers, except where the oil was thick.

Burl's reasoning had been of the simplest sort. He had contemplated a situation—not deliberately but because he had to—and presently his mind showed him a way out of it. It was a way specifically suited to the situation. Here he faced something different. Presently he applied the answer of one problem to a second problem. Oil on his body had let him go free of things that would stick to him. Here things stuck to his feet; so he oiled them.

And it worked. Burl strode away, almost—but not completely—untroubled by the bothersome pebbles and bits of discarded armor. Then he halted to regard himself with astonished appreciation. He was still thirty-five miles from his tribe; he was naked and unarmed, utterly ignorant of wood and fire and weapons other than the one he had lost. But he

paused to observe with some awe that he was very
wonderful indeed.

He wanted to display himself. But his spear was
gone. So Burl found it necessary to think again. And
the remarkable thing about it was that he succeeded.

In a surprisingly brief time he had come up with
a list of answers. He was naked, so he would find
garments for himself. He was weaponless: he would
find himself a spear. He was hungry and he would seek
food. Since he was far from his tribe, he would go to
them. And this was, in a fashion, quite obviously
thought; but it was not obvious on the forgotten planet
because it had been futile—up to now. The importance
of such thought in the scheme of things was that men
had not been thinking even so simply as this, living only
from minute to minute. Burl was fumbling his way into
a habit of thinking from problem to problem. And that
was very important indeed.

Even in the advanced civilization of other planets,
few men really used their minds. The great majority
of people depended on machines not only for computations but decisions as well. Any decisions not made
by machines most men left to their leaders. Burl's
tribesfolk thought principally with their stomachs,
making few if any decisions on any other basis—though
they did act, very often, under the spur of fear. Fear-
inspired actions, however, were not thought out. Burl
was thinking out his actions.

There would be consequences.

He faced upstream and began to move again, slowly
and warily, his eyes keenly searching out the way ahead,
ears alert for the slightest sound of danger. Gigantic
butterflies, riotous in coloring, fluttered overhead
through the hazy air. Sometimes a grasshopper hurtled
from one place to another like a projectile, its transparent wings beating frantically. Now and then a wasp

sped by, intent upon its hunting, or a bee droned heavily alone, anxious and worried, striving to gather pollen in a nearly flowerless world.

Burl marched on. From somewhere far behind him came a very faint sound. It was a shrill noise, but very distant indeed. Absorbed in immediate and nearby matters, Burl took no heed. He had the limited local viewpoint of a child. What was near was important and what was distant could be ignored. Anything not imminent still seemed to him insignificant—and he was preoccupied.

The source of this sound was important, however. Its origin was a myriad of clickings compounded into a single noise. It was, in fact, the far-away but yet perceptible sound of army ants on the march. The locusts of Earth were very trivial nuisances compared to the army ants of this planet.

Locusts, in past ages on Earth, had eaten all green things. Here in the lowlands were only giant cabbages and a few rank, tenacious growths. Grasshoppers were numerous here, but could never be thought of as a plague; they were incapable of multiplying to the size of locust hordes. Army ants, however . . .

But Burl did not notice the sound. He moved forward briskly though cautiously, searching the fungus-landscape for any sign of garments, food, and weapons. He confidently expected to find all of them within a short distance. Indeed, he did find food very soon. No more than a half mile ahead he found a small cluster of edible fungi.

With no special elation, Burl broke off a food supply from the largest of them. Naturally, he took more than he could possibly eat at one time. He went on, nibbling at a big piece of mushroom abstractedly, past a broad plain, more than a mile across and broken into odd little hillocks by gradually ripening mushrooms which were unfamiliar to him. In several places the ground had been pushed aside by rounded objects, only the tips showing. Blood-red hemispheres seemed to be forcing themselves through the soil, so they might reach the outer air. Careful not to touch any of them, Burl examined the hillocks curiously as he entered the plain. They were strange, and to Burl most strange things meant danger. In any event, he had two conscious purposes now. He wanted garments and weapons.

Reaching the farther side of the plain, Burl found himself threading the aisles of a fungus forest in which the growths were misshapen travesties of the trees which could not live here. Bloated yellow limbs branched off from rounded swollen trunks. Here and there a pear-shaped puffball, Burl's height and half his height again, waited until a chance touch should cause it to shoot upward a curling puff of infinitely fine dust.

He continued to move with caution. There were dangers here, but he went forward steadily. He still held a great mass of edible mushroom under one arm and from time to time broke off a fragment, chewing it meditatively. But always his eyes searched here and there for threats of harm.

Behind him the faint, shrill outcry had risen only slightly in volume. It was still too far away to attract his notice. Army ants, however, were working havoc in the distance. By thousands and millions, myriads of them advanced across the fungoid soil. They clambered over every eminence. They descended into every depression. Their antennae waved restlessly. Their mandibles were extended threateningly. The ground was black with them, each one more than ten inches long.

A single such creature, armored and fearless as it was, could be formidable enough to an unarmed and naked man like Burl. The better part of discretion would be avoidance. But numbering in the thousands and millions, they were something which could not be avoided. They advanced steadily and rapidly; the chorus of shrill stridulations and clickings marking their progress.

Great, inoffensive caterpillars crawling over the huge cabbages heard the sound of their coming, but were too stupid to flee. The black multitudes blanketed the rank vegetables. Tiny, voracious jaws tore at the flaccid masses of greasy flesh.

The caterpillars strove to throw off their assailants by writhings and contortions—uselessly. The bees fought their entrance into the monster hives with stings and wing-beats. Moths took to the air in daylight with dazzled, blinded eyes. But nothing could withstand the relentless hordes of small black things that reeked of formic acid and left the ground behind them empty of life.

Before the horde was a world of teeming life, where mushrooms and other fungi fought with thinning numbers of cabbages and mutant earth-weeds for a foothold. Behind the black multitude was—nothing. Mushrooms, cabbages, bees, wasps, crickets, grubs— every living thing that could not flee before the creeping black tide reached it was lost, torn to bits by tiny mandibles.

Even the hunting spiders and tarantulas fell before the black host. They killed many in their desperate self-defense, but the army ants could overwhelm anything— anything at all—by sheer numbers and ferocity. Killed or wounded ants served as food for their sound comrades. Only the web spiders sat unmoved and immovable in their colossal snares, secure in the knowledge that their gummy webs could not be invaded along the slender supporting cables.

3. THE PURPLE HILLS

The army ants flowed over the ground like a surging, monstrous, inky tide. Their vanguard reached the river and recoiled. Burl was perhaps five miles away when they changed their course. The change was made without confusion, the leaders somehow communicating the altered line of march to those behind them.

Back on Earth, scientists had gravely debated the question of how ants conveyed ideas to each other. Honeybees, it was said, performed elaborate ritual dances to exchange information. Ants, it had been observed, had something less eccentric. A single ant, finding a bit of booty too big for it to manage alone, would return to its city to secure the help of others. From that fact men had deduced that a language of gestures made with crossed antennae must exist.

Burl had no theories. He merely knew facts, but he did know that ants could and did pass information to one another. Now, however, he moved cautiously along toward the sleeping-place of his tribe in complete

ignorance of the black blanket of living creatures
spreading over the ground behind him.

A million tragedies marked the progress of the insect
army. There was a tiny colony of mining bees, their
habits unchanged despite their greater size, here on
the forgotten planet. A single mother, four feet long,
had dug a huge gallery with some ten off-shooting cells,
in which she had laid her eggs and fed her grubs with
hard-gathered pollen. The grubs had waxed fat and
large, become bees, and laid eggs in their turn within
the same gallery their mother had dug out for them.

Ten bulky insects now foraged busily to feed their
grubs within the ancestral home, while the founder of
the colony had grown draggled and wingless with the
passing of time. Unable to bring in food, herself, the
old bee became the guardian of the hive. She closed
the opening with her head, making a living barrier
within the entrance. She withdrew only to grant admis-
sion or exit to the duly authorized members—her
daughters.

The ancient concierge of the underground dwelling
was at her post when the wave of army ants swept over.
Tiny, evil-smelling feet trampled upon her and she
emerged to fight with mandible and sting for the sanc-
tity of her brood. Within moments she was a shaggy
mass of biting ants. They rent and tore at her chitinous armor. But she fought on madly, sounding a
buzzing alarm to the colonists yet within.

They came out, fighting as they came: ten huge bees,
each four to five feet long and fighting with legs and
jaws, with wing and mandible, and with all the ferocity of so many tigers. But the small ants covered them,
snapping at their multiple eyes, biting at the tender
joints in their armor—and sometimes releasing the
larger prey to leap upon an injured comrade, wounded
by the monster they battled together.

Such a fight, however, could have but one end. Struggle as the bees might, they were powerless against their unnumbered assailants. They were being devoured even as they fought. And before the last of the ten was down the underground gallery had been gutted both of the stored food brought by the adult defenders and the last morsels of what had been young grubs, too unformed to do more than twitch helplessly, inoffensively, as they were torn to shreds.

When the army ants went on there were merely an empty tunnel and a few fragments of tough armor, unappetizing even to the ants.

Burl heard them as he meditatively inspected the scene of a tragedy of not long before. The rent and scraped fragments of a great beetle's shiny casing lay upon the ground. A greater beetle had come upon the first and slain him. Burl regarded the remains of the meal.

Three or four minims, little ants barely six inches long, foraged industriously among the bits. A new ant-city was to be formed and the queen lay hidden half a mile away. These were the first hatchlings. They would feed their younger kindred until they grew large enough to take over the great work of the ant-city. Burl ignored the minims. He searched for a weapon of some sort. Behind him the clicking, high-pitched roar of the horde of army ants increased in volume.

He turned away disgustedly. The best thing he could find in the way of a weapon was a fiercely-toothed hind-leg. When he picked it up an angry whine rose from the ground. One of the minims had been struggling to detach a morsel of flesh from the leg-joint. Burl had snatched the tidbit from him.

The little creature was surely no more than half a foot long, but it advanced angrily upon Burl, shrilling a challenge. He struck with the beetle's leg and crushed the ant. Two of the other minims appeared, attracted by the noise the first had made. They discovered the crushed body of their fellow, unceremoniously dismembered it, and bore it away in triumph.

Burl went on, swinging the toothed limb in his hand. The sound behind him became a distant whispering, high-pitched and growing steadily nearer. The army ants swept into a mushroom forest and the yellow, umbrella-like growths soon swarmed with the black creatures.

A great bluebottle fly, shining with a metallic luster, stood beneath a mushroom on the ground. The mushroom was infected with maggots which exuded a solvent pepsin that liquefied the firm white meat. They swam ecstatically in the liquid gruel, some of which dripped and dripped to the ground. The bluebottle was sipping the dark-colored liquid through its long proboscis, quivering with delight as it fed on the noisomeness.

Burl drew near and struck. The fly collapsed in a quivering heap. Burl stood over it for an instant and pondered.

The army ants were nearer, now. They swarmed down into a tiny valley, rushing into and through a little brook over which Burl had leaped. Since ants can remain underwater for a long time without drowning, the small stream was not even dangerous. Its current did sweep some of them away. A great many of them, however, clung together until they choked its flow by the mass of their bodies, the main force marching across the bridge they constituted.

The ants reached a place about a quarter of a mile to the left of Burl's line of march, perhaps a mile from the spot where he stood over the dead bluebottle. There was an expanse of some acres in which the giant, rank cabbages had so far succeeded in their competition with the world of fungi. The pale, cross-shaped flowers of the cabbages formed food for many bees. The leaves fed numberless grubs and worms. Under the fallen-away dead foliage—single leaves were twenty feet across at their largest—crickets hid and fed.

The ant-army flowed into this space, devouring every living thing it encountered. A terrible din arose. The crickets hurtled away in erratic leapings. They shot aimlessly in any direction. More than half of them landed blindly in the carpeting of clicking black bodies which were the ants from whose vanguard they had fled. Their blind flight had no effect save to give different individuals the opportunity to seize them as they fell and instantly begin to devour them. As they were torn to fragments, horrible screamings reached Burl's ears.

A single such cry of agony would not have attracted Burl's attention. He lived in a world of nightmare horror. But a chorus of creatures in torment made him look up. This was no minor horror. Something wholesale was in progress. He jerked his head about to see what it was.

A wild stretch of sickly yellow fungus was interspersed here and there with a squat toadstool, or a splash of vivid color where one of the many rusts had found a foothold. To the left a group of branched fungoids clustered in silent mockery of a true forest. Burl saw the faded green of the cabbages.

With the sun never shining on the huge leaves save through the cloud-bank overhead, the cabbages were not vivid. There were even some moldy yeasts of a brighter green and slime much more luridly tinted. Even so, the cabbages were the largest form of true vegetation Burl had ever seen. The nodding white cruciform flowers stood out plainly against the yellowish, pallid green of the leaves. But as Burl gazed at them, the green slowly became black.

Three great grubs, in lazy contentment, were eating ceaselessly of the cabbages on which they rested. Suddenly first one and then another began to jerk spasmodically. Burl saw that around each of them a rim of black had formed. Then black motes milled all over them.

The grubs became black-covered with biting, devouring ants. The cabbages became black. The frenzied contortions of the grubs told of the agonies they underwent as they were literally devoured alive. And then Burl saw a black wave appear at the nearer edge of the stretch of yellow fungus. A glistening, living flood flowed forward over the ground with a roar of clickings and a persistent overtone of shrill stridulations.

Burl's scalp crawled. He knew what this meant. And he did not pause to think. With a gasp of pure panic he turned and fled, all intellectual preoccupation forgotten.

The black tide came on after him.

He flung away the edible mushroom he had carried under his arm. Somehow, though, he clung to the sharp-toothed club as he darted between tangled masses of fungus, ignoring now the dangers that ordinarily called for vast caution.

Huge flies appeared. They buzzed about him loudly. Once he was struck on the shoulder by one of them— at least as large as his hand—and his skin torn by its swiftly vibrating wings.

He brushed it away and sped on. But the oil with which he was partly covered had turned rancid, now, and the fetid odor attracted them. There were half a dozen—then a dozen—creatures the size of pheasants, droning and booming as they kept pace with his wild flight.

A weight pressed onto his head. It doubled. Two of the disgusting creatures had settled upon his oily hair to sip the stuff through their hairy feeding-tubes. Burl shook them off with his hand and raced madly on, his ears attuned to the sounds of the ants behind him.

That clicking roar continued, but in Burl's ears it was almost drowned out by the noise made by the halo of flies accompanying him. Their buzzing had deepened in pitch with the increase in size of all their race. It was now the note close to the deepest bass tone of an organ. Yet flies—though greatly enlarged on the forgotten planet—had not become magnified as much as some of the other creatures. There were no great heaps of putrid matter for them to lay their eggs in. The ants were busy scavengers, carting away the debris of tragedies in the insect world long before it could acquire the gamey flavor beloved of fly-maggots. Only in isolated spots were the flies really numerous. In such places they clustered in clouds.

Such a cloud began to form about Burl as he fled. It seemed as though a miniature whirlwind kept pace with him—a whirlwind composed of furry, revolting bodies and multi-faceted eyes. Fleeing, Burl had to swing his club before him to clear the way. Almost every stroke was interrupted by an impact against some thinly-armored body which collapsed with the spurting of reddish liquid.

Then an anguish as of red-hot iron struck upon Burl's back. One of the stinging flies had thrust its sharp-tipped proboscis into his flesh to suck the blood. Burl uttered a cry and ran full-tilt into the stalk of a blackened, draggled toadstool.

There was a curious crackling as of wet punk. The toadstool collapsed upon itself with a strange splashing sound. A great many creatures had laid their eggs in it, until now it was a seething mass of corruption and ill-smelling liquid.

When the toadstool crashed to the ground, it

crumbled into a dozen pieces, spattering the earth for yards all about with stinking stuff in which tiny, headless maggots writhed convulsively.

The deep-toned buzzing of the flies took on a note of solemn satisfaction. They settled down upon this feast. Burl staggered to his feet and darted off again. Now he was nothing but a minor attraction to the flies, only three or four bothering to come after him. The others settled by the edges of the splashing fluid, quickly absorbed in an ecstasy of feasting. The few still hovering about his head, Burl killed—but he did not have to smash them all. The remaining few descended to feast on their fallen comrades twitching feebly at his feet.

He ran on and passed beneath the wide-spreading leaves of an isolated giant cabbage. A great grasshopper crouched on the ground, its tremendous radially-opening jaws crunching the rank vegetation. Half a dozen great worms ate steadily of the leaves that supported them. One had swung itself beneath an overhanging leaf—which would have thatched houses for men—and was placidly anchoring itself for the spinning of a cocoon in which to sleep the sleep of metamorphosis.

A mile away, the great black tide of army ants advanced relentlessly. The great cabbage, the huge grasshopper, and all the stupid caterpillars on the leaves would presently be covered with small, black demons. The cocoon would never be spun. The caterpillars would be torn into thousands of furry fragments and devoured. The grasshopper would strike out with its terrific, unguided strength, crushing its assailants with blows of its great hind-legs and powerful jaws. But it would die, making terrible sounds of torment as the ants consumed it piecemeal.

The sound of the ants' advance overwhelmed all other noises now. Burl ran madly, his breath coming in great gasps, his eyes wide with panic. Alone of the world about him, he knew the danger that followed him. The insects he passed went about their business with that terrifying, abstracted efficiency found only in the insect world.

Burl's heart pounded madly from his running. The breath whistled in his nostrils—and behind him the flood of army ants kept pace. They came upon the feasting flies. Some took to the air and escaped. Others were too absorbed in their delicious meal. The twitching maggots, stranded by the scattering of their soupy broth, were torn to shreds and eaten. The flies who were seized vanished into tiny maws. And the serried-ranks of ants moved on.

Burl could hear nothing else, now, but the clickings of their limbs and the stridulating challenges and cross-challenges they uttered. Now and then another sound pierced the noises made by the ants themselves: a cricket, perhaps, seized and dying, uttering deep-bass cries of agony.

Before the horde there was a busy world which teemed with life. Butterflies floated overhead on lazy wings; grubs waxed fat and huge; crickets feasted; great spiders sat quietly in their lairs, waiting with implacable patience for prey to fall into the trap-doors and snares; great beetles lumbered through the mushroom forests, seeking food and making love in monstrous, tragic fashion.

Behind the wide front of the army ants was—chaos. Emptiness. Desolation. All life save that of the army ants was exterminated, though some bewildered flying creatures still fluttered helplessly over the silent landscape. Yet even behind the army ants little bands of stragglers from the horde marched busily here and there, seeking some trace of life that had been overlooked by the main body.

Burl put forth his last ounce of strength. His limbs trembled. His breathing was agony. Sweat stood out upon his forehead. He ran for his life with the desperation of one who knows that death is at his heels. He ran as if his continued existence among the million tragedies of the single day were the purpose for which the universe had been created.

There was redness in the west and in the cloud-bank overhead. To the east gray sky became a deeper gray— much deeper. It was not yet time for the creatures of the day to seek their hiding-places, nor for the night-insects to come forth. But in many secret spots there were vague and sleepy stirrings.

Heedless of the approaching darkness Burl sped over an open space a hundred yards across. A thicket of beautifully golden mushrooms barred his way. Danger lay there. He dodged aside and saw in the gray dusk a glistening sheet of white, barely a yard above the ground. It was the web of the morning-spider which, on Earth, was noted only in hedges and such places when the dew of earliest dawn exposed it as a pattern-less plate of diamond-dust. There were anchor-cables, of course, but no geometry. Tidy housewives—also on Earth—used to mop it out of corners as a filmy fabric of irritating gossamer. On the forgotten planet it was a net with strength and bird-lime qualities that increased day by day, as its spinner moved restlessly over the surface, always trailing sticky cord behind itself.

Burl had no choice but to avoid it, even though he lost ground to the ant-horde roaring behind him. And night was definitely on the way. It was inconceivable that a human should travel in the lowlands after dark. It literally could not be done over the normal nightmare terrain. Burl had not only to escape the army ants, but find a hiding-place quickly if he was to see

tomorrow's light. But he could not think so far ahead,
just now.

He blundered through a screen of puffballs that shot
dusty powder toward the sky. Ahead, a range of
strangely colored hills came into view—purple, green,
black and gold—melting into each other and branch-
ing off, inextricably mingled. They rose to a height of
perhaps sixty or seventy feet. A curious grayish haze
had gathered above them. It seemed to be a layer of
thin vapor, not like mist or fog, clinging to certain parts
of the hills, rising slowly to coil and gather into an
indefinitely thicker mass above the ridges.

The hills themselves were not geological features,
but masses of fungus that had grown and cannibalized,
piling up upon themselves to the thickness of carboniferous vegetation. Over the face of the hills grew every
imaginable variety of yeast and mold and rust. They
grew within and upon themselves, forming freakish
conglomerations that piled up into a range of hills,
stretching across the lunatic landscape for miles.

Burl blundered up the nearest slope. Sometimes the
surface was a hard rind that held him up. Sometimes
his feet sank—perhaps inches, perhaps to mid-leg. He
scrambled frantically. Panting, gasping, staggering from
the exhaustion of moving across the fungus quicksand,
he made his way to the top of the first hill, plunged
down into a little valley on the farther side, and up
another slope. He left a clear trail behind him of
disturbed and scurrying creatures that had inevitably
found a home in the mass of living stuff. Small sinu-
ous centipedes scuttled here and there, roused by his
passage. At the bottom of his footprints writhed fat
white worms. Beetles popped into view and vanished
again.

A half mile across the range and Burl could go no
farther. He stumbled and fell and lay there, gasping

hoarsely. Overhead the gray sky had become a deep-red which was rapidly melting into that redness too deep to be seen except as black. But there was still some light from the west.

Burl sobbed for breath in a little hollow, his sharp-toothed club still clasped in his hands. Something huge, with wings like sails, soared in silhouette against the sunset. Burl lay motionless, breathing in great gasps, his limbs refusing to lift him.

The sound of the army ants continued. At last, above the crest of the last hillock he had surmounted, two tiny glistening antennae appeared, then the small, deadly shape of an army ant. The forerunner of its horde, it moved deliberately forward, waving its antennae ceaselessly. It made its way toward Burl, tiny clickings coming from its limbs.

A little wisp of vapor swirled toward the ant. It was the vapor that had gathered over the whole range of hills as a thin, low cloud. It enveloped the ant which seemed to be thrown into a strange convulsion, throwing itself about, legs moving aimlessly. If it had been an animal instead of an insect, it would have choked and gasped. But ants breathe through air-holes in their abdomens. It writhed helplessly on the spongy stuff across which it had been moving.

Burl was conscious of a strange sensation. His body felt remarkably warm. It felt hot. It was an unparalleled sensation, because Burl had no experience of fire or the heat of the sun. The only warmth he had ever known was when huddling together with his tribesmen in some hiding-place to avoid the damp chill of the night.

Then, the heat of their breath and flesh helped to combat discomfort. But this was a fiercer heat. It was intolerable. Burl moved his body with a tremendous effort and for a moment the fungus soil was cool beneath him. Then the sensation of hotness began again and increased until Burl's skin was reddened and inflamed.

The tenuous vapor, too, seemed to swirl his way. It made his lungs smart and his eyes water. He still breathed in painful gasps, but even that short period of rest had done him some good. But it was the heat that drove him to his feet again. He crawled painfully to the crest of the next hill. He looked back.

This was the highest hill he had come upon and he could see most of the purple range in the deep, deep dusk. Now he was more than half-way through the hills. He had barely a quarter-mile to go, northward. But east and west the range of purple hills was a ceaseless, undulating mass of lifts and hollows, of ridges and spurs of all imaginable colorings.

And at the tips of most of them were wisps of curling gray.

From his position he could see a long stretch of the hills not hidden by the surrounding darkness. Back along the way he had come, the army ants now swept up into the range of hills. Scouts and advance-guard parties scurried here and there. They stopped to devour the creatures inhabiting the surface layers. But the main body moved on inexorably.

The hills, though, were alive; not upheavals of the ground but festering heaps of insanely growing fungus, hollowed out in many places by tunnels, hiding-places, and lurking-places. These the ants invaded. They swept on, devouring everything. . . .

Burl leaned heavily upon his club and watched dully. He could run no more. The army ants were spreading everywhere. They would reach him soon.

Far to the right, the vapor thickened. A thin column of smoke arose in the dim half-light. Burl did not know smoke, of course. He could not conceivably guess that deep down in the interior of the insanely growing hills, pressure had killed and oxidation had carbonized the once-living material. By oxidation the temperature down below had been raised. In the damp darkness of the bowels of the hills spontaneous combustion had begun.

The great mounds of tinder-like mushroom had begun to burn very slowly, quite unseen. There had been no flames because the hills' surface remained intact and there was no air to feed the burning. But when the army ants dug ferociously for fugitive small things, air was admitted to tunnels abandoned because of heat.

Then slow combustion speeded up. Smolderings became flames. Sparks became coals. A dozen columns of fume-laden smoke rose into the heavens and gathered into a dense pall above the range of purple hills. And Burl apathetically watched the serried ranks of army ants march on toward the widening furnaces that awaited them.

They had recoiled from the river instinctively. But their ancestors had never known fire. In the Amazon basin, on Earth, there had never been forest fires. On the forgotten planet there had never been fires at all, unless the first forgotten colonists tried to make them. In any case the army ants had no instinctive terror of flame. They marched into the blazing openings that appeared in the hills. They snapped with their mandibles at the leaping flames, and sprang to grapple with the burning coals.

The blazing areas widened as the purple surface was consumed. Burl watched without comprehension—even without thankfulness. He stood breathing more and more easily until the glow from approaching flames reddened his skin and the acrid smoke made tears flow from his eyes. Then he retreated slowly, leaning on his club and often looking back.

Night had fallen, but yet it was light to the army
ants. They marched on, shrilling their defiance. They
poured devotedly—and ferociously—into the inferno
of flame. At last there were only small groups of stragglers from the great ant-army scurrying here and there
over the ground their comrades had stripped of all life.
The bodies of the main army made a vast malodor,
burning in the furnace of the hills.

There had been pain in that burning; agony such
as no one would willingly dwell upon. But it came of
the insane courage of the ants, attacking the burning
stuff with their horny jaws, rolling over and over with
flaming lumps of charcoal clutched in their mandibles.
Burl heard them shrilling their war-cry even as they
died. Blinded, antennae singed off, legs shriveling, they
yet went forward to attack their impossible enemy.

Burl made his way slowly over the hills. Twice he
saw small bodies of the vanished army. They had passed
between the widening furnaces and furiously devoured
all that moved as they forged ahead. Once Burl was
spied, and a shrill cry sounded, but he moved on and
only a single ant rushed after him. Burl brought down
his club and a writhing body remained to be eaten by
its comrades when they came upon it.

And now the last faint traces of light had vanished
in the west. There was no real brightness anywhere
except the flames of the burning hills. The slow, slow
nightly rain that dripped down all through the dark
hours began. It made a pattering noise upon the
unburnt part of the hills.

Burl found firm ground beneath his feet. He listened
keenly for sounds of danger. Something rustled heavily
in a thicket of toadstools a hundred feet away. There
were sounds of preening, and of feet delicately placed
here and there upon the ground. Then a great body
took to the air with the throbbing beat of mighty wings.

A fierce down-current of air smote Burl, and he looked upward in time to glimpse the outline of a huge moth passing overhead. He turned to watch the line of its flight, and saw the fierce glow filling all the horizon. The hills burned brighter as the flames widened.

He crouched beneath a squat toadstool and waited for the dawn. The slow-dripping rain kept on, falling with irregular, drum-like beats upon the tough top of the toadstool.

He did not sleep. He was not properly hidden, and there was always danger in the dark. But this was not the darkness Burl was used to. The great fires grew and spread in the masses of ready-carbonized mushroom. The glare on the horizon grew brighter through the hours. It also came nearer.

Burl shivered a little, as he watched. He had never even dreamed of fire before, and even the overhanging clouds were lighted by these flames. Over a stretch at least a dozen miles in length and from half a mile to three miles across, the seething furnaces and columns of flame-lit smoke sent illumination over the world. It was like the glow the lights of a city can throw upon the sky. And like the flitting of aircraft above a city was the assembly of fascinated creatures of the night.

Great moths and flying beetles, gigantic gnats and midges grown huge upon this planet, fluttered and danced above the flames. As the fire came nearer, Burl could see them: colossal, delicately-formed creatures sweeping above the white-hot expanse. There were moths with riotously-colored wings of thirty-foot spread, beating the air with mighty strokes, their huge eyes glowing like garnets as they stared intoxicatedly at the incandescence below them.

Burl saw a great peacock-moth soaring above the

hills with wings all of forty feet across. They fluttered
like sails of unbelievable magnificence. And this was
when all the separate flames had united to form a
single sheet of white-hot burning stuff spread across
the land for miles.

Feathery antennae of the finest lace spread out
before the head of the peacock-moth; its body was of
softest velvet. A ring of snow-white fur marked where
its head began. The glare from below smote the
maroon of its body with a strange effect. For one
instant it was outlined clearly. Its eyes shone more redly
than any ruby's fire. The great, delicate wings were
poised in flight. Burl caught the flash of flame upon
the two great iridescent spots on the wings. Shining
purple and bright red, all the glory of chalcedony and
of chrysoprase was reflected in the glare of burning
fungi.

And then Burl saw it plunge downward, straight into
the thickest and fiercest of the leaping flames. It flung
itself into the furnace as a willing, drunken victim of
their beauty.

Flying beetles flew clumsily above the pyre also,
their horny wing-cases stiffly outstretched. In the light
from below they shone like burnished metal. Their
clumsy bodies, with spurred and fierce-toothed limbs,
darted through the flame-lit smoke like so many gro-
tesque meteors.

Burl saw strange collisions and still stranger meet-
ings. Male and female flying creatures circled and spun
in the glare, dancing their dance of love and death.
They mounted higher than Burl could see, drunk with
the ecstasy of living, and then descended to plunge
headlong in the roaring flames below.

From every side the creatures came. Moths of
brightest yellow, with furry bodies palpitant with life,
flew madly to destruction. Other moths of a deepest

black, with gruesome symbols on their wings, swiftly came to dance above the glow like motes in sunlight.

And Burl crouched beneath a toadstool, watching while the perpetual, slow raindrops fell and fell, and a continuous hissing noise came from where the rain splashed amid the flames.

4. A KILLER OF MONSTERS

The night wore on, while the creatures above the firelight danced and died, their numbers ever reinforced by fresh arrivals. Burl sat tensely still, his eyes watching everything while his mind groped for an explanation of what he saw. At last the sky grew dimly gray, then brighter, and after a long time it was day. The flames of the burning hills seemed to dim and die as all the world became bright. After a long while Burl crawled from his hiding-place and stood erect.

No more than two hundred paces from where he stood, a straight wall of smoke rose from the still-smoldering fungus-range. Burl could see the smoke rising for miles on either hand. He turned to continue on his way, and saw the remains of one of the tragedies of the night.

A great moth had flown into the flames, been horribly scorched, and floundered out again. Had it been able to fly, it would have returned to its devouring deity; but now it lay upon the ground, its antennae hopelessly seared. One beautiful wing was nothing but gaping holes. The eyes had been dimmed by flame. The exquisitely tapering limbs lay broken and crushed by the violence of landing. The creature was helpless on the ground, only the stumps of its antennae moving restlessly and the abdomen pulsating slowly as it drew pain-racked breaths.

Burl drew near. He raised his club.

When he moved on there was a velvet cloak cast over his shoulders, gleaming with all the colors of the rainbows. A gorgeous mass of soft blue moth-fur was about his middle, and he had bound upon his forehead two yard-long fragments of the moth's magnificent antennae.

He strode on slowly, clad as no man had been clad in all the ages before him. After a while another victim of the holocaust—similarly blundered out to die—yielded him a spear that was longer and sharper and much more deadly than his first. So he took up his journey to Saya looking like a prince of Ind upon a bridal journey—though surely no mere prince ever wore such raiment.

For many miles, Burl threaded his way through an extensive forest of thin-stalked toadstools. They towered high over his head, colorful, parasitic molds and rusts all about their bases. Twice he came upon open glades where bubbling pools of green slime festered in corruption. Once he hid himself as a monster scarabeus beetle lumbered by three yards away, clanking like some mighty machine.

Burl saw the heavy armor and inward-curving jaws of the monster. He almost envied him his weapons. The time was not yet come, though, when Burl and his kind would hunt such giants for the juicy flesh within their armored limbs. Burl was still a savage, still ignorant, still essentially timid. His only significant advance had been that where at first he had fled without reasoning, now he paused to see if he need flee.

He was a strange sight, moving through the shadowed lanes of the forest in his cloak of velvet. The fierce-toothed leg of a fighting beetle rested in a strip of sinew about his waist, ready for use. His new spear was taller than himself. He looked like a conqueror. But he was still a fearful and feeble creature, no match for the monstrous creatures about him. He was weak—and in that lay his greatest hope. Because if he were strong, he would not need to think.

Hundreds of thousands of years before, his ancestors had been forced to develop brains as penalty for the lack of claws or fangs. Burl was sunk as low as any of them, but he had to combat more horrifying enemies, more inexorable dangers, and many times more crafty antagonists. His ancestors had invented knives and spears and flying missiles, but the creatures about Burl had weapons a thousand times more deadly than the ones that had defended the first humans.

The fact, however, simply put a premium on the one faculty Burl had which the insect world has not.

In mid-morning he heard a discordant, deep-bass bellow, coming from a spot not twenty yards from where he moved. He hid in panic, waiting for an instant, listening.

The bellow came again, but this time with a querulous note. Burl heard a crashing and plunging as of some creature caught in a snare. A mushroom tumbled with a spongelike sound, and the thud was followed by a tremendous commotion. Something was fighting desperately against something else, but Burl did not know what creatures were in combat.

He waited, and the noise died gradually away. Presently his breath came more slowly and his courage returned. He stole from his hiding-place and would have made away, but new curiosity held him back. Instead of creeping from the scene, he moved cautiously toward the source of the noise.

Peering between two cream-colored stalks he saw a wide, funnel-shaped snare of silk spread out before him, some twenty yards across and as many deep. The individual threads could be plainly seen, but in the mass it seemed a fabric of sheerest, finest texture. Held up by tall mushrooms, it was anchored to the ground below and drew away to a small point through which a hole led to some as yet unseen recess. This was the trap of a labyrinth spider.

Burl's hair stood on end from sheer fright, but he was the slave of an idea.

The tunnel and the nest at the end did not rest on the ground, but were suspended in the air by cables. The gray labyrinth-spider bulged the fabric. It lay in luxurious comfort, waiting for victims to approach.

There was sweat on Burl's face as he raised his spear. The bare idea of attacking a spider was horrifying. But actually he was in no danger whatever before the instant of the spear-thrust, because web-spiders never, never, leave their webs to hunt.

So Burl sweated, and grasped his spear with agonized firmness—and thrust it into the bulge that was the spider's body in its nest. He thrust with hysterical fury.

And then he ran as if the devil were after him.

It was a long time before he dared come back, his heart in his throat. All was still. He had missed the horrid convulsions of the wounded spider; he had not heard the frightful gnashings of its fangs at the piercing weapon, nor seen the silken threads of the tunnel ripped and torn in the spider's death-struggle. Burl came back to quietness. There was a great rent in the silken tunnel, and a puddle of ill-smelling stuff lay upon the ground. From time to time another droplet fell from the spear to join it. And the great spider had fallen half through its own enlargement of the rent made by the spear in the wall of the nest.

Burl stared. Even when he saw it, the thing was not easy to believe. The dead eyes of the spider looked at him with mad, frozen malignity. The fangs were still raised to kill. The hairy legs were still braced as if to enlarge further the gaping hole through which it had partly fallen.

Then Burl felt exultation. His tribe had been furtive vermin for almost forty generations, fleeing from the mighty insects, hiding from them, and when caught waiting helplessly for death, screaming shrilly in horror. But he, Burl, had turned the tables. He, a man, had killed a spider! His breast expanded. Always his tribesmen went quietly and fearfully, making no sound. But a sudden, surprising, triumphant yell burst from Burl's lips—the first hunting-cry of man upon the forgotten planet in two thousand years.

Next second, of course, his pulse almost stopped in sheer terror because he had made such a noise. He listened fearfully. The insect world was oblivious to him. Presently, shuddering but infinitely proud, he drew near his prey. He carefully withdrew his spear, poised to flee if the spider stirred. It did not. It was dead. The blood upon the spear was revolting. Burl wiped it off on a leathery toadstool. Then. . . .

He thought of Saya and his tribesmen. Trembling even as he gloated over his own remarkable self, he shifted the spider and worked it out of the nest. Presently he moved off with the belly of the spider upon his back and two of its hairy legs over his shoulders. The other limbs of the monster hung limp, trailing on the ground behind him.

Marching, then, he was the first such spectacle in

history. His velvet cloak shining with its iridescent spots, the yard-long scraps of golden antennae bound to his forehead, a spear in his hand, and the hideous bulk of a gray spider for burden—Burl was a very strange sight indeed.

He believed that other creatures fled before him because of the thing he carried. He tended to grow haughty. But actually, of course, insects do not know fear. They recognize their own specific enemies. That is necessary. But the life of the lowlands on the forgotten planet went on abstractedly, despite the splendid feat of one man.

Burl marched. He came upon a valley full of torn and tattered mushrooms. There was not a single yellow top among them. Every one had been infested with maggots that had liquefied the tough meat of the mushroom-tops, causing it to drip to the ground below. The liquid was gathered in a golden pool in the center of the small depression. Burl heard a loud and deep-toned humming before he saw the valley. Then he stopped and looked down.

He saw the golden pond, its surface reflecting the gray sky and the darkened stumps of mushrooms on the hillside which looked as if they had been blackened by a running flame. A small brooklet of golden liquid trickled over a rocky ledge, and all round the edges of the pond and brook, in ranks and rows, by hundreds and by thousands and it seemed by millions, were the green-gold bodies of great flies.

They were small compared to other insects. The fleshflies laid their eggs by the hundreds in decaying carcasses. The others chose mushrooms to lay their eggs in. To feed the maggots that would hatch, a relatively great quantity of food was needed; therefore, the flies must remain comparatively small, or the body of a single grasshopper would furnish food for only a few maggots instead of the hundreds it must support. There

must also be a limit to the size of worms if hundreds
were to feast upon a single fungus.

But there was no limitation to the greediness of the
adult creatures. There were bluebottles and green-bottles
and all the flies of metallic luster, gathered at a Lucullan
feast of corruption. The buzzing of those swarming above
the golden pool was a tremendous sound. The flying
bodies flashed and glittered as they flew back and forth,
seeking a place to alight and join in the orgy.

The glittering bodies clustered in already-found
places were motionless as if carved from metal. Burl
watched them. And then he saw motion overhead.

A slender, brilliant shape appeared, darting swiftly
through the air, enlarging into a needle-like body with
transparent, shining wings and two huge eyes. It circled
and enlarged again, becoming a shimmering dragonfly, twenty feet and more in length. It poised itself
abruptly above the pool, and then darted down, its jaws
snapping viciously. They snapped again and again. Burl
could not follow their slashings. And with each snap
the glittering body of a fly vanished.

A second dragonfly appeared and a third. They
swooped above the golden pool, snapping in mid-air,
making their abrupt and angular turns, creatures of
incredible ferocity and beauty. In that mass of buzzing creatures, even the most voracious appetite must
soon have been sated, but the slender creatures still
darted about in frenzied destruction.

And all this while the loud, contented, deep-bass
humming went on as before. Their comrades were
slaughtered by the hundreds not forty feet above their
heads, but still the glittering rows of red-eyed flies
gorged themselves upon the fluid of the pond. The
dragonflies feasted until they were unable to devour
even a single one more of their chosen prey. But even
then they continued to sweep madly above the pool,

striking down the buzzing flies though their bodies must perforce remain uneaten.

Some of the dead flies, crushed to pulp by the angry dragonflies, dropped among their feasting brothers. Presently, one of them placed its disgusting proboscis upon the mangled creature. It sipped daintily from the contents of the broken armor. Another joined it and another. In a little while a cluster of them pushed against each other for a chance to join them in a cannibalistic feast.

Burl turned aside and went on, leaving the dragonflies still at their massacre and the flies absorbed and ecstatic at their feast. The feast, indeed, was improved by the rain of murdered brethren from overhead.

Only a few miles farther on, Burl came upon a familiar landmark. He knew it well, but had always kept at a safe distance from it. A mass of rock had heaved itself up from the almost level plain over which he traveled to form an out-jutting cliff. At one point the rock overhung, forming an inverted ledge—a roof over nothingness— which had been preempted by a hairy monster and made into a fairylike dwelling. A white hemisphere clung to the rock, firmly anchored by long cables.

Burl knew the place as one to be feared. A clotho spider had built itself a nest there, from which it emerged to hunt the unwary. Within the silken globe was a monstrosity, resting upon cushions of softest silk. The exterior had been beautiful once. But if one went too near one of the little inverted arches seemingly closed by panels of silk it would open and out would rush a creature from a dream of hell.

Surely Burl knew this place. Hung upon the walls of the fairy palace were trophies. They had a purpose, of course. Stones and boulders hung there, too, to hold the structure firm against the storm-winds that rarely blew. But amid the stones and fragments of insect-armor there was a very special decoration: the shrunken, desiccated skeleton of a man.

The death of that man had saved Burl's life two years before. They had been together, seeking a new source of edible mushroom. The clotho spider was a hunter, not a spinner of webs. It had sprung suddenly from behind a great puffball as the two men froze in horror. Then it had come forward and deliberately chosen its victim. It did not choose Burl.

Now he looked with half-frightened speculation at the lair of his ancient enemy. Some day, perhaps. . . .

But now he passed on. He went past the thicket in which the great moths hid by day, past the slimy pool in which something unknown but terrible lurked. He penetrated the little forest of mushrooms that glowed at night and the place where the truffle-hunting beetles chirped thunderously during the dark hours.

And then he saw Saya. He caught a flash of pink skin vanishing behind a squat toadstool, and he ran forward calling her name. She emerged, and saw the figure with the horrible bulk of the spider on its back. She cried out in horror, and Burl understood. He let his burden fall, running swiftly to her.

They met. Saya waited timidly until she saw who this man was, and then she was astounded indeed. With golden plumes rising from his head, a velvet cloak about his shoulders, blue moth-fur about his middle, and a spear in his hand—and a dead spider behind him!—this was not the Burl she had known.

He took her hands, babbling proudly. She stared at him and at his victim—but the language of men had diminished sadly—struggling to comprehend. Presently her eyes glowed. She pulled at his wrists.

When they found the other tribesmen, they were carrying the dead spider between them, Saya looking more proud than Burl.

5. MEAT OF MAN'S KILLING!

In their climb up from savagery, the principal handicap from which men have always suffered is the fact that they are human. Or it can be said that human beings always have to struggle against the obstacle which is simply that they are men. To Burl his splendid return to the tribe called for a suitable reaction. He expected them to take note that he was remarkable, unparalleled, and in all ways admirable. He expected them to look at him with awe. He rather hoped that the sight of him would involve something like ecstasy.

And as a matter of fact, it did. For fully an hour they gathered around him while he used his—and their—scanty vocabulary to tell them of his unique achievements and adventures during the past two days and nights. They listened attentively and with appropriate admiration and vicarious pride.

This in itself was a step upward. Mostly their talk was of where food might be found and where danger lurked. Strictly practical data connected with the pressing business of getting enough to eat and staying alive. The sheer pressure of existence was so great that the humans Burl knew had altogether abandoned such luxuries as boastful narrative. They had given up tradition. They did not think of art in even its most primitive forms, and the only craft they knew was the craftiness which promoted simple survival. So for them to listen to a narrative which did not mean either food or even a lessening of danger to themselves was a step upward on the cultural scale.

But they were savages. They inspected the dead spider, shuddering. It was pure horror. They did not touch it—the adults not at all—and even Dik and Tet not for a very long time. Nobody thought of spiders as food. Too many of them had been spiders' food.

But presently even the horror aroused by the spider palled. The younger children quailed at sight of it, of course, but the adults came to ignore it. Only the two gangling boys tried to break off a furry leg with which to charge and terrify the younger ones still further. They failed to get it loose because they did not think of cutting it. But they had nothing to cut it with anyhow.

Old Jon went wheezing off, foraging. He waved a hand to Burl as he went. Burl was indignant. But it was true that he had brought back no food. And people must eat.

Tama went off, her tongue clacking, with Lona the half-grown girl to help her find and bring back something edible. Dor, the strongest man in the tribe, went away to look where he thought there might be edible mushrooms full-grown again. Cori left with her children—very carefully on watch for danger to them— to see what she could find.

In little more than an hour Burl's audience had diminished to Saya. Within two hours ants found the spider where it had been placed for the tribe to admire. Within three hours there was nothing left of it. During the fourth hour—as Burl struggled to dredge up some new, splendid item to tell Saya for the tenth time, or thereabouts—during the fourth hour one of the tribeswomen beckoned to Saya. She left with a flashing backward smile for Burl. She went, actually, to help dig up underground fungi—much like truffles—discovered by the older woman. She undoubtedly expected to share them with Burl.

But in five hours it was night and Burl was very indignant with his tribesfolk. They had shifted the location of the hiding-place for the night, and nobody had thought to tell him. And if Saya wished to come for Burl, to lead him to that place, she did not dare for the simple reason that it was night.

For a long time after he found a hiding-place, Burl fumed bitterly to himself. He was very much of a human being, differing from his fellows—so far—mainly because he had been through experiences not shared by them. He had resolved a subjective dilemma of sorts by determining to return to his tribe. He had discovered a weapon which, at first, had promised—and secured—foodstuff, and later had saved him from a tarantula. His discovery that fish-oil was useful when applied to spider-snares and things sticking to the feet was of vast importance to the tribe. Most remarkable of all, he had deliberately killed a spider. And he had experienced triumph. Temporarily he had even experienced admiration.

The adulation was a thing which could never be forgotten. Human appetites are formed by human experiences. One never had an appetite for a thing one has not known in some fashion. But no human being who has known triumph is ever quite the same again, and anybody who has once been admired by his fellows is practically ruined for life—at least so far as being independent of admiration is concerned.

So during the dark hours, while the slow rain dripped in separate, heavy drops from the sky, Burl first coddled his anger—which was a very good thing for a member of a race grown timorous and furtive—and then began to make indignant plans to force his tribesmen to yield him more of the delectable sensations he alone had begun to know.

He was not especially comfortable during the night. The hiding-place he had chosen was not water-tight. Water trickled over him for several hours before he discovered that his cloak, though it would not keep him dry—which it would have done if properly disposed— would still keep the same water next to his skin where his body could warm it. Then he slept. When morning came he felt singularly refreshed. For a savage, he was unusually clean, too.

He woke before dawn with vainglorious schemes in his head. The sky grew gray and then almost white. The overhanging cloud bank seemed almost to touch the earth, but gradually withdrew. The mist among the mushroom-forests grew thinner, and the slow rain ceased reluctantly. When he peered from his hiding-place, the mad world he knew was, as far as he could see, quite mad, as usual. The last of the night-insects had vanished. The day-creatures began to venture out.

Not too far from the crevice where he'd hidden was an ant-hill, monstrous by standards on other planets. It was piled up not of sand but gravel and small boulders. Burl saw a stirring. At a certain spot the smooth, outer surface crumbled and fell into an invisible opening. A spot of darkness appeared. Two slender, thread-like antennae popped out. They withdrew and popped out again. The spot enlarged until there was a sizeable opening. An ant appeared, one of the warrior-ants of this particular breed. It stood fiercely over the opening, waving its antennae agitatedly as if striving to sense some danger to its metropolis.

He was fourteen inches long, this warrior, and his mandibles were fierce and strong. After a moment, two other warriors thrust past him. They ran about the whole extent of the ant-hill, their legs clicking, antennae waving restlessly.

They returned, seeming to confer with the first, then went back down into the city with every appearance of satisfaction. As if they made a properly reassuring report, within minutes afterward, a flood of black, ill-smelling workers poured out of the opening and dispersed about their duties.

The city of the ants had begun its daily toil. There were deep galleries underground here: granaries, storage-vaults, refectories, and nurseries, and even a royal apartment in which the queen-ant reposed. She was waited upon by assiduous courtiers, fed by royal stewards, and combed and caressed by the hands of her subjects and children. A dozen times larger than her loyal servants, she was no less industrious than they in her highly specialized fashion. From the time of waking to the time of rest she was queen-mother in the most literal imaginable sense. At intervals, to be measured only in minutes, she brought forth an egg, perhaps three inches in length, which was whisked away to the municipal nursery. And this constant, insensate increase in the population of the city made all its frantic industry at once possible and necessary.

Burl came out and spread his cloak on the ground. In a little while he felt a tugging at it. An ant was tearing off a bit of the hem. Burl slew the ant angrily and retreated. Twice within the next half-hour he had to move swiftly to avoid foragers who would not directly attack him because he was alive—unless he seemed to threaten danger—but who lusted after the fabric of his garments.

This annoyance—and Burl would merely have taken it as a thing to be accepted a mere two days before— this annoyance added to Burl's indignation with the world about him. He was in a very bad temper indeed when he found old Jon, wheezing as he checked on the possibility of there being edible mushrooms in a thicket of poisonous, pink-and-yellow amanitas.

Burl haughtily commanded Jon to follow him. Jon's untidy whiskers parted as his mouth dropped open in astonishment. Burl's tribe was so far from being really a tribe that for anybody to give a command was astonishing. There was no social organization, absolutely no tradition of command. As a rule life was too uncertain for anybody to establish authority.

But Jon followed Burl as he stamped on through the morning mist. He saw a small movement and shouted imperatively. This was appalling! Men did not call attention to themselves! He gathered up Dor, the strongest of the men. Later, he found Jak who some day would wear an expression of monkey-like wisdom. Then Tet and Dik, the half-grown boys, came trooping to see what was happening.

Burl led onward. A quarter of a mile and they came upon a great, gutted shell which had been a rhinoceros beetle the day before. Today it was a disassembled mass of chitinous armor. Burl stopped, frowning portentously. He showed his quaking followers how to arm themselves. Dor picked up the horn hesitantly, Burl showing him how to use it. He stabbed out awkwardly with the sharp fragment of armor. Burl showed others how to use the leg-sections for clubs. They tested them without conviction. In any sort of danger, they would trust to their legs and a frantically effective gift for hiding.

Burl snarled at his tribesmen and led them on. It was unprecedented. But because of that fact there was no precedent for rebellion. Burl led them in a curve. They glanced all about apprehensively.

When they came to an unusually large and attractive clump of golden edible mushrooms, there were murmurings. Old Jon was inclined to go and load himself and retire to some hiding-place for as long as the food lasted. But Burl snarled again.

Numbly they followed on—Dor and Jon and Jak and the two youngsters. The ground inclined upward. They came upon puffballs. There was a new kind visible, colored a lurid red, that did not grow like the others. It seemed to begin and expand underground, then thrust away the soil above in its development. Its taut, angry-red parchment envelope seemed to swell from a reservoir of subterranean material. Burl and the others had never seen anything like it.

They climbed higher. As other edible mushrooms came into view Burl's followers cheered visibly. This was a new tribal ground anyhow and it had not been fully explored. But Burl was leading them to quantities of food they had never suspected before.

Quaintly, it was Burl himself who began to feel an uncomfortable dryness in his throat. He knew what he was about. His followers did not suspect because to them what he intended was simply inconceivable. They couldn't suspect it because they couldn't imagine anybody doing such a thing. It simply couldn't be thought of at all.

It is rather likely that Burl began to regret that he had thought of it. It had come to him first as an angry notion in the night. Then the idea had developed as a suitable punishment for his abandonment. By dawn it was an ambition so terrifying that it fascinated him. Now he was committed to it in his own mind, and the

only way to keep his knees from knocking together was
to keep moving. If his followers had protested now, he
would have allowed himself to be persuaded. But he
heard more pleased murmurs. There was more edible
stuff, in quantity. But there were no ant-trails here, no
sounds of foraging beetles. This was an area which
Burl's tribesmen could clearly see was almost devoid
of dangerous life. They seemed to brighten a little.
This, they seemed to think, would be a good place to
move to.

But Burl knew better. There were few ground-
insects here because the area was hunted out. And Burl
knew what had done the hunting.

He expected the others to realize where they were
when they dodged around a clump of the new red
puffballs and saw bald rock before them and a falling-
away to emptiness beyond. Even then they could have
retreated, but it did not enter their heads that Burl
could do anything like this.

They didn't know where they were until Burl held
up his hand for silence almost at the edge of the
rock-knob which rose a hundred feet sheer, curving
out a little near its top. They looked out
uncomprehendingly at the mist-filled air and the
nightmare landscape fading into its grayness. A tiny
spider, the very youngest of hatchlings and barely four
inches across, stealthily stalked another vastly smaller
mite. The other was the many-legged larva of the oil-
beetle. The larva itself had been called—on other
planets by other men—the bee-louse. It could easily hide in the thick fur of a giant bumble-bee. But
this one small creature never practiced that ability.
The hatchling spider sprang and the small midge died.
When the spider had grown and, being grown, spun
a web, it would slay great crickets with the same
insane ferocity.

Burl's followers saw first this and then certain three-quarter-inch strands of dirty silk that came up over the edge of the precipice. As one man after another realized where he was, he trembled violently. Dor turned gray. Jon and Jak were paralyzed with horror. They couldn't run.

Seeing the others even more frightened than himself filled Burl with a wholly unwarranted courage. When he opened his mouth, they cringed. If he shouted then at least one, more likely several, of them would die.

And this was because some forty or fifty feet down the mold-speckled precipice hung a drab-white object nearly hemispherical, some six feet in its half-diameter. A number of little semi-circular doors were fixed about its sides like arches. Though each one seemed to be a doorway, only one would open.

The thing had been oddly beautiful at first glance. It was held fast to the inward-sloping stone by cables, one or two of which stretched down toward the ground. Others reached up over the precipice-edge to hold it fast. It was a most unusual engineering feat, yet something more than that: this was also an ogre's castle. Ghastly trophies were fastened to the outer walls and hung by silken cords below it. Here was the hind-leg of one of the smaller beetles, there the wing-case of a flying creature. Here a snail-shell—the snails of Earth would hardly have recognized their descendant—and there a boulder weighing forty pounds or more. The shrunken head-armor of a beetle, the fierce jaws of a cricket, the pitiful shreds of dozens of creatures—all had once provided meals for the monster in the castle. And dangling by the longest cord of all was the shrunken, shriveled body of a long-dead man.

Burl glared at his tribesmen, clamping his jaws tight lest they chatter. He knew, as did the others, that any

noise would bring the clotho spider swinging up its
anchor-cables to the cliff-top. The men didn't dare
move. But every one of them—and Burl was among
the foremost—knew that inside the half-dome of gruesome relics the monster reposed in luxury and ease.
It had eight furry, attenuated legs and a face that was
a mask of horror. The eyes glittered malevolently above
needle-sharp mandibles. It was a hunting-spider. At any
moment it might leave the charnel-house in which it
lived to stalk and pursue prey.

Burl motioned the others forward. He led one of
them to the end of a cable where it curled up over
the edge for an anchorage. He ripped the end free—
and his flesh crawled as he did so. He found a boulder and knotted the end of the cable about it. In a
whisper that imitated a spider's ferocity, Burl gave the
man orders. He plucked a second quaking tribesman
by the arm. With the jerky, uncontrolled movements
of a robot, Dor allowed himself to be led to a second
cable.

Burl commanded in a frenzy. He worked with stiff
fingers and a dry throat, not knowing how he could
do this thing. He had formed a plan in anger which
he somehow was carrying out in a panic. Although his
followers were as responsive as dead men, they obeyed
him because they felt like dead men, unable to resist.
After all, it was simple enough. There were boulders
at the top of the precipice and silken cables hung taut
over the edge. As Burl fastened a heavy boulder to each
cable he could find, he loosened the silken strand until
it hung tight only at the very edge of the more-than-
vertical fall.

He took his post—and his followers gazed at him
with the despairing eyes of zombies—and made a
violent, urgent gesture. One man dumped his boulder
over the precipice's edge. Burl cried out shrilly to the

others, half-mad with his own terror. There was a ripping sound. The other men dumped their boulders over, fleeing with the movement—the paralysis of horror relieved by that one bit of exertion.

Burl could not flee. He panted and gasped, but he had to see. He stared down the dizzy wall. Boulders ripped and tore their way down the cliff-wall, pulling the cables loose from the face of the precipice. They shot out into space and jerked violently at the half-globular nest, ripping it loose from its anchorage.

Burl cried out exultantly. And as he cried out the shout became a bubbling sound; for although the ogre's silken castle did swing clear, it did not drop the sixty feet to the hard ground below. There was one cable Burl had missed, hidden by rock-tripe and mold in a depressed part of the cliff-top. The spider's house was dangling crazily by that one strand, bobbing erratically to and fro in mid-air.

And there was a convulsive struggle inside it. One of the arch-doors opened and the spider emerged. It was doubtless confused, but spiders simply do not know terror. Their one response to the unusual is ferocity. There was still one cable leading up the cliff-face— the thing's normal climbing-rope to its hunting-ground above. The spider leaped for this single cable. Its legs grasped the cord. It swarmed upward, poison fangs unsheathed, mandibles clashing in rage. The shaggy hair of its body seemed to bristle with insane ferocity. The skinny articulated legs fairly twinkled as it rose. It made slavering noises, unspeakably horrifying.

Burl's followers were already in panic-stricken flight. He could hear them crashing through obstacles as they ran glassy-eyed from the horror they only imagined, but which Burl could not but encounter. Burl shivered, his body poised for equally frenzied but quite hope-less flight. But his first step was blocked. There was a boulder behind him, standing on end, reaching up to his knee. He could not take the first step without dodging it.

It was not the Burl of the terror-filled childhood who acted then. It was the throw-back, the atavism to a bolder ancestry. While the Burl who was a product of his environment was able to know only the stunned sensations of purest panic, the other Burl acted on a sounder basis of desperation. The emerging normal human seized the upright boulder. He staggered to the rock-face with it. He dumped it down the line of the descending cable.

Humans do have ancestral behavior-patterns built into their nervous systems. A frightened small child does not flee; it swarms up the nearest adult to be carried away from danger. At ten a child does not climb but runs. And there is an age when it is normal for a man to stand at bay. This last instinct can be conditioned away. In Burl's fellows and his immediate forbears it had been. But things had happened to Burl to break that conditioning.

He flung the pointed boulder down. For the fraction of a second he heard only the bubbling, gnashing sounds the spider made as it climbed toward him. Then there was a quite indescribable cushioned impact. After that, there were seconds in which Burl heard nothing whatever—and then a noise which could not be described either, but was the impact of the spider's body on the ground a hundred feet below, together with the pointed boulder it had fought insanely during all its fall. And the boulder was on top. The noise was sickening.

Burl found himself shaking all over. His every muscle was tense and strained. But the spider did not crawl over the edge of the precipice and something had hit far below.

A long minute later he managed to look.

The nest still dangled at the end of the single cable, festooned with its gruesome trophies. But Burl saw the spider. It was, of course, characteristically tenacious of life. Its legs writhed and kicked, but the body was crushed and mangled.

As Burl stared down, trying to breathe again, an ant drew near the shattered creature. It stridulated. Other ants came. They hovered restlessly at the edge of the death-scene. One loathsome leg did not quiver. An ant moved in on it.

The ants began to tear the dead spider apart, carrying its fragments to their city a mile away.

Up on the cliff-top Burl got unsteadily to his feet and found that he could breathe. He was drenched in sweat, but the shock of triumph was as overwhelming as any of the terrors felt by ancestors on this planet.

On no other planet in the Galaxy could any human experience such triumph as Burl felt now because never before had human beings been so completely subjugated by their environment. On no other planet had such an environment existed, with humans flung so helplessly upon its mercy.

Burl had been normal among his fellows when he was as frightened and furtive as they. Now he had been given shock treatment by fate. He was very close to normal for a human being newly come to the forgotten planet, save that he had the detailed information which would enable a normal man to cope with the nightmare environment. What he lacked now was the habit.

But it would be intolerable for him to return to his former state of mind.

He walked almost thoughtfully after his fled followers. And he was still a savage in that he was remarkably matter-of-fact. He paused to break off a huge piece of the edible golden mushrooms his fellow-men had noticed on the way up. Lugging it easily, he went back down over the ground that had looked so astonishingly free of inimical life—which it was because of the spider that had used it as a hunting-preserve.

Burl began to see that it was not satisfactory to be one of a tribe of men who ran away all the time. If one man with a spear or stone could kill spiders, it was ridiculous for half a dozen men to run away and leave that one man the job alone. It made the job harder.

It occurred to Burl that he had killed ants without thinking too much about it, but nobody else had. Individual ants could be killed. If he got his followers to kill foot-long ants, they might in time battle the smaller, two-foot beetles. If they came to dare so much, they might attack greater creatures and ultimately attempt to resist the real predators.

Not clearly but very dimly, the Burl who had been shocked back to the viewpoint which was normal to the race of men saw that human beings could be more than the fugitive vermin on which other creatures preyed. It was not easy to envision, but he found it impossible to imagine sinking back to his former state. As a practical matter, if he was to remain as leader his tribesmen would have to change.

It was a long time before he reached the neighborhood of the hiding-place of which he had not been told the night before. He sniffed and listened. Presently he heard faint, murmurous noises. He traced them, hearing clearly the sound of hushed weeping and excited, timid chattering. He heard old Tama shrilly bewailing fate and the stupidity of Burl in getting himself killed.

He pushed boldly through the toadstool-growth and found his tribe all gathered together and trembling. They were shaken. They chattered together—not discussing or planning, but nervously recalling the terrifying experience they had gone through.

Burl stepped through the screen of fungi and men gaped at him. Then they leaped up to flee, thinking he might be pursued. Tet and Dik babbled shrilly. Burl cuffed them. It was an excellent thing for him to do. No man had struck another man in Burl's memory. Cuffings were reserved for children. But Burl cuffed the men who had fled from the cliff-edge. And because they had not been through Burl's experiences, they took the cuffings like children.

He took Jon and Jak by the ear and heaved them out of the hiding-place. He followed them, and then drove them to where they could see the base of the cliff from whose top they had tumbled stones—and then run away. He showed them the carcass of the spider, now being carted away piecemeal by ants. He told them angrily how it had been killed.

They looked at him fearfully.

He was exasperated. He scowled at them. And then he saw them shifting uneasily. There were clickings. A single, foraging black ant—rather large, quite sixteen inches long—moved into view. It seemed to be wandering purposelessly, but was actually seeking carrion to take back to its fellows. It moved toward the men. They were alive, therefore it did not think of them as food—though it could regard them as enemies.

Burl moved forward and struck with his club. It was butchery. It was unprecedented. When the creature lay still he commanded one of his followers to take it up. Inside its armored legs there would be meat. He mentioned the fact, pungently. Their faces expressed amazed wonderment.

There was another clicking. Another solitary ant. Burl handed his club to Dor, pushing him forward. Dor hesitated. Though he was not afraid of one wandering ant, he held back uneasily. Burl barked at him.

Dor struck clumsily and botched the job. Burl had

to use his spear to finish it. But a second bit of prey lay before the men.

Then, quite suddenly, this completely unprecedented form of foraging became understandable to Burl's followers. Jak giggled nervously.

An hour later Burl led them back to the tribe's hiding-place. The others had been terror-stricken, not knowing where the men had gone. But their terror changed to mute amazement when the men carried huge quantities of meat and edible mushroom into the hiding-place. The tribe held what amounted to a banquet.

Dik and Tet swaggered under a burden of ant-carcass. This was not, of course, in any way revolting. Back on Earth, even thousands of years before, Arabs had eaten locusts cooked in butter and salted. All men had eaten crabs and other crustaceans, whose feeding habits were similar to those of ants. If Burl and his tribesmen had thought to be fastidious, ants on the for-gotten planet would still have been considered edible, since they had not lost the habits of extreme cleanli-ness which made them notable on Earth.

This feast of all the tribe, in which men had brought back not only mushrooms to be eaten, but actual prey—small prey—of their hunting, was very probably the first such occasion in at least thirty generations of the forty-odd since the planet's unintended coloniza-tion. Like the other events, which began with Burl trying to spear a fish with a rhinoceros-beetle's horn, it was not only novel, on that world, but would in time have almost incredibly far-reaching consequences. Perhaps the most significant thing about it was its timing. It came at very nearly the latest instant at which it could have done any good.

There was a reason which nobody in the tribe would ever remember to associate with the significance of this banquet. A long time before—months in terms of Earth time—there had been a strong breeze that blew for three days and nights. It was an extremely unusual windstorm. It had seemed the stranger, then, because during all its duration everyone in the tribe had been sick, suffering continuously. When the windstorm had ended, the suffering ceased. A long time passed and nobody remembered it any longer.

There was no reason why they should. Yet, since that time there had been a new kind of thing growing among the innumerable molds and rusts and toadstools of the lowlands. Burl had seen them on his travels, and the expeditionary force against the clotho spider had seen them on the journey up to the cliff-edge. Red puffballs, developing first underground, were now pushing the soil aside to expose taut, crimson parchment spheres to the open air. The tribesmen left them alone because they were strange; and strange things were always dangerous. Puffballs they were familiar with—big, misshapen things which shot at a touch a powder into the air. The particles of powder were spores—the seed from which they grew. Spores had remained infinitely small even on the forgotten planet where fungi grew huge. Only their capacity for growth had increased. The red growths were puffballs, but of a new and different kind.

As the tribe ate and admired, the hunters boasting of their courage, one of the new red mushrooms reached maturity.

This particular growing thing was perhaps two feet across, its main part spherical. Almost eighteen inches of the thing rose above ground. A tawny and menacing red, the sphere was contained in a parchment-like skin that was pulled taut. There was internal tension. But the skin was tough and would not yield, yet the inexorable pressure of life within demanded that it stretch. It was growing within, but the skin without had ceased to grow.

This one happened to be on a low hillside a good half mile from the place where Burl and his fellows banqueted. Its tough, red parchment skin was tensed unendurably. Suddenly it ripped apart with an explosive tearing noise. The dry spores within billowed out and up like the smoke of a shell-explosion, spurting skyward for twenty feet and more. At the top of their ascent they spread out and eddied like a cloud of reddish smoke. They hung in the air. They drifted in the sluggish breeze. They spread as they floated, forming a gradually extending, descending dust-cloud in the humid air.

A bee, flying back toward its hive, droned into the thin mass of dust. It was preoccupied. The dust-cloud was not opaque, but only a thick haze. The bee flew into it.

For half a dozen wing-beats nothing happened. Then the bee veered sharply. Its deep-toned humming rose in pitch. It made convulsive movements in mid-air. It lost balance and crashed heavily to the ground. There its legs kicked and heaved violently but without purpose. The wings beat furiously but without rhythm or effect. Its body bent in paroxysmic flexings. It stung blindly at nothing.

After a little while the bee died. Like all insects, bees breathe through spiracles—breathing holes—in their abdomens. This bee had flown into the cloud of red dust which was the spore-cloud of the new mushrooms.

The cloud drifted slowly along over the surface of yeasts and molds, over toadstools and variegated fungus monstrosities. It moved steadily over a group of ants at work upon some bit of edible stuff. They were seized with an affliction like that of the bee. They writhed, moved convulsively. Their legs thrashed about. They died.

The cloud of red dust settled as it moved. By the time it had traveled a quarter-mile it had almost all settled to the ground.

But a half-mile away there was another skyward-spurting uprush of red dust which spread slowly with the breeze, A quarter-mile away another plumed into the air. Farther on, two of them spouted their spores toward the clouds almost together.

Living things that breathed the red dust writhed and died. And the red-dust puffballs were scattered everywhere.

Burl and his tribesmen feasted, chattering in hushed tones of the remarkable fact that men ate meat of their own killing.

6. RED DUST

It was very fortunate indeed that the feast took place when it did. Two days later it would probably have been impossible, and three days later it would have been too late to do any good. But coming when it did, it made the difference which was all the difference in the world.

Only thirty hours after the feasting which followed the death of the clotho spider, Burl's fellows—from Jon to Dor to Tet and Dik and Saya—had come to know a numb despair which the other creatures of his world were simply a bit too stupid to achieve.

It was night. There was darkness over all the lowlands, and over all the area of perhaps a hundred square miles which the humans of Burl's acquaintance really knew. He, alone of his tribe, had been as much as forty miles from the foraging-ground over which they wandered. At any given time the tribe clung together for comfort, venturing only as far as was necessary to find food. Although the planet possessed continents, they knew less than a good-sized county of it. The planet owned oceans, and they knew only small brooks and one river which, where they knew it, was assuredly less than two hundred yards across. And they faced stark disaster that was not strictly a local one, but beyond their experience and hopelessly beyond their ability to face.

They were superior to the insects about them only in the fact they realized what was threatening them.

The disaster was the red puffballs.

But it was night. The soft, blanketing darkness of a cloud-wrapped world lay all about. Burl sat awake, wrapped in his magnificent velvet cloak, his spear beside him and the yard-long golden plumes of a moth's antennae bound to his forehead for a headdress. About him and his tribesmen were the swollen shapes of fungi, hiding the few things that could be seen in darkness. From the low-hanging clouds the nightly rain dripped down. Now a drop and then another drop; slowly, deliberately, persistently, moisture fell from the skies.

There were other sounds. Things flew through the blackness overhead—moths with mighty wing-beats that sometimes sent rhythmic wind-stirrings down to the tribe in its hiding-place. There were the deep pulsations of sound made by night-beetles aloft. There were the harsh noises of grasshoppers—they were rare—senselessly advertising their existence to nearby predators. Not too far from where Burl brooded came bright chirrupings where relatively small beetles roamed among the mushroom-forests, singing cheerfully in deep bass voices. They were searching for the underground tidbits which took the place of truffles their ancestors had lived on back on Earth.

All seemed to be as it had been since the first humans were cast away upon this planet. And at night, indeed, the new danger subsided. The red puffballs did not burst after sunset. Burl sat awake, brooding in a new sort of frustration. He and all his tribe were plainly doomed—yet Burl had experienced too many satisfying sensations lately to be willing to accept the fact.

The new red growths were everywhere. Months ago a storm-wind blew while somewhere, not too far distant, other red puffballs were bursting and sending their spores into the air. Since it was only a windstorm, there was no rain to wash the air clean of the lethal dust. The new kind of puffball—but perhaps it was not new: it could have thriven for thousands of years where it was first thrown as a sport from a genetically unstable parent—the new kind of puffball would not normally be spread in this fashion. By chance it had.

There were dozens of the things within a quarter-mile, hundreds within a mile, and thousands upon thousands within the area the tribe normally foraged in. Burl had seen them even forty miles away, as yet immature. They would be deadly at one period alone— the time of their bursting. There were limitations even to the deadliness of the red puffballs, though Burl had not yet discovered the fact. But as of now, they doomed the tribe.

One woman panted and moaned in her exhausted sleep, a little way from where Burl tried to solve the problem presented by the tribe. Nobody else attempted to think it out. The others accepted doom with fatalistic hopelessness. Burl's leadership might mean extra food, but nothing could counter the doom awaiting them—so their thoughts seemed to run.

But Burl doggedly reviewed the facts in the darkness, while the humans about him slept the sleep of those without hope and even without rebellion. There had been many burstings of the crimson puffballs. As many as four and five of the deadly dust-clouds had been seen spouting into the air at the same time. A small boy of the tribe had breathlessly told of seeing a hunting-spider killed by the red dust. Lana, the half-grown girl, had come upon one of the gigantic rhinoceros-beetles belly-up on the ground, already the prey of ants. She had snatched a huge, meat-filled joint and run away, faster than the ants could follow. A far-ranging man had seen a butterfly, with wings ten yards across, die in a dust-cloud. Another woman—Cori—had been nearby when a red cloud settled slowly over long, solid lines of black worker-ants bound on some unknown mission. Later she saw other workers carrying the dead bodies back to the ant-city to be used for food.

Burl still sat wakeful and frustrated and enraged as the slow rain fell upon the toadstools that formed the tribe's lurking-place. He doggedly went over and over the problem. There were innumerable red puffballs. Some had burst. The others undoubtedly would burst. Anything that breathed the red dust died. With thousands of the puffballs around them it was unthinkable that any human in this place could escape breathing the red dust and dying. But it had not always been so. There had been a time when there were no red puff-balls here.

Burl's eyes moved restlessly over the sleeping forms limned by a patch of fox-fire. The feathery plumes rising from his head were outlined softly by the phosphorescence. His face was lined with a frown as he tried to think his own and his fellows' way out of the predicament. Without realizing it, Burl had taken it upon himself to think for his tribe. He had no reason to. It was simply a natural thing for him to do so, now that he had learned to think—even though his efforts were crude and painful as yet.

Saya woke with a start and stared about. There had been no alarm, merely the usual noises of distant

murders and the songs of singers in the night. Burl
moved restlessly. Saya stood up quietly, her long hair
flowing about her. Sleepy-eyed, she moved to be near
Burl. She sank to the ground beside him, sitting up—
because the hiding-place was crowded and small—and
dozed fitfully. Presently her head drooped to one side.
It rested against his shoulder. She slept again.

This simple act may have been the catalyst which
gave Burl the solution to the problem. Some few days
before, Burl had been in a far-away place where there
was much food. At the time he'd thought vaguely of
finding Saya and bringing her to that place. He remembered now that the red puffballs flourished there as
well as here—but there had been other dangers in
between, so the only half-formed purpose had been
abandoned. Now, though, with Saya's head resting
against his shoulder, he remembered the plan. And then
the stroke of genius took place.

He formed the idea of a journey which was not a
going-after-food. This present dwelling-place of the
tribe had been free of red puffballs until only recently.
There must be other places where there were no red
puffballs. He would take Saya and his tribesmen to such
a place.

It was really genius. The people of Burl's tribe had
no purposes, only needs—for food and the like. Burl
had achieved abstract thought—which previously had
not been useful on the forgotten planet and, therefore,
not practiced. But it was time for humankind to take
a more fitting place in the unbalanced ecological system of this nightmare world, time to change that
unbalance in favor of humans.

When dawn came, Burl had not slept at all. He was
all authority and decision. He had made plans.

He spoke sternly, loudly—which frightened people
conditioned to be furtive—holding up his spear as he

issued commands. His timid tribesfolk obeyed him meekly. They felt no loyalty to him or confidence in his decisions yet, but they were beginning to associate obedience to him with good things. Food, for one.

Before the day fully came, they made loads of the remaining edible mushroom and uneaten meat. It was remarkable for humans to leave their hiding-place while they still had food to eat, but Burl was implacable and scowling. Three men bore spears at Burl's urging. He brandished his long shaft confidently as he persuaded the other three to carry clubs. They did so reluctantly, even though previously they had killed ants with clubs. Spears, they felt, would have been better. They wouldn't be so close to the prey then.

The sky became gray over all its expanse. The indefinite bright area which marked the position of the sun became established. It was part-way toward the center of the sky when the journey began. Burl had, of course, no determined course, only a destination—safety. He had been carried south, in his misadventure on the river. There were red puffballs to southward, therefore he ruled out that direction. He could have chosen the east and come upon an ocean, but no safety from the red spore-dust. Or he could have chosen the north. It was pure chance that he headed west.

He walked confidently through the gruesome world of the lowlands, holding his spear in a semblance of readiness. Clad as he was, he made a figure at once valiant and rather pathetic. It was not too sensible for one young man—even one who had killed two spiders—to essay leading a tiny tribe of fearful folk across a land of monstrous ferocity and incredible malignancy, armed only with a spear from a dead insect's armor. It was absurd to dress up for the enterprise in a velvety cloak made of a moth's wing, blue moth-fur for a loin-cloth, and merely beautiful golden plumes bobbing above his forehead.

Probably, though, that gorgeousness had a good effect upon his followers. They surely could not reassure each other by their numbers! There was a woman with a baby in her arms—Cori. Three children of nine or ten, unable to resist the instinct to play even on so perilous a journey, ate almost constantly of the lumps of food-stuff they had been ordered to carry. After them came Dik, a long-legged adolescent boy with eyes that roved anxiously about. Behind him were two men. Dor with a short spear and Jak hefting a club, both of them badly frightened at the idea of fleeing from dangers they knew and were terrified by, to other dangers unknown and, consequently, more to be feared. The others trailed after them. Tet was rear-guard. Burl had separated the pair of boys to make them useful. Together they were worthless.

It was a pathetic caravan, in a way. In all the rest of the Galaxy, man was the dominant creature. There was no other planet from one rim to the other where men did not build their cities or settlements with unconscious arrogance—completely disregarding the wishes of lesser things. Only on this planet did men hide from danger rather than destroy it. Only here could men be driven from their place by lower life-forms. And only here would a migration be made on foot, with men's eyes fearful, their bodies poised to flee at sight of something stronger and more deadly than themselves.

They marched, straggling a little, with many waverings aside from a fixed line. Once Dik saw the trapdoor of a trapdoor-spider's lair. They halted, trembling, and went a long way out of their intended path to avoid it. Once they saw a great praying-mantis a good half-mile off, and again they deviated from their proper route.

Near midday their way was blocked. As they moved onward, a great, high-pitched sound could be heard ahead of them. Burl stopped; his face grew pinched. But it was only a stridulation, not the cries of creatures being devoured. It was a horde of ants by the thousands and hundreds of thousands, and nothing else.

Burl went ahead to scout. And he did it because he did not trust anybody else to have the courage or intelligence to return with a report, instead of simply running away if the news were bad. But it happened to be a sort of action which would help to establish his position as leader of his tribe.

Burl moved forward cautiously and presently came to an elevation from which he could see the cause of the tremendous waves of sound that spread out in all directions from the level plain before him. He waved to his followers to join him, and stood looking down at the extraordinary sight.

When they reached his side—and Saya was first— the spectacle had not diminished. For quite half a mile in either direction the earth was black with ants. It was a battle of opposing armies from rival ant-cities. They snapped and bit at each other. Locked in vise-like embraces, they rolled over and over upon the ground, trampled underfoot by hordes of their fellows who surged over them to engage in equally suicidal combat. There was, of course, no thought of surrender or of quarter. They fought by thousands of pairs, their jaws seeking to crush each other's armor, snapping at each other's antennae, biting at each other's eyes. . . .

The noise was not like that of army-ants. This was the agonizing sound of ants being dismembered while still alive. Some of the creatures had only one or two or three legs left, yet struggled fiercely to entangle another enemy before they died. There were mad cripples, fighting insanely with head and thorax only, their abdomens sheared away. The whining battle-cry of the multitude made a deafening uproar.

From either side of the battleground a wide path led back toward separate ant-cities which were invisible from Burl's position. These highways were marked by hurrying groups of ants—reinforcements rushing to the fight. Compared to the other creatures of this world the ants were small, but no lumbering beetle dared to march insolently in their way, nor did any carnivores try to prey upon them. They were dangerous. Burl and his tribesfolk were the only living things remaining near the battle-field—with one single exception.

That exception was itself a tribe of ants, vastly less in number than the fighting creatures, and greatly smaller in size as well. Where the combatants were from a foot to fourteen inches long, these guerilla-ants were no more than the third of a foot in length. They hovered industriously at the edge of the fighting, not as allies to either nation, but strictly on their own account. Scurrying among the larger, fighting ants with marvelous agility, they carried off piecemeal the bodies of the dead and valiantly slew the more gravely wounded for the same purpose.

They swarmed over the fighting-ground whenever the tide of battle receded. Caring nothing for the origin of the quarrel and espousing neither side, these opportunists busily salvaged the dead and still-living debris of the battle for their own purposes.

Burl and his followers were forced to make a two-mile detour to avoid the battle. The passage between bodies of scurrying reinforcements was a matter of some difficulty. Burl hurried the others past a route to the front, reeking of formic acid, over which endless regiments and companies of ants moved frantically to join in the fight. They were intensely excited. Antennae waving wildly, they rushed to the front and instantly flung themselves into the fray, becoming lost and indistinguishable in the black mass of fighting creatures.

The humans passed precariously between two hurrying battalions—Dik and Tet pausing briefly to burden themselves with prey—and hurried on to leave as many miles as possible behind them before nightfall. They never knew any more about the battle. It could have started over anything at all—two ants from the different cities may have disputed some tiny bit of carrion and soon been reinforced by companions until the military might of both cities was engaged. Once it had started, of course, the fighters knew whom to fight if not why they did so. The inhabitants of the two cities had different smells, which served them as uniforms.

But the outcome of the war would hardly matter. Not to the fighters, certainly. There were many red mushrooms in this area. If either of the cities survived at all, it would be because its nursery-workers lived upon stored food as they tended the grubs until the time of the spouting red dust had ended.

Burl's folk saw many of the red puffballs burst during the day. More than once they came upon empty, flaccid parchment sacs. More often still they came upon red puffballs not yet quite ready to emit their murderous seed.

That first night the tribe hid among the bases of giant puffballs of a more familiar sort. When touched they would shoot out a puff of white powder resembling smoke. The powder was harmless fortunately and the tribe knew that fact. Although not toxic, the white powder was identical in every other way to the terrible red dust from which the tribe fled.

That night Burl slept soundly. He had been without rest for two days and a night. And he was experienced in journeying to remote places. He knew that they were no more dangerous than familiar ones. But the rest of the tribe, and even Saya, were fearful and terrified. They waited timorously all through the dark hours for menacing sounds to crash suddenly through the steady dripping of the nightly rain around them.

The second day's journey was not unlike the first. The following day, they came upon a full ten-acre patch of giant cabbages bigger than a family dwelling. Something in the soil, perhaps, favored vegetation over fungi. The dozens of monstrous vegetables were the setting for riotous life: great slugs ate endlessly of the huge green leaves—and things preyed on them; bees came droning to gather the pollen of the flowers. And other things came to prey on the predators in their turn.

There was one great cabbage somewhat separate from the rest. After a long examination of the scene, Burl daringly led quaking Jon and Jak to the attack. Dor splendidly attacked elsewhere, alone. When the tribe moved on, there was much meat, and everyone— even the children—wore loin-cloths of incredibly luxurious fur.

There were perils, too. On the fifth day of the tribe's journey Burl suddenly froze into stillness. One of the hairy tarantulas which lived in burrows with a concealed trapdoor at ground-level, had fallen upon a scarabeus beetle and was devouring it only a hundred yards ahead. The tribesfolk trembled as Burl led them silently back and around by a safe detour.

But all these experiences were beginning to have an effect. It was becoming a matter of course that Burl should give orders which others should obey. It was even becoming matter-of-fact that the possession of food was not a beautiful excuse to hide from all danger, eating and dozing until all the food was gone. Very gradually the tribe was developing the notion that the purpose of existence was not solely to escape awareness of peril, but to foresee and avoid it. They had no clear-cut notion of purpose as yet. They were simply outgrowing purposelessness. After a time they even looked about them with dim stirrings of an attitude other than a desperate alertness for danger.

Humans from any other planet, surely, would have been astounded at the vistas of golden mushrooms stretching out in forests on either hand and the plains with flaking surfaces given every imaginable color by the molds and rusts and tiny flowering yeasts growing upon them. They would have been amazed by the turgid pools the journeying tribe came upon, where the water was concealed by a thick layer of slime through which enormous bubbles of foul-smelling gas rose to enlarge to preposterous size before bursting abruptly.

Had they been as ill-armed as Burl's folk, though, visitors from other planets would have been at least as timorous. Lacking highly specialized knowledge of the ways of insects on this world even well-armed visitors would have been in greater danger.

But the tribe went on without a single casualty. They had fleeting glimpses of the white spokes of symmetrical spider-webs whose least thread no member of the tribe could break.

Their immunity from disaster—though in the midst of danger—gave them a certain all-too-human concentration upon discomfort. Lacking calamities, they noticed their discomforts and grew weary of continual traveling. A few of the men complained to Burl.

For answer, he pointed back along the way they had come. To the right a reddish dust-cloud was just settling, and to the rear rose another as they looked.

And on this day a thing happened which at once gave the complainers the rest they asked for, and proved the fatality of remaining where they were. A child ran aside from the path its elders were following. The ground here had taken on a brownish hue. As the child stirred up the surface mold with his feet, dust that had settled was raised up again. It was far too thin to have any visible color. But the child suddenly screamed, strangling. The mother ran frantically to snatch him up.

The red dust was no less deadly merely because it had settled to the ground. If a storm-wind came now— but they were infrequent under the forgotten planet's heavy bank of clouds—the fallen red dust could be raised up again and scattered about until there would be no living thing anywhere which would not gasp and writhe—and die.

But the child would not die. He would suffer terribly and be weak for days. In the morning he could be carried.

When night began to darken the sky, the tribe searched for a hiding-place. They came upon a shelf-like cliff, perhaps twenty or thirty feet high, slanting toward the line of the tribesmen's travel. Burl saw black spots in it—openings. Burrows. He watched them as the tribe drew near. No bees or wasps went in or out. He watched long enough to be sure.

When they were close, he was certain. Ordering the others to wait, he went forward to make doubly sure. The appearance of the holes reassured him. Dug months before by mining-bees, gone or dead now, the entrances to the burrows were weathered and bedraggled. Burl explored, first sniffing carefully at each opening. They were empty. This would be shelter for the night. He called his followers, and they crawled into the three-foot tunnels to hide.

Burl stationed himself near the outer edge of one of them to watch for signs of danger. Night had not quite fallen. Jon and Dor, hungry, went off to forage a little way beyond the cliff. They would be cautious and timid, taking no risks whatever.

Burl waited for the return of his explorers. Meanwhile he fretted over the meaning of the stricken child. Stirred-up red dust was dangerous. The only time when there would be no peril from it would be at night, when the dripping rainfall of the dark hours turned the surface of this world into thin slime. It occurred to Burl that it would be safe to travel at night, so far as the red dust was concerned. He rejected the idea instantly. It was unthinkable to travel at night for innumerable other reasons.

Frowning, he poked his spear idly at a tumbled mass of tiny parchment cup-like things near the entrance of a cave. And instantly movement became visible. Fifty, sixty, a hundred infinitesimal creatures, no more than half an inch in length, made haste to hide themselves among the thimble-sized paper-like cups. They moved with extraordinary clumsiness and immense effort, seemingly only by contortions of their greenish-black bodies. Burl had never seen any creature progress in such a slow and ineffective fashion. He drew one of the small creatures back with the point of his spear and examined it from a safe distance.

He picked it up on his spear and brought it close to his eyes. The thing redoubled its frenzied movements. It slipped off the spear and plopped upon the soft moth-fur he wore about his middle. Instantly, as if it were a conjuring-trick, the insect vanished. Burl searched for minutes before he found it hidden deep in the long, soft hairs of his garment, resting motionless and seemingly at ease.

It was the larval form of a beetle, fragments of whose armor could be seen near the base of the clayey cliff-side. Hidden in the remnants of its egg-casings, the brood of minute things had waited near the opening of the mining-bee tunnel. It was their gamble with destiny when mining-bee grubs had slept through metamorphosis and come uncertainly out of the tunnel for the first time, that some or many of the larvae might snatch the instant's chance to fasten to the bees' legs and writhe upward to an anchorage in their fur. It happened that this particular batch of eggs had been laid after the emergence of the grubs. They had no possible chance of fulfilling their intended role as parasites on insects of the order hymenoptera. They were simply and matter-of-factly doomed by the blindness of instinct, which had caused them to be placed where they could not possibly survive.

On the other hand, if one or many of them had found a lurking-place, the offspring of their host would have been doomed. The place filled by oil-beetle larvae in the scheme of things is the place—or one of the places—reserved for creatures that limit the number of mining-bees. When a bee-louse-infested mining-bee has made a new tunnel, stocked it with honey for its young, and then laid one egg to float on that pool of nourishment and hatch and feed and ultimately grow to be another mining-bee—at that moment of egg-laying, one small bee-louse detaches itself. It remains zestfully in the provisioned cell to devour the egg for which the provisions were accumulated. It happily consumes those provisions and, in time, an oil-beetle crawls out of the tunnel a mining-bee so laboriously prepared.

Burl had no difficulty in detaching the small insect and casting it away, but in doing so he discovered that others had hidden themselves in his fur without his knowledge. He plucked them away and found more. While savages can be highly tolerant of vermin too small to be seen, they feel a peculiar revolt against serving as host to creatures of sensible size. Burl reacted violently—as once he had reacted to the discovery of a leech clinging to his heel. He jerked off his loin-cloth and beat it savagely with his spear.

When it was clean, he still felt a wholly unreasonable sense of humiliation. It was not clearly thought out, of course. Burl feared huge insects too much to hate them. But that small creatures should fasten upon him produced a completely irrational feeling of outrage. For the first time in very many years or centuries a human being upon the forgotten planet felt that he had been insulted. His dignity had been assailed. Burl raged.

But as he raged, a triumphant shout came from nearby. Jon and Dor were returning from their foraging, loaded down with edible mushroom. They, also, had taken a step upward toward the natural dignity of men. They had so far forgotten their terror as to shout in exultation at their find of food. Up to now, Burl had been the only man daring to shout. Now there were two others.

In his overwrought state this was also enraging. The result of hurt vanity on two counts was jealousy, and the result of jealousy was a crazy foolhardiness. Burl ground his teeth and insanely resolved to do something so magnificent, so tremendous, so utterly breathtaking that there could be no possible imitation by anybody else. His thinking was not especially clear. Part of his motivation had been provided by the oil-beetle larvae. He glared about him at the deepening dusk, seeking some exploit, some glamorous feat, to perform immediately, even in the night.

He found one.

7. JOURNEY THROUGH DEATH

It was late dusk and the reddened clouds overhead were deepening steadily toward black. Dark shadows hung everywhere. The clay cliff cut off all vision to one side, but elsewhere Burl could see outward until the graying haze blotted out the horizon. Here and there, bees droned homeward to hive or burrow. Sometimes a slender, graceful wasp passed overhead, its wings invisible by the swiftness of their vibration.

A few butterflies lingered hungrily in the distance, seeking the few things they could still feast upon. No moth had wakened yet to the night. The cloud-bank grew more somber. The haze seemed to close in and shrink the world that Burl could see.

He watched, raging, for the sight that would provide him with the triumph to end all triumphs among his followers. The soft, down-reaching fingers of the night touched here and there and the day ended at those spots. Then, from the heart of the deep redness to the west a flying creature came. It was a beautiful thing—a yellow emperor butterfly—flapping eastward with great sail-like velvet wings that seemed black against the sunset. Burl saw it sweep across the incredible sky, alight delicately, and disappear behind a mass of toadstools clustered so thickly they seemed nearly a hillock and not a mass of growing things.

Then darkness closed in completely, but Burl still stared where the yellow emperor had landed. There was that temporary, utter quiet when day-things were hidden and night-things had not yet ventured out. Foxfire glowed. Patches of pale phosphorescence— luminous mushrooms—shone faintly in the dark.

Presently Burl moved through the night. He could imagine the yellow emperor in its hiding-place, delicately preening slender limbs before it settled down to rest until the new day dawned. He had noted landmarks, to guide himself. A week earlier and his blood would have run cold at the bare thought of doing what he did now. In mere coolheaded detachment he would have known that what he did was close to madness. But he was neither cool-headed nor detached.

He crossed the clear ground before the low cliff. But for the fox-fire beacons he would have been lost instantly. The slow drippings of rain began. The sky was dead black. Now was the time for night-things to fly, and male tarantulas to go seeking mates and prey. It was definitely no time for adventuring.

Burl moved on. He found the close-packed toadstools by the process of running into them in the total obscurity. He fumbled, trying to force his way between them. It could not be done; they grew too close and too low. He raged at this impediment. He climbed.

This was insanity. Burl stood on spongy mushroom-stuff that quivered and yielded under his weight. Somewhere something boomed upward, rising on fast-beating wings into blackness. He heard the pulsing drone of four-inch mosquitoes close by. He moved forward, the fungus support swaying, so that he did not so much walk as stagger over the close-packed mushroom heads. He groped before him with this spear and panted a little. There was a part of him which was bitterly afraid, but he raged the more furiously because if once he gave way even to caution, it would turn to panic.

Burl would have made a strange spectacle in daylight, gaudily clothed as he was in soft blue fur and velvet cloak, staggering over swaying insecurity, coddling ferocity in himself against the threat of fear.

Then his spear told him there was emptiness ahead. Something moved, below. He heard and felt it stirring the toadstool-stalks on which he stood.

Burl raised his spear, grasping it in both hands. He plunged down with it, stabbing fiercely.

The spear struck something vastly more resistant than any mushroom could be. It penetrated. Then the stabbed thing moved as Burl landed upon it, flinging him off his feet, but he clung to the firmly imbedded weapon. And if his mouth had opened for a yell of victory as he plunged down, the nature of the surface on which he found himself, and the kind of movement he felt, turned that yell into a gasp of horror.

It wasn't the furry body of a butterfly he had landed on; his spear hadn't pierced such a creature's soft flesh. He had leaped upon the broad, hard back of a huge, meat-eating, nocturnal beetle. His spear had pierced not the armor, but the leathery joint-tissue between head and thorax.

The giant creature rocketed upward with Burl clinging to his spear. He held fast with an agonized strength. His mount rose from the blackness of the ground into the many times more terrifying blackness of the air.

It rose up and up. If Burl could have screamed, he would have done so, but he could not cry out. He could only hold fast, glassy-eyed.

Then he dropped. Wind roared past him. The great insect was clumsy at flying. All beetles are. Burl's weight and the pain it felt made its flying clumsier still. There was a semi-liquid crashing and an impact. Burl was torn loose and hurled away. He crashed into the spongy top of a mushroom and came to rest with his naked shoulder hanging halfway over some invisible drop. He struggled.

He heard the whining drone of his attempted prey. It rocketed aloft again. But there was something wrong with it. With his weight applied to the spear as he was torn free, Burl had twisted the weapon in the wound. It had driven deeper, multiplying the damage of the first stab.

The beetle crashed to earth again, nearby. As Burl struggled again, the mushroom-stalk split and let him gently to the ground.

He heard the flounderings of the great beetle in the darkness. It mounted skyward once more, its wing-beats no longer making a sustained note. It thrashed the air irregularly and wildly.

Then it crashed again.

There was seeming silence, save for the steady drip-drip of the rain. And Burl came out of his half-mad fear: he suddenly realized that he had slain a victim even more magnificent than a spider, because this creature was meat.

He found himself astonishedly running toward the spot where the beetle had last fallen.

But he heard it struggle aloft once more. It was wounded to death. Burl felt certain of it this time. It floundered in mid-air and crashed again.

He was within yards of it before he checked

himself. Now he was weaponless, and the gigantic
insect flung itself about madly on the ground, striking out with colossal wings and limbs, fighting it knew
not what. It struggled to fly, crashed, and fought its
way off the ground—ever more weakly—then smashed
again into mushrooms. There it floundered horribly
in the darkness.

Burl drew near and waited. It was still, but pain
again drove it to a senseless spasm of activity.

Then it struck against something. There was a ripping noise and instantly the close, peppery, burning
smell of the red dust was in the air. The beetle had
floundered into one of the close-packed red puffballs,
tightly filled with the deadly red spores. The red dust
would not normally have been released at night. With
the nightly rain, it would not travel so far or spread
so widely.

Burl fled, panting.

Behind him he heard his victim rise one last time,
spurred to impossible, final struggle by the anguish
caused by the breathed-in red dust. It rose clumsily
into the darkness in its death-throes and crashed to the
ground again for the last time.

In time to come, Burl and his followers might learn
to use the red-dust puffballs as weapons—but not how
to spread them beyond their normal range. But now,
Burl was frightened. He moved hastily sidewise. The
dust would travel down-wind. He got out of its possible path.

There could be no exultation where the red dust
was. Burl suddenly realized what had happened to him.
He had been carried aloft an unknown though not-great
distance, in an unknown direction. He was separated
from his tribe, with no faintest idea how to find them
in the darkness. And it was night.

He crouched under the nearest huge toadstool and

waited for the dawn, listening dry-throated for the sound of death coming toward him through the night.

But only the wind-beats of night-fliers came to his ears, and the discordant notes of gray-bellied truffle-beetles as they roamed the mushroom thickets, seeking the places beneath which—so their adapted instincts told them—fungoid dainties, not too much unlike the truffles of Earth, awaited the industrious miner. And, of course, there was that eternal, monotonous dripping of the rain-drops, falling at irregular intervals from the sky.

Red puffballs did not burst at night. They would not burst anyhow, except at one certain season of their growth. But Burl and his folk had so far encountered the over-hasty ones, bursting earlier than most. The time of ripeness was very nearly here, though. When day came again, and the chill dampness of the night was succeeded by the warmth of the morning, almost the first thing Burl saw in the gray light was a tall spouting of brownish-red stuff leaping abruptly into the air from a burst red parchment-like sphere.

He stood up and looked anxiously all around. Here and there, all over the landscape, slowly and at intervals, the plumes of fatal red sprang into the air. There was nothing quite like it anywhere else. An ancient man, inhabiting Earth, might have likened the appearance to that of a scattered and leisurely bombardment. But Burl had no analogy for them.

He saw something hardly a hundred yards from where he had hidden during the night. The dead beetle lay there, crumpled and limp. Burl eyed it speculatively. Then he saw something that filled him with elation. The last crash of the beetle to the ground had driven his spear deeply between the joints of the corselet and neck. Even if the red dust had not finished the creature, the spear-point would have ended its life.

He was thrilled once more by his superlative great-ness. He made due note that he was a mighty slayer. He took the antennae as proof of his valor and hacked off a great barb-edged leg for meat. And then he remembered that he did not know how to find his fellow-tribesmen. He had no idea which way to go.

Even a civilized man would have been at a loss, though he would have hunted for an elevation from which to look for the cliff hiding-place of the tribe. But Burl had not yet progressed so far. His wild ride of the night before had been at random, and the chase after the wounded beetle no less dictated by chance. There was no answer.

He set off anxiously, searching everywhere. But he had to be alert for all the dangers of an inimical world while keeping, at the same time, an extremely sharp eye out for bursting red puffballs.

At the end of an hour he thought he saw familiar things. Then he recognized the spot. He had come back to the dead beetle. It was already the center of a mass of small black bodies which pulled and hacked at the tough armor, gnawing out great lumps of flesh to be carried to the nearest ant-city.

Burl set off again, very carefully avoiding any place that he recognized as having been seen that morning. Sometimes he walked through mushroom-thickets—dangerous places to be in—and sometimes over rela-tively clear ground colored exotically with varicolored fungi. More than once he saw the clouds of red stuff spurting in the distance. Deep anxiety filled him. He had no idea that there were such things as points of the compass. He knew only that he needed desperately to find his tribesfolk again.

They, of course, had given him up for dead. He had vanished in the night. Old Tama complained of him shrilly. The night, to them, meant death. Jon quaked watchfully all through it. When Burl did not come to the feast of mushroom that Jon and Dor had brought back, they sought him. They even called timidly into the darkness. They heard the throbbing of huge wings as a great creature rose desperately into the sky, but they did not associate that sound with Burl. If they had, they would have been instantly certain of his fate.

As it was, the tribe's uneasiness grew into terror which rapidly turned to despair. They began to tremble, wondering what they would do with no bold chieftain to guide them. He was the first man to command allegiance from others in much too long a period, on the forgotten planet, but the submission of his followers had been the more complete for its novelty. His loss was the more appalling. Burl had mistaken the triumphant shout of the foragers. He'd thought it independence of him—rivalry. Actually, the men dared to shout only because they felt secure under his leadership. When they accepted the fact that he had vanished—and to disappear in the night had always meant death—their old fears and timidity returned. To them it was added despair.

They huddled together and whispered to one another of their fright. They waited in trembling silence through all the long night. Had a hunting-spider appeared, they would have fled in as many directions as there were people, and undoubtedly all would have perished. But day came again, and they looked into each other's eyes and saw the selfsame fear. Saya was probably the most pitiful of the group. Her face was white and drawn beyond that of any one else.

They did not move when day brightened. They remained about the bee-tunnels, speaking in hushed tones, huddled together, searching all the horizon for enemies. Saya would not eat, but sat still, staring before her in numbed grief. Burl was dead.

Atop the low cliff a red puffball glistened in the
morning light. Its tough skin was taut and bulging,
resisting the pressure of the spores within. Slowly, as
the morning wore on, some of the moisture that kept
the skin stretchable dried. The parchment-like stuff
contracted. The tautness of the spore-packed envelope
grew greater. It became insupportable.

With a ripping sound, the tough skin split across and
a rush of the compressed spores shot skyward.

The tribesmen saw and cried out and fled. The red
stuff drifted down past the cliff-edge. It drifted toward
the humans. They ran from it. Jon and Tama ran fast-
est. Jak and Cori and the others were not far behind.
Saya trailed, in her despair.

Had Burl been there, matters would have been
different. He had already such an ascendancy over the
minds of the others that even in panic they would have
looked to see what he did. And he would have dodged
the slowly drifting death-cloud by day, as he had during
the night. But his followers ran blindly.

As Saya fled after the others she heard shrieks of
fright to the left and ran faster. She passed by a thick
mass of distorted fungi in which there was a sudden
stirring and panic lent wings to her feet. She fled
blindly, panting. Ahead was a great mass of stuff—red
puffballs—showing here and there among great fanlike growths, some twelve feet high, that looked like
sponges.

She fled past them and swerved to hide herself from
anything that might be pursuing by sight. Her foot
slipped on the slimy body of a shell-less snail and she
fell heavily, her head striking a stone. She lay still.

Almost as if at a signal a red puffball burst among
the fanlike growths. A thick, dirty-red cloud of dust
shot upward, spread and billowed and began to settle
slowly toward the ground again. It moved as it settled,

flowing over the inequalities of the ground as a monstrous snail or leach might have done, sucking from all breathing creatures the life they had within them. It was a hundred yards away, then fifty, then thirty. . . .

Had any member of the tribe watched it, the red dust might have seemed malevolently intelligent. But when the edges of the dust-cloud were no more than twenty yards from Saya's limp body, an opposing breeze sprang up. It was a vagrant, fitful little breeze that halted the red cloud and threw it into some confusion, sending it in a new direction. It passed Saya without hurting her, though one of its misty tendrils reached out as if to snatch at her in slow-motion. But it passed her by.

Saya lay motionless on the ground. Only her breast rose and fell shallowly. A tiny pool of red gathered near her head.

Some thirty feet from where she lay, there were three miniature toadstools in a clump, bases so close together that they seemed but one. From between two of them, however, two tufts of reddish thread appeared. They twinkled back and forth and in and out. As if reassured, two slender antennae followed, then bulging eyes and a small, black body with bright-red scalloped markings upon it.

It was a tiny beetle no more than eight inches long—a sexton or burying-beetle. Drawing near Saya's body it scurried onto her flesh. It went from end to end of her figure in a sort of feverish haste. Then it dived into the ground beneath her shoulder, casting back a little shower of hastily-dug dirt as it disappeared.

Ten minutes later, another small creature appeared, precisely like the first. Upon the heels of the second came a third. Each made the same hasty examination and dived under her unmoving form.

Presently the ground seemed to billow at a spot

along Saya's side and then at another. Ten minutes after
the arrival of the third beetle, a little rampart had
reared itself all about Saya's body, following her outlines precisely. Then her body moved slightly, in little
jerks, seeming to settle perhaps half an inch into the
ground.

The burying-beetles were of that class of creatures
which exploited the bodies of the fallen. Working
from below, they excavated the earth. When there
was a hollow space below they turned on their backs
and thrust up with their legs, jerking at the body
until it sank into the space they had made ready.
The process would be repeated until at last all their
dead treasures had settled down below the level of
the surrounding ground. The loosened dirt then fell
in at the sides, completing the inhumation. Then,
in the underground darkness, it was the custom
for the beetles to feast magnificently, gorging
themselves upon the food they had hidden from
other scavengers—and of course rearing their young
also upon its substance.

Ants and flies were rivals of these beetles and not
infrequently the sexton-beetles came upon carrion after
ants had taken their toll, and when it already swarmed
with maggots. But in this case Saya was not dead. The
fact that she still lived, though unconscious, was the
factor that had given the sexton-beetles this splendid
opportunity.

She breathed gently and irregularly, her face drawn
with the sorrow of the night before, while the desperately hurrying beetles swarmed about beneath her body,
channeling away the soil so she would sink lower and
lower into it. She descended slowly, a half-inch by a
half-inch. The bright-red tufts of thread appeared again
and a beetle made its way to the open air. It moved
hastily about, inspecting the progress of the work.

It dived below again. Another inch and, after a long time, another, were excavated.

Matters still progressed when Burl stepped out from a group of overshadowing toadstools and halted. He cast his eyes over the landscape and was struck by its familiarity. He was, in fact, very near the spot he had left the night before in that maniacal ride on the back of a flying beetle. He moved back and forth, trying to account for the feeling of recognition.

He saw the low cliff, then, and moved eagerly toward it, passing within fifty feet of Saya's body, now more than half-buried in the ground. The loose dirt around the outline of her figure was beginning to topple in little rivulets upon her. One of her shoulders was already half-screened from view. Burl passed on, unseeing.

He hurried a little. In a moment he recognized his location exactly. There were the mining-bee burrows. There was a thrown-away lump of edible mushroom, cast aside as the tribesfolk fled.

His feet stirred up a fine dust, and he stopped short. A red puffball had burst here. It fully accounted for the absence of the tribe, and Burl sweated in sudden fear. He thought instantly of Saya. He went carefully to make sure. This was, absolutely, the hiding place of the tribe. There was another mushroom-fragment. There was a spear, thrown down by one of the men in his flight. Red dust had settled upon the spear and the mushroom-fragments.

Burl turned back, hurrying again, but taking care to disturb the dust no more than he could possibly help.

The little excavation into which Saya was sinking inch by inch was not in his path. Her body no longer lay above the ground, but in it. Burl went by, frantic with anxiety about the tribe, but about Saya most of all.

Her body quivered and sank a fraction into the ground. Half a dozen small streams of earth were tumbling upon her. In minutes she would be wholly hidden from view.

Burl went to beat among the mushroom-thickets, in quest of the bodies of his tribesfolk. They could have staggered out of the red dust and collapsed beyond. He would have shouted, but the deep sense of loneliness silenced him. His throat ached with grief. He searched on. . . .

There was a noise. From a huge clump of toadstools—perhaps the very one he had climbed over in the night—there came the sound of crashings and the breaking of the spongy stuff. Twin tapering antennae appeared, and then a monster beetle lurched into the open space, its ghastly mandibles gaping sidewise.

It was all of eight feet long and supported by six crooked, saw-toothed legs. Huge, multiple eyes stared with preoccupation at the world. It advanced deliberately with clankings and clashings as of a hideous machine. Burl fled on the instant, running directly away from it.

A little depression lay in the ground before him. He did not swerve, but made to jump over it. As he leaped he saw the color of bare flesh, Saya, limp and helpless, sinking slowly into the ground with tricklings of dirt falling down to cover her. It seemed to Burl that she quivered a little.

Instantly there was a terrific struggle within Burl. Behind him was the giant meat-eating beetle; beneath him was Saya whom he loved. There was certain death lurching toward him on evilly crooked legs—and the life he had hoped for lay in a shallow pit. Of course, he thought Saya dead.

Perhaps it was rage, or despair, or a simple human

madness which made him act otherwise than rationally. The things which raise humans above brute creation, however, are only partly reasonable. Most human emotions—especially the creditable ones—cannot be justified by reason, and very few heroic actions are based upon logical thought.

Burl whirled as he landed, his puny spear held ready. In his left hand he held the haunch of a creature much like the one which clanked and rattled toward him. With a yell of insane defiance—completely beyond justification by reason—Burl flung that meat-filled leg at the monster.

It hit. Undoubtedly, it hurt. The beetle seized it ferociously. It crushed it. There was meat in it, sweet and juicy.

The beetle devoured it. It forgot the man standing there, waiting for death. It crunched the leg-joint of a cousin or brother, confusing the blow with the missile that had delivered it. When the tidbit was finished it turned and lumbered off to investigate another mushroom thicket. It seemed to consider that an enemy had been conquered and devoured and that normal life could go on.

Then Burl stooped quickly, and dragged Saya from the grave the sexton-beetles had labored so feverishly to provide for her. Crumbled soil fell from her shoulders, from her face, and from her body. Three little eight-inch beetles with black-and-red markings scurried for cover in terrified haste. Burl carried Saya to a resting-place of soft mold to mourn over her.

He was a completely ignorant savage, save that he knew more of the ways of insects than anybody anywhere else—the Ecological Service, which had stocked this planet, not being excepted. To Burl the unconsciousness of Saya was as death itself. Dumb misery smote him, and he laid her down gently and quite literally wept. He had been beautifully pleased with himself for having slain one flying beetle. But for Saya's seeming death, he would have been almost unbearable with pride over having put another to flight. But now he was merely a broken-hearted, very human young man.

But a long time later Saya opened her eyes and looked about bewilderedly.

They were in considerable danger for some time after that, because they were oblivious to everything but each other. Saya rested in half-incredulous happiness against Burl's shoulder as he told her jerkily of his attempt on a night-bound butterfly, which turned out to be a flying beetle that took him aloft. He told of his search for the tribe and then his discovery of her apparently lifeless body. When he spoke of the monster which had lurched from the mushroom thicket, and of the desperation with which he had faced it, Saya looked at him with warm, proud eyes. But Burl was abruptly struck with the remarkable convenience of that discovery. If his tribesmen could secure an ample supply of meat, they might defend themselves against attack by throwing it to their attackers. In fact, insects were so stupid that almost any object thrown quickly enough and fast enough, might be made to serve as sacrifices instead of themselves.

A timid, frightened whisper roused them from their absorption. They looked up. The boy Dik stood some distance away, staring at them wide-eyed, almost convinced that he looked upon the living dead. A sudden movement on the part of either of them would have sent him bolting away. Two or three other bobbing heads gazed affrightedly from nearby hiding-places. Jon was poised for flight.

The tribe had come back to its former hiding-place

simply as a way to reassemble. They had believed both Burl and Saya dead, and they accepted Burl's death as their own doom. But now they stared.

Burl spoke—fortunately without arrogance—and Dik and Tet came timorously from their hiding-places. The others followed, the tribe forming a frightened half-circle about the seated pair. Burl spoke again and presently one of the bravest—Cori—dared to approach and touch him. Instantly a babble of the crude labial language of the tribe broke out. Awed exclamations and questions filled the air.

But Burl, for once, showed some common sense. Instead of a vainglorious recital, he merely cast down the long tapering antennae of the flying-beetle. They looked, and recognized their origin.

Then Burl curtly ordered Dor and Jak to make a chair of their hands for Saya. She was weak from her fall and the loss of blood. The two men humbly advanced and obeyed. Then Burl curtly ordered the march resumed.

They went on, more slowly than on previous days, but nonetheless steadily. Burl led them across-country, marching in advance with a matter-of-fact alertness for signs of danger. He felt more confidence than ever before. It was not fully justified, of course. Jon now retrieved the spear he had discarded. The small party fairly bristled with weapons. But Burl knew that they were liable to be cast away as impediments if flight seemed necessary.

As he led the way Burl began to think busily in the manner that only leaders find necessary. He had taught his followers to kill ants for food, though they were still uneasy about such adventures. He had led them to attack great yellow grubs upon giant cabbages. But they had not yet faced any actual danger, as he had done. He must drive them to face something. . . .

The opportunity came that same day, in late afternoon. To westward the cloud-bank was barely beginning to show the colors that presage nightfall, when a bumblebee droned heavily overhead, making for its home burrow. The little, straggling group of marching people looked up and saw the scanty load of pollen packed in the stiff bristles of the bee's hind-legs. It sped onward heavily, its almost transparent wings mere blurs in the air.

It was barely fifty feet above the ground. Burl dropped his glance and tensed. A slender-waisted wasp was shooting upward from an ambush among the noisome fungi of this plain.

The bee swerved and tried to escape. The wasp overhauled it. The bee dodged frantically. It was a good four feet in length—as large as the wasp, certainly—but it was more heavily built and could not make the speed of which the wasp was capable. It dodged with less agility. Twice, in desperation, it did manage to evade the plunging dives of the wasp, but the third time the two insects grappled in midair almost over the heads of the humans.

They tumbled downward in a clawing, biting, tangle of bodies and legs. They hit the ground and rolled over and over. The bee struggled to insert her barbed sting in the more supple body of her adversary. She writhed and twisted desperately.

But there came an instant of infinite confusion and the bee lay on her back. The wasp suddenly moved with that ghastly skilled precision of a creature performing an incredible feat instinctively, apparently unaware that it is doing so. The dazed bee was swung upright in a peculiarly artificial pose. The wasp's body curved, and its deadly, rapier-sharp sting struck. . . .

The bee was dead. Instantly. As if struck dead by lightning. The wasp had stung in a certain place in the neck-parts where all the nerve-cords pass. To sting there, the wasp had to bring its victim to a particular pose. It was precisely the trick of a *desnucador*, the butcher who kills cattle by severing the spinal cord. For the wasp's purposes the bee had to be killed in this fashion and no other.

Burl began to give low-toned commands to his followers. He knew what was coming next, and so did they. When the sequel of the murder began he moved forward, his tribesmen wavering after him. This venture was actually one of the least dangerous they could attempt, but merely to attack a wasp was a hair-raising idea. Only Burl's prestige plus their knowledge made them capable of it.

The second act of the murder-drama was gruesomeness itself. The pirate-wasp was a carnivore, but this was the season when the wasps raised young. Inevitably there was sweet honey in the half-filled crop of the bee. Had she arrived safely at the hive, the sweet and sticky liquid would have been disgorged for the benefit of bee-grubs. The wasp avidly set to work to secure that honey. The bee-carcass itself was destined for the pirate-wasp's own offspring, and that squirming monstrosity is even more violently carnivorous than its mother. The parent wasp set about extracting the dead bee's honey, before taking the carcass to its young one, because honey is poisonous to the pirate-wasp's grub. Yet insects cannot act from solicitude or anything but instinct. And instinct must be maintained by lavish rewards.

So the pirate-wasp sought its reward—an insane, insatiable, gluttonous satisfaction in the honey that was poison to its young. The wasp rolled its murdered victim upon its back again and feverishly pressed on the limp body to force out the honey. And this was the reason for its precise manner of murder. Only when

killed by the destruction of all nerve-currents would the
bee's body be left limp like this. Only a bee killed in this
exact fashion would yield its honey to manipulation.

The honey appeared, flowing from the dead bee's
mouth. The wasp, in trembling, ghoulish ecstasy,
devoured it as it appeared. It was lost to all other sights
or sensations but its feast.

And this was the moment when Burl signaled for
the attack. The tribesmen's prey was deaf and blind
and raptured. It was aware of nothing but the delight
it savored. But the men wavered, nevertheless, when
they drew near. Burl was first to thrust his spear
powerfully into the trembling body.

When he was not instantly destroyed the others took
courage. Dor's spear penetrated the very vitals of the
ghoul. Jak's club fell with terrific force upon the wasp's
slender waist. There was a crackling, and the long,
spidery limbs quivered and writhed. Then Burl struck
again and the creature fell into two writhing halves.

They butchered it rather messily, but Burl noticed
that even as it died, sundered and pierced with spears,
its long tongue licked out in one last rapturous taste
of the honey that had been its undoing.

Some time later, burdened with the pollen-laden legs
of the great bee, the tribe resumed its journey.

Now Burl had men behind him. They were still
timid and prone to flee at the least alarm, but they
were vastly more dependable than they had been. They
had attacked and slain a wasp whose sting would have
killed any of them. They had done battle under the
leadership of Burl, whose spear had struck the first
blow. They were sharers of his glory and, therefore,
much more nearly like the followers of a chieftain
ought to be.

Their new spirit was badly needed. The red puffballs were certainly no less numerous in the new

territory the tribe traversed than in the territory they had left. And the season of their ripening was further advanced. More and more of the ground showed the deadly rime of settled death-dust. To stay alive was increasingly difficult. When the full spore-casting season arrived, it would be impossible. And that season could not be far away.

The very next day after the killing of the wasp, survival despite the red dust had begun to seem unimaginable. Where, earlier, one saw a red-dust cloud bursting here and there at intervals, on this day there was always a billowing mass of lethal vapor in the air. At no time was the landscape free of a moving mist of death. Usually there were three or four in sight at once. Often there were half a dozen. Once there were eight. It could be guessed that in one day more they would ripen in such monstrous numbers that anything which walked or flew or crawled must breathe in the spores and perish.

And that day, just at sunset, the tribe came to the top of a small rise in the ground. For an hour they had been marching and countermarching to avoid the suddenly-billowing clouds of dust. Once they had been nearly hemmed in when three of the dull-red mists seemed to flow together, enclosing the three sides of a circle. They escaped then only by the most desperate of sprinting.

But now they came to the little hillock and halted. Before them stretched a plain, all of four miles wide, colored a brownish brick-red by the red puffballs. The tribe had seen mushroom forests—they had lived in them—and knew of the dangers that lurked there. But the plain before them was not simply dangerous; it was fatal. To right and left it stretched as far as the eye could see, but away on its farther edge Burl caught a glimpse of flowing water.

Over the plain itself a thin red haze seemed to float. It was simply a cloud of the deadly spores, dispersed and indefinite, but constantly replenished by the freshly bursting puffballs. While the tribesfolk stood and watched, thick columns of dust rose here and there and at the other place, too many to count. They settled again but left behind enough of the fine powder to keep a thin red haze over all the plain. This was a mass of literally millions of the deadly growths. Here was one place where no carnivorous beetles roamed and where no spiders lurked. There were nothing here but the sullen columns of dust and the haze that they left behind.

And of course it would be nothing less than suicide to try to go back.

8. A FLIGHT CONTINUES

Burl kept his people alive until darkness fell. He had assigned watchers for each direction and when flight was necessary the adults helped the children to avoid the red dust. Four times they changed direction after shrill-voiced warnings. When night settled over the plain they were forced to come to a halt.

But the puffballs were designed to burst by day. Stumbled into, they could split at any time, and the humans did hear some few of the tearing noises that denoted a spore-spout in the darkness. But after slow nightly rain began they heard no more.

Burl led his people into the plain of red puffballs as soon as the rain had lasted long enough to wash down the red haze still hanging in the air and turn the fallen spores to mud.

It was an enterprise of such absolute desperation that very likely no civilized man would have tried it. There were no stars, for guidance, nor compasses to show the way. There were no lights to enable them to dodge the deadly things they strove to escape, and there was no possibility of their keeping a straight course in the darkness. They had to trust to luck in perhaps the longest long-shot that humans ever accepted as a gamble.

Quaintly, they used the long antennae of a dead flying-beetle as sense-organs for themselves. They entered the red plain in a long single file, Burl leading the way with one of the two feathery whips extended before him. Saya helped him check on what lay in the darkness ahead, but made sure not to leave his side. Others trailed behind, hand in hand.

Progress was slow. The sky was utter blackness, of course, but nowhere in the lowlands is there an absolute black. Where fox-fire doesn't burn without consuming, there are mushrooms with glows of their own. Rusts sometimes shone faintly. Naturally there were no fireflies or glow-worms of any sort; but neither were there any living things to hunt the tiny tribe as it moved half-blindly in single file through the plain of red puffballs. Within half an hour even Burl did not believe he had kept to his original line. An hour later they realized despairingly that they were marching helpless through puffballs which would make the air unbreathable at dawn. But they marched on.

Once they smelled the rank odor of cabbages. They followed the scent and came upon them, glowing palely with parasitic molds on their leaves. And there were living things here: huge caterpillars eating and eating, even in the dark, against the time of metamorphosis. Burl could have cried out infuriatedly at them because they were—so he assumed—immune to the death of the red dust. But the red dust was all about, and the smell of cabbages was not the smell of life.

It could have been, of course. Caterpillars breathe like all insects at every stage of their development. But furry caterpillars breathe through openings which are covered over with matted fur. Here, that matted fur acted to filter the air. The eggs of the caterpillars had been laid before the puffballs were ready to burst. The time of spore-bearing would be over before the grubs were butterflies or moths. These creatures were safe against all enemies—even men. But men groped and blundered in the darkness simply because they did not think to take the fur garments they wore and hold them to their noses to serve as gas-masks or air-filters. The time for that would come, but not yet.

With the docility of despair, Burl's tribe followed him through all the night. When the sky began to pale in the east, they numbly resigned themselves to death. But still they followed.

And in the very early gray light—when only the very ripest of the red puffballs spouted toward a still-dark sky—Burl looked harassedly about him and could have groaned. He was in a little circular clearing, the deadly red things all about him. There was not yet light enough for colors to appear. There was merely a vast stillness everywhere, and a mocking hint of the hot and peppery scent of death-dust—now turned to mud—all about him.

Burl dropped in bitter discouragement. Soon the misty dust-clouds would begin to move about; the reddish haze would form above all this space.

Then, quite suddenly, he lifted his head and whooped. He had heard the sound of running water.

His followers looked at him with dawning hope. Without a word to them, Burl began to run. They followed hastily and quickened their pace when his voice came back in a shout of triumph. In a moment they had emerged from the tangle of fungus growths to stand upon the banks of a wide river—the same river whose gleam Burl had seen the day before, from the farther side of the red puffball plain.

Once before, Burl had floated down a river upon a mushroom raft. That journey had been involuntary. He had been carried far from his tribe and Saya, his heart filled with desolation. But now he viewed the swiftly-running current with delight.

He cast his eyes up and down the bank. Here and there it rose in a low bluff and thick shelf-fungi stretched out above the water. They were adaptations of the fungi that once had grown on trees and now fed upon the incredibly nourishing earth-banks formed of dead growing things. Burl was busy in an instant, stabbing the relatively hard growths with his spear and striving to wrench them free. The tribesmen stared blankly, but at a snapped order they imitated him.

Soon two dozen masses of firm, light fungus lay upon the shore. Burl began to explain what they were for, but Dor remonstrated. They were afraid to part from him. If they might embark on the same fungus-raft, it would be a different matter. Old Tama scolded him shrilly at the thought of separation. Jon trembled at the mere idea.

Burl cast an apprehensive glance at the sky. Day was rapidly approaching. Soon the red puffballs would burst and shoot their dust-clouds into the air. This was no time to make stipulations. Then Saya spoke softly.

Burl made the suggested great sacrifice. He took the gorgeous velvet cloak of moth-wing from his shoulder and tore it into a dozen long, irregular pieces along the lines of the sinews reinforcing it. He planted his spear upright in the largest raft, fastening the other cranky craft to it with the improvised lines.

In a matter of minutes the small flotilla of rafts bobbed in the stream. One by one, Burl settled the folk upon them with stern commands about movement. Then he shoved them out from the bank. The collection of uneasy, floating things moved slowly out from shore to where the current caught them. Burl and Saya sat on the same section of fungus, the other trustful but frightened tribes-people clustered timorously about.

As they began to move between the mushroom-lined banks of the river, and as the mist of night-time lifted from its surface, columns of red dust spurted sullenly upward on the plain. In the light of dawn the deadly red haze was forming once more over the puffball plain.

By that time, however, the unstable rafts were speeding down the river, bobbing and whirling in the stream, with wide-eyed people as their passengers gazing in wonderment at the shores.

Five miles downstream, the red growths became less numerous and other forms of fungus took their places. Molds and rusts covered the ground as grass did on more favored planets. Toadstools showed their creamy, rounded heads, and there were malformed things with swollen trunks and branches mocking the trees that were never seen in these lowlands. Once the tribesmen saw the grisly bulk of a hunting-spider outlined on the river-bank.

All through the long day they rode the current, while the insect life that had been absent in the neighborhood of the death-plain became abundant again. Bees once more droned overhead, and wasps and dragonflies. Four-inch mosquitoes appeared, to be driven off with blows. Glittering beetles made droning or booming noises as they flew. Flies of every imaginable metallic hue flew about. Huge butterflies danced above the steaming land and running river in seeming ecstasy at simply being alive.

All the thousand-and-one forms of insect life flew and crawled and swam and dived where the people of the rafts could see them. Water-beetles came lazily to the surface to snap at other insects on the surface. The shell-covered boats of caddis-flies floated in the eddies and backwaters.

The day wore on and the shores flowed by. The tribesmen ate of their food and drank of the river. When afternoon came the banks fell away and the current slackened. The shores became indefinite. The river merged itself into a vast swamp from which came a continual muttering.

The water seemed to grow dark when black mud took the place of the clay that had formed its bed. Then there appeared floating green things which did not move with the flowing water. They were the leaves of the water-lilies that managed to survive along with cabbages and a very few other plants in the midst of a fungus world. Twelve feet across, any one of the green leaves might have supported the whole of Burl's tribe.

They became so numerous that only a relatively narrow, uncovered stream flowed between tens of acres of the flat, floating leaves. Here and there colossal waxen blossoms could be seen. Three men could hide in those enormous flowers. They exhaled an almost overpowering fragrance into the air.

And presently the muttering sound that had been heard far away grew in volume to an intermittent deep-bass roar. It seemed to come from the banks on either side. It was the discordant croaking of frogs, eight feet in length, which lived and throve in this swamp. Presently the tribesfolk saw them: green giants sitting immobile upon the banks, only opening their huge mouths to croak.

Here in the swamps there was such luxuriance of insect life that a normal tribal hunting-ground—in which tribesmen were not yet accustomed to hunt— would seem like a desert by comparison. Myriads of little midges, no more than three or four inches across their wings, danced above the water. Butterflies flew low, seemingly enamored of their reflections in the glassy water.

The people watched as if their eyes would become engorged by the strange new things they saw. Where the river split and split and divided again, there was nothing with which they were familiar. Mushrooms did not grow here. Molds, yes. But there were cattails, with stalks like trees, towering thirty feet above the waterways.

After a long, long time though, the streams began to rejoin each other. Then low hills loomed through the thicker haze that filled the air here. The river flowed toward and through them. And here a wall of high mountains rose toward the sky, but their height could not be guessed. They vanished in the mist even before the cloudbank swallowed them.

The river flowed through a river-gate, a water-gap in the mountains. While day still held fully bright, the bobbing rafts went whirling through a narrow pass with sheer walls that rose beyond all seeing in the mist. Here there was even some white water. Above it, spanning a chasm five hundred feet across, a banded spider had flung its web. The rafts floated close enough to see the spider, a monster even of its kind, its belly swollen to a diameter of yards. It hung motionless in the center of the snare as the humans swept beneath it.

Then the mountains drew back and the tribe was in a valley where, look as they might, there was no single tawny-red puffball from whose spreading range the tribesmen were refugees. The rafts grounded and they waded ashore while still the day held. And there was food here in plenty.

But darkness fell before they could explore. As a matter of precaution Burl and his folk found a hiding-place in a mushroom-thicket and hid until morning. The night-sounds were wholly familiar to them. The noise of katydids was louder than usual— the feminine sound of that name gives no hint of the sonorous, deep-toned notes the enlarged creatures uttered—and that implied more vegetation as compared with straight fungoid flora. A great many fire-flies glowed in the darkness shrouding the hiding-place, indicating that the huge snails they fed on were plentiful. The snails would make very suitable prey for the tribesmen also. But men were not yet established in their own minds as predators.

They were, though, definitely no longer the furtive vermin they had been. They knew there were such things as weapons. They had killed ants for food and a pirate-wasp as an exercise in courage. To some degree they were acquiring Burl's own qualities. But they were still behind him—and he still had some way to go.

The next day they explored their new territory with a boldness which would have been unthinkable a few weeks before. The new haven was a valley, spreading out to a second swamp at its lower end. They could not know it, but beyond the swamp lay the sea. Exploring, because of strictly practical purposes and not for the sake of knowledge, they found a great trapdoor in the earth, sure sign of the lair of a spider. Burl considered that before many days the monster would have to be dealt with. But he did not yet know how it could be done.

His people were rapidly becoming a tribe of men, but they still needed Burl to think for them. What he could not think out, so far, could not be done. But a part of the proof that they needed Burl to think for them lay in the fact that they did not realize it. They gathered facts about their environment. The nearest ant-city was miles away. That meant that they would encounter its scouting foragers rather than working-parties. The ant-city would be a source of small prey—a notion that would have been inconceivable a little while ago. There were numerous giant cabbages in the valley and that meant there were big, defenseless slugs to spear whenever necessary.

They saw praying-mantises—the adults were eighteen feet tall and as big as giraffes, but much less desirable neighbors—and knew that they would have to be avoided. But there were edible mushrooms on every hand. If one avoided spiders and praying-mantises and the meat-eating beetles; if one were safely hidden at night against the amorous male spiders who took time off from courtship to devour anything living that came their way; and if one lived at high-tension alertness, interpreting every sound as possible danger and every unknown thing as certain peril, then one could live quite comfortably in this valley.

For three days the tribesmen felt that they had found a sort of paradise. Jon had his belly full to bursting all day long. Tet and Dik became skilled ant-hunters. Dor found a better spear and practiced thoughtfully with it.

There were no red puffballs here. There was food. Burl's folk could imagine no greater happiness. Even old Tama scolded only rarely. They surely could not conceive of any place where a man might walk calmly about with no danger at all of being devoured. This was paradise!

And it was a deplorable state of affairs. It is not good for human beings to feel secure and experience contentment. Men achieve only by their wants or through their fears. Back at their former foraging-ground, the tribe would never have emulated Burl with any passion so long as they could survive by traditional behavior. Before the menace of the red puffballs developed, he had brought them to the point of killing ants, with him present and ready to assist. They would have stayed at about that level. The red dust had forced their flight. During that flight they had achieved what was— compared to their former timidity—prodigies of valor.

But now they arrived at paradise. There was food. They could survive here in the fashion of the good old days before they learned the courage of desperation. They did not need Burl to keep them alive or to feed them. They tended to disregard him. But they did not disperse. Social grouping is an instinct in human beings as it is in cattle or in schools of fish. Also, when Burl was available there was a sense of pleasant confidence. He had gotten them out of trouble before. If more trouble came, he would get them out of it again. But why look for trouble?

Burl's tribesmen sank back into a contented lethargy. They found food and hid themselves until it was all consumed. A part of the valley was found where they were far enough from visible dangers to feel blissfully safe. When they did move, though still with elaborate caution, it was only to forage for food. And they did not need to go far because there was plenty of food. They slipped back. Happier than they had ever been, the foragers finally began to forget to take their new spears or clubs with them. They were furtive vermin in a particularly favorable environment.

And Burl was infuriated. He had known adulation. He was cherished, to be sure, but adulation no longer came his way. Even Saya . . .

An ironically natural change took place in Saya. When Burl was a chieftain, she looked at him with worshipful eyes. Now that he was as other men, she displayed coquetry. And Burl was of that peculiarly direct-thinking sort of human being who is capable of leadership but not of intrigue. He was vain, of course.

But he could not engage in elaborate maneuvers to build up a romantic situation. When Saya archly remained with the women of the tribe, he considered that she avoided him. When she coyly avoided speech with him, he angrily believed that she did not want his company.

When they had been in the valley for a week Burl went off on a bitter journey by himself. Part of his motivation, probably, was a childish resentment. He had been the great man of the tribe. He was no longer so great because his particular qualities were not needed. And—perhaps with some unconscious intent to punish them for their lessened appreciation—he went off in a pet.

He still carried spear and club, but the grandeur of his costume had deteriorated. His cloak was gone. The moth-antennae he had worn bound to his forehead were now so draggled that they were ridiculous. He went off angrily to be rid of his fellows' indifference.

He found the upward slopes which were the valley's literal boundaries. They promised nothing. He found a minor valley in which a labyrinth spider had built its shining snare. Burl almost scorned the creature. He could kill it if he chose, merely by stabbing it though the walls of its silken nest as it waited for unlucky insects to blunder into the intricate web. He saw praying-mantises. Once he came upon that extraordinary egg-container of the mantis tribe: a gigantic leaf-shaped mass of solidified foam, whipped out of some special plastic compound which the mantis secretes, and in which the eggs are laid.

He found a caterpillar wrapped in its thick cocoon and, because he was not foraging and not particularly hungry, he inspected it with care. With great difficulty he even broke the strand of silk that formed it, unreeling several feet in curiosity. Had he meditated,

Burl would have seen that this was cord which could be used to build snares as spiders did. It could also be used to make defenses in which—if built strongly and well—even hunting-spiders might be tangled and dispatched.

But again he was not knowingly looking for things to be of use. He coddled his sense of injury against the tribe. He punished them by leaving them.

He encountered a four-foot praying-mantis that raised its saw-toothed forelimbs and waited immobile for him to come within reach. He had trouble getting away without a fight. His spear would have been a clumsy weapon against so slender a target and the club certainly not quick enough to counter the insect's lightning-like movements.

He was bothered. That day he hunted ants. The difficulty was mainly that of finding individual ants, alone, who could be slaughtered without drawing hordes of others into the fight. Before nightfall he had three of them—foot-long carcasses—slung at his belt. Near sunset he came upon another fairly recent praying-mantis hatchling. It was almost an ambush. The young monster stood completely immobile and waited for him to walk into its reach.

Burl performed a deliberate experiment—something that had not been done for a very long time on the forgotten planet. The small, grisly creature stood as high as Burl's shoulders. It would be a deadly antagonist. Burl tossed it a dead ant.

It struck so swiftly that the motion of its horrible forearms could not be seen. Then it ignored Burl, devouring the tidbit.

It was a discovery that was immediately and urgently useful.

On the second day of his aimless journey Burl saw something that would be even more deadly and appalling than the red dust had been for his kind. It was a female black hunting-spider, the so-called American tarantula. When he glimpsed the thing the blood drained from Burl's face.

As the monster moved out of sight Burl, abandoning any other project he might have intended, headed for the place his tribe had more or less settled in. He had news which offered the satisfaction of making him much-needed again, but he would have traded that pleasure ten hundred times over for the simple absence of that one creature from this valley. That female tarantula meant simply and specifically that the tribe must flee or die. This place was not paradise!

The entry of the spider into the region had preceded the arrival of the people. A giant, even of its kind, it had come across some pass among the mountains for reasons only it could know. But it was deadliness beyond compare. Its legs spanned yards. The fangs were needle-sharp and feet in length—and poisoned. Its eyes glittered with insatiable, insane blood-lust. Its coming was ten times more deadly to the humans— as to the other living creatures of the valley—than a Bengal tiger loosed in a human city would have been. It was bad enough in itself, but it brought more deadly disaster still behind it.

Bumping and bouncing behind its abdomen as it moved, fastened to its body by dirtied silken ropes, this creature dragged a burden which was its own ferocity many times multiplied. It was dragging an egg-bag larger than its body—which was feet in diameter. The female spider would carry this ghastly burden— cherishing it—until the eggs hatched. And then there would be four to five hundred small devils loose in the valley. From the instant of their hatching they would be as deadly as their parent. Though the offspring would be small—with legs spanning no more than a

foot—their bodies would be the size of a man's fist and
able to leap two yards. Their tiny fangs would be no
less envenomed than their mother's. In stark, maniacal hatred of all other life they would at least equal
the huge gray horror which had begot them.

Burl told his tribesmen. They listened, eyes large
with fright but not quite afraid. The thing had not yet
happened. When Burl insistently commanded that they
follow him on a new journey, they nodded uneasily but
slipped away. He could not gather the tribe together.
Always there were members who hid from him—and
when he went in search of them, the ones he had
gathered vanished before he could return.

There were days of bright light and murder, and
nights of slow rain and death in the valley. The great
creatures under the cloud-bank committed atrocities
upon each other and blandly dined upon their victims.
Unthinkingly solicitous parents paralyzed creatures to
be left living and helpless for their young to feed on.
There were enormities of cruelty done in the matter-
of-fact fashion of the insect world. To these things the
humans were indifferent. They were uneasy, but like
other humans everywhere they would not believe the
worst until the worst arrived.

Two weeks after their coming to the valley, the worst
was there. When that day came the first gray light of
dawn found the humans in a shivering, terrified group
in a completely suicidal position. They were out in the
open—not hidden but in plain view. They dared not
hide any more. The furry gray monster's brood had
hatched. The valley seemed to swarm with small gray
demons which killed and killed, even when they could
not devour. When they encountered each other they
fought in slavering fury and the victors in such duels
dined upon their brethren. But always they hunted for
more things to kill. They were literally maniacs—and

they were too small and too quick to fight with spears or clubs.

So now, at daybreak, the humans looked about despairingly for death to come to them. They had spent the night in the open lest they be trapped in the very thickets that had formerly been their protection. They were in clear sight of the large gray murderer, if it should pass that way. And they did not dare hide because of that ogreish creature's brood.

The monster appeared. A young girl saw it and cried out chokingly. It had not seen them. They watched it leap upon and murder a vividly-colored caterpillar near the limit of vision in the morning-mist. It was in the tribe's part of the valley. Its young swarmed everywhere. The valley could have been a paradise, but it was doomed to become a charnel-house.

And then Burl shook himself. He had been angry when he left his tribe. He had been more angry when he returned and they would not obey him. He had remained with them, petulantly silent, displaying the offended dignity he felt and elaborately refusing to acknowledge any overtures, even from Saya. Burl had acted rather childishly. But his tribesmen were like children. It was the best way for him to act.

They shivered, too hopeless even to run away while the shaggy monster feasted a half-mile away. There were six men and seven women besides himself, and the rest were children, from gangling adolescents to one babe in arms. They whimpered a little. Then Saya looked imploringly at Burl—coquetry forgotten now. The others whimpered more loudly. They had reached that stage of despair, now, when they could draw the monster to them by blubbering in terror.

This was the psychological moment. Burl said dourly: "Come!"

He took Saya's hand and started away. There was

but one direction in which any human being could
think to move in this valley, at this moment. It was the
direction away from the grisly mother of horrors. It
happened to be the way up the valley wall. Burl started
up that slope. Saya went with him.

Before they had gone ten yards Dor spoke to his
wife. They followed Burl, with their three children.
Five yards more, and Jak agitatedly began to bustle his
family into movement. Old Jon, wheezing, frantically
scuttled after Burl, and Cori competently set out with
the youngest of her children in her arms and the others
marching before her. Within seconds more, all the tribe
was in motion.

Burl moved on, aware of his following, but ignoring it. The procession continued in his wake simply
because it had begun to do so. Dik, his adolescent
brashness beaten down by terror, nevertheless regarded
Burl's stained weapon with the inevitable envy of the
half-grown for achievement. He saw something half-
buried in the soil and—after a fearful glance behind—
he moved aside to tug at it. It was part of the armor
of a former rhinoceros beetle. Tet joined him. They
made an act of great daring of lingering to find themselves weapons as near as possible to Burl's.

A quarter-mile on, the fugitives passed a struggling
milkweed plant, no more than twenty feet high and
already scabrous with scale and rusts upon its lower
parts. Ants marched up and down its stalk in a steady
single file, placing aphids from their nearby ant-city
on suitable spots to feed—and to multiply as only
parthenogenetic aphids can do. But already, on the far
side of the milkweed, an ant-lion climbed up to do
murder among them. The ant-lion, of course, was the
larval form of a lace-wing fly. The aphids were its
predestined prey.

Burl continued to march, holding Saya's hand. The

reek of formic acid came to his nostrils. He ignored it. Ants were as much prey to his tribesmen, now, as crabs and crayfish to other, shore-dwelling tribesmen on long-forgotten Earth. But Burl was not concerned with food, now. He stalked on toward the mountain-slopes.

Dik and Tet brandished their new weapons. They looked fearfully behind them. The monster from whom they fled was lost in its gruesome feasting—and they were a long way from it, now. There was a steady, single-file procession of ants, with occasional gaps in the line. The procession passed the line through one of those gaps.

Beyond it, Tet and Dik conferred. They dared each other. They went scrambling back to the line of ants. Their weapons smote. The slaughtered ants died instantly and were quickly dragged from the formic-acid-scented path. The remaining ants went placidly on their way. The weapons struck again.

The two adolescents had to outdo each other. But they had as much food as they could carry. Gloating—each claiming to have been most daring and to have the largest bag of game—they ran panting after the tribe. They grandly distributed their take of game. It was a form of boasting. But the tribesfolk accepted the gifts automatically. It was, after all, food.

The two gangling boys, jabbering at each other, raced back once more. Again they returned with dangling masses of foodstuff—half-scores of foot-long creatures whose limbs, at least, contained firm meat.

Behind, the ant-lion made his onslaught into the stupidly feasting aphids, and warrior-ants took alarm and thrust forward to offer battle. Tumult arose upon the milkweed.

But Burl led his followers toward the mountainside. He reached a minor eminence and looked about him. Caution was the price of existence on this world.

Two hundred feet away, a small scurrying horror
raged and searched among the rough-edged layers of
what on other worlds was called paper-mold or rock-
tripe. Here it was thick as quilting, and infinitesimal
creatures denned under it. The sixteen-inch spider
devoured them, making gluttonous sounds. But it was
busy, and all spiders are relatively short-sighted.

Burl turned to Saya, and realized that all his tribe
had followed him fearfully even to this small height
he'd climbed only to look around from. Dor had taken
advantage of Burl's pause. There was an empty cricket-
shell partly overwhelmed by the fungoid soil. He tore
free a now-hollow, sickle-shaped jaw. It was curved and
sharp and deadly if properly wielded. Dor had seen
Burl kill things. He had even helped. Now, very grimly,
he tried to imagine killing something all alone. Jak saw
him working on the sickle-shaped weapon. He tugged
at the cricket's ransacked carcass for another weapon.
Dik and Tet vaingloriously pretended to fight between
themselves with their recently acquired instruments for
killing. Jon wheezed and panted. Old Tama complained
to herself in whispers, not daring to make sounds in
the daylight. The rest waited until Burl should lead
them further.

When Burl turned angry eyes upon them—he was
beginning to do such things deliberately, now—they all
regarded him humbly. Now they remembered that they
had been hungry and he had gotten food for them, and
they had been paralyzed by terror, and he dared to
move. They definitely had a feeling of dependence
upon him, for the present moment only. Later, their
feeling of humbleness would diminish. In proportion
as he met their needs for leadership, they would tend
to try to become independent of him. His leadership
would be successful in proportion as he taught them
to lead themselves. But Burl perceived this only dimly.

At the moment it was pleasing to have all his tribe regard him so worshipfully, even if not in quite the same fashion as Saya. He was suddenly aware that now—at any rate while they were so frightened—they would obey him. So he invented an order for them to obey.

"I carry sharp things," he said sternly. "Some of you have gotten sharp things. Now everybody must carry sharp things, to fight with."

Humbly, they scattered to obey. Saya would have gone with them, but Burl held her back. He did not quite know why. It could have been that the absolute equality of the sexes in cravenness was due to end, and for his own vanity Burl would undertake the defense of Saya. He did not analyze so far. He did not want her to leave him, so he prevented it.

The tribesfolk scattered. Dor went with his wife, to help her arm herself. Jak uneasily followed his. Jon went timorously where the picked-over remnant of the cricket's carcass might still yield an instrument of defense. Cori laid her youngest child at Burl's feet while she went fearfully to find some toothed instrument meeting Burl's specification of sharpness.

There was a stifled scream. A ten-year-old boy—he was Dik's younger brother—stood paralyzed. He stared in an agony of horror at something that had stepped from behind a misshapen fungoid object fifty yards from Burl, but less than ten yards from him.

It was a pallidly greenish creature with a small head and enormous eyes. It stood upright, like a man, and it was a few inches taller than a man. Its abdomen swelled gracefully into a leaf-like form. The boy faced it, paralyzed by horror, and it stood stock-still. Its great, hideously spined arms were spread out in a pose of hypocritical benediction.

It was a partly-grown praying mantis, not too long

hatched. It stood rigid, waiting benignly for the boy to come closer or try to flee. If he had fled, it would fling itself after him with a ferocity beside which the fury of a tiger would be kittenish. If he approached, its fanged arms would flash down, pierce his body, and hold him terribly fast by the needle-sharp hooks that were so much worse than trap-claws. And of course it would not wait for him to die before it began its meal.

All the small party of humans stood frozen. It may be questioned whether they were filled with horror for the boy, or cast into a deeper abyss of despair by the sight of a half-grown mantis. Only Burl, so far, had any notion of actually leaving the valley. To the rest, the discovery of one partly mature praying mantis meant that there would be hundreds of others. It would be impossible to evade the tiny, slavering demons which were the brood of the great spider. It would be impossibility multiplied to live where a horde of small—yet vastly larger—fiends lived, raising their arms in a semblance of blessing before they did murder.

Only Burl was capable of thought, and this was because vanity filled him. He had commanded and had been obeyed. Now obedience was forgotten because there was this young mantis. If the men had dreamed of fighting it, it could have destroyed any number of them by sheer ferocity and its arsenal of knives and daggers. But Burl was at once furious and experienced. He had encountered such a middle-sized monster, when alone, and deliberately had experimented with it. In consequence he could dare to rage. He ran toward the mantis. He swung the small corpse of an ant—killed by Tet only minutes since—and hurled it past the terror-fascinated boy. He had hurled it at the mantis.

It struck. And insects simply do not think. Something

hurtled at the ghastly young creature. Its arms struck ferociously to defend itself. The ant was heavy. Poised upright in its spectral attitude, the mantis was literally flung backward. But it rolled over, fighting the dead ant with that frenzy which is not so much ferocity as mania.

The small boy fled, hysterically, once the insect's attention was diverted.

The human tribe gathered around Burl many hundreds of yards away, again uphill. He was their rendezvous because of the example set by Cori. She had left her baby with Burl. When Burl dashed from the spot, Saya had quite automatically followed the instinct of any female for the young of its kind. She'd snatched up the baby before she fled. And—of course—she'd joined Burl when the immediate danger was over.

The floor of the valley seemed a trifle indistinct, from here. The mist that hung always in the air partly veiled the details of its horrors. It was less actual, not quite as deadly as it once had seemed.

Burl said fiercely to his followers:

"Where are the sharp things?"

The tribesfolk looked at one another, numbly. Then Jon muttered rebelliously, and old Tama raised her voice in shrill complaint. Burl had led them to this! There had been only the red dust in the place from which they had come, but here was a hunting-spider and its young and also a new hatching of mantises! They could dodge the red dust, but how could they escape the deaths that waited them here? Ai! Ai! Burl had persuaded them to leave their home and—brought them here to die. . . .

"I," said Burl haughtily, "am not going to stay here. I go to a place where there are neither spiders nor mantises. Come!"

He held out his hand to Saya. She gave the child

to Cori and confidently moved to follow him. Burl
stalked grandly away and she went with him. He went
uphill. Naturally! There were spiders and mantises in
the valley—so many that to stay there meant death.
So he moved to go somewhere else.

And this was the climactic event that changed the
whole history of humanity upon the forgotten planet.
Up to this point, there may have been other individuals
who had accomplished somewhat of Burl's kind of
leadership. A few may have learned courage. It is
possible that some even led their tribesfolk upon
migrations in search of safer lands to live in. But until
Burl led his people out of a valley filled with food, up
a mountainside toward the unknown, it was simply
impossible for humans to rise permanently above the
status of hunted vermin; at the mercy of monstrous
mindless creatures; whose forbears had most ironically
been brought to this planet to prepare it for humans
to live on.

Burl was the first man to lead his fellows toward
the heights.

9. THERE IS SUCH A THING AS SUNSHINE

The sun that shone upon the forgotten planet was actually very near. It shone on the top of the cloud-bank, and the clouds glowed with dazzling whiteness. It shone on the mountain-peaks where they penetrated the mist, and the peaks were warmed, and there was no snow anywhere despite the height. There were winds, here where the sun yielded sensible heat. The sky was very blue. At the edge of the plateau—from which the cloud-banks were down instead of up—the mountainsides seemed to descend into a sea of milk. Great undulations in the mist had the semblance of waves, which moved with great deliberation toward the shores. They seemed sometimes to break in slow-motion against the mountain-walls where they were cliff-like, and sometimes they seemed to flow up gentler inclinations like water flowing up a beach. But all of this was very deliberate indeed, because the cloud-waves were sometimes twenty miles from crest to crest.

The look of things was different on the highlands. This part of the unnamed world, no less than the lowlands, had been seeded with life on two separate occasions. Once the seeding was with bacteria and molds and lichens to break up the rocks and make soil of them, and once with seeds and insect-eggs and such living things as might sustain themselves immediately they were hatched. But here on the highlands the different climatic conditions had allowed other seedlings and creatures to survive together.

Here molds and yeasts and rusts were stunted by the sunlight. Grasses and weeds and trees survived, instead. This was an ideal environment for plants that needed sunlight to form chlorophyll, with which to make use of the soil that had been formed. So on the highlands the vegetation was almost earthlike. And there was a remarkable side-effect on the fauna which had been introduced in the same manner and at the same time as the creatures down below. In coolness which amounted to a temperate climate, there developed no such frenzy of life as made the nightmare jungles under the clouds. Plants grow at a slower rate than fungi, and less luxuriantly. There was no vast supply of food for large-sized plant-eaters. Insects which were to survive, here, could not grow to be monsters. Moreover, the nights here were chill. Very many insects grow torpid in the cool of a temperate-zone night, but warm up to activity soon after sunrise. But a large creature, made torpid by cold, will not revive so quickly. If large enough, it will not become fully active until close to dark. On the plateau, the lowland monsters would starve in any case. But more— they would have only a fraction of each day of full activity.

So there was a necessary limit to the size of the creatures that lived above the clouds. To humans from other planets, the life on the plateau would not have seemed horrifying at all. Save for the absence of birds to sing, and a lack of small mammals to hunt or merely to enjoy, the untouched, sunlit plateau with its warm days and briskly chill nights would have impressed most civilized men as an ideal habitation.

But Burl and his followers were hardly prepared to see it that way at first glance. If told about it in advance, they would have thought of it with despair.

But they did not know beforehand. They toiled upward, their leader moved by such ridiculous motives of pride and vanity as have caused men to achieve greatness throughout all history. Two great continents were discovered back on Earth by a man trying to get spices to hide the gamey flavor of half-spoiled meat, and the power that drives mile-long space-craft was first discovered and tamed by men making bombs to destroy their fellows. There were precedents for foolish motives producing results far from foolishness.

The trudging, climbing folk crawled up the hillside. They reached a place high above the valley Burl had led them to. That valley grew misty in appearance. Presently it could no longer be seen at all. The mist they had taken for granted, all their lives, hid from them everything but the slanting stony wall up which they climbed. The stone was mostly covered by bluish-green rock-tripe in partly overlapping sheets. Such stuff is always close behind the bacteria which first attack a rock-face. On a slope, it clings while soil is washed downward as fast as it is formed. The people never ate rock-tripe, of course. It produces frightening cramps. In time they might learn that when thoroughly dried it can be cooked to pliability again and eaten with some satisfaction. But so far they neither knew dryness nor fire.

Nor had they ever known such surroundings as

presently enveloped them. A slanting rocky mountainside, which stretched up frighteningly to the very sky. Grayness overhead. Grayness also to one side, the side away from the mountain. And equal grayness below. The valley from which they had come could no longer be seen even as a different shading of the mist. And as they scrambled and trudged after Burl, his followers gradually became aware of the utter strangeness of all about them. For one result, they grew sick and dizzy. To them it seemed that all solidity was slowly tilting. Had they been superstitious, they might have thought of demons preparing to punish them for daring to come to such a place. But—quaintly enough—Burl's followers had developed no demonology. Your typical savage is resolved not to think, but he does have leisure to—want. He makes gods and devils out of his nightmares, and gambles on his own speculations to the extent of offering blackmail to demons if they will only let him alone or—preferably—give him more of the things he wants.

But the superstitions of savages involve the payment of blackmail in exact proportion to their prosperity. The Eskimos of Earth lived always on the brink of starvation. They could not afford the luxury of tabus and totem animals whose flesh must not be eaten, and forbidden areas which might contain food.

Religion there was, among Burl's people, but superstition was not. No humans, anywhere, can live without religion, but on Earth Eskimos did with a minimum of superstitions—they could afford no more—and the humans of the forgotten planet could not afford any at all.

Therefore they climbed desperately despite the unparalleled state of things about them. There was no horizon, but they had never seen a horizon. Their feeling was that what had been "down" was now partly "behind" and they feared lest a toppling universe ultimately let them fall toward that grayness they considered the sky.

But all kept on. To lag behind would be to be abandoned in this place where all known sensations were turned topsy-turvy. None of them could imagine turning back. Even old Tama, whimpering in a whisper as she struggled to keep up, merely complained bitterly of her fate. She did not even think of revolt. If Burl had stopped, all his followers would have squatted down miserably to wait for death. They had no thought of adventure or any hope of safety. The only goodnesses they could imagine were food and the nearness of other humans. They had food—nobody had abandoned any of the dangling ant-bodies Tet and Dik had distributed before the climb began. They would not be separated from their fellows.

Burl's motivation was hardly more distinct. He had started uphill in a judicious mixture of fear and injured vanity and desperation. There was nothing to be gained by going back. The terrors at hand were no greater than those behind, so there was no reason not to go ahead.

They came to a place where the mountain-flank sank inward. There was a flat space, and behind it a winding canyon of sorts like a vast crack in the mountain's substance. Burl breasted the curving edge and found flatness beyond it. He stopped short.

The mouth of the canyon was perhaps fifty yards from the lip of the downward slope. So much space was practically level, and on it were toadstools and milkweed—two of them—and there was food. It was a small, isolated asylum for life such as they were used to. They could—it was possible that they could—have found a place of safety here.

But the possibility was not the fact. They saw the

spider-web at once. It was slung between the opposite canyon walls by cables all of two hundred feet long.
The radiating cables reached down to anchorages on
stone. The snare-threads, winding out and out in that
logarithmic spiral whose properties men were so astonished to discover, were fully a yard apart. The web was
for giant game. It was empty now, but Burl saw the
telegraph-cord which ran from the very center of the
web to the web-maker's lurking-place. There was a
rocky shelf on the canyon wall. On it rested the spider, almost invisible against the stone, with one furry
leg touching the cable. The slightest touch on any part
of the web would warn it instantly.

Burl's followers accumulated behind him. Old Jon's
wheezing was audible. Tama ceased her complaints to
survey this spot. It might be—it could be—a haven,
and she would have to find new and different things
to complain about in consequence. The spider-web
itself, of course, was no reason for them to be alarmed.
Web-spiders do not hunt. Their males do, but they are
rarely in the neighborhood of a web save at mating-
time. The web itself was no reason not to settle here.
But there was a reason.

The ground before the web—between the web and
themselves—was a charnel-house of murdered creatures. Half-inch-thick wing-cases of dead beetles and
the cleaned-out carapaces of other giants. The oviposi-
tor of an ichneumon-fly—six feet of springy, slender,
deadly-pointed tube—and the abdomen-plates of bees
and the draggled antennae of moths and butterflies.

Something very terrible lived in this small place. The
mountainsides were barren of food for big flying things.
Anything which did fly this high for any reason would
never land on sloping foodless stone. It would land
here. And very obviously it would die. Because
something—something—killed things as they came. It

denned back in the canyon where they could not see it. It dined here.

The humans looked and shivered, all but Burl. He cast his eyes about for better weapons than he possessed. He chose for himself a magnificent lance grown by some dead thing for its own defense. He pulled it out of the ground.

It was utterly silent, here on the heights. No sounds from the valley rose so high. There was no noise except the small creakings made as Burl strove to free the new, splendid weapon for himself.

That was why he heard the gasp which somebody uttered in default of a scream that would not be uttered. It was a choked, a strangled, an inarticulate sobbing noise.

He saw its cause.

There was a thing moving toward the folk from the recesses of the canyon. It moved very swiftly. It moved upon stilt-like, impossibly attenuated legs of impossible length and inconceivable number. Its body was the thickness of Burl's own. And from it came a smell of such monstrous foetor that any man, smelling it, would gag and flee even without fear to urge him on. The creature was a monstrous millipede, forty feet in length, with features of purest, unadulterated horror.

It did not appear to plan to spring. Its speed of movement did not increase as it neared the tribesfolk. It was not rushing, like the furious charge of the murderers Burl's tribe knew. It simply flowed sinuously toward them with no appearance of haste, but at a rate of speed they could not conceivably outrun.

Sticklike legs twitched upward and caught the spinning body of an ant. The creature stopped, and turned its head about and seized the object its side-legs had grasped. It devoured it. Burl shouted again and again.

There was a rain of missiles upon the creature. But

they were not to hurt it, but to divert its incredibly automaton-like attention. Its legs seized the things flung to it. It was not possible to miss. Ten, fifteen, twenty of the items of small-game were grasped in mid-air, as if they were creatures in flight.

Burl's shoutings took effect. His people fled to the side of the level lip of ground. They climbed frantically past the opening of the valley. They fled toward the heights.

Burl was the last to retreat. The monstrous millipede stood immobile, trapped for the moment by the gratification of all its desires. It was absorbed by the multitude of tiny tidbits with which it had been provided.

It was a fact to Burl's honor that he debated a frantic attack upon the monster in its insane absorption. But the strangling stench was deterrent enough. He fled, the last of his band of fugitives to leave the place where the monstrous creature lived and preyed. As he left it, it was still crunching the small meals, one by one, with which the folk had supplied it.

They went on up the mountain-flank. It was not to be supposed, of course, that the creature could not move above the slanting rock-surface. Unquestionably it roamed far and wide, upon occasion. But its own foetid reek would make impossible any idea of trailing the humans by scent. And, climbing desperately as the humans did, it would be unable to see them when they were past the first protuberance of the mountain.

In twenty minutes they slackened their pace. Exhaustion prompted it. Caution ordered it. Because here they saw another small island of flatness in the slanting universe which was all they could see save mist. It was simply a place where boulders had piled up, and soil had formed, and there was a miniature haven for life other than molds which could grow on naked stone.

Actually, there was a space a hundred feet by fifty on which wholly familiar mushrooms grew. It was a thicket like a detached section of the valley itself. Well-known edible fungi grew here. There were gray puff-balls. And from it came the cheerful loud chirping of some small beetle, arrived at this spot nobody could possibly know how, but happily ensconced in a sepa-rate bit of mushroom-jungle remote from the dangers of the valley. If it was small enough, it would even be safe from the reeking horror of the canyon just below it.

They broke off edible mushrooms here and ate. And this could have been safety for them—save for the giant millipede no more than half a mile below. Old Jon wheezed querulously that here was food and there was no need for them to go further, just now. Here was food. . . .

Burl regarded him with knitted brows. Jon's reac-tion was natural enough. The tribesfolk had never tended to think for the future because it was impos-sible to make use of such planning. Even Burl could easily enough have accepted the fact that this was safety for the moment and food for the moment. But it happened that to settle down here until driven out would—and at this moment—have deprived him of the authority he had so recently learned to enjoy.

"You stay," he said haughtily, to Jon. "I go on, to a better place where nothing is to be feared at all!"

He held out his hand to Saya. He assailed the slope again, heading upward in the mist.

His tribe followed him. Dik and Tet, of course, because they were boys and Burl led on to high adven-tures in which so far nobody had been killed. Dor followed because—he being the strongest man in the tribe—he had thoughtfully realized that his strength was not as useful as Burl's brains and other qualities.

Cori followed because she had children, and they were safer where Burl led than anywhere else. The others followed to avoid being left alone.

The procession toiled on and up. Presently Burl noticed that the air seemed clearer, here. It was not the misty, only half transparent stuff of the valley. He could see for miles to right and left. He realized the curvature of the mountain-face. But he could not see the valley. The mist hid that.

Suddenly he realized that he saw the cloudbank overhead as an object. He had never thought of it specifically before. To him it had been simply the sky. Now he saw an indefinite lower surface which yet definitely hid the heights toward which he moved. He and his followers were less than a thousand feet below it. It appeared to Burl that presently he would run into an obstacle which would simply keep him from going any further. The idea was disheartening. But until it happened he obstinately climbed on.

He observed that the thing which was the sky did not stay still. It moved, though slowly. A little higher, he could see that there were parts of it which were actually lower than he was. They moved also, but they moved away from him as often as they moved toward him. He had no experience of any dangerous thing which did not leap at its victims. Therefore he was not afraid.

In fact, presently he noticed that the whiteness which was the cloud-layer seemed to retreat before him. He was pleased. Weak things like humans fled from enemies. Here was something which fled at his approach! His followers undoubtedly saw the same thing. Burl had killed spiders. He was a remarkable person. This unknown white stuff was afraid of him. Therefore it was wise to stay close to Burl. Burl found his vanity inflamed by the fact that always—even at its thickest—the white cloud-stuff never came nearer than some dozens of feet. He swaggered as he led his people up.

And presently there was brightness about them. It was a greater brightness than the tribesfolk had ever known. They knew daylight as a grayness in which one could see. Here was a brightness that shone. They were not accustomed to brightness.

They were not accustomed to silence, either. The noises of the valley were like all the noises of the lowlands. They had been in the ears of every one of the human beings since they could hear at all. They had gradually diminished as the valley dropped behind them. Now, in the radiant white mist which was the cloud-layer, there were no sounds at all, and the fact was suddenly startling.

They blinked in the brightness. When they spoke to each other, they spoke in whispers. The stone underfoot was not even lichen-covered, here. It was bare and bright and glistened with wetness. The light they experienced took on a golden tint. All of these things were utterly unparalleled, but the stillness was a hush instead of a menacing silence. The golden light could not possibly be associated with fear. The people of the forgotten planet felt, most likely, the sort of promise in this shining tranquility which before they had known only in dreams. But this was no dream.

They came up through the surface of a sea of mist, and they saw before them a shore of sunshine. They saw blue and sky and sunlight for the first time. The light smote their skins and brilliantly colored furry garments. It glittered in changing, ever-more-colorful flashes upon cloaks made of butterfly wings. It sparkled on the great lance carried by Burl in the lead, and the quite preposterous weapons borne by his followers.

The little party of twenty humans waded ashore

through the last of the thinning white stuff which was cloud. They gazed about them with wondering, astonished eyes. The sky was blue. There was green grass. And again there was sound. It was the sound of wind blowing among trees, and of things living in the sunshine.

They heard insects, but they did not know what they heard. The shrill small musical whirrings; the high-pitched small cries which made an elfin melody everywhere—these were totally strange. All things were new to their eyes, and an enormous exultation filled them. From deep-buried ancestral memories they somehow knew that what they saw was right, was normal, was appropriate and proper, and that this was the kind of world in which humans belonged, rather than the seething horror of the lowlands. They breathed clean air for the first time in many generations.

Burl shouted in his triumph, and his voice echoed among trees and hillsides.

10. MEN CLIMB UP TO SAVAGERY

They had food for days. They had brought mushrooms from the isolated thicket not too far beneath the clouds. There were the ants that Dik and Tet had distributed grandly, and not all of which had been used to secure escape from the canyon of the millipede. Had they found other food immediately, they would have settled down comfortably in the fashion normal to creatures whose idea of bliss is a secure hiding-place and food on hand so they do not have to leave it. Somehow they believed that this high place of bright light and new colors was secure. But they had no hiding-place. And though they did accept with the unreasoning faith of children and savages that there were no enemies here, they still wanted one.

They found a cave. It was small, so that it would be crowded with all of them in it, but as it turned out, this was fortunate. At some time it had been occupied by some other creature, but the dirt which floored it had settled flat and showed no tracks. It retained faint traces of a smell which was unfamiliar but not unpleasing—it held no connotation of danger. Ants stank of formic acid plus the musky odor of their particular city. One could identify not only the kind of ant, but its home city, by sniffing at an ant-trail. Spiders had their own hair-raising odor. The smell of a praying-mantis was acrid, and all beetles reeked of decay. And of course there were those bugs whose main defense was an effluvium which tended to strangle all but the smell's happy possessor. This faint smell in the cave was different. The humans thought vaguely that it might possibly be another kind of man.

Actually, it was the smell of a warm-blooded animal. But Burl and his fellows knew of no warm-blooded creature but themselves.

They had come above the clouds a bare two hours before sunset—of which they knew nothing. For an hour they marveled, staying close together. They were especially astounded by the sun, since they could not bear to look at it. But presently, being savages, they accepted it matter-of-factly.

They could not cease to wonder at the vegetation about them. They were accustomed only to gigantic fungi and the few straggling plants which tried so desperately to bear seed before they were devoured. Here they saw many plants and no fungi, and they did not see anything they recognized as insects. They looked only for large things.

They were astounded by the slenderness and toughness of the plants. Grass fascinated them, and weeds. A large part of their courage came from the absence of debris upon the ground. The hunting-grounds of spiders were marked by grisly remnants of finished meals, and where mantises roamed there were bits of transparent beetle-wings and sharp spiny bits of armor not tasty enough to be consumed. Here, in the first hour of their exploration, they saw no sign that an insect like the lowland ones had ever been in this place at all. But they could not believe the monsters never came. They correctly—and pessimistically—assumed that their coming was only rare.

The cave was a great relief. Trees did not grow close enough to give them a feeling of safety, though they were ludicrously amazed at the invincible hardness of tree trunks. They had never known anything but insect-armor and stone which was as hard as the trunks of those growing things. They found nothing to eat, but they were not yet hungry. They did not worry about food while they still had remnants from their climb.

When the sun sank low and crimson colorings filled the west, they were less happy. They watched the glory of their first sunset with scared, incredulous eyes. Yellows and reds and purples reared toward the zenith. It became possible to look at the sun directly. They saw it descend behind something they could not guess at. Then there was darkness.

The fact stunned them. So night came like this!

Then they saw the stars for the first time, as they came singly into being. And the folk from the lowland crowded frantically into the cave with its faint odor of having once been occupied by something else. They filled the cave tightly. But Burl had some reluctance to admit his terror. He and Saya were the last to enter.

And nothing happened. Nothing. The sounds of sunset continued. They were strange but soothing and somehow—again ancestral memory spoke comfortingly—they were the way night-sounds ought to be. Burl and the others could not possibly know it, but for the first time in forty generations on the forgotten planet, human beings were in an environment really suited to them. It had a rightness and a goodness which was obvious in spite of its novelty. And because of Burl's own special experiences, he was a little bit better able to estimate novelties than the rest. He listened to the night-noises from close by the cave's small entrance. He heard the breathing of his tribesfolk. He felt the heat of their bodies, keeping the crowded enclosure warm enough for all. Saya held fast to his hand, for the reassurance of the contact. He was wakeful, and thinking very busily and painfully, but Saya was not thinking at all. She was simply proud of Burl.

She felt, to be sure, a tumult which was fear of the unknown and relief from much greater fear of the familiar. She felt warm, prideful memories of the sight of Burl leading and commanding the others. She had absorbing fresh memories of the look and feel of sunshine, and mental pictures of sky and grass and trees which she had never seen before. Confusedly she remembered that Burl had killed a spider, no less, and he had shown how to escape a praying-mantis by flinging at it an ant, and he had grandly led the others up a mountainside it had never occurred to anybody else to climb. And the giant millipede would have devoured them all, but that Burl gave commands and set the example, and he had marched magnificently up the mountainside when it seemed that all the cosmos twisted and prepared to drop them into an inverted sky.

Saya dozed. And Burl sat awake, listening, and presently with fast-beating heart he slipped out of the entrance to the cave and stared about him in the night.

There was coolness such as he had never known before, but night-fall was not long past. There were smells in the air he had never before experienced— green things growing, and the peculiar clean odor of wind that has been bathed in sunshine, and the oddly satisfying smell of resinous trees.

But Burl raised his eyes to the heavens. He saw the stars in all their glory, and he was the first human in two thousand years and more to look at them from this planet. There were myriads upon myriads of them, varying in brightness from stabbing lights to infinitesimal twinklings. They were of every possible color. They hung in the sky above him, immobile and unthreatening. They had not descended. They were very beautiful.

Burl stared. And then he noticed that he was breathing deeply, with a new zest. He was filling his lungs with clean, cool, fragrant air such as men were intended to breathe from the beginning, and of which Burl and many others had been deprived. It was almost intoxicating to feel so splendidly alive and unafraid.

There was a slight sound. Saya stood beside him, trembling a little. To leave the others had required great courage, but she had come to realize that if Burl was in danger she wished to share it.

They heard the nightwind and the orchestra of nightsingers. They wandered aside from the cave-mouth and Saya found completely primitive and satisfying pride in the courage of Burl, who was actually not afraid of the dark! Her own uneasiness became something which merely added savor to her pride in him. She followed him wherever he went, to examine this and consider that in the nighttime. It gave her enormous satisfaction at once to think of danger and to feel so safe because of his nearness.

Presently they heard a new sound in the night. It was very far away, and not in the least like any sound they had ever heard before. It changed in pitch as insect-cries do not. It was a baying, yelping sound. It rose, and held the higher note, and abruptly dropped in pitch before it ceased. Minutes later it came again. Saya shivered, but Burl said thoughtfully:

"That is a good sound."

He didn't know why. Saya shivered again. She said reluctantly:

"I am cold."

It had been a rare sensation in the lowlands. It came only after one of the infrequent thunderstorms, when wetted human bodies were exposed to the gusty winds that otherwise never blew. But here the nights grew cold after sundown. The heat of the ground would radiate to outer space with no clouds to intercept it, and before dawn the temperature might drop nearly to freezing. On a planet so close to its sun, however, there would hardly be more than light hoar-frost at any time.

The two of them went back to the cave. It was warm there, because of the close packing of bodies and many breaths. Burl and Saya found places to rest and dozed off, Saya's hand again trustfully in Burl's.

He still remained awake for a long time. He thought of the stars, but they were too strange to estimate. He thought of the trees and grass. But most of his impressions of this upper world were so remote from previous knowledge that he could only accept them as they were and defer reflecting upon them until later. He did feel an enormous complacency at having led his followers here, though.

But the last thing he actually thought about, before his eyes blinked shut in sleep, was that distant howling noise he had heard in the night. It was totally novel in kind, and yet there was something buried among the items of his racial heritage that told him it was good.

He was first awake of all the tribesmen and he looked out into the cold and pallid grayness of before-dawn. He saw trees. One side was brightly lighted by comparison, and the other side was dark. He heard the tiny singing noises of the inhabitants of this place. Presently he crawled out of the cave again.

The air was biting in its chill. It was an excellent reason why the giant insects could not live here, but it was invigorating to Burl as he breathed it in. Presently he looked curiously for the source of the peculiar one-sided light.

He saw the top of the sun as it peered above the eastern cloud-bank. The sky grew lighter. He blinked and saw it rise more fully into view. He thought to look upward, and the stars that had bewildered him were nearly gone. He ran to call Saya.

The rest of the tribe waked as he roused her. One by one, they followed to watch their first sunrise. The men gaped at the sun as it filled the east with colorings, and rose and rose above the seemingly steaming layer of clouds, and then appeared to spring free of the horizon and swim on upward.

The women stared with all their eyes. The children blinked, and shivered, and crept to their mothers for warmth. The women enclosed them in their cloaks, and they thawed and peered out once more at the glory of sunshine and the day. Very soon, too, they realized that warmth came from the great shining body in the sky. The children presently discovered a game. It was the first game they had ever played. It consisted of running into a shaded place until they shivered, and then of running out into warm sunshine once more. Until this, dawning fear was the motive for such playing as they did. Now they gleefully made a game of sunshine.

In this first morning of their life above the clouds, the tribesmen ate of the food they had brought from below. But there was not an indefinite amount of food left. Burl ate, and considered darkly, and presently summoned his followers' attention. They were quite contented and for the moment felt no need of his guidance. But he felt need of admiration.

He spoke abruptly:

"We do not want to go back to the place we came from," he said sternly. "We must look for food here, so we can stay for always. Today we find food."

It was a seizure of the initiative. It was the linking of what the folk most craved with obedience to Burl. It was the device by which dictators seize power, and it was the instinctive action of a leader.

The eating men murmured agreement. There was a certain definite idea of goodness—not virtue, but of things desirable—associated with what Burl did and what he commanded. His tribe was gradually forming a habit of obedience, though it was a very fragile habit up to now.

He led them exploring as soon as they had eaten. All of them, of course. They straggled irregularly behind him. They came to a brook and regarded it with amazement. There were no leeches. No greenish algae. No foaming masses of scum. It was clear! Greatly daring, Burl tasted it. He drank the first really potable water in a very long time for his race on this planet. It was not fouled by drainage through molds or rusts.

Dor drank after him. Jak. Cori tasted, and instantly bade her children drink. Even old Tama drank suspiciously, and then raised her voice in shrill complaint that Burl had not led them to this place sooner. Tet and Dik became convinced that there were no deadly things lurking in it, and splashed each other. Dik slipped and sat down hard on white stuff that yielded and almost splashed. He got up and looked fearfully at what he thought might be a deadly slime. Then he yelped shrilly.

He had sat down on and crushed part of a bed of mushrooms. But they were tiny, clean, and appetizing.

They were miniatures of the edible mushrooms the tribe fed on.

Burl smelled and finally tasted one. It was, of course, nothing more nor less than a perfectly normal edible mushroom, growing to the size that mushrooms originally grew on Earth. It grew on a shaded place in enormously rich soil. It had been protected from direct sunlight by trees, but it had not had the means or the stimulus to become a monster.

Burl ate it. He carefully composed his features. Then he announced the find to his followers. There was food here, he told them sternly, but in this splendid world to which he had led them, food was small. There would be no great enemies here, but the food would have to be sought in small objects instead of great ones. They must look at this place and seek others like it, in order to find food.

The tribesmen were doubtful. But they plucked mushrooms—whole ones—instead of merely breaking off parts of their tops. With deep astonishment they recognized the miniature objects as familiar things ensmalled. These mushrooms had the same savor, but they were not coarse or stringy or tough like the giants. They melted in the mouth. Life in this place to which Burl had led them was delectable! Truly the doings of Burl were astonishing!

When the oldest of Cori's children found a beetle on a leaf, and they recognized it, and instead of being bigger than a man and a thing to flee from, it was less than an inch in size and helpless against them. They were entranced. From that moment onward they would really follow Burl anywhere, in the happy conviction that he could only bring good to everybody.

The opinion could have drawbacks, and it need not be always even true, but Burl did nothing to discourage it.

And then, near midday, they made a discovery even greater than that of familiar food in unfamiliar sizes. They were struggling, at the time, through a vast patch of bushes with thorns on them—they were not used to thorns—which they deeply distrusted. Eventually they would find out that the glistening dark fruit were blackberries, and would rejoice in them, but at this first encounter they were uneasy. In the midst of such an untouched berry-patch they heard noises in the distance.

The sound was made up of cries of varying pitch, some of which were loud and abrupt, and others longer and less loud. The people did not understand them in the least. They could have been cries of human beings, perhaps, but they were not cries of pain. Also they were not language. They seemed to express a tremendous, zestful excitement. They had no overtone of horror. And Burl and his folk had known of no excitement among insects except frenzy. They could not imagine what sort of tumult this could be.

But to Burl these sounds had something of the timbre of the yelping noises of the night before. He had felt drawn to that sound. He liked it. He liked this.

He led the way boldly toward the agitated noises. Presently—after a mile or so—he and his people came out of breast-high weeds. Saya was immediately behind him. The others trailed, Tama complaining bitterly that there was no need to track down sounds which could only mean danger. They emerged in a space of bare stone above a small and grassy amphitheatre. The tumult came from its center.

A pack of dogs was joyously attacking something that Burl could not see clearly. They were dogs. They barked zestfully, and they yelped and snarled and yapped in a dozen different voices, and they were having a thoroughly good time—though it might not be so good for the thing they attacked.

One of them sighted the humans. He stopped stock-still and barked. The others whirled and saw the humans as they came out into view. The tumult ceased abruptly.

There was silence. The tribesmen saw creatures with four legs only. They had never before seen any living thing with fewer than six, except men. Spiders had eight. The dogs did not have mandibles. They did not have wing-cases. They did not act like insects. It was stupefying!

And the dogs saw men, whom they had never seen before. Much more important, they smelled men. And the difference between man-smell and insect-smell was so vast—because through hundreds of generations the dogs had not smelled anything with warm blood save their own kind—the difference in smell was so great in kind that the dogs did not react with suspicion, but with a fascinated curiosity. This was an unparalleled smell. It was, even in its novelty, an overwhelmingly satisfying smell.

The dogs regarded the men with their heads on one side, sniffing in the deepest possible amazement—amazement so intense that they could not possibly feel hostility. One of them whined a little because he did not understand.

11. WARM BLOOD IS A BOND

Peculiarly enough, it was a matter of topography. The plateau which reached above the clouds rose with a steep slope from the valley from which a hunting-spider's brood had driven the men. This was on the eastern edge of the plateau. On the west, however, the highland was subject to an indentation which almost severed it. No more than twenty miles from where Burl's group had climbed to sunshine, there was a much more gradual slope downward. There, mushroom-forests grew almost to the cloud-layer. From there, giant insects strayed up and onto the plateau itself.

They could not live above the clouds, of course. There was not food enough for their insatiable hunger. Especially at night, it was too cold to allow them to stay active. But they did stray from their normal environment, and some of them did reach the sunshine, and perhaps some of them blundered back down to their mushroom-forests again. But those which did not stumble back were chilled to torpor during their first night underneath the stars. They were only partly active on the second day—if, indeed, they were active at all. Few or none recovered from their second night's coldness. None at all kept their full ferocity and deadliness.

And this was how the dogs survived. They were certainly descended from dogs on the wrecked spaceship—the *Icarus*—whose crew had landed on this planet some forty-odd human generations since. The humans of today had no memories of the ship, and the dogs surely had no traditions. But just because those early dogs had less intelligence, they had more useful instincts. Perhaps the first generations of castaways bred dogs in their first few desperate centuries, hoping that dogs could help them survive. But no human civilization could survive in the lowlands. The humans went back to the primitive state of their race and lived as furtive vermin among monsters. Dogs could not survive there, though humans did linger on, so somehow the dogs took to the heights. Perhaps dogs survived their masters. Perhaps some were abandoned or driven away. But dogs had reached the highlands. And they did survive because giant insects blundered up after them, and could not survive in a proper environment for dogs and men.

There was even reason for the dogs remaining limited in number, and keenly intelligent. The food-supply was limited. When there were too many dogs, their attacks on stumbling insect giants were more desperate and made earlier, before the monsters' ferocity was lessened. So more dogs died. Then there was an adjustment of the number of dogs to the food-supply. There was also a selection of those too intelligent to attack rashly. Yet these who had insufficient courage would not eat.

In short, the dogs who now regarded men with bright, interested eyes were very sound dogs. They had the intelligence needed for survival. They did not attack anything imprudently, but they also knew that it was not necessary to be more than reasonably wary of insects in general—not even spiders unless they were very newly arrived from the steaming lowlands. So the dogs regarded men with very much the same astonished interest with which the men regarded the dogs.

Burl saw immediately that the dogs did not act with the blind ferocity of insects, but with an interested, estimative intelligence strikingly like that of men. Insects never examined anything. They fled or they fought. Those who were not carnivorous had no interest in anything but food, and those who were meat-eaters lumbered insanely into battle at the bare sight of possible prey. The dogs did neither. They sniffed and they considered.

Burl said sharply to his followers:

"Stay here!"

He walked slowly down into the amphitheatre. Saya followed him instantly. Dogs moved warily aside. But they raised their noses and sniffed. They were long, luxurious sniffs. The smell of human kind was a good smell. Dogs had lived hundreds of their generations without having it in their nostrils, but before that there were thousands of generations to whom that smell was a necessity.

Burl reached the object the dogs had been attacking. It lay on the grass, throbbing painfully. It was the larva of an azure-blue moth which spread ten-foot wings at nightfall. The time for its metamorphosis was near, and it had traveled blindly in search of a place where it could spin its cocoon safely and change to its winged form. It had come to another world, the world above the clouds. It could find no proper place. Its stores of fat had protected it somewhat from the chill. But the dogs had found it as it crawled blindly.

Burl considered. It was the custom of wasps to sting creatures like this at a certain special spot, apparently marked for them by a tuft of dark fur.

Burl thrust home with his lance. The point pierced that particular spot. The creature died quickly and without agony. The thought to kill was an inspiration. Then instinct followed. Burl cut off meat for his tribesmen. The dogs offered no objection. They were well-fed enough. Burl and Saya, together, carried the meat back to the other tribesfolk. On the way Burl passed within two yards of a dog which regarded him with extreme intentness and almost a wistful expression. Burl's smell did not mean game. It meant—something the dog struggled helplessly to remember. But it was good.

"I have killed the thing," said Burl to the dog, in the tone of one addressing an equal. "You can go and eat it now. I took only part of it."

Burl and his people ate of what he had brought back. Many of the dogs—most of them—went to the feast Burl had left. Presently they were back. They had no reason to be hostile. They were fed. The humans offered them no injury, and the humans smelled of something that appealed to the deepest well-springs of canine nature.

Presently the dogs were close about the humans. They were fascinated. And the humans were fascinated in return. Each of the people had a little of the feeling that Burl had experienced as the tribal leader. In the intent, absorbed and wholly unhostile regard of the dogs, even children felt flattered and friendly. And surely in a place where everything else was so novel and so satisfactory, it was possible to imagine friendliness with creatures which were not human, since assuredly they were not insects.

A similar state of mind existed among the dogs.

Saya had more meat than she desired. She glanced among the members of the tribe. All were supplied. She tossed it to a dog. He jerked away alertly, and then sniffed at it where it had dropped. A dog can always eat. He ate it.

"I wish you would talk to us," said Saya hopefully.

The dog wagged his tail.

"You do not look like us," said Saya interestedly, "but you act like we do. Not like the—Monsters."

The dog looked significantly at meat in Burl's hand. Burl tossed it. The dog caught it with a quick snap, swallowed it, wagged his tail briefly and came closer. It was a completely incredible action, but dogs and men were blood-kin on this planet. Besides, there was racial-memory rightness in friendship between men and dogs. It was not hindered by any past experience of either. They were the only warm-blooded creatures on this world. It was a kinship felt by both.

Presently Burl stood up and spoke politely to the dog.

He addressed him with the same respect he would have given to another man. In all his life he had never felt equal to an insect, but he felt no arrogance toward this dog. He felt superior only to other men.

"We are going back to our cave," he said politely. "Maybe we will meet again."

He led his tribe back to the cave in which they had spent the previous night. The dogs followed, ranging on either side. They were well-fed, with no memory of hostility to any creature which smelled of warm blood. They had an instinct without experience to dull it. The latter part of the journey back to the tribal cave was—if anybody had been qualified to notice it— remarkably like a group of dogs taking a walk with a group of people. It was companionable. It felt right.

That night Burl left the cave, as before, to look at the stars. This time Saya went with him matter-of-factly. But as they came out of the cave-entrance there was a stirring. A dog rose and stretched himself elaborately, yawning the while. When Burl and Saya moved away, he trotted amiably with them.

They talked to it, and the dog seemed pleased. It wagged its tail.

When morning came, the dogs were still waiting hopefully for the humans to come out. They appeared to expect the people to take another nice long walk, on which they would accompany them. It was a brand-new satisfaction they did not want to miss. After all, from a dog's standpoint, humans are made to take long walks with, among other things. The dogs greeted the people with tail-waggings and cordiality.

The dogs made a great difference in the adjustment of the tribe to life upon the plateau. Their friendship assured the new status of human life. Burl and his fellows had ceased to be fugitive game for any insect murderer. They had hoped to become unpursued for-agers, because they could hardly imagine anything else. But when the dogs joined them, they were immediately raised to the estate of hunters. The men did not domesticate the dogs. They made friends with them. The dogs did not subjugate themselves to the men. They joined them, at first tentatively, and then with worshipful enthusiasm. And the partnership was so inevitably a right one that within a month it was as if it had always been.

Actually, save for a mere two thousand years, it had been.

At the end of a month the tribe had a permanent encampment. There were caves at a suitable distance from the slope up which most wanderers from the lowlands came. Cori's oldest child found the chrysalis

of a giant butterfly, whose caterpillar form had so
offensive an odor that the dogs had not attacked it. But
when it emerged from the chrysalis, men and dogs
together assailed it before it could take flight. They
ended the enterprise with warm mutual approval. The
humans had acquired great wings with which to make
warm cloaks—very useful against the evening chill.
Dogs and men, alike, had feasted.

Then, one dawning, the dogs made a vast outcry
which awoke the tribesmen. Burl led the rush to the
spot. They did battle with a monster nocturnal beetle,
less chilled than most such invaders. In the gray dawn
light Burl realized that the darting, yapping dogs kept
the creature's full attention. He crippled, and then
killed it with his spear. The feat appeared to earn him
warm admiration from the dogs. Burl wore a moth's
feathery antenna again, bound to his forehead like a
knight's plumes. He looked very splendid.

The entire pattern of human life changed swiftly,
as if an entire revelation had been granted to men. The
ground was often thorny. One man pierced his foot.
Old Tama, scolding him for his carelessness, bound a
strip of wing-fabric about it so he could walk. The
injured foot was more comfortable than the one still
unhurt. Within a week the women were busily contriv-
ing divers forms of footgear to achieve greater comfort for everybody. One day Saya admired glistening
red berries and tried to pluck one, and they stained
her fingers. She licked her fingers to clean them—and
berries were added to the tribe's menu. A veritable orgy
of experiment began, which is a state of things which
is extremely rare in human affairs. A race with an
established culture and tradition does not abandon old
ways of doing things without profound reason. But men
who have abandoned their old ways can discover astonishingly useful new ones.

Already the dogs were established as sentries and watchmen, and as friends to every member of the tribe. By now mothers did not feel alarmed if a child wandered out of sight. There would be dogs along. No danger could approach a child without vociferous warning from the dogs. Men went hunting, now, with zestful tail-wagging dogs as companions in the chase. Dor killed a torpid minotaur beetle alone, save for assisting dogs, and Burl felt a twinge of jealousy. But then Burl, himself, battled a black male spider in a lone duel, with dogs to help. By the time a stray monster from the lowlands reached this area, it was dazed and half-numbed by one night of continuous chill. Even the black spider could not find the energy to leap. It fought like a fiend, yet sluggishly. Burl killed this one while the dogs kept it busy, and the dogs were reproachful because he carried it back to the tribal headquarters before dividing it among his assistants. Afterward, he realized that though he could have avoided the fight he would have been ashamed to do so, while the dogs barked and snapped at its furry legs.

It was while things were in this state that the way of life for human beings on the forgotten planet was settled for all time. Burl and Saya went out early one morning with the dogs, to hunt for meat for the village. Hunting was easiest in the early hours, while creatures that strayed up the night before were still sluggish with cold. Often, hunting was merely butchery of an enfeebled monster to whom any effort at all was terribly difficult.

This morning they strode away briskly. The dogs roved exuberantly through the brush before them. They were some five miles from the village when the dogs bayed game. And Burl and Saya ran to the spot with ready spears, which was something of a change from their former actions on notice of a carnivore abroad.

They found the dogs dancing and barking around one of the most ferocious of the meat-eating beetles. It was not unduly large, to be sure. Its body might have been four feet long, or thereabouts. But its horrible gaping mandibles added a good three feet more.

Those scythe-like weapons gaped wide—opening sidewise as insects' jaws do—as the beetle snapped hideously at its attackers, swinging about as the dogs dashed at it. Its legs were spurred and spiked and armed with dagger-like spines. Burl plunged into the fight.

The great mandibles clicked and clashed. They were capable of disemboweling a man or snapping a dog's body in half without effort. There were whistling noises as the beetle breathed through its abdominal spiracles. It fought furiously, making ferocious charges at the dogs who tormented and bewildered it. But they created the most zestfully excited of tumults.

Burl and Saya were, of course, at least as absorbed and excited as the dogs, or they would have noticed the thing that was to make so much difference to every human being, not only on the plateau but still down in the lowlands. This unnoticed thing was beyond their imagining. There had been nothing else like it on this world in many hundreds of years. It was half a dozen miles away and perhaps a thousand feet high when Burl and Saya prepared to intervene professionally on behalf of the dogs. It was a silvery needle, floating unsupported in the air. As they entered the battle, it swerved and moved swiftly in their direction. It was silent, and they did not notice. They knew of no reason to scan the sky in daytime. And there was business on hand, anyhow.

Burl leaped in toward the beetle with a lance-thrust at the tough integument where an armored leg joined the creature's body. He missed, and the beetle whirled.

Saya flashed her cloak before the monster so that it seemed a larger and a nearer antagonist. As the creature whirled again, Burl stabbed and a hind-leg crumpled.

Instantly the thing was limping. A beetle does not use its legs like four-legged creatures. A beetle moving shifts the two end legs on one side and the central leg on the other, so that it always stands on an adjustable tripod of limbs. It cannot adjust readily to crippling. A dog snatched at a spiny lower leg and crunched, and darted away. The machine-like monster uttered a formless, deep-bass cry and was spurred to unbelievable fierceness. The fight became a thing of furious movement and joyous uproar, with Burl striking once at a multiple eye so the pain would deflect it from a charge at Saya, and Saya again deflecting it with her cloak and once breathlessly trying to strike it with her shorter spear.

They struck it again, and a third time, and it sank horribly to the ground, all three legs on one side crippled. The remaining three thrust and thrust and struggled senselessly—and suddenly it was on its back, still striking its gigantic jaws frantically in the hope of murder. But then Burl struck home between two armor-plates where a ganglion was almost exposed. The blow killed it instantly.

Burl and Saya were smiling at each other when there was a monstrous sound of crashing trees. They whirled. The dogs pricked up their ears. One of them barked defiantly.

Something huge—truly huge! —had settled to the ground a bare two hundred yards away. It was metal, and there were ports in its sides, and it was quite beyond imagining. Because, of course, no spaceship had landed on this planet in forty-odd human generations.

A port opened as they stared at it. Men came out.

Burl and Saya were barbarically attired, but they had been fighting some sort of local monster—the men on the spaceship could not quite grasp what they had seen—and they had been helped by dogs. Human beings and dogs, together, always mean some sort of civilization.

The dogs gave an impression of a very high level indeed. They trotted confidently over to the ship, and they sniffed cautiously at the men who had landed. Then their behavior was admirable. They greeted the new-come men with the self-confident cordiality of dogs who are on the best possible terms with human beings, and there was no question of any suspicion by anybody. The attitude of a man toward a dog is a perfectly valid indication of his character, if not of his technical education. And the newcomers knew how to treat dogs.

So Burl and Saya went forward, with the confident pleasure with which well-raised children and other persons of innate dignity greet strangers.

The ship was the *Wapiti*, a private cruiser doing incidental exploration for the Biological Survey in the course of a trip after good hunting. It had touched on the forgotten planet, and it would never be forgotten again.

EPILOGUE

The survey-ship *Tethys* made the first landing on the forgotten planet, and the *Orana* followed, and some centuries later the *Ludred*. Then the planet was forgotten until the *Wapiti* arrived. The arrival of the *Wapiti* was as much an accident as the loss of the records which caused the planet to be overlooked for some thousands of years. Somebody had noticed that the sun around which it circled was of a type which usually has useful planets, but there was no record that it had ever been visited. So a request to the sportsmen on the *Wapiti* had caused them to turn aside. They considered, anyhow, that it would be interesting to land on a brand-new world or two. They considered it fascinating to find human beings there before them. But they could not understand the use of such primitive weapons or garments of such barbaric splendor. They had trouble, too, because in forty-odd generations the speech of the universe had changed, while Burl and Saya spoke a very archaic language indeed.

But there was an educator on the *Wapiti*. It was

quite standard apparatus—simply basic education for a human child, so that one's schoolyears could be begun with a backlog of correct speech, and reading, with the practical facts of mathematics, sanitation, and the general information that any human being anywhere needs to know. Children use it before they start school, and they absorb its information quite painlessly. It is rare that an adult needs it. But Burl and Saya did.

Burl was politely invited to wear the head-set, and he politely obliged. He found himself equipped with a new language and what seemed to him an astonishing amount of information. Among the information was the item that he was going to have—as an adult—a severe headache. Which he did. Also included was the fact that the making of records for such educators was so laborious a process that it took generations to compile one master-record for the instruments.

Burl, with a splitting headache, nevertheless urged Saya to join him in getting an education. And she did. And thereafter they were able to converse with the sportsmen on the *Wapiti* comfortably enough—except for their headaches.

And all this led to extremely satisfactory arrangements. Sportsmen could not but be enthusiastic about the hunting of giant insects with dogs and spears. The sportsmen on the *Wapiti* wanted some of that kind of sport. Burl's fellow tribesmen were delighted to oblige, though they had not quite the zest of Burl. They had to acquire educations in their turn, so they could talk to their new hunting-companions. But the hunting was magnificent. The *Wapiti* abandoned its original plans and settled down for a stay.

Presently Burl's casual talk of the lowlands produced results. An atmosphere-flier came out of the ship's storage-compartments. And through the educator Burl was now a civilized man. He had not the specialized later information of his guests, but he had knowledge they could not dream of, and which it would take much of a century to put in recordable form for an educator.

So an atmosphere-flier went down into the lowlands through the cloud-banks. There were three men on board. They had good hunting. Magnificent hunting. Even more importantly, they found another cluster of human beings who lived as fugitives among the insect giants. They brought them to the plateau, a few at a time. Sportsmen stayed in the lowlands with modern weapons, hunting enthusiastically, while the transfer took place.

In all, the *Wapiti* stayed for two months Earthtime. When it left, its sportsmen had such trophies as would make them envied of all other hunters in three star-clusters. They left behind weapons and atmosphere-fliers and their library and tools. But they took with them enthusiasm for the sport on the once-forgotten planet, and rather warm feelings of friendship for Burl.

They sent their friends back. The next ship to come in found a small city on the plateau, with a population of three hundred souls, all civilized by educator. Naturally, they'd had no trouble building civilized dwellings or practicing sanitation, or developing a neatly adapted culture-pattern for their particular environment. This second ship brought more weapons and fliers and news from the first party about commercial demand for the incredibly luxurious moth-fur, to be found on only one planet in all the galaxy.

The fourth ship to land on the plateau was a trading-ship anxious to load such furs for recklessly bidding merchants in a dozen interplanetary marts. There were then nearly a thousand people living on the plateau. They had a natural monopoly, not of moth-fur and butterfly-wing fabric, and panels of iridescent chitin for luxurious decoration, but of the strictly practical and detailed knowledge of insect habits which made it possible to obtain them. Off-planet visitors who tried to hunt without local knowledge did not come back from the lowlands. In time, Burl firmly enacted a planetary law which forbade the inexperienced to go below the cloud-layer.

Because, of course, a government had to be formed for the planet. But men with the basic education of citizens everywhere did not fumble it. They had a job to do which was more important than anybody's vanity. It was a job which gave deep and abiding satisfaction. When naked, trembling folk were found in the mushroom-jungles and brought to the plateau, they had one instant, feverish desire as soon as they got over the headache from the educator.

They wanted to go back to the lowlands. It was profitable, to be sure. But it was even more of a satisfaction to hunt and kill the monsters that had hunted and killed men for so long. It felt good, too, to find other humans and bring them out to sunshine.

So nowadays the forgotten planet has ceased to be forgotten. It is hardly necessary to name it, because its name is known through all the Galaxy. Its population is not large, so far, but it is an interesting place to live in. In the popular mind, it is the most glamorous of all possible worlds, and for easily understandable reasons. The inhabitants of its capital city wear moth-fur garments and butterfly-wing cloaks for the benefit of their fellows in the lowlands. There is no day but fliers take off and dive down into the mists. When human hunters are in the lowlands, they dress as the lowlanders they used to be, so that lowlanders who may spy them will be sure that they are men, and friends, and come to them to be raised to proper dignity above the insects. It is not unusual for a man to be brought up to sunshine, and have his session with the educator, and be flying his own assigned atmosphere-flier within a week, diving back above what used to be the place where he was hunted, but where he has become the hunter.

It is a very pleasant arrangement. The search for more humans in the lowlands is a prosperous business, even when it is unsuccessful. The wings of white Morpho butterflies bring the highest prices, but even a common swallow-tail is riches, and the fur of caterpillars—duly processed—goes into the holds of the planet-owned space-line ships with the care given elsewhere to platinum and diamonds.

And also it is good sport. The planet is a sportsman's paradise. There are not too many visitors. Nobody may go hunting without an experienced host. And off-planet sportsmen tend to feel somewhat queasy after a session as guest of the folk who have made Burl their planet-president. Visitors are not so much alarmed at fighting flying beetles in mid-air, even though the beetles may compare with the hunters' craft in size and are terrifically tenacious of life. The thing that appalls strangers is the insistence of Burl's fellow-citizens—no longer only tribesmen—upon fighting spiders on the ground. With their memories, they like it that way. It's more satisfactory.

Not long ago the Planet President of Sumor XI was Burl's guest for a hunt. Sumor XI is a highly civilized planet, and life there has become tame. Its president is an ardent hunter. He liked Burl, who is still all hard muscle despite his graying hair. He and Saya have a very comfortable dwelling, and now that their children are grown they have room in it even for a planet president, if he comes as a sportsman guest. The Planet President of Sumor XI even liked the informal atmosphere of a house where pleasantly self-possessed dogs curl up comfortably on rugs of emperor-moth down that elsewhere are beyond price.

But the President of Sumor XI was embarrassed on his visit. He and Burl are both hunters, and they are highly congenial. But the President of Sumor XI was upset on his last flight to the lowlands. Burl got out of the atmosphere-flier alone, and for pure deep personal satisfaction he fought a mastodon-sized wolf spider with nothing but a spear.

He killed the creature, of course. But the President of Sumor XI was embarrassed. He wouldn't have dared try it. He felt that, however sporting it might be, it was too risky a thing for a Planet President to do.

But Saya took it for granted.

THE PLANET EXPLORER

SOLAR CONSTANT

Bordman woke that morning when the partly-opened port of his sleeping-cabin closed of itself and the room-warmer began to whir. He found himself burrowed deep under his covering, and when he got his head out of it the already-bright room was bitterly cold and his breath made a fog about his head.

He thought uneasily *it's colder than yesterday!* But a Senior Colonial Survey Officer is not supposed to let himself seem disturbed in public, and the only way to follow that rule is to follow it in private too. So Bordman composed his features, while gloom filled him. When one has just received senior service rating and is on one's very first independent survey of a new colonial installation, the unexpected can be appalling. The unexpected was definitely here, on Lani III.

He'd been a Survey Candidate on Khali II and Taret and Arepo I, all of which were tropical, and a Junior Officer on Menes III and Thotmes—one a semi-arid planet and the other temperate-volcanic—and he'd done an assistant job on Saril's solitary world, which

was nine-tenths water. But this first independent survey on his own was another matter. Everything was
wholly unfamiliar. An ice-planet with a minus point one
habitability rating was upsetting in its peculiarities. He
knew what the books said about glacial-world conditions, but that was all.

The denseness of the fog his breath made seemed
to grow less as the room-warmer whirred and whirred.
When by the thinness of the mist he guessed the
temperature to be not much under freezing, he climbed
out of his bunk and went to the port to look out. His
cabin, of course, was in one of the drone-hulls that had
brought the colony's equipment to Lani III. The other
emptied hulls were precisely ranged in order outside.
They were connected by tubular galleries, and painstakingly leveled. They gave an impression of impassioned tidiness among the upheaved, ice-coated
mountains all about.

He gazed down the long valley in which the colony
lay. There were monstrous slanting peaks on either side
that partly framed the morning sun. Their flanks were
ice. The sky was pale, and the sun had four sun-dogs
geometrically about it. Normal post-midnight temperatures in this valley ranged around ten below zero—and
this was technically summer. But it was colder than ten
below zero now. At noon there were normally tiny
trickling rills of surface-thaw running down the sunlit sides of the mountains, but they froze again at night.
And this was a sheltered valley, warmer than most of
the planet's surface. The sun had its sun-dogs every
day, on rising. There were nights when the brighter
planets had star-pups, too.

The phone-plate lighted and dimmed and lighted
and dimmed. They did themselves well on Lani III;
the parent world was in this same solar system, making supply easy. That was rare. Bordman stood before

the plate and it cleared. Herndon's face peered unhappily out of it. He was even younger than Bordman, and inclined to lean on the supposedly vast experience of a Senior Officer of the Colonial Survey.

"Well?" said Bordman, feeling undignified in his sleeping garments.

"We're picking up a beam from home," said Herndon anxiously. "But we can't make it out."

Because the third planet of the sun Lani was being colonized from the second, inhabited world, communication with the colony's base was possible. A tight beam could span the distance, which was only light-minutes across at conjunction, and not much over a light-hour at opposition, as now. But the beam communication had been broken for the past few weeks, and shouldn't be possible again for some weeks more. The sun lay between. One wouldn't expect normal sound-and-picture transmission until the parent planet had moved past the scrambler-fields of Lani. But something had come through. It would be reasonable for it to be pretty much hash when it arrived.

"They aren't sending words or pictures," said Herndon. "The beam is wobbly and we don't know what to make of it. It's a signal, all right, and on the regular frequency. But there are all sorts of stray noises and still in the midst of it there's some sort of signal we can't make out. It's like a whine, only it stutters. It's a broken-up sound of one pitch."

Bordman rubbed his chin. He remembered a course in information theory just before he'd graduated from the Service Academy. Signals were made by pulses, pitch-changes, and frequency-variations. Information was what couldn't be predicted without information. And he remembered with gratitude a seminar on the history of communication, just before he'd gone out on his first field job as a Survey Candidate.

"Hm," he said with a trace of self-consciousness. "Those noises, the stuttering ones. Would they be, on the whole, of no more than two different durations? Like—hm— Bzz bzz bzzzzzzz bzz?"

He felt that he lost dignity by making such ribald sounds. But Herndon's face brightened.

"That's it!" he said relievedly. "That's it! Only they're high-pitched like—" His voice went falsetto. "Bz bz bz bzzz bz bz." Bordman thought, *we sound like two idiots.* He said:

"Record everything you get, and I'll try to decode it." He added, "Before there was voice communication there were signals by light and sound in groups of long and short units. They came in groups, to stand for letters, and things were spelled out. Of course there were larger groups which were words. Very crude system, but it worked when there was a lot of interference, as in the early days. If there's some emergency, your home world might try to get through the sun's scrambled-field that way."

"Undoubtedly!" said Herndon, with even greater relief. "No question, that's it!"

He regarded Bordman with respect as he clicked off. His image faded.

He thinks I'm wonderful, thought Bordman wryly. *Because I'm Colonial Survey. But all I know is what's been taught me. It's bound to show up sooner or later. Damn!*

He dressed. From time to time he looked out the port again. The intolerable cold of Lani III had intensified, lately. There was some idea that sunspots were the cause. He couldn't make out sunspots with the naked eye, but the sun did look pale, with its accompanying sundogs, the result of microscopic ice-crystals suspended in the air. There was no dust on this planet, but there was plenty of ice! It was in the air and on the ground and even under it. To be sure, the drills for the foundation of the great landing-grid had brought up cores of frozen humus along with frozen clay, so there must have been a time when this world had known clouds and seas and vegetation. But it was millions, maybe hundreds of millions of years ago. Right now, though, it was only warm enough to have an atmosphere and very slight and partial thawings in direct sunlight, in sheltered spots, at midday. It couldn't support life, because life is always dependent on other life, and there is a temperature below which a natural ecological system can't maintain itself. And for the past few weeks, the climate had been such that even human-supplied life looked dubious.

Bordman slipped on his Colonial Survey uniform with its palm-tree insignia. Nothing could be much more inappropriate than palm-tree symbols on a planet with sixty feet of permafrost, Bordman reflected. *The construction gang calls it a blast, instead of a tree, because we blow up when they try to dodge specifications. But specifications have to be met! You can't bet the lives of a colony or even a ship's crew on half-built facilities!*

He marched down the corridor from his sleeping-room, with the dignity he tried to maintain for the sake of the Colonial Survey. It was a pretty lonely business, being dignified all the time. If Herndon didn't look so respectful it would have been pleasant to be more friendly. But Herndon revered him. Even his sister Riki . . .

But Bordman put her firmly out of his mind. He was on Lani III, which had very valuable mineral resources that made colonization worthwhile, to check and approve the colony installations. There was the giant landing-grid for spaceships, which took power from the ionosphere to bring space vessels gently to the ground, and also to supply the colony's power needs. It likewise lifted visiting space craft the necessary five planetary diameters out when they took off again. There was power storage in the remote event of disaster to that giant device. There was a food reserve and the necessary resources for its indefinite stretching in case of need. That usually meant hydroponic installations. All these things had had to be finished, operable, and inspected by a duly qualified Colonial Survey officer before the colony could be licensed for unlimited use.

It was all very normal and official, but Bordman was the newest Senior Survey Officer on the list, and this was the first of his independent operations. He felt inadequate at times.

He passed through the vestibule between this dronehull and the next and went directly to Herndon's office. Herndon, like himself, was newly endowed with authority. He was actually a mining-and-minerals man and a youthful prodigy in that field, but when the director of the colony was taken ill while a supply-ship was aground, he went back to the home planet and command devolved on Herndon. *I wonder,* thought Bordman, *if he feels as shaky as I do.*

When he entered the office, Herndon sat listening to a literal hash of noises coming out of a speaker on his desk. The cryptic signal had been relayed to him, and a recorder stored it as it came. There were cacklings and squeals and moaning sounds, sputters and rumbles and growls. But behind the facade of confusion there was a tiny, interrupted, high-pitched noise. It was a monotone whining not to be confused with the random sounds accompanying it. Sometimes it faded almost to inaudibility, and sometimes it was sharp and clear. But it was a distinctive sound in itself, and it was made up of short whines and longer ones of two durations only.

"I've put Riki at making a transcription of what we've got," said Herndon with relief as he saw Bordman. "She'll make short marks for the short sounds, and long ones for the long. I've told her to try to separate the groups. We've got a full half-hour of it, already."

Bordman made an inspired guess.

"I would expect it to be the same message repeated over and over," he said. He added, "And I think it would be decoded by guessing at the letters in two-letter and three-letter words, as clues to longer ones. That's quicker than statistical analysis of frequency."

Herndon instantly pressed buttons under his phone-plate. He relayed the information to his sister, as if it were gospel. *But it wasn't,* Bordman thought. *It's simply a trick remembered from boyhood, when I was interested in secret languages. My interest faded when I realized I had no secrets to record or transmit.*

Herndon turned from the phone-plate.

"Riki says she's already learned to recognize some groups," he reported, "but thanks for the advice. Now what?"

Bordman sat down. "It seems to me," he observed, "that the increased cold out here might not be local. Sunspots—"

Herndon wordlessly handed over a sheet of paper with observation figures on top and a graph below them, which related the observations to each other. They were the daily, at-first-routine, measurements of the solar constant from Lani III. The graph-line almost ran off the paper at the bottom.

"To look at this," he admitted, "you'd think the sun was going out. Of course it can't be," he added hastily. "Not possibly. But there is an extraordinary number of sunspots. Maybe they'll clear. But meanwhile the amount of heat reaching us is dropping. As far as I know there's no parallel for it. Night temperatures are thirty degrees lower than they should be. Not only here, either, but at all the robot weather-stations that have been spotted around the planet. They average forty below zero minimum, instead of ten. And—there is that terrific lot of sunspots. . . ."

Bordman frowned. Sunspots are things about which nothing can be done. Yet the habitability of a borderline planet, anyhow, could very well depend on them. An infinitesimal change in sun-heat can make a serious change in any planet's temperature. In the books, the ancient mother planet Earth was said to have entered glacial periods through a drop of only three degrees in the planet-wide temperature, and to have been tropic almost to its poles from a rise of only six. It had been guessed that those changes on the planet where humanity began had been caused by a coincidence of sunspot maxima.

Lani III was already glacial to its equator. Sunspots could account for worsening conditions here, perhaps. *That message from the inner planet could be bad,* thought Bordman, *if the solar constant drops and stays down awhile.* But aloud he said:

"There couldn't be a really significant permanent change. Not quickly, anyhow. Lani's a Sol-type star, and they aren't variables, though of course any dynamic system like a sun will have cyclic modifications of one sort or another. But they usually cancel out."

He sounded encouraging, even to himself.

There was a stirring behind him; Riki Herndon had come silently into her brother's office. She looked pale. She put some papers down on the desk.

"That's true," she said. "But while cycles sometimes cancel, sometimes they enhance each other. That's what's happening."

Bordman scrambled to his feet, flushing. Herndon said sharply:

"What? Where'd you get that stuff, Riki?"

She nodded at the sheaf of papers she'd just laid down.

"That's the news from home." She nodded again, to Bordman. "You were right. It was the same message, repeated over and over. And I decoded it like children decode each other's secret messages. I did that to Ken once. He was twelve, and I decoded his diary, and I remember how angry he was that I'd found out he didn't have any secrets."

She tried to smile. But Herndon wasn't listening. He read swiftly. Bordman saw that the under sheets were rows of dots and dashes, painstakingly transcribed and then decoded. There were letters under each group of marks.

Herndon was very white when he'd finished. He handed the sheet to Bordman. Riki's handwriting was precise and clear. Bordman read:

"FOR YOUR INFORMATION THE SOLAR CON-
STANT IS DROPPING RAPIDLY DUE TO COINCI-
DENCE OF CYCLIC VARIATIONS IN SUNSPOT
ACTIVITY WITH PREVIOUS UNOBSERVED LONG
CYCLES APPARENTLY INCREASING THE
EFFECT MAXIMUM IS NOT YET REACHED AND
IT IS EXPECTED THAT THIS PLANET WILL
BECOME UNINHABITABLE FOR A TIME
ALREADY KILLING FROSTS HAVE DESTROYED
CROPS IN SUMMER HEMISPHERE IT IS IMPROB-
ABLE THAT MORE THAN A SMALL PART OF
THE POPULATION CAN BE SHELTERED AND
WARMED THROUGH DEVELOPING GLACIAL
CONDITIONS WHICH WILL REACH TO EQUA-
TOR IN TWO HUNDRED DAYS THE COLD

CONDITIONS ARE COMPUTED TO LAST TWO
THOUSAND DAYS BEFORE NORMAL SOLAR
CONSTANT RECURS THIS INFORMATION IS
SENT YOU TO ADVISE IMMEDIATE DEVELOP-
MENT OF HYDROPONIC FOOD SUPPLY AND
OTHER PRECAUTIONS MESSAGE ENDS FOR
YOUR INFORMATION THE SOLAR CONSTANT IS
DROPPING RAPIDLY DUE TO COINCIDENCE OF
CYCLIC—"

Bordman looked up. Herndon's face was ghastly.
Bordman said:

"Kent IV is the nearest world your planet could hope
to get help from. A mail liner will make it in two
months. Kent IV might be able to send three ships—
to get here in two months more. That's no good!"

He felt sick. Human-inhabited planets are far apart.
There is on an average between four and five light-
years of distance between suns, two months' spaceship
journey apart. And not all stars are Sol-type or have
inhabited planets. Colonized worlds are like isolated
islands in an unimaginably vast ocean, and the ships
that ply between them at thirty light-speeds seem
merely to creep. In ancient days on the mother-planet
Earth, men sailed for months between ports, in their
clumsy sailing-ships. There was no way to send messages faster than they could travel. Nowadays there was
little improvement. News of the Lani disaster could not
be transmitted. It had to be carried, as between stars,
and carriage was slow and response to news of disaster was no faster.

The inner planet, Lani II, had twenty million inhabitants, as against the three hundred people in the colony
on Lani III. The outer planet was already frozen, but
there would be glaciation on the inner world in two
hundred days. Glaciation and human life are practically

exclusive. Human beings can survive only so long as food and power hold out, and shelter against really bitter cold cannot be quickly improvised for twenty million people. And, of course, there could be no help on any adequate scale. News of the need for it would travel too slowly. It would take five Earth-years to get a thousand ships to Lani II, and a thousand ships could not rescue more than one per cent of the population. But in five years there would not be nearly so many people left alive.

"Our people," said Riki in a thin voice, "all of them. Mother and father and the others. All our friends. Home is going to be like that!"

She jerked her head toward a port which let in the frigid colony-world's white daylight.

Bordman was aware of an extreme unhappiness on her account. For himself of course, the tragedy was less. He had no family, and very few friends. But he could see something that had not occurred to them as yet.

"Of course," he said, "it's not only their trouble. If the solar constant is really dropping like that, things out here will be pretty bad, too. A lot worse than they are now. We'll have to get to work to save ourselves!"

Riki did not look at him. Bordman bit his lips. It was plain that their own fate did not concern them immediately. When one's home world is doomed, one's personal safety seems a trivial matter.

There was silence save for the cackling, confused noises that came out of the speaker on Herndon's desk.

"We," said Bordman, "are right now in the conditions they'll face a good long time from now."

Herndon said dully:

"We couldn't live here without supplies from home. Or even without the equipment we brought. But they can't get supplies from anywhere, and they can't make such equipment for everybody! They'll die!" He swallowed. "They—they know it, too. So they warn us to try to save ourselves because they can't help us any more."

There are many reasons why a man can feel shame that he belongs to a race which can do the things that some men do. But sometimes there are reasons to be proud as well. The home world of this colony was doomed, but it sent a warning to the tiny colony so that they could try to save themselves.

"I wish we were there to—share what they have to face," said Riki. Her voice sounded as if her throat hurt. "I don't want to keep on living if everybody who ever cared about us is going to die!"

Bordman felt lonely. He could understand that nobody would want to live as the only human alive. Nobody would want to live as a member of the only group of people left alive. And everybody thinks of his home planet as all the world there is. *I don't think that way,* thought Bordman. *But maybe it's the way I'd feel about living if Riki were to die.* It would be natural to want to share any danger or any disaster she faced.

"L-look!" he said, stammering a little. "You don't see! It isn't a case of your living while they die! If your home world becomes like this, what will this be like? We're farther from the sun, colder to start with. Do you think we'll live through anything they can't take? Food supplies or no, equipment or no, do you think we've got a chance? Use your brains!"

Herndon and Riki stared at him. And then some of the strained look left Riki's face and body. Herndon blinked, and said slowly: "Why, that's so! We were thought to be taking a terrific risk when we came here. But it'll be as much worse here. Of course! We are in the same fix they're in!"

He straightened a little. Color actually came back into his face. Riki managed to smile. And then Herndon said almost naturally:

"That makes things look more sensible. We've got to fight for our lives too! And we've very little chance of saving them. What do we do about it, Bordman?"

The sun was halfway toward mid-sky, still attended by its sun-dogs, though they were fainter than at the horizon. The sky was darker. The icy mountain peaks reached skyward, serene and utterly aloof from the affairs of men. The city was a fleet of metal hulks, neatly arranged on the valley floor, emptied of the material they had brought for the building of the colony. Not far away, the landing-grid stood. It was a gigantic skeleton of steel, rising from legs of unequal length bedded in the hillsides and reaching two thousand feet toward the stars. Human figures, muffled almost past recognition, moved about a catwalk three-quarters of the way up. There was a tiny glittering below where they moved. The men were using sonic ice-breakers to shatter the frost which formed on the framework at night. Falling shards of crystal made a liquid-like flashing. The landing-grid needed to be cleared every ten days or so. Left uncleared, it would acquire an increasingly thick coating of ice, and in time it could collapse. But long before that time it would have ceased to operate, and without its operation there could be no space-travel. Rockets for lifting spaceships were impossibly heavy, for practical use. But the landing-grids could lift them out to the unstressed space where Lawlor drives could work, and draw them to ground with cargoes they couldn't possibly have carried if they'd needed rockets.

Bordman reached the base of the grid on foot. He was dwarfed by the ground-level upright beams. He went through the cold-lock to the small control house at the grid's base.

He nodded to the man on standby as he got out of his muffling garments.

"Everything all right?" he asked.

The standby operator shrugged. Bordman was Colonial Survey. It was his function to find fault, to expose inadequacies in the construction and operation of colony facilities. *It's natural for me to be disliked by men whose work I inspect,* thought Bordman. *If I approve it doesn't mean anything, and if I protest, it's bad.*

"I think," he said, "that there ought to be a change in maximum no-drain voltage. I'd like to check it."

The operator shrugged again. He pressed buttons under a phone-plate.

"Shift to reserve power," he commanded, when a face appeared in the plate. "Gotta check no-drain juice."

"What for?" demanded the face in the plate.

"You-know-who's got ideas," said the grid operator scornfully. "Maybe we've been skimping something. Maybe there's some new specification we didn't know about. Maybe anything! But shift to reserve power."

The face in the screen grumbled. Bordman swallowed. It was not a Survey officer's privilege to maintain discipline. And anyhow, there was no particular virtue in discipline here and now. He watched the current-demand dial. It stood a little above normal day-drain, which was understandable. The outside temperature was down. There was more power needed to keep the dwellings warm, and there was always a lot of power needed in the mine the colony had been formed to exploit. The mine had to be warmed for the men who worked to develop it.

The current-demand needle dropped abruptly, hung steady, and dropped again and again as additional parts of the colony's power uses were switched to reserve. The needle hit bottom. It stayed there.

Bordman had to walk around the standby man to get at the voltmeter. He pushed in the contact plugs, read the no-drain voltage, licked his lips, and made a note. He reversed the leads, so it would read backward. He took another reading. He drew in his breath very quietly.

"Now I want the power turned on in sections," he told the operator. "The mine first, maybe. It doesn't matter. But I want to get voltage readings at different power take-offs."

The operator looked pained. He spoke with unnecessary elaboration to the face in the phone-plate, and grudgingly went through the process by which Bordman measured the successive drops in voltage with power drawn from the ionosphere. The current available from a layer of ionized gas is, in effect, the current-flow through a conductor with marked resistance. It is possible to infer a gas's ionization from the current it yields. The cold-lock door opened. Riki Herndon came in, panting a little.

"There's another message from home," she said sharply. Her voice seemed strained. "They picked up our answering-beam and are giving the information you asked for."

"I'll be along," said Bordman. "I just got some information here."

He got into his cold-garments again, and followed her out of the control-hut.

"The figures from home aren't good," said Riki, when mountains visibly rose on every hand around them. "Ken says they're much worse than he thought. The rate of decline in the solar constant's worse than we figured or could believe."

"I see," said Bordman, inadequately.

"It's absurd!" said Riki angrily. "There've been

sunspots and sunspot cycles all along—I learned about
them in school. I learned about a four-year and a seven-
year cycle, and that there were others. They should
have known, they should have calculated in advance!
Now they talk about sixty-year cycles coming in with
a hundred-and-thirty-year cycle to pile up with all the
others. . . . What's the use of scientists if they don't do
their work right and twenty million people die of it?"

Bordman did not consider himself a scientist, but
he winced. Riki raged as they moved over the slippery
ice. Her breath was an intermittent cloud about her
shoulders, and there was white frost on the front of
her cold-garments. Even so quickly the moisture of her
breath congealed.

He held out his hand quickly as she slipped, once.

"But they'll beat it!" said Riki in a sort of angry
pride. "They're starting to build more landing-grids,
back home. Hundreds of them! Not for ships to land
by, but to draw power from the ionosphere. They figure
that one ship-size grid can keep nearly three square
miles of ground warm enough to live on. They'll roof
over the streets of cities and pile snow on top for
insulation. Then they'll plant food-crops in the streets
and gardens, and do what hydroponic growing they can.
They're afraid they can't do it fast enough to save
everybody, but they'll try!"

Bordman clenched his hands inside their bulky
mittens.

"Well?" demanded Riki. "Won't that do the trick?"

"No."

"Why not?"

"I just took readings on the grid, here. The voltage
and the conductivity of the layer we draw power from,
both depend on ionization. When the intensity of
sunlight drops, the voltage drops and the conductivity drops too. It's harder for less power to flow to the

area the grid can tap—and the voltage pressure is lower to drive it."

"Don't say any more!" cried Riki. "Not another word!"

Bordman was silent. They went down the last small slope, and passed the opening of the mine, a great drift which bored straight into the mountain. Looking into it, they saw the twin rows of brilliant roof-lights going toward the heart of the stony monster.

They had almost reached the village when Riki said in a stifled voice:

"How bad is it?"

"Very," admitted Bordman. "We have here the conditions the home planet will have in two hundred days. Originally we could draw less than a fifth the power they count on from a grid on Lani II."

Riki ground her teeth. "Go on," she said.

"Ionization here is down ten per cent," said Bordman. "That means the voltage is down, somewhat more. A great deal more. And the resistance of the layer is greater. Very much greater. When they need power most, on the home planet, they won't draw more from a grid than we do now. It won't be enough."

They reached the village. There were steps to the cold-lock of Herndon's office-hull. They were ice-free, because like the village walkways they were warmed to keep frost from depositing on them. Bordman made a mental note.

In the cold-lock, the warm air pouring in was almost stifling. Riki said defiantly:

"You might as well tell me now!"

"We usually can draw one-fifth as much power, here, as the same sized grid would yield on your home world," he said. "We are drawing—call it sixty per cent of normal. A shade over one-tenth of what they expect to draw when the real cold hits them. Their estimates are nine times too high. One grid won't warm three square miles of city. About a third of one is closer. But—"

"That won't be the worst," said Riki in a choked voice. "Is that right? How much good will a grid do?"

Bordman did not answer.

The inner cold-rock door opened. Herndon sat at his desk, even paler than before, listening to the hash of noises that came out of the speaker. He tapped on the desk-top, quite unconscious of the action. He looked almost desperately at Bordman.

"Did she tell you?" he asked in a numb voice. "They hope to save maybe half the population. All the children anyhow. . . ."

"They won't," said Riki bitterly.

"Better go transcribe the new stuff that's come in," said her brother. "We might as well know what it says."

Riki went out of the office. Bordman shed his cold-garments. He said:

"The rest of the colony doesn't know what's up yet. The operator at the grid didn't, certainly. But they have to know."

"We'll post the messages on the bulletin board," said Herndon. "I wish I could keep it from them. It's not fun to live with. I—might as well not tell them just yet."

"To the contrary," insisted Bordman. "They've got to know right away! You're going to issue orders and they'll need to understand how urgent they are."

Herndon looked hopeless.

"What's the good of doing anything?" When Bordman frowned, he added: "Seriously, is there any use? You're all right. A Survey Ship's due to take you away. It's not coming because they know there's something wrong, but because your job should be finished about now. But it can't do any good! It would be insane for it to land at home. It couldn't carry away more than a few dozen refugees, and there are twenty million people who're going to die. It might offer to take some of us, but I don't think many of us would go. I wouldn't. I don't think Riki would."

"I don't see—"

"What we've got right here," said Herndon, "is what they're going to have back home. And worse. But there's no chance for us to keep alive here! You are the one who pointed it out. I've been figuring, and the way the solar-constant curve is going—I plotted it from the figures they gave us—it couldn't possibly level out until the oxygen, anyhow, is frozen out of the atmosphere here. We aren't equipped to stand anything like that, and we can't get equipped. There isn't equipment to let us stand it indefinitely. Anyhow, the maximum cold conditions will last two thousand days back home—six Earth years. And there'll be storage of cold in frozen oceans and piled-up glaciers. It'll be twenty years before home will be back to normal in temperature, and the same here. Is there any point in trying to live—just barely to survive—for twenty years before there'll be a habitable planet to go back to?"

Bordman said irritably:

"Don't be a fool! Doesn't it occur to you that this planet is a perfect experiment station, two hundred days ahead of the home world, where ways to beat the whole business can be tried? If we can beat it here, they can beat it there!"

Herndon said:

"Can you name one thing to try here?"

"Yes," snapped Bordman. "I want the walk-heaters and the step-heaters outside turned off. They use power to keep walkways clear of frost and door-steps not slippery. I want to save that heat!"

Herndon said, "And when you've saved it, what will you do with it?"

"Put it underground to be used as needed!" Bordman said. "Store it in the mine! I want to put every heating-device we can contrive to work in the mine, to heat the rock. I want to draw every watt the grid will yield and warm up the inside of the mountain while we can draw power to do it with. I want the deepest part of the mine too hot to enter! We'll lose a lot of heat, of course. It's not like storing electric power. But we can store heat now, and the more we store the more will be left when we need it!"

Herndon thought. Presently he stirred slightly.

"Do you know, that is an idea. . . ." He looked up. "Back home there was a shale-oil deposit up near the ice-caps. It wasn't economical to mine it. So they put heaters down in boreholes and heated up the whole shale deposit. Drill-holes let out the hot oil vapors to be condensed. They got out every bit of oil without disturbing the shale. And then the shale stayed warm for years! Farmers bulldozed soil over it and raised crops with glaciers all around them. That could be done again. They could be storing up heat back home!"

Then he drooped.

"But they can't spare power to warm up the ground under cities. They need all the power they've got to build roofs. . . . And it takes time to build grids."

Bordman snapped:

"Yes, if they're building regulation ones. By the time they were finished they'd be useless. The ionization here is dropping already. But they don't need to build grids that will be useless later. They can weave cables together on the ground and hang them in the air by helicopters. They wouldn't hold up a landing ship for an instant, but they'll draw power right away. They'll even power the helis that hold them up! Of course, they'll have defects; they'll have to come down in high winds, for example. They won't be too dependable. But they can put heat in the ground to come out under roofs, to grow food by, to save lives by. What's the matter with them?"

Herndon stirred again. His eyes ceased to be dull and lifeless.

"I'll give the orders for turning off the sidewalks. And I'll send what you just said back home. They should like it."

He looked respectfully at Bordman.

"I guess you know what I'm thinking right now," he said.

Bordman flushed. He felt that Herndon was unduly impressed. Herndon didn't see that the device wouldn't solve anything. It would merely postpone the effects of a disaster. It could not possibly prevent them.

"It ought to be done," he said. "There'll be other things to be done, too."

"Then when you tell them to me," said Herndon, "they'll get done! I'll have Riki put this into that pulse-code you explained to us and she'll get it off right away."

He stood up.

"I didn't explain the code to her," insisted Bordman. "She was already translating it when you gave her my suggestion."

"All right," said Herndon. "I'll get this sent back at once."

He hurried out of the office. *This,* thought Bordman irritably, *is how reputations are made, I suppose. I'm getting one.* But his own reaction was extremely inappropriate. If the people of Lani II did suspend helicopter-supported grids of wire in the atmosphere, they could warm masses of underground rock and stone and earth. They could establish what were practically reservoirs of life-giving heat under their cities. They could contrive that the warmth from below would rise only as it was needed. *But—*

Two hundred days to conditions corresponding to the colony-planet. Then two thousand days of minimum-heat conditions. Then very, very slow return to normal temperature, long after the sun was back to its previous brilliance. They couldn't store enough heat for so long. It couldn't be done. It was ironic that in the freezing of ice and the making of glaciers the planet itself could store cold.

Also, there would be monstrous storms and blizzards on Lani II as cold conditions got worse. The wire-grids could be held aloft for shorter and shorter periods, and each time they would pull down less power than before. Their effectiveness would diminish even faster than the need for effectiveness increased.

Bordman felt even deeper depression as he worked out the facts. His proposal was essentially futile. It would be encouraging, and to a very slight degree and for a certain short time it would palliate the situation on the inner planet. But in the long run its effect would be zero.

He was embarrassed, too, that Herndon was so admiring. Herndon would tell Riki that he was marvelous. She might—though cagily—be inclined to agree. But he wasn't marvelous. This trick of a flier-supported grid was not new. It had been used on Saril to supply power for giant peristaltic pumps emptying a polder that had been formed inside a ring of indifferently upraised islands.

All I know, thought Bordman bitterly, *is what somebody's showed me or I've read in books. And nobody's showed or written how to handle a thing like this!*

He went to Herndon's desk. Herndon had made a new graph of the solar-constant observations forwarded from home. It was a strictly typical curve of the results of coinciding cyclic change. It was the curve of a series of frequencies at the moment when they were all precisely in phase. From this much one could extrapolate and compute.

Bordman took a pencil, frowning. His fingers clumsily formed equations and solved them. The result was just about as bad as it could be. The change in brightness of the sun Lani would not be enough to be observed on Kent IV, the nearest other inhabited world, when the light reached there four years from now. Lani would never be classed as a variable star, because the total change in light and heat would be relatively minute. The formula for computing planetary temperatures is not simple. Among its factors are squares and cubes of the variables. Worse, the heat radiated from a sun's photosphere varies not as the square or cube, but as the fourth power of its absolute temperature.

Bordman's computations were not pure theory. The data came from Sol itself, where alone in the galaxy there had been daily solar-constant measurements for three hundred years. The rest of his deductions were based ultimately on Earth observations, too. Most scientific data had to refer back to Earth to get an adequate continuity. And there could be no possible doubt about the sunspot data, because Sol and Lani were of the same type and nearly equal size.

Using the figures on the present situation, Bordman reluctantly arrived at the fact that here, on this already-frozen world, the temperature would drop gradually until CO_2 froze out of the atmosphere. When that happened, the temperature would plummet until there was no really significant difference between it and that of empty space. It is carbon dioxide which is responsible for the greenhouse effect, by which a planet is in thermal equilibrium only at a temperature above its surroundings, as a greenhouse in sunlight is warmer than the outside air.

The greenhouse effect would vanish soon on the colony world. When it vanished on the mother planet . . .

Bordman found himself thinking, *If Riki won't leave when the Survey ship comes, I'll resign from the Service. I'll have to if I'm to stay. And I won't go unless she does.*

"If you want to come, it's all right," said Bordman ungraciously.

He waited while Riki slipped into the bulky cold-garments that were needed out-of-doors in the day-time, and were doubly necessary at night. There were heavy boots with inches-thick insulating soles, made in one piece with the many-layered trousers. There was an air-puffed, insulated over-tunic with its hood and mittens which were a part of the sleeves.

"Nobody goes outside at night," she said when they stood together in the cold-lock.

"I do," he told her. "I want to find out something."

The outer door opened and he stepped out. He held his arm for her, because the steps and walkway were no longer heated. Now they were covered with a filmy layer of something which was not frost, but a faint bloom of powder—microscopic snow-crystals frozen out of the air by the unbearable chill of night.

There was no moon, of course, yet the ice-clad mountains glowed faintly. The drone-hulls arranged in such an orderly fashion were dark against the frosted ground. There was silence, stillness, the feeling of ancient quietude. No wind stirred anywhere. Nothing moved, nothing lived. The soundlessness was enough to crack the eardrums.

Bordman threw back his head and gazed at the sky for a very long time. Nothing. He looked down at Riki.

"Look at the sky," he commanded.

She raised her eyes. She had been watching him. But as she gazed upward she almost cried out. The sky was filled with stars in innumerable variety. But the brighter ones were as stars had never been seen before. Just as the sun in daylight had been accompanied by its sun-dogs—pale phantoms of itself ranged about it—so the brighter distant suns now shone from the center of rings of their own images. They no longer had the look of random placing. Those which were most distinct were patterns in themselves, and one's eyes strove instinctively to grasp the greater pattern in which such seeming artifacts must belong.

"Oh—beautiful!" cried Riki softly.

"Look!" he insisted. "Keep looking!"

She continued to gaze, moving her eyes about hopefully. It was such a sight as no one could have imagined. Every tint and every color, every possible degree of brightness appeared. And there were groups of stars of the same brilliance which almost made triangles, but not quite. There were rose-tinted stars which almost formed an arc, but did not. And there were arrays which were almost lines and nearly formed squares and polygons, but never actually achieved them.

"It's beautiful," said Riki. "But what must I look for?"

"Look for what isn't there," he ordered.

She looked, and the stars were unwinking, but that was not extraordinary. They filled all the firmament, without the least space in which some tiny sparkle of light was not to be found. But that was not remarkable, either. Then there was a vague flickering grayish glow somewhere, indefinite. It vanished. Then she realized.

"There's no aurora!" she exclaimed.

"That's it," said Bordman. "There've always been auroras here. But no longer. We may be responsible. I wish I thought it wise to turn everything back to reservoir power for a while. We could find out. But we can't afford it."

"I looked at it when we first landed," admitted Riki. "It was unbelievable. But it was terribly cold, out of shelter. And it happened every night, so I said to myself I'd look tomorrow, and then tomorrow again. So it got so I never looked at all."

Bordman kept his eyes where that faint gray flickering had been. And, once one realized, it was astonishing that the former nightly play of ghostly colors should be absent.

"The aurora," he said, "happens in the very upper limits of the air, fifty-seventy-ninety miles up, when God-knows-what emitted particles from the sun come streaking in, drawn by the planet's magnetic field. The aurora's a phenomenon of ions. We tap the ionosphere a long way down from where it plays, but I'm wondering if we stopped it."

"We?" said Riki, shocked. "We humans?"

"We tap the ions of their charges," he said somberly, "that the sunlight made by day. We're pulling in all the power we can. I wonder if we've drained the aurora of its energy, too."

Riki was silent. Bordman gazed, still searching. But he shook his head.

"It could be," he said in a carefully detached voice. "We didn't draw much power by comparison with the amount that came. But the ionization is an ultra-violet effect. Atmospheric gases don't ionize too easily. After all, if the solar constant dropped a very little, it might mean a terrific drop in the ultraviolet part of the spectrum—and that's what makes ions of oxygen and nitrogen and hydrogen and such. The ion-drop could easily be fifty times as great as the drop in the solar constant. And we're drawing power from the little that's left."

Riki stood very still. The cold was horrible. Had there been a wind, it could not have been endured for an instant. But the air was motionless. Yet its coldness was so great that the inside of one's nostrils ached, and the inside of one's chest was aware of chill. Even through the cold-garments there was the feeling as of ice without.

"I'm beginning," said Bordman, "to suspect that I'm a fool. Or maybe I'm an optimist. It might be the same thing. I could have guessed that the power we could draw would drop faster than our need for power increased. If we've drained the aurora of its light, we're scraping the bottom of the barrel. And it's a shallower barrel than one would suspect."

There was stillness again. Riki stood mousy-quiet. *When she realizes what this means,* thought Bordman grimly, *she won't admire me so much. Her brother's built me up. But I've been a fool, figuring out excuses to hope. She'll see it.*

"I think," said Riki, "that you're telling me that after all we can't store up heat to live on, down in the mine."

"We can't," agreed Bordman. "Not much, nor long. Not enough to matter."

"So we won't live as long as Ken expects?"

"Not nearly as long," said Bordman. "He's hoping we can find out things to be useful back on Lani II. But we'll lose the power we can get from our grid long before even their new grids are useless. We'll have to start using our reserve power a lot sooner. It'll be gone—and us with it—before they're really in straits for living-heat."

Riki's teeth began to chatter.

"This sounds like I'm scared," she said angrily, "but

I'm not! I'm just freezing. If you want to now, I'd a lot rather have it the way you say. I won't have to grieve over anybody, and they'll be too busy to grieve for me. . . . Let's go inside while it's still warm."

He helped her back into the cold-lock, and the outer door closed. She was shivering uncontrollably when the warmth came, pouring in.

They went into Herndon's office. He came in as Riki was peeling off the top part of her cold-garments. She still shivered. He glanced at her and said to Bordman:

"There's been a call from the grid-control shack. It looks like there's something wrong, but they can't find anything. The grid is set for maximum power-collection, but it's bringing in only fifty thousand kilowatts!"

"We're on our way back to savagery," said Bordman, with an attempt at irony.

It was true. A man can produce two hundred fifty watts from his muscles for a reasonable length of time. When he has no more power, he is a savage. When he gains a kilowatt of energy from the muscles of a horse, he is a barbarian, but the new power cannot be directed wholly as he wills. When he can apply it to a plow he has high barbarian culture, and when he adds still more he begins to be civilized. Steam-power put as much as four kilowatts to work for every human being in the first industrialized countries, and in the mid-twentieth century there was sixty kilowatts per person in the more advanced nations. Nowadays, of course, a modern culture assumed five hundred as a minimum. But there was less than half that in the colony on Lani III. And its environment made its own demands.

"There can't be any more," said Riki, trying to control her shivering. "We're even using the aurora and there isn't any more power. It's running out. We'll go even before the people at home, Ken."

Herndon's features looked pinched.

"But we can't! We mustn't!" He turned to Bordman. "We do them good, back home! There was panic. Our report about cable grids has put heart in people. They're setting to work magnificently! So we're some use. They know we're worse off then they are, and as long as we hold on they'll be encouraged. We've got to keep going somehow!"

Riki breathed deeply until her shivering stopped. Then she said:

"Haven't you noticed, Ken, that Mr. Bordman has the viewpoint of his profession? His business is finding things wrong. He was deposited in our midst to detect defects in what we did and do. He has the habit of looking for the worst. But I think he can turn the habit to good use. He did turn up the idea of cable-grids."

"Which," said Bordman, "turns out to be no good at all. They'd be some good if they weren't needed, really. But the conditions that make them necessary make them useless!"

Riki shook her head.

"They are useful!" she said. "They're keeping people at home from despairing. Now, though, you've got to think of something else. If you think of enough things, one will do good the way you want, more than just making people feel better."

"What does it matter how people feel?" he demanded bitterly, "What difference do feelings make? One can't change facts!"

Riki said firmly:

"We humans are the only creatures in the universe who don't do anything else. Every other creature accepts facts. It lives where it is born, and it feeds on the food that is there for it, and it dies when the facts of nature require it to. We humans don't. Especially we women! We won't let men do it, either. When we don't like facts—mostly about ourselves—we change them. But important facts we disapprove of—we ask men to change them for us. And they do!"

She faced Bordman. Rather incredibly, she grinned at him.

"Will you please change the facts that look so annoying just now, please? Please?" Then she elaborately pantomimed an over-feminine girl's look of wide-eyed admiration. "You're so big and strong! I just know you can do it—for me!"

She abruptly dropped the pretense and moved toward the door. She half-turned then, and said detachedly:

"But about half of that is true."

The door slid shut behind her. It suddenly occurred to Bordman that she knew a Colonial Survey ship was due to stop by here to pick him up. She believed he expected to be rescued, even though the rest of the colony could not be, and most of it wouldn't consent to leave their kindred when the death of mankind in this solar system took place. He said awkwardly:

"Fifty thousand kilowatts isn't enough to land a ship."

Herndon frowned. Then he said:

"Oh. You mean the Survey ship that's to pick you up can't land? But it can go in orbit and put down a rocket landing-boat for you."

"I wasn't thinking of that. I'd something more in mind. I rather like your sister. She's pretty wonderful. But there are some other women here in the colony, too. About a dozen all told. As a matter of self-respect I think we ought to get them away on the Survey ship. I agree that they wouldn't consent to go. But if they had no choice—if we could get them on board the grounded ship, and they suddenly found themselves—well—kidnapped and outward-bound not by their own fault. They could be faced with the accomplished fact that they had to go on living."

Herndon said evenly:

"That's been in the back of my mind for some time. Yes, I'm for that. But if the Survey ship can't land—"

"I believe I can land it regardless," said Bordman. "I can find out, anyhow. I'll need to try things. I'll need help. But I want your promise that if I can get the ship to ground you'll conspire with her skipper and arrange for them to go on living."

Herndon looked at him.

"Some new stuff, in a way," said Bordman uncomfortably. "I'll have to stay aground to work it. It's also part of the bargain that I shall. And of course your sister can't know about it, or she can't be fooled into living."

Herndon's expression changed a little.

"What'll you do? Of course it's a bargain."

"I'll need some metals we haven't smelted so far," said Bordman. "Potassium if I can get it, sodium if I can't, and at worst I'll settle for zinc. Cesium would be best, but we've found no traces of it."

Herndon said thoughtfully:

"No-o-o. I think I can get you sodium and potassium, from rocks. I'm afraid no zinc. How much?"

"Grams," said Bordman. "Trivial quantities. And I'll need a miniature landing-grid built. Very miniature."

Herndon shrugged his shoulders.

"It's over my head. But just to have work to do will be good for everybody. We've been feeling more frustrated here than any other humans in history. I'll go round up the men who'll do the work. You talk to them."

The door closed behind him. Bordman got out of his cold-clothing. He thought, *She'll rage when she finds her brother and I have deceived her.* Then he thought of the other women. *If any of them are married, we'll have to see if there's room for their husbands. I'll have to dress up the idea. Make it look like reason for hope, or the women would find out. But not many can go. . . .*

He knew roughly how many extra passengers could be carried on a Survey ship, even in such an emergency as this. Living-quarters were not luxurious, at best. Everything was cramped and skimped. Survey ships were rugged, tiny vessels which performed their duties amid tedium and discomfort and peril for all on board. But one of them could carry away a very few unwilling refugees to Kent IV.

He settled down at Herndon's desk to work out the thing to be done.

It was not unreasonable. Tapping the ionosphere for power was something like pumping water out of a pipe-well in sand. If the water-table was high, there was pressure to force the water to the pipe, and one could pump fast. If the water-table was low, water couldn't flow fast enough. The pump would suck dry. In the ionosphere, the level of ionization was at once like the pressure and the size of the sand-grains. When the level was high, the flow was vast because the sand-grains were large and the conductivity high. But as the level lessened, so did the size of the sand-grains. There was less to draw, and more resistance to its flow.

However, there had been one tiny flicker of auroral light over by the horizon. There was still power aloft. If Bordman could in a fashion prime the pump, if he could increase the conductivity by increasing the ions present around the place where their charges were drawn away, he could increase the total flow. It would be like digging a brick well where a pipe well had been.

A brick well draws water from all around its circumference.

So Bordman computed carefully. It was ironic that he had to go to such trouble simply because he didn't have test-rockets like the Survey uses to get a picture of a planet's weather-pattern. They rise vertically for fifty miles or so, trailing a thread of sodium vapor behind them. The trail is detectable for some time, and ground instruments record each displacement by winds blowing in different directions at different speeds, one over the other. Such a rocket with its loading slightly changed would do all Bordman had in mind. But he didn't have one, so something much more elaborate was called for.

A landing-grid has to be not less than half a mile across and two thousand feet high because its field has to reach out five planetary diameters to handle ships that land and take off. To handle solid objects it has to be accurate, though power can be drawn with an improvisation. To thrust a sodium vapor bomb anywhere from twenty to fifty miles high, he'd need a grid only six feet wide and five high. It could throw much higher, of course, and hold what it threw. But doubling the size would make accuracy easier.

He tripled the dimensions. There would be a grid eighteen feet across and fifteen high. Tuned to the casing of a small bomb, it could hold it steady at seven hundred fifty thousand feet, far beyond necessity. He began to make the detail drawings.

Herndon came back with half a dozen chosen colonists. They were young men, technicians rather than scientists. Some of them were several years younger than Bordman. There were grim and stunned expressions on some faces, but one tried to pretend nonchalance, and two seemed trying to suppress fury at the monstrous occurrence that would destroy not only their own lives, but everything they remembered on the planet which was their home. They looked almost challengingly at Bordman.

He explained. He was going to put a cloud of metallic vapor up in the ionosphere. Sodium if he had to, potassium if he could, zinc if he must. Those metals were readily ionized by sunlight, much more readily than atmospheric gases. In effect, he was going to supply a certain area of the ionosphere with material to increase the efficiency of sunshine in providing electric power. As a sideline, there would be increased conductivity from the normal ionosphere.

"Something like this was done centuries ago, back on Earth," he explained. "They used rockets, and made sodium-vapor clouds as much as twenty and thirty miles long. Even nowadays the Survey uses test rockets with trails of sodium vapor. It will work to some degree. We'll find out how much."

He felt Herndon's eyes upon him. They were almost dazedly respectful. But one of the technicians said:

"How long will those clouds last?"

"That high, three or four days," Bordman told him. "They won't help much at night, but they should step up power-intake while the sun shines on them."

A man in the back said, "Hup!" The significance was, "Let's go!"

Somebody else said feverishly, "What do we do? Got working drawings? Who makes the bombs? Who does what? Let's get at this!"

Then there was confusion, and Herndon vanished. Bordman suspected he'd gone to have Riki put this theory into dot-and-dash code for beam-transmission back to Lani II. But there was no time to stop him. These men wanted precise information and it was half an hour before the last of them had gone out with free-hand sketches, and had come back for further explanation of a doubtful point, and other men had come in to demand a share in the job.

When he was alone again, Bordman thought, *Maybe it's worth doing because it'll get Riki on the Survey ship. But they think it means saving the people back home!*

Which it didn't. Taking energy out of sunlight is taking energy out of sunlight, no matter how you do it. Take it out as electric power, and there's less heat left. Warm one place with electric power, and everywhere else is a little colder. There's an equation. On this colony-world it wouldn't matter, but on the home world it would. The more there was trickery to gather heat, the more heat would be needed. . . . Again it might postpone the death of twenty million people, but it would never, never prevent it.

The door slid aside and Riki came in. She stammered a little.

"I just coded what Ken told me to send back home. It will—it will do everything! It's wonderful! I wanted to tell you!"

"Consider," Bordman said, in a desperate attempt to take it lightly, "that I've taken a bow."

He tried to smile. It was not a success. And Riki suddenly drew a deep breath and looked at him in a new fashion.

"Ken's right," she said softly. "He says you can't get conceited. You're not satisfied with yourself even now, are you?" She smiled. "But what I like is that you aren't really smart. A woman can make you do things. I have!"

He looked at her uneasily. She grinned.

"I, even I, can at least pretend to myself that I helped bring this about! If I hadn't said please change the facts that are so annoying, and if I hadn't said you were big and strong and clever. . . . I'm going to tell myself for the rest of my life that I helped make you do it!"

Bordman swallowed.

"I'm afraid," he said, "that it won't work again."

She cocked her head on one side.

"No?"

He stared at her apprehensively. And then with a bewildering change of emotional reaction, he saw that her eyes were filled with tears. She stamped her foot.

"You're horrible!" she cried. "Here I came in, and—and if you think you can get me kidnapped to safety without even telling me that you 'rather like' me, as you told my brother, or that I'm 'pretty wonderful—'"

He was stunned that she knew. She stamped her foot again. "For Heaven's sake!" she wailed. "Do I have to *ask* you to kiss me?"

During the last night of preparation, Bordman sat by a thermometer registering the outside temperature. He hovered over it as one might over a sick child. He watched it and sweated, though the inside temperature of the drone-hull was lowered to save power. There was nothing he could actually do. At midnight the thermometer said it was seventy degrees below zero Fahrenheit. At halfway to dawn it was eighty degrees below zero Fahrenheit. The hour before dawn it was eighty-five degrees below zero. Then he sweated profusely. The meaning of the slowed descent was that carbon dioxide was being frozen out of the upper layers of the atmosphere. The frozen particles were drifting slowly downward, and as they reached lower and faintly warmer levels they returned to the state of gas. But there was a level, above the CO_2, where the temperature was plummeting.

The height to which carbon dioxide existed was

dropping. Slowly, but inexorably. And above the carbon-dioxide level there was no bottom limit to the temperature. The greenhouse effect was due to CO_2. Where it wasn't, the cold of space moved down. If at ground-level the thermometer read ever-so-slightly less than one hundred nine below zero, then everything was finished. Without the greenhouse effect, the night side of the planet would lose its remaining heat with a rush. Even the day side, once cold enough, would lose heat to emptiness as fast as it came from the sun. Minus one hundred nine point three was the critical reading. If it went down to that it would plunge to a hundred and fifty or two hundred degrees below zero, or more. And it would never come up again.

There would be rain at nightfall, a rain of oxygen frozen to a liquid and splashing on the ground. Human life would be impossible, in any shelter and under any conditions. Even spacesuits would not protect against an atmosphere sucking heat from it at that rate. A spacesuit can be heated against the loss of temperature due to radiation in a vacuum. It could not be heated against nitrogen which would chill it irresistibly by contact.

But, as Bordman sweated over it, the thermometer steadied at minus eighty-five degrees. When the dawn came, it rose to seventy. By mid-morning, the temperature in bright sunshine was no lower than sixty-five degrees below zero.

But there was no bounce left in Bordman when Herndon came for him.

"Your phone-plate's been flashing," said Herndon, "and you didn't answer. Must have had your back to it. Riki's over in the mine, watching them get things ready. She was worried that she couldn't call you. Asked me to find out what was the trouble."

"Has she got something to heat the air she breathes?" asked Bordman.

"Naturally," said Herndon. He added curiously, "What's the matter?"

"We almost took our licking," Bordman told him. "I'm afraid for tonight, and tomorrow night too. If the CO2 freezes—"

"We'll have power!" Herndon insisted. "We'll build ice-tunnels and ice-domes. We'll build a city under ice, if we have to. But we'll have power!"

"I doubt it very much," said Bordman. "I wish you hadn't told Riki of the bargain to get her away from here when the Survey ship comes."

Herndon grinned.

"Is the little grid ready?" asked Bordman.

"Everything's set," said Herndon. "It's in the mine-tunnel with radiant heaters playing on it. The bombs are ready. We made enough to last for months, while we were at it. No use taking chances."

Bordman looked at him queerly. Then he said: "We might as well go out and try the thing, then."

He put on the cold-garments as they were now modified for the increased frigidity. Nobody could breathe air at minus sixty-five degrees without getting his lungs frost-bitten. So there was now a plastic mask to cover one's face, and the air one breathed outdoors was heated as it came through a wire-gauze snout. But still it was not wise to stay out of shelter for too long a time.

Bordman and Herndon went out-of-doors. They stepped out of the cold-lock and gazed about them. The sun seemed markedly paler and now it had lost its sun-dogs again. Ice-crystals no longer floated in the almost congealed air. The sky was dark. It was almost purple, and it seemed to Bordman that he could detect faint flecks of light in it. They would be stars, shining in the daytime.

There seemed no one about at all, only the white coldness of the mountains. But there was a movement at the mine-drift, and something came out of it. Four men appeared, muffled up like Bordman himself. They rolled the eighteen-foot grid out of the mine-mouth, moving it on those inflated bags which are so much better than rollers for rough terrain. They looked absurdly like bears with steaming noses in their masks and clothing. They had some sort of powered pusher with them and they got the metal cage to the very top of a rounded stone upcrop which rose in the center of the valley.

"We picked that spot," said Herndon's muffled voice through the chill, "because by shifting the grid's position it can be aimed, and be on a solid base. Right?"

"Quite all right," said Bordman. "We'll go work it."

The two men walked across the valley, in which nothing moved except the padded figures of the four technicians. Their wire-gauze breathing-masks seemed to emit smoke. They waved to Bordman in greeting.

I'm popular again, he thought drearily, *but it doesn't matter. Getting the Survey ship to ground won't help now, since Riki's forewarned. And this trick won't solve anything permanently on the home planet. It'll just postpone things.*

Even when Riki, muffled like the rest, waved to him from the mouth of the tunnel, his spirits did not lift. The thing he wanted was to look forward to years and years of being with Riki. He wanted, in fact, to look forward to forever. And there might not *be* a tomorrow.

"I had the control-board rolled out here," she called through her mask. "It's cold, but you can watch."

It wouldn't be much to watch. If everything went all right, some dial-needles would kick over violently and their readings would go up and up. But they

wouldn't be readings of temperature. Presently the big
grid would report increased power from the sky. But
tonight the temperature would drop a little farther.
Tomorrow night it would drop further still. When it
reached one hundred nine point three degrees below
zero at ground-level, that would be the finish.

Another of the figures that looked like a bear now
went out of the mine-mouth, trudging toward the grid.
It carried a muffed, well-wrapped object in its arms.
It stopped and crept between the spokes of the grid,
and put the object on the stone. Bordman traced cables
with his eyes, from the grid to the control-board, and
from the board back to the reserve-power storage cells,
deep in the mountain.

"The grid's tuned to the bomb," said Riki, close
beside him. "I checked that myself!"

The bear-like figure out in the valley jerked at the
bomb. There was a small rising cloud of grayish vapor.
It continued. The figure climbed hastily out of the grid.
When the man was clear, Bordman threw a switch.

There was a thin whining sound, and the wrapped,
smoking object leaped upward. It seemed to fall toward
the sky. There was no more of drama than that. An
object the size of a basketball fell upward, swiftly, until
it disappeared.

Bordman sat quite still, watching the control-board
dials. Presently he corrected this, and shifted that. He
did not want the bomb to have too high an upward
velocity. At a hundred thousand feet it would find very
little air to stop the rise of the vapor it was to release.

The field-focus dial reached its indication of one
hundred thousand feet. Bordman reversed the lift-
switch. He counted, and then switched the power off.
The small, thin whine ended.

He threw the power-intake switch. The power-yield
needle stirred. The minute grid was drawing power like

its vaster counterpart, but its field was infinitesimal by comparison. It drew power as a soda-straw might draw water from wet sand.

Then the intake-needle kicked. It swung sharply, and wavered, and then began a steady, even, climbing movement across the markings on the dial-face. Riki was not watching that.

"They see something!" she panted. "Look at them!"

The four men who had trundled the smaller grid to its place, now stared upward. They flung out their arms. One of them jumped up and down. They leaped. They practically danced. "Let's go see," said Bordman.

He went out of the tunnel with Riki. They gazed upward. And directly overhead, where the sky was darkest blue and where it had seemed that stars shone through the daylight, there was a minute cloud. But it grew. Its edges were yellow, saffron-yellow. It expanded and spread. Presently it began to thin. As it thinned, it began to shine. It was luminous. And the luminosity had a strange, familiar quality.

Somebody came panting down the tunnel, from inside the mountain.

"The grid—" he panted. "The big grid! It's pumping power! Big power! BIG power!"

But Bordman was looking at the sky, as if he did not quite believe his eyes. The cloud now expanded very slowly, but still it grew. And it was not regular in shape. The bomb had not shattered quite evenly, and the vapor had poured out more on one side than the other. There was a narrow, arching arm of brightness. . . .

"It looks," said Riki breathlessly, "like a comet!"

And then Bordman froze in every muscle. He stared at the cloud he had made aloft, and his hands clenched in their mittens, and he swallowed behind his cold-mask.

"Th-that's it," he said in a hushed voice. "It's—very much like a comet. I'm glad you said that! We can make something even more like a comet. We can use all the bombs we've made, right away, to make it. And we've got to hurry so it won't get any colder tonight!"

Which, of course, sounded like insanity. Riki looked apprehensively at him. But Bordman had just thought of something. And nobody had taught it to him and he hadn't gotten it out of books. But he'd seen a comet.

The new idea was so promising that he regarded it with anguished unease for fear it would not hold up. It was an idea that really ought to change the facts resulting naturally from a lowered solar constant in a Sol-type star.

Half the colony set to work to make more bombs when the effect of the first bomb showed up. The men were not very efficient, at first, because they tended to want to stop work and dance from time to time. But they worked with an impassioned enthusiasm. They made more bomb-casings, and they prepared more sodium and potassium metal and more fuses, and more insulation to wrap around the bombs to protect them from the cold of airless space.

Because these were to go out to airlessness. The miniature grid could lift and hold a bomb steady in its field-focus at seven hundred and fifty thousand feet. But if a bomb was accelerated all the way out to that point, and the field was then snapped off . . . Why, it wasn't held anywhere! It kept on going with its attained velocity. And it burst when its fuse decided that it should, whereupon immediately a mass of sodium and potassium vapor, mixed with the fumes of high explosive, flung itself madly in all directions, out between the stars. Absolute vacuum tore the compressed gasified metals apart. The separate atoms, white-hot from the explosion, went swirling through sunlit space. The sunlight was dimmed a trifle, to be sure. But individual atoms of the lighter alkaline-earth metals have marked photoelectric properties. In sunshine these gas molecules ionized, and therefore spread more widely, and did not coalesce into even microscopic droplets.

They formed, in fact, a cloud in space. An ionized cloud, in which no particle was too large to be responsive to the pressure of light. The cloud acted like the gases of a comet's tail. It was a comet's tail, though there was no comet. And it was an extraordinary comet's tail because it is said that you can put a comet's tail in your hat, at normal atmospheric pressure. But this could not have been put in a hat. Even before it turned to gas, it was the size of a basketball. And, in space, it glowed.

It glowed with the brightness of the sunshine on it, which was light that would normally have gone away through the interstellar dark. And it filled one corner of the sky. Within one hour it was a comet tail ten thousand miles long, which visibly brightened the daytime heavens. And it was only the first of such reflecting clouds.

The next bomb set for space exploded in a different quarter, because Bordman had had the miniature grid wrestled around the upcrop to point in a new and somewhat more carefully chosen line. The next spattered brilliance in a different section still. And the brilliance lasted.

Bordman flung his first bombs recklessly, because there would be more, and because he was desperately anxious to hang as many comet-tails as possible around the colony-planet before nightfall. He didn't want it to get any colder.

And it didn't. In fact, there wasn't exactly any real nightfall on Lani III that night.

The planet turned on its axis, to be sure. But around

it, quite close by, there hung gigantic streamers of shining gas. At their beginning, those streamers bore a certain resemblance to the furry wild-animal tails that little boys like to have hanging down from hunting-caps. Only they shone. And as they developed they merged, so that there was an enormous shining curtain about Lani III, draperies of metal-mist to capture sunlight that would otherwise have been wasted, and to diffuse much of it on Lani III. At midnight there was only one spot in all the night sky where there was really darkness. That was overhead, directly outward from the planet, opposite from the sun. Gigantic shining streamers formed a wall, a tube, of comet-tail material, yet many times more dense and therefore more bright, which shielded the colony world against the dark and cold, and threw upon it a shining, warming brightness.

Riki maintained stoutly that she could feel the warmth from the sky, but that was improbable. However, heat certainly did come from somewhere. The thermometer did not fall at all, that night. It rose. It was up to fifty below zero at dawn. During the day— they sent out twenty more bombs that second day— it was up to twenty degrees below zero. By the day after, there were competent computations from the home planet, and the concrete results of abstruse speculation, and the third day's bombs were placed with optimum spacing for heating purposes.

By dawn of the fourth day the air was a balmy five degrees below zero, and the day after that there was a small running stream in the valley at midday.

There was talk of stocking the stream with fish, on the morning the Survey ship came in. The great landing-grid gave out a deep-toned, vibrant, humming note, like the deepest possible note of the biggest organ that could be imagined. A speck appeared high up in a pale-blue sky with trimmings of golden gas clouds.

The Survey ship came down and down and settled as a shining silver object in the very center of the gigantic red-painted landing-grid.

Her skipper came to find Bordman. He was in Herndon's office. The skipper struggled to keep sheer blankness out of his expression.

"What the hell?" he demanded. "This is the damnedest sight in the whole Galaxy, and they tell me you're responsible! There've been ringed planets before, and there've been comets and who knows what! But shining gas-pipes aimed at the sun, half a million miles across! And there are two of them—both the occupied planets!"

Herndon explained why the curtains hung in space. There was a drop in the solar constant. . . .

The skipper exploded. He wanted facts! Details! Something to report!

Bordman was automatically on the defensive when the skipper swung his questions at him. A Senior Colonial Survey officer is not revered by the Survey ship-service officers. Men like Bordman can be a nuisance to a hard-working ship's officer. They have to be carried to unlikely places for their work of checking over colonial installations. They have to be put down on hard-to-get-at colonies, and they have to be called for, sometimes, at times and places which are inconvenient. So a man in Bordman's position is likely to feel unpopular.

"I'd just finished the survey here," he said defensively, "when a cycle of sunspot cycles matured. All the sunspot periods got in phase, and the solar constant dropped. So I naturally offered what help I could to meet the situation."

The skipper regarded him incredulously.

"But it couldn't be done!" he said. "They told me how you did it, but it couldn't be done! Do you realize that these vapor curtains will make fifty borderline worlds fit for use? Half a pound of sodium vapor a week!" He gestured helplessly. "They tell me the amount of heat reaching the surface here has been upped by fifteen per cent! D'you realize what *that* means?"

"I haven't been worrying about it," admitted Bordman. "There was a local situation and something had to be done. I—er—remembered things, and Riki suggested something I mightn't have thought of. So it's worked out like this." Then he said abruptly: "I'm not leaving. I'll let you take my resignation back. I think I'm going to settle here. It'll be a long time before we get really temperate-climate conditions here, but we can warm up a valley like this for cultivation, and it's going to be a rather satisfying job. It's a brand-new planet with a brand-new ecological system to be established."

The skipper of the Survey ship sat down hard. Then the sliding door of Herndon's office opened and Riki came in. The skipper stood up again. Bordman awkwardly made the introduction. Riki smiled.

"I'm telling him," said Bordman, "that I'm resigning from the Service to settle down here."

Riki nodded. She put her hand in proprietary fashion on Bordman's arm. The Survey skipper cleared his throat.

"I'm not going to carry your resignation," he said. "There've got to be detailed reports on how this business works. Dammit, if vapor clouds in space can be used to keep a planet warm, they can be used to shade a planet, too! If you resign, somebody else will have to come out here to make observations and work out the details of the trick. Nobody could be gotten here in less than a year! You've got to stay here to build up a report, and you ought to be available for consultation when this thing's to be done somewhere else. I'll report that I insisted as a Survey emergency—"

Riki said confidently:

"Oh, that's all right! He'll do that! Of course! Won't you?"

Bordman nodded. He thought, *I've been lonely all my life. I've never belonged anywhere. But nobody could possibly belong anywhere as thoroughly as I'll belong here when it's warm and green and even the grass on the ground is partly my doing. But Riki'll like for me still to be in the Service. Women like to see their husbands wearing uniforms.*

Aloud he said:

"Of course. If it really needs to be done. Though you realize that there's nothing really remarkable about it. Everything *I've* done has been what I was taught, or read in books."

"Hush!" said Riki. "You're wonderful!"

And so they were married, and Bordman was very, very happy. But people who can serve their fellow-men are never left alone. We humans get into so many predicaments!

Bordman had lived contentedly on Lani III for only three years when there was an emergency on Kalen IV and no other qualified Space Survey officer could possibly be gotten to the spot in time to handle it. A special ship raced to ask him to act, just for this once. And, reluctantly, he went to do what he could, with the assurance to Riki that he would be back in three months. But he was gone two years, and his youngest child did not remember him when he came back.

He stayed home one year, and then there was an emergency on Seth IV. That kept him only four months, but before he could get back to Lani he was urgently required to check out a colony on Aleph I, whose colonists could not enter into possession until a short-handed Survey service licensed it. Then there was another call. . . .

In the first ten years of his marriage, Bordman spent less than five with his family. But he didn't like it. When he'd been married fifteen years he'd made it clear at Headquarters that he was only carrying on until a new class graduated from Space Survey training. Then he was going home to stay.

SAND DOOM

Bordman knew there was something wrong when the throbbing, acutely uncomfortable vibration of rocket-blasts shook the ship. Rockets were strictly emergency devices these days, so when they were used there was obviously an emergency.

He sat still. He had been reading in the passenger-lounge of the *Warlock*—a very small lounge indeed—but as a Senior Colonial Survey Officer with considerable experience he was well-traveled enough to know when things did not go right. He looked up from the book-screen, waiting. Nobody came to explain the eccentricity of a spaceship using rockets. The explanation would have been immediate on a regular liner, but the *Warlock* was practically a tramp. This trip it carried just two passengers. Passenger service was not yet authorized to the planet, and would not be until Bordman had made the report he was on his way to compile. At the moment, though, the rockets blasted, and stopped, and blasted again. There was something definitely wrong.

The *Warlock*'s other passenger came out of her
cabin. She looked surprised. She was Aletha Redfeather,
a very lovely Amerind. It was extraordinary that a girl
could be so self-sufficient on a tedious space-voyage,
and Bordman approved of her. She was making the
journey to Xosa II as a representative of the Amerind
Historical Society, but she'd brought her own book-reels
and some elaborate fancy-work which—woman-
fashion—she used to occupy her hands. She hadn't
been at all a nuisance. Now she tilted her head on one
side as she looked inquiringly at Bordman.

"I'm wondering too," he told her, just as an especially sustained and violent shuddering of rocket-
impulsion made his chair legs thutter on the floor.

There was a long period of stillness. Then another
violent but much shorter blast. A shorter one still.
Presently there was a half-second blast which must have
been from a single rocket-tube because of the mild
shaking it produced. After that there was nothing at
all.

Bordman frowned to himself. He'd been anticipat-
ing groundfall within a matter of hours, certainly. He'd
just gone through his spec-book carefully and re-
familiarized himself with the work he was to survey
on Xosa II. It was a perfectly commonplace minerals-
planet development, and he'd expected to clear it FE—
fully established—and probably TP and NQ ratings as
well, indicating that tourists were permitted and no
quarantine was necessary. Considering the aridity of the
planet, no bacteriological dangers could be expected
to exist, and if tourists wanted to view its monstrous
deserts and inferno-like wind-sculptures, they should
be welcome.

But the ship had used rocket-drive in the planet's
near vicinity. Emergency. Which was ridiculous. This
was a perfectly routine sort of voyage. Its purpose was

the delivery of heavy equipment—specifically a smelter—and a Senior Colonial Survey Officer to report the completion of primary development.

Aletha waited, as if for more rocket-blasts. Presently she smiled at some thought that had occurred to her.

"If this were an adventure story," she said, "the loudspeaker would now announce that the ship had established itself in an orbit around the strange, uncharted planet first sighted three days ago, and that volunteers were wanted for a boat landing."

Bordman demanded impatiently:

"Do you bother with adventure stories? They're nonsense! A pure waste of time!"

Aletha smiled again.

"My ancestors," she told him, "used to hold tribal dances and make medicine and boast about how many scalps they'd taken and how they did it. It was satisfying—and educational for the young. Adolescents became familiar with the idea of what we nowadays call adventure. They were partly ready for it when it came. I suspect your ancestors used to tell each other stories about hunting mammoths and such. So I think it would be fun to hear that we were in orbit and that a boat landing was in order."

Bordman grunted. There were no longer adventures. The universe was settled, civilized. Of course there were still frontier planets—Xosa II was one—but pioneers had only hardships. Not adventures.

The ship-phone speaker clicked. It said curtly:

"Notice. We have arrived at Xosa II and have established an orbit about it. Landing will be made by boat."

Bordman's mouth dropped open.

"What the devil's this?" he demanded.

"Adventure, maybe," said Aletha. Her eyes crinkled very pleasantly when she smiled. She wore the modern Amerind dress—a sign of pride in the ancestry

which now implied such diverse occupations as interstellar steel construction and animal husbandry and
llano-planet colonization. "If it were adventure, as the
only girl on this ship I'd have to be in the landing party,
lest the tedium of orbital waiting make the—" her smile
widened to a grin—"the pent-up restlessness of trouble-
makers in the crew—"

The ship phone clicked again.

*"Mr. Bordman. Miss Redfeather. According to advices
from the ground, the ship may have to stay in orbit
for a considerable time. You will accordingly be landed
by boat. Will you make yourselves ready, please, and
report to the boat-blister?"* The voice paused and
added, *"Hand luggage only, please."*

Aletha's eyes brightened. Bordman felt the shocked
incredulity of a man accustomed to routine when
routine is broken. Of course, survey ships made boat
landings from orbit, and colony ships let down robot
hulls by rocket when there was as yet no landing-grid
for the handling of a ship. But never before in his
experience had an ordinary freighter, on a routine
voyage to a colony ready for a degree-of-completion
survey, ever landed anybody by boat.

"This is ridiculous!" said Bordman, fuming.

"Maybe it's adventure," said Aletha. "I'll pack."

She disappeared into her cabin. Bordman hesitated.
Then he went into his own. The colony on Xosa II had
been established two years before. Minimum-comfort
conditions had been realized within six months. A temporary landing-grid for light supply ships was up within
a year. It had permitted stockpiling, and it had been
taken down to be rebuilt as a permanent grid with every
possible contingency provided for. The eight months
since the last ship landing was more than enough for
the rebuilding of the gigantic, spidery, half-mile-high
structure which would handle this planet's interstellar

commerce. There was no excuse for an emergency. A
boat landing was nonsensical! He surveyed the contents
of his cabin. Most of the cargo of the *Warlock* was
smelter equipment which was to complete the outfit-
ting of the colony. It was to be unloaded first. By the
time the ship's holds were wholly empty, the smelter
would be operating. The ship would wait for a full cargo
of pig metal. Bordman had expected to live in this cabin
while he worked on the survey he'd come to make and
to leave again with the ship.

Now he was to go aground by boat. He fretted. The
only emergency equipment he could possibly need was
a heat-suit. He doubted the urgency of that. But he
packed some clothing for indoors, and then defiantly
included his spec-book and the volumes of definitive
data to which specifications for structures and colonial
establishments always referred. He'd get to work on
his report immediately after he landed.

He went out of the passenger-lounge to the boat-
blister. An engineer's legs projected from the boat port.
Bordman consciously acted according to the best traditions of passengers.

"What's the trouble?" he asked.

"We can't land," said the engineer shortly.

He went away—according to the tradition by which
ships' crews are always scornful of passengers.

Bordman scowled. Then Aletha came, carrying a not-
too-heavy bag. Bordman put it in the boat, disapproving
of the crampedness of the craft. But this wasn't a lifeboat. It was a landing-boat. A lifeboat had Lawlor drive
and could travel light-years, but in the place of rockets and rocket fuel it had air purifiers and water
recovery units and food stores. It couldn't land without a landing-grid aground, but it could get to a civilized planet. This landing boat could land without a
grid, but its air wouldn't last long.

"Whatever's the matter," said Bordman darkly, "it's incompetence somewhere!"

But he couldn't figure it out. This was a cargo-ship. Cargo-ships neither took off nor landed under their own power. It was too costly of fuel they would have to carry. So landing-grids used local power—which did not have to be lifted—to heave ships out into space, and again used local power to draw them to ground again. Therefore ships carried fuel only for actual space flight, which was economy. Yet landing-grids had no moving parts, and while they did have to be monstrous structures they actually drew power from planetary ionospheres. So with no moving parts to break down and no possibility of the failure of a power-source, landing-grids couldn't fail! So there couldn't be an emergency to make a ship ride orbit around a planet which had a landing-grid.

The engineer came back. He carried a mail sack full of letter-reels. He waved his hand. Aletha crawled into the landing boat port. Bordman followed. Four people, with considerable crowding, could have gotten into the little ship. Three pretty well filled it. The engineer followed them and sealed the port.

"Sealed off," he said into the microphone before him.

The exterior-pressure needle moved halfway across the dial. The interior-pressure needle stayed steady.

"All tight," said the engineer.

The exterior-pressure needle flicked to zero. There were clanking sounds. The long halves of the boat-blister stirred and opened, and abruptly the landing boat was in an elongated cup in the hull plating, and above them there were many, many stars. The enormous disk of a nearby planet floated into view around the hull. It was monstrous and blindingly bright. It was of a tawny color, with great, irregular areas of yellow and patches of bluishness. But most of it was the color of sand. And all its colors varied in shade—some places lighter and some darker—and over at one edge there was blinding whiteness which could not be anything but an ice cap. Bordman knew that there was no ocean or sea or lake on all this whole planet, and the ice-cap was more nearly hoar-frost than such mile-deep glaciation as would be found at the poles of a maximum-comfort world.

"Strap in," said the engineer over his shoulder. "No-gravity coming, and then rocket-push: Settle your heads."

Bordman irritably strapped himself in. He saw Aletha busy at the same task, her eyes shining. Without warning, there came a sensation of acute discomfort. It was the landing boat detaching itself from the ship and the diminishment of the ship's closely-confined artificial gravity field. That field suddenly dropped to nothingness, and Bordman had the momentary sickish dizziness that flicked-off gravity always produces. At the same time his heart pounded unbearably in the instinctive, racial-memory reaction to the feel of falling.

Then roarings. He was thrust savagely back against his seat. His tongue tried to slide back into his throat. There was an enormous oppression on his chest and he found himself thinking panicky profanity.

Simultaneously the vision ports went black, because they were out of the shadow of the ship. The landing boat turned—but there was no sensation of centrifugal force—and they were in a vast obscurity with merely a dim phantom of the planetary surface to be seen. Behind them a blue-white sun shone terribly. Its light was warm—hot—even though it came through the polarized, shielding ports.

"Did you say," panted Aletha happily—breathless

because of the acceleration—"that there weren't any
adventures?"

Bordman did not answer. But he did not count
discomfort as an adventure.

The engineer did not look out the ports at all. He
watched the screen before him. There was a vertical
line across the side of the lighted screen. A blip moved
downward across it, showing their height in thousands
of miles. After a long time the blip reached the bottom, and the vertical line became double and another
blip began to descend. It measured height in hundreds
of miles. A bright spot—a square—appeared at one side
of the screen. A voice muttered metallically, and suddenly seemed to shout, and then muttered again.
Bordman looked out one of the black ports and saw
the planet as if through smoked glass. It was a ghostly
reddish thing which filled half the cosmos. It had
mottlings, and its edge was curved. That would be the
horizon.

The engineer moved controls and the white square
moved. It went across the screen. He moved more
controls. It came back to the center. The height-in-
hundreds blip was at the bottom now, and the vertical line tripled and a tens-of-miles-height blip crawled
downward.

There were sudden, monstrous plungings of the
landing boat. It had hit the outermost fringes of atmosphere. The engineer said words it was not appropriate for Aletha to hear. The plungings became more
violent. Bordman held on, to keep from being shaken
to pieces despite the straps, and stared at the murky
surface of the planet. It seemed to be fleeing from
them and they to be trying to overtake it. Gradually,
very gradually, its flight appeared to slow. They were
down to twenty miles, then.

Quite abruptly the landing boat steadied. The square

spot bobbled about in the center of the astrogation-screen. The engineer worked controls to steady it.

The ports cleared a little. Bordman could see the ground below more distinctly. There were patches of every tint that mineral coloring could produce, and vast stretches of tawny sand. A little while more, and he could see the shadows of mountains. He made out mountain-flanks which should have had valleys between them and other mountain-flanks beyond, but they were joined by tawny flatnesses instead. These, he knew, would be the sand-plateaus which had been observed on this planet and which had only a still-disputed explanation. But he could see areas of glistening yellow and dirty white, and splashes of pink and streaks of ultramarine and gray and violet, and the incredible red of iron oxide covering square miles—too much to be believed.

The landing boat's rockets cut off. It coasted. Presently the horizon tilted and all the dazzling ground below turned sedately beneath them. Then came staccato instructions from a voice-speaker, which the engineer obeyed. The landing boat swung low—below the tips of giant mauve mountains with a sand-plateau beyond them—and its nose went up. It stalled.

Then the rockets roared again—and now, with air about them, they were horribly loud—and the boat settled down and down upon its own tail of fire.

A blinding mass of dust and rocket-fumes cut off all sight of everything else. Then a crunching crash, and the engineer swore peevishly to himself. He cut the rockets again. Finally.

Bordman found himself staring straight up, still strapped in his chair. The boat had settled on its own tail fins, and his feet were higher than his head. He felt ridiculous. He saw the engineer at work unstrapping himself, and duplicated the action, but it was absurdly difficult to get out of the chair.

Aletha managed more gracefully. She didn't need help.

"Wait," said the engineer ungraciously, "till somebody comes."

So they waited, using what had been chair-backs for seats.

The engineer moved a control and the windows cleared further. They saw the surface of Xosa II. There was no living thing in sight. The ground itself was pebbles and small rocks and minor boulders—all apparently tumbled from the starkly magnificent mountains to one side. There were monstrous, many-colored cliffs and mesas, every one eaten at in the unmistakable fashion of wind erosion. Through a notch in the mountain wall before them a strange, fan-shaped, frozen formation appeared. If such a thing had been credible, Bordman would have said that it was a flow of sand simulating a waterfall. And everywhere was a blinding brightness and the look and feel of blistering sunshine. But there was not one single leaf or twig or blade of grass. This was pure desert. This was Xosa II.

Aletha regarded it with bright eyes.

"Beautiful!" she said happily. "Isn't it?"

"Personally," said Bordman, "I never saw a place that looked less homelike or attractive."

Aletha laughed.

"My eyes see it differently."

Which was true. It was accepted, nowadays, that humankind might be one species but was many races, and each saw the cosmos in its own fashion. On Kalmet III there was a dense, predominantly Asiatic population which terraced its mountainsides for agriculture and deftly mingled modern techniques with social customs not to be found on—say—Demeter I, where there were many red tiled stucco towns and very many olive groves. In the llano planets of the Equis cluster, Amerinds—Aletha's kin—rode over plains dotted with the descendants of buffalo and antelope and cattle brought from ancient Earth. On the oases of Rustam IV there were date palms and riding camels and much argument about what should be substituted for the direction of Mecca at the times for prayer, while wheat fields spanned provinces on Canna I and highly civilized emigrants from the continent of Africa on Earth stored jungle-gums and lustrous gems in the warehouses of their space-port city of Timbuk.

So it was natural for Aletha to look at this wind-carved wilderness otherwise than as Bordman did. Her racial kin were the pioneers of the stars these days. Their heritage made them less than appreciative of urban life. Their inborn indifference to heights made them the steel construction men of the cosmos, and more than two thirds of the landing-beam grids in the whole galaxy had their coup-feather symbols on the key posts. But the planet government on Algonka V was housed in a three-thousand-foot stone tepee, and the best horses known to men were raised by ranchers with bronze skins and high cheekbones on the llano planet Chagan.

Now, here, in the *Warlock*'s landing boat, the engineer snorted. A vehicle came around a cliff wall, clanking its way on those eccentric caterwheels that new-founded colonies find so useful. The vehicle glittered. It crawled over tumbled boulders, and flowed over fallen scree. It came briskly toward them.

"That's my cousin Ralph!" said Aletha in pleased surprise.

Bordman blinked and looked again. He did not quite believe his eyes. But they told the truth. The figure

controlling the ground car was Indian—Amerind—
wearing a breechclout and thick-soled sandals and three
streamlined feathers in a band about his head. Moreover, he did not ride in a seat. He sat astride a semi-
cylindrical part of the ground car, over which a gaily
colored blanket had been thrown.

The ship's engineer rumbled disgustedly. But then
Bordman saw how sane this method of riding was—
here. The ground vehicle lurched and swayed and
rolled and pitched and tossed as it came over the
uneven ground. To sit in anything like a chair would
have been foolish. A back rest would throw one forward in a frontward lurch, and give no support in case
of a backward one. A sidewise tilt would tend to throw
one off. Riding a ground car as if in a saddle was sense!

But Bordman was not so sure about the costume.
The engineer opened the port and spoke hostilely out
of it:

"D'you know there's a lady in this thing?"

The young Indian grinned. He waved his hand to
Aletha, who pressed her nose against a viewport. And
just then Bordman did understand the costume or lack
of it. Air came in the open exit-port. It was hot and
dessicated. It was furnace-like!

"How, 'Letha," called the rider on the caterwheel
steed. "Either dress for the climate or put on a heat-
suit before you come out of there!"

Aletha chuckled. Bordman heard a stirring behind
him. Then Aletha climbed to the exit-port and swung
out. Bordman heard a dour muttering from the engineer. Then he saw her greeting her cousin. She had
slipped out of the conventionalized Amerind outfit to
which Bordman was accustomed. Now she was clad as
Anglo-Saxon girls dressed for beaches on the cool-
temperature planets.

For a moment Bordman thought of sunstroke, with

his own eyes dazzled by the still partly-filtered sunlight. But Aletha's Amerind coloring was perfectly suited
to sunshine even of this intensity. Wind blowing upon
her body would cool her skin. Her thick, straight black
hair was at least as good protection against sunstroke
as a heat-helmet. She might feel hot, but she would
be perfectly safe. She wouldn't even sunburn. But he,
Bordman . . .

He grimly stripped to underwear and put on the
heat-suit from his bag. He filled its canteens from the
boat's water tank. He turned on the tiny, battery-
powered motors. The suit ballooned out. It was
intended for short periods of intolerable heat. The
motors kept it inflated—away from his skin—and
cooled its interior by the evaporation of sweat plus
water from its canteen tanks. It was a miniature air-
conditioning system for one man, and it should enable
him to endure temperatures otherwise lethal to someone with his skin and coloring. But it would use a lot
of water.

He climbed to the exit port and went clumsily down
the exterior ladder to the tail fin. He adjusted his
goggles. He went over to the chattering young Indians, young man and girl, and held out his gloved hand.

"I'm Bordman," he said. "Here to make a degree-
of-completion survey. What's wrong that we had to land
by boat?"

Aletha's cousin shook hands cordially.

"I'm Ralph Redfeather," he said. "Project engineer.
About everything's wrong. Our landing-grid's gone. We
couldn't contact your ship in time to warn it off. It was
in our gravity field before it answered, and its Lawlor
drive couldn't take it away—not working because of the
gravity stresses. Our power, of course, went with the
landing-grid. The ship you came in can't get back, and
we can't send a distress message anywhere, and our

best estimate is that the colony will be wiped out—
thirst and starvation—in six months. I'm sorry you and
Aletha have to be included."

Then he turned to Aletha and said amiably:

"How's Mike Thundercloud and Sally Whitehorse
and the gang in general, 'Letha?"

The *Warlock* rolled on in her newly-established orbit
about Xosa II. The landing boat was aground, having
removed the two passengers. It would come back.
Nobody on the ship wanted to stay aground, because
they knew the conditions and the situation below—
unbearable heat and the complete absence of hope. But
nobody had anything to do. The ship had been maintained in standard operating condition during its two-
month voyage from Trent to here. No repairs or
overhaulings were needed. There was no maintenance
work to speak of. There would be only standby watches
until something happened, and nothing to do on those
watches. There would be off-watch time for twenty-
one out of every twenty-four hours, and no purpose-
ful activity to fill even half an hour of it. In a matter
of—probably—years, the *Warlock* should receive aid.
She might be towed out of her orbit to space—five
diameters out—in which the Lawlor drive could function, or the crew might simply be taken off. But
meanwhile, those on board were as completely frustrated as the colony. They could not do anything at all
to help themselves.

In one fashion the crewmen were worse off than the
colonists. The colonists had at least the colorful prospect of death before them. They could prepare for it
in their several ways. But the members of the *Warlock*'s
crew had nothing ahead but tedium. The skipper faced
the future with extreme distaste.

❖   ❖   ❖

The ride to the colony was torment. Aletha rode behind her cousin on the saddle blanket, and apparently suffered little if at all. But Bordman could only ride in the ground car's cargo space, along with the sack of mail from the ship. The ground was unbelievably rough and the jolting intolerable. The heat was literally murderous. In the metal cargo space, the temperature reached a hundred and sixty degrees in the sunshine—and given enough time, food will cook in no more heat than that. Of course a man has been known to enter an oven and stay there while a roast was cooked, and to come out alive. But the oven wasn't throwing him violently about or bringing sun heated—blue-white-sun heated—metal to press his heat-suit about him. The suit did make survival possible, but that was all. The contents of its canteens gave out just before arrival, and for a short time Bordman had only sweat for his suit to work with. It kept him alive by forced ventilation, but he arrived in a state of collapse. He drank the iced salt water they gave him and went to bed. He'd get back his strength with a proper sodium level in his blood. But he slept for twelve hours straight.

When he got up, he was physically normal again, but abysmally ashamed. It did no good to remind himself that Xosa II was rated minimum-comfort class D—a blue-white sun and a mean temperature of one hundred ten degrees. Africans could do steel construction work in the open, protected only by insulating shoes and gloves. But Bordman could not venture out-of-doors except in a heat-suit. He could not stay long then. It was not a weakness. It was a matter of genetics. But he was ashamed.

Aletha nodded to him when he found the Project Engineer's office. It occupied one of the hulls in which colony-establishment materials had been lowered by rocket power. There were forty of the hulls, and they had been emptied and arranged for intercommunication, so that an individual could change his quarters and ordinary associates from time to time and colony-fever—frantic irritation with one's companions—was minimized.

Aletha sat at a desk, busily making notes from a loose-leaf volume before her. The wall behind the desk was fairly lined with similar volumes.

"I made a spectacle of myself!" said Bordman.

"Not at all!" Aletha assured him. "It could happen to anybody. I wouldn't do too well on Timbuk."

There was no answer to that. Timbuk was essentially a jungle planet, barely emerging from the carboniferous stage. Its colonists thrived because their ancestors had lived on the shores of the Gulf of Guinea, on Earth. But Anglos did not find its climate healthful, nor would many other races. Amerinds died there quicker than most.

"Ralph's on the way here now," added Aletha. "He and Dr. Chuka were out picking a place to leave the records. The sand-dunes here are terrible, you know. When an explorer ship does come to find out what's happened to us, these buildings could be covered up completely. Any place could be. It isn't easy to pick a record cache that's quite sure to be found."

"When," said Bordman, "there's nobody left alive to point it out. Is that it?"

"That's it," agreed Aletha. "It's pretty bad all around. I didn't plan to die just yet."

Her voice was perfectly normal. Bordman snorted. As a Senior Colonial Survey Officer, he'd been around. But he'd never yet known a human colony to be extinguished when it was properly equipped and after a proper presettlement survey. He'd seen panic, but never real cause for a matter-of-fact acceptance of doom.

There was a clanking noise outside the hulk which was the Project Engineer's headquarters. Bordman couldn't see clearly through the filtered ports, so he reached over and opened a door. The brightness outside struck his eyes like a blow. He blinked them shut instantly and turned away. But he'd seen a glistening, caterwheel ground car stopping not far from the doorway.

He stood wiping tears from his light-dazzled eyes as footsteps sounded outside. Aletha's cousin came in, followed by a huge man with remarkably dark skin. The dark man wore eyeglasses with a curiously thick, corklike nosepiece to insulate the necessary metal of the frame from his skin. It would blister if it touched bare flesh.

"This is Dr. Chuka," said Redfeather pleasantly, "Mr. Bordman. Dr. Chuka's the director of mining and mineralogy here."

Bordman shook hands with the ebony-skinned man. He grinned, showing startlingly white teeth. Then he began to shiver.

"It's like a freeze-box in here," he said in a deep voice. "I'll get a robe and be with you."

He vanished through a doorway, his teeth chattering audibly. Aletha's cousin took half a dozen deliberate deep breaths and grimaced.

"I could shiver myself," he admitted, "but Chuka's really acclimated to Xosa. He was raised on Timbuk."

Bordman said curtly:

"I'm sorry I collapsed on landing. It won't happen again. I came here to do a degree-of-completion survey that should open the colony to normal commerce, let the colonist's families move in, tourists, and so on. But I was landed by boat instead of normally, and I am told the colony is doomed. I would like an official statement of the degree of completion of the colony's facilities and an explanation of the unusual points I have just mentioned."

The Indian blinked at him. Then he smiled faintly. The dark man came back, zipping up an indoor warmth-garment. Redfeather dryly brought him up to date by repeating what Bordman had just said. Chuka grinned and sprawled comfortably in a chair.

"I'd say," he remarked, in that astonishingly deep-toned voice of his, "I'd say sand got in our hair. And our colony. And the landing-grid. There's a lot of sand on Xosa. Wouldn't you say that was the trouble?"

The Indian said with deliberate gravity: "Of course wind had something to do with it."

Bordman fumed. "I think you know," he said, "that as a Senior Colonial Survey Officer, I have authority to give any orders needed for my work. I give one now. I want to see the landing-grid, if it is still standing. I take it that it didn't fall down?"

Redfeather flushed beneath the bronze pigment of his skin. It would be hard to offend a steelman more than to suggest that his work did not still stand up.

"I assure you," he said politely, "that it did not fall down."

"Your estimate of its degree of completion?"

"Eighty per cent," said Redfeather.

"You've stopped work on it?"

"Work on it has been stopped," agreed the Indian.

"Even though the colony can receive no more supplies until it is completed?"

"Just so," said Redfeather without expression.

"Then I issue a formal order that I be taken to the landing-grid site immediately!" said Bordman angrily. "I want to see what sort of incompetence is responsible! Will you arrange that at once?"

Redfeather said in a completely emotionless voice:

"You want to see the site of the landing-grid. Very good. Immediately."

He turned and walked out into the incredible, blinding sunshine. Bordman blinked at the momentary blast of light, and then began to pace up and down the office. He fumed. He was still ashamed of his collapse from the heat during the travel from the landed rocket-boat to the colony. Therefore he was touchy and irritable. But the order he had given was strictly justifiable.

He heard a small noise and whirled. Dr. Chuka, huge and black and spectacled, rocked back and forth in his seat, suppressing laughter.

"Now, what the devil does that mean?" demanded Bordman suspiciously. "It certainly isn't ridiculous to ask to see the structure on which the life of the colony finally depends!"

"Not ridiculous," said Doctor Chuka. "It's—hilarious!"

He boomed laughter in the office with the rounded ceiling of a remade robot hull. Aletha smiled with him, though her eyes were grave.

"You'd better put on a heat-suit," she said to Bordman.

He fumed again, tempted to defy all common sense because its dictates were not the same for everybody. But he marched away, back to the cubbyhole in which he had awakened. He donned the heat-suit that had not protected him adequately before, but had certainly saved his life, and filled the canteens topping full—he suspected he hadn't done so the last time. He went back to the Project Engineer's office with a feeling of being burdened and absurd.

Out a filter-window, he saw that men with skins as dark as Dr. Chuka's were at work on a ground car. They were equipping it with a sunshade and curious shields like wings. Somebody pushed a sort of caterwheel handtruck toward it. They put big, heavy tanks into its cargo space. Dr. Chuka had disappeared, but Aletha was back at work making notes from the loose-leaf volume on the desk.

"May I ask," asked Bordman with some irony, "what your work happens to be just now?"

She looked up.

"I thought you knew!" she said in surprise. "I'm here for the Amerind Historical Society. I can certify coups. I'm taking coup-records for the Society. They'll go in the record cache Ralph and Dr. Chuka are arranging, so no matter what happens to the colony, the record of the coups won't be lost."

"Coups?" demanded Bordman. He knew that Amerinds painted feathers on the key posts of steel structures they'd built, and he knew that the posting of such "coup-marks" was a cherished privilege and undoubtedly a survival or revival of some American Indian tradition back on Earth. But he did not know what they meant.

"Coups," repeated Aletha matter-of-factly. "Ralph wears three eagle-feathers. You saw them. He has three coups. Pinions, too! He built the landing-grids on Norlath and— Oh, you don't know!"

"I don't," admitted Bordman, his temper not of the best because of what seemed unnecessary condescensions on Xosa II.

Aletha looked surprised.

"In the old days," she explained, "back on Earth, if a man scalped an enemy, he counted coup. The first to strike an enemy in a battle counted coup, too—a lesser one. Nowadays a man counts coups for different things, but Ralph's three eagle-feathers mean he's entitled to as much respect as a warrior in the old days who, three separate times, had killed and scalped an enemy warrior in the middle of his own camp. And he is, too!"

Bordman grunted.

"Barbarous, I'd say!"

"If you like," said Aletha. "But it's something to be proud of and one doesn't count coup for making a lot of money." Then she paused and said curtly: "The word 'snobbish' fits it better than 'barbarous.' We are snobs! But when the head of a clan stands up in Council in the Big Tepee on Algonka, representing his clan, and men have to carry the ends of the feather headdress with all the coups the members of his clan have earned—why—one is proud to belong to that clan." She added defiantly, "Even watching it on a vision-screen!"

Dr. Chuka opened the outer door. Blinding light poured in. He did not enter, and his body glistened with sweat.

"Ready for you, Mr. Bordman."

Bordman adjusted his goggles and turned on the motors of his heat-suit. He went out the door.

The heat and light outside was like a blow. He darkened the goggles again and made his way heavily to the waiting, now-shaded ground car. He noted that there were other changes besides the sunshade. The cover deck of the cargo space was gone, and there were cylindrical riding seats like saddles in the back. The odd lower shields reached out sidewise from the body, barely above the caterwheels. He could not make out their purpose and irritably failed to ask.

"All ready," said Redfeather. "Dr. Chuka's coming with us. If you'll get in here, please. . . ."

Bordman climbed awkwardly into the boxlike back of the car. He bestrode one of the cylindrical arrangements. With a saddle on it, it would undoubtedly have been a comfortable way to cover impossibly bad terrain in a mechanical carrier. He waited. About him there were the squatty hulls of the space barges which

had been towed here by a colony ship, each one once
equipped with rockets for landing. Emptied of their
cargos, they bad been huddled together into the three
separate, adjoining communities. There were separate
living-quarters and mess-halls and recreation-rooms for
each, and any colonist lived in the community of his
choice and shifted at pleasure, or visited, or remained
solitary. For mental health a man has to be assured
of his free will, and over-regimentation is deadly in any
society. With men psychologically suited to colonize,
it is fatal.

Above—but at a distance, now—was the monstrous
scarp of mountains, colored in glaring and unnatural
tints. Immediately about there was raw rock. But it was
peculiarly smooth, as if sand-grains had rubbed over
it for uncountable aeons and carefully worn away every
trace of unevenness. Half a mile to the left, dunes
began and went away to the horizon. The nearer ones
were small, but they gained in size with distance from
the mountains—which evidently affected the surface-
winds hereabouts—and the edge of seeing was visibly
not a straight line. The dunes yonder must be gigantic. But of course on a world the size of ancient Earth,
and which was waterless save for snow-patches at its
poles, the size to which sand-dunes could grow had no
limit. The surface of Xosa II was a sea of sand, on
which islands and small continents of wind-swept rock
were merely minor features.

Dr. Chuka adjusted a small metal object in his hand.
It had a tube dangling from it. He climbed into the
cargo space and fastened it to one of the two tanks
previously loaded.

"For you," he told Bordman. "Those tanks are full
of compressed air at rather high pressure—a couple
of thousand pounds. Here's a reduction valve with an
adiabatic expansion feature, to supply extra air to your

heat-suit. It will be pretty cold, expanding from so high a pressure. Bring down the temperature a little more."

Bordman again felt humiliated. Chuka and Redfeather, because of their races, were able to move about nine-tenths naked in the open air on this planet, and they thrived. But he needed a special refrigerated costume to endure the heat. More, they provided him with sunshades and refrigerated air that they did not need for themselves. They were thoughtful of him. He was as much out of his element where they fitted perfectly, as he would have been making a degree-of-completion survey on an underwater project. He had to wear what was practically a diving suit and use a special air-supply to survive!

He choked down the irritation his own inadequacy produced.

"I suppose we can go now," he said as coldly as he could. Aletha's cousin mounted the control saddle—though it was no more than a blanket—and Dr. Chuka mounted beside Bordman. The ground car got under way. It headed for the mountains.

The smoothness of the rock was deceptive. The caterwheel car lurched and bumped and swayed and rocked. It rolled and dipped and wallowed. Nobody could have remained in a normal seat on such terrain, but Bordman felt hopelessly undignified riding what amounted to a hobbyhorse. Under the sunshade it was infuriatingly like a horse on a carrousel. That there were three of them together made it look even more foolish. He stared about, trying to take his mind from his own absurdity. His goggles made the light endurable, but he felt ashamed.

"Those side-fins," said Chuka's deep voice pleasantly, "the bottom ones, makes things better for you. The shade overhead cuts off direct sunlight, and they cut

off the reflected glare. It would blister your skin even
if the sun never touched you directly."

Bordman did not answer. The caterwheel car went
on. It came to a patch of sand—tawny sand, heavily
mineralized. There was a dune here. Not a big one for
Xosa II, no more than a hundred feet high. But they
went up its leeward, steeply slanting side. All the planet
seemed to tilt insanely as the caterwheels spun. They
reached the dune's crest, where it tended to curl over
and break like a water-comber, and here the wheels
struggled with sand precariously ready to fall, and
Bordman had a sudden perception of the sands of Xosa
II as the oceans that they really were. The dunes were
waves which moved with infinite slowness, but the
irresistible force of storm-seas. Nothing could resist
them. Nothing!

They traveled over similar dunes for two miles. Then
they began to climb the approaches to the mountains.
And Bordman saw for the second time—the first had
been through the ports of the landing boat—where
there was a notch in the mountain wall and sand had
flowed out of it like a waterfall, making a beautifully
symmetrical cone-shaped heap against the lower cliffs.
There were many such falls. In one place there was
a sand-cascade. Sand had poured over a series of rocky
steps, piling up on each in turn to its very edge, and
then spilling again to the next.

They went up a crazily slanting spur of stone, whose
sides were too steep for sand to lodge on, and whose
narrow crest had a bare thin coating of powder.

The landscape looked like a nightmare. As the car
went on, wobbling and lurching and dipping, the
heights on either side made Bordman tend to dizziness. The coloring was impossible. The aridness, the
dessication, the lifelessness of everything about was
somehow shocking. Bordman found himself straining

his eyes for the merest, scrubbiest of bushes and for however stunted and isolated a wisp of grass.

The journey went on for an hour. Then there came a straining climb up a now-windswept ridge of eroded rock, and then the attainment of its highest point— and then the ground car went onward for a hundred yards and stopped.

They had reached the top of the mountain range, and there was doubtlessly another range beyond. But they could not see it. Here, as the place to which they had climbed so effortfully, there were no more rocks. There was no valley. There was no descending slope. There was sand. This was one of the sand-plateaus which were a unique feature of Xosa II. And Bordman knew, now, that the disputed explanation was the true one.

Winds, blowing over the mountains, carried sand as on other worlds they carried moisture and pollen and seeds and rain. Where two mountain ranges ran across the course of long-blowing winds, the winds eddied above the valley between. They dropped sand into it. The equivalent of trade winds, Bordman considered, in time would fill a valley to the mountain tops, just as trade winds provide moisture in equal quantity on other worlds, and civilizations have been built upon them. But—

"Well?" said Bordman challengingly.

"This is the site of the landing-grid," said Redfeather.

"Where?"

"Here," said the Indian. "A few months ago there was a valley here. The landing-grid had eighteen hundred feet of height built. There was to be four hundred feet more—the lighter top construction justifies my figure of eighty per cent completion. Then there was a storm."

It was hot. Horribly, terribly hot, even here on a

plateau at mountaintop height. Dr. Chuka looked at Bordman's face and bent down in the vehicle. He turned a stopcock on one of the air tanks brought for Bordman's needs. Immediately Bordman felt cooler. His skin was dry, of course; the circulated air dried sweat as fast as it appeared. But he had the dazed, feverish feeling of a man in an artificial fever box. He'd been fighting it for some time. Now the coolness of the expanded air was almost deliriously refreshing.

Dr. Chuka produced a canteen. Bordman drank thirstily. The water was slightly salted to replace salt lost in sweat.

"A storm, eh?" asked Bordman, after a time of contemplation of his inner sensations as well as the scene of disaster before him. There'd be some hundreds of millions of tons of sand in even a section of this plateau. It was unthinkable that it could be removed except by a long-time sweep of changed trade winds along the length of the valley. "But what has a storm to do—?"

"It was a sandstorm," said Redfeather curtly. "Probably there was a sunspot flareup. We don't know. But the pre-colonization survey spoke of sandstorms. The survey team even made estimates of sandfall in various places as so many inches per year. Here all storms drop sand instead of rain. But there must have been a sunspot flare because this storm blew for"—his voice went flat and deliberate because it was stating the unbelievable—"this storm blew for two months. We did not see the sun in all that time. And we couldn't work, naturally. So we waited it out. When it ended, there was this sand-plateau where the survey had ordered the landing-grid to be built. The grid was under it. It is still under it. The top of eighteen hundred feet of steel is buried two hundred feet down in the sand you see. Our unfabricated building-steel is piled ready for erection—under two thousand feet of sand. Without anything but stored power it is hardly practical"— Redfeather's tone was sardonic—"for us to try to dig it out. There are hundreds of millions of tons of stuff to be moved. If we could get the sand away, we could finish the grid. If we could finish the grid, we'd have power enough to get the sand away—in a few years, and if we could replace the machinery that wore out handling it. And if there wasn't another sandstorm."

He paused. Bordman took deep breaths of the cooler air. He could think more clearly.

"If you will accept photographs," said Redfeather, "you can check that we actually did the work."

Bordman saw the implications. The colony had been formed of Amerinds for the steel work and Africans for the labor. The Amerinds were congenitally averse to the handling of complex mining-machinery underground and the control of modern high speed smelting operations. Both races could endure this climate and work in it, provided that they had cooled sleeping-quarters. But they had to have power. Power not only to work with, but to live by. The air cooling machinery that made sleep possible also condensed from the cool air that minute trace of water-vapor it contained and that they needed for drink. But without power they would thirst. Without the landing-grid and the power it took from the ionosphere, they could not receive supplies from the rest of the universe. So they would starve.

Bordman said:

"I'll accept the photographs. I even accept the statement that the colony will die. I will prepare my report for the cache Aletha tells me you're preparing. And I apologize for any affront I may have offered you."

Dr. Chuka nodded. He regarded Bordman with benign warmth. Ralph Redfeather said cordially enough:

"That's perfectly all right. No harm done."

"And now," said Bordman, "since I have authority to give any orders needed for my work, I want to survey the steps you've taken to carry out those parts of your instructions dealing with emergencies. I want to see right away what you've done to beat this state of things. I know they can't be beaten, but I intend to leave a report on what you've tried!"

A fist-fight broke out in the crew's quarters within two hours after the *Warlock* had established its orbit— a first reaction to their catastrophe. The skipper went through the ship and painstakingly confiscated every weapon. He locked them up. He, himself, already felt the nagging effect of jangling nerves. There was nothing to do. He didn't know when there would ever be anything to do. It was a condition to produce hysteria.

It was night. Outside and above the colony there were uncountable myriads of stars. They were not the stars of Earth of course, but Bordman had never been on Earth. He was used to unfamiliar constellations. He stared out a port at the sky, and noted that there were no moons. He remembered, when he thought, that Xosa II had no moons. There was a rustling of paper behind him. Aletha Redfeather turned a page in a looseleaf volume and made a note. The wall behind her held many more such books. From them could be extracted the detailed history of every bit of work that had been done by the colony-preparation crews. Separate, tersely-phrased items could be assembled to make a record of individual men.

There had been incredible hardships at first, and heroic feats. There had been an attempt to ferry water-supplies down from the pole by aircraft. It was not practical, even to build up a reserve of fluid. Winds carried sand particles here as on other worlds they carried moisture. Aircraft were abraded as they flew. The last working flier made a forced landing five hundred miles from the colony. A caterwheel expedition went out and brought the crew in. The caterwheel trucks were armored with silicone plastic, resistant to abrasion, but when they got back they had to be scrapped. Men had been lost in sudden sand squalls, and heroic searches made for them, and once or twice rescues. There had been cave-ins in the mines, and other accidents.

Bordman went to the door of the hull which was Ralph Redfeather's office. He opened it, and stepped outside.

It was like stepping into an oven. The sand was still hot from the sunshine just ended. The air was so utterly dry that Bordman instantly felt it sucking at the moisture of his nasal passages. In ten seconds his feet— clad in indoor footwear—were uncomfortably hot. In twenty the soles of his feet felt as if they were blistering. He would die of the heat even at night, here! Perhaps he could endure the outside near dawn, but he raged a little. Here Amerinds and Africans lived and throve, but he could live unprotected for no more than an hour or two—and that only at one special time of the planet's rotation!

He went back in, ashamed of the discomfort of his feet and angrily letting them feel scorched rather than admit to it.

Aletha turned another page.

"Look here!" said Bordman. "No matter what you say, you're going to go back on the *Warlock* before—"

She raised her eyes.

"We'll worry about that when the time comes. But I think not. I'd rather stay here."

"For the present, perhaps," snapped Bordman. "But before things get too bad you go back to the ship! They've rocket fuel enough for half a dozen landings of the landing boat. They can lift you out of here."

Aletha shrugged.

"Why leave here to board a derelict? The *Warlock*'s practically that. What's your honest estimate of the time before a ship equipped to help us gets here?"

Bordman would not answer. He'd done some figuring. It had been a two-month journey from Trent, the nearest Survey base, to here. The *Warlock* had been expected to remain aground until the smelter it brought could load it with pig-metal. Which could be as little as two weeks, but would surprise nobody if it was two months instead. So the ship would not be considered due back on Trent for four months. It would not be considered overdue for at least two more. It would be six months before anybody seriously wondered why it wasn't back with its cargo. There'd be a wait for lifeboats to come in, should there have been a mishap in space. Eventually a report of non-communication would be made to the Colonial Survey headquarters on Canna III. But it would take three months for that report to be received, and six more for a confirmation—even if ships made the voyages exactly at the most favorable intervals—and then there should at least be a complaint from the colony. There were lifeboats aground on Xosa II, for emergency communication, and if a lifeboat didn't bring news of a planetary crisis, no crisis would be considered to exist. Nobody could imagine a landing-grid failing.

Maybe in a year somebody would think that maybe somebody ought to ask around about Xosa II. It would be much longer before somebody put a note on somebody else's desk that would suggest that when or if a suitable ship passed near Xosa II, or if one should be

available for the inquiry, it might be worth while to
have the non-communication from the planet looked
into. Actually, to guess at three years before another
ship arrived would be the most optimistic of estimates.

"You're a civilian," said Bordman. "When the food
and water run low, you go back to the ship. You'll at
least be alive when somebody does come to see what's
the matter here!"

Aletha said mildly:

"Maybe I'd rather not be alive. Will you go back to
the ship?"

Bordman flushed. He wouldn't. But he said:

"I can order you sent on board, and your cousin will
carry out the order."

"I doubt it very much," said Aletha.

She returned to her task.

There were crunching footsteps outside the hulk.
Bordman winced a little. With insulated sandals, it was
normal for these colonists to move from one part of
the colony to another in the open, even by daylight.
He, Bordman, couldn't take out-of-doors at night!

Men came in. There were dark men with rippling
muscles under glistening skin, and bronze Amerinds
with coarse straight hair. Ralph Redfeather was with
them. Dr. Chuka came in last of all.

"Here we are," said Redfeather. "These are our
foremen. Among us, I think we can answer any questions you want to ask."

He made introductions. Bordman didn't try to
remember the names. Abeokuta and Northwind and
Sutata and Tallgrass and T'chka and Spottedhorse and
Lewanika. . . . They were names which in combination
would only be found in a very raw, new colony. But
the men who crowded into the office were wholly at
ease, in their own minds as well as in the presence of
a Senior Colonial Survey Officer. They nodded as they

were named, and the nearest shook hands. Bordman knew that he'd have liked their looks under other circumstances. But he was humiliated by the conditions on this planet. They were not. They were apparently only sentenced to death by them.

"I have to leave a report," said Bordman—and he was somehow astonished to know that he did expect to leave a report rather than make one: he accepted the hopelessness of the colony's future—"I have to leave a report on the degree-of-completion of the work here. But since there's an emergency, I have also to leave a report on the measures taken to meet it." The report would be futile, of course. As futile as the coup-records Aletha was compiling, which would be read only after everybody on the planet was dead. But Bordman knew he'd write it. It was unthinkable that he shouldn't.

"Redfeather tells me," he added, "that the power in storage can be used to cool the colony buildings—and therefore condense drinking water from the air—for just about six months. There is food for about six months also. If one lets the buildings warm up a little, to stretch the fuel, there won't be enough water to drink. Go on half rations to stretch the food, and there won't be enough water to last and the power will give out anyhow. No profit there!"

There were nods. The matter had been thrashed out long before.

"There's food in the *Warlock* overhead," Bordman went on, "but they can't use the landing boat more than a few times. It can't use ship fuel. No refrigeration to hold it stable. They couldn't land more than a ton of supplies all told. There are five hundred of us here. No help there!"

He looked from one to another.

"So we live comfortably," he told them with irony, "until our food and water and minimum night comfort run out together. Anything we do to try to stretch anything is useless because of what happens to something else. Redfeather tells me you accept the situation. What are you doing, since you accept it?"

Dr. Chuka said amiably:

"We've picked a storage place for our records, and our miners are blasting out space in which to put away the record of our actions to the last possible moment. It will be sand-proof. Our mechanics are building a broadcast unit we'll spare a tiny bit of fuel for. It will run twenty-odd years, broadcasting directions so it can be found regardless of how the terrain is changed by drifting sand."

"And," said Bordman, "the fact that nobody will be here to give directions."

Chuka added benignly, "We're doing a great deal of singing, too. My people are—ah—religious. When we are no longer here—there have been boastings that there'll be a well-practiced choir ready to go to work in the next world."

White teeth showed in grins. Bordman was almost envious of men who could grin at such a thought. But he went on:

"And I understand that athletics have also been much practiced?"

Redfeather said:

"There's been time for it. Climbing teams have counted coup on all the worst mountains within three hundred miles. There's been a new record set for the javelin, adjusted for gravity, and Johnny Cornstalk did a hundred yards in eight point four seconds. Aletha has the records and has certified them."

"Very useful!" said Bordman sardonically. Then he disliked himself for saying it even before the bronze-skinned men's faces grew studiedly impassive.

Chuka waved his hand.

"Wait, Ralph! Lewanika's nephew will beat that within a week!"

Bordman was ashamed again because Chuka had spoken to cover up his own bad temper.

"I take it back," he said irritably. "What I said was uncalled for. I shouldn't have said it. But I came here to do a completion survey and what you've been giving me is material for an estimate of morale. It's not my line! I'm a technician, first and foremost. We're faced with a technical problem!"

Aletha spoke suddenly from behind him.

"But these are men, first and foremost, Mr. Bordman. And they're faced with a very human problem—how to die well. They seem to be rather good at it, so far."

Bordman ground his teeth. He was again humiliated. In his own fashion he was attempting the same thing. But just as he was genetically not qualified to endure the climate of this planet, he was not prepared for a fatalistic or pious acceptance of disaster. Amerind and African, alike, these men instinctively held to their own ideas of what the dignity of a man called upon him to do when he could not do anything but die. But Bordman's idea of his human dignity required him to be still fighting: still scratching at the eyes of fate or destiny when he was slain. It was in his blood or genes or the result of training. He simply could not, with self-respect, accept any physical situation as hopeless even when his mind assured him that it was.

"I agree," he said, "but I still have to think in technical terms. You might say that we are going to die because we cannot land the *Warlock* with food and equipment. We cannot land the *Warlock* because we have no landing-grid. We have no landing-grid because it and all the materials to complete it are buried under millions of tons of sand. We cannot make a new, light-supply-ship type of landing-grid because we have no smelter to make beams, nor power to run it if we had, yet if we had the beams we could get the power to run the smelter we haven't got to make the beams. And we have no smelter, hence no beams, no power, no prospect of food or help because we can't land the *Warlock*. It is strictly a circular problem. Break it at any point and all of it is solved."

One of the dark men muttered something under his breath to those near him. There were chuckles.

"Like Mr. Woodchuck," explained the man, when Bordman's eyes fell on him. "When I was a little boy there was a story like that."

Bordman said icily:

"The problem of coolness and water and food is the same sort of problem. In six months we could raise food—if we had power to condense moisture. We've chemicals for hydroponics—if we could keep the plants from roasting as they grew. Refrigeration and water and food are practically another circular problem."

Aletha said tentatively:

"Mr. Bordman—"

He turned, annoyed. Aletha said almost apologetically:

"On Chagan there was a—you might call it a woman's coup given to a woman I know. Her husband raises horses. He's mad about them. And they live in a sort of home on caterwheels out on the plains—the llanos. Sometimes they're months away from a settlement. And she loves ice cream and refrigeration isn't too simple. But she has a Doctorate in Human History. So she had her husband make an insulated tray on the roof of their prefabricated tepee, and she makes her ice cream there."

Men looked at her. Her cousin said amusedly:

"That should rate some sort of technical coup feather!"

"The Council gave her a brass pot—official," said Aletha. "Domestic science achievement." To Bordman she explained: "Her husband put a tray on the roof of their house, insulated from the heat of the house below. During the day there's an insulated cover on top of it, insulating it from the heat of the sun. At night she takes off the top cover, pours her custard, thin, in the tray. Then she goes to bed. She has to get up before daybreak to scrape it up, but by then the ice cream is frozen. Even on a warm night." She looked from one to another. "I don't know why. She said it was done in a place called Babylonia on Earth, many thousands of years ago."

Bordman blinked. Then he said:

"Damn! Who knows how much the ground temperature drops here before dawn?"

"I do," said Aletha's cousin. "The top sand temperature falls forty-odd degrees. Warmer underneath, of course. But the air here is almost cool when the sun rises. Why?"

"Nights are cooler on all planets," said Bordman, "because every night the dark side radiates heat to empty space. There'd be frost everywhere every morning if the ground didn't store up heat during the day. If we prevent daytime heat storage—cover a patch of ground before dawn and leave it covered all day—and uncover it all night while shielding it from warm winds—we've got refrigeration! The night sky is empty space itself—two hundred eighty below zero!"

There was a murmur, then argument. The foremen of the Xosa II colony preparation crew were strictly practical men, but they had the habit of knowing why some things were practical. One does not do modern steel construction in contempt of theory, nor handle modern mining tools without knowing why as well as how they work. This proposal sounded like something that was based on reason—that should work to some degree. But how well? Anybody could guess that it should cool something at least twice as much as the normal night temperature drop. But somebody produced a calculator and began to juggle it. He announced his results. Others questioned, and then verified it. Nobody paid much attention to Bordman. But there was a hum of discussion, in which Redfeather and Chuka were immediately included. By calculation, it appeared that if the air on Xosa II was really as clear as the bright stars and deep day sky color indicated, every second night a total drop of one hundred eighty degrees temperature could be secured by radiation to interstellar space—if there were no convection currents, and they could be prevented by—

It was the convection current problem which broke the assembly into groups with different solutions. But it was Dr. Chuka who boomed at all of them to try all three solutions and have them ready before daybreak, so the assembly left the hulk, still disputing enthusiastically. Somebody had recalled that there were dewponds in the one arid area on Timbuk, and somebody else remembered that irrigation on Delmos III was accomplished that same way. And they recalled how it was done. . . .

Voices went away in the oven-like night outside. Bordman grimaced, and again said:

"Darn! Why didn't I think of that myself?"

"Because," said Aletha, smiling, "you aren't a Doctor of Human History with a horse-raising husband and a fondness for ice cream. Even so, a technician was needed to break down the problems here into really simple terms." Then she said, "I think Bob Running Antelope might approve of you, Mr. Bordman."

Bordman fumed to himself.

"Who's he?—Just what does that whole comment mean?"

"I'll tell you," said Aletha, "when you've solved one or two more problems."

Her cousin came back into the room. He said with gratification:

"Chuka can turn out silicone-wool insulation, he says. Plenty of material, and he'll use a solar mirror to get the heat he needs. Plenty of temperature to make silicones! How much area will we need to pull in four thousand gallons of water a night?"

"How do I know?" demanded Bordman. "What's the moisture-content of the air here, anyhow?" Then he said, "Tell me! Are you using heat exchangers to help cool the air you pump into the buildings, before you use power to refrigerate it? It would save some power—"

The Indian project engineer said:

"Let's get to work on this! I'm a steel man myself, but—"

They settled down. Aletha turned a page.

The *Warlock* spun around the planet. The members of its crew withdrew into themselves. In even two months of routine tedious voyaging to this planet there had been the beginnings of irritation with the mannerisms of other men. Now there would be years of it. Within two days of its establishment in orbit, the *Warlock* was manned by men already morbidly resentful of fate, with the psychology of prisoners doomed to close confinement for an indeterminate but ghastly period. On the third day there was a second fist fight. A bitter one.

Fist fights are not healthy symptoms in a space ship which cannot hope to make port for a matter of years.

❖   ❖   ❖

It took three weeks for the problem to be seen as the ultimately simple thing it really was. Bordman had called it a circular problem, but he hadn't seen its true circularity. It was actually—like all circular problems—inherently an unstable set of conditions. It began to fall apart simply because he saw that mere refrigeration would break its solidity.

In one week there were ten acres of desert covered with silicone-wool felt in great strips. By day a reflective surface was uppermost, and at sundown caterwheel trucks hooked on to towlines and neatly pulled it over on its back, to expose gridded black-body surfaces to the starlight. The gridding was precisely designed so that winds blowing across it did not make eddies in the grid squares. The chilled air in those pockets remained undisturbed, and there was no conduction of heat downward by eddy currents, while there was admirable radiation of heat out to space. This was in the manner of the night sides of all planets, only somewhat more efficient.

In two weeks there was a water yield of three thousand gallons per night, and in three weeks more there were similar grids over the colony houses and a vast roofed cooling shed for pre-chilling air to be used by the refrigeration systems themselves. The fuel store—stored power—was thereupon stretched to three times its former calculated usefulness. The situation was no longer a simple and neat equation of despair.

Then something else happened. One of Dr. Chuka's assistants was curious about a certain mineral. He used the solar furnace that had made the silicone wool to smelt it. And Dr. Chuka saw him. After one blank moment he bellowed laughter and went to see Ralph Redfeather. Whereupon Amerind steel workers sawed apart a robot hull that was no longer a fuel tank because its fuel was gone, and they built a demountable solar mirror some sixty feet across—which African mechanics deftly powered—and suddenly there was a spot of incandescence even brighter than the sun of Xosa II, down on the planet's surface. It played upon a mineral cliff, and monstrous smells developed and even the African mining-technicians put on goggles because of the brightness. Presently there were little rolls of molten metal and slag trickling—and separating as they trickled—hesitantly down the cliffside. Dr. Chuka beamed and slapped his sweating thighs, and Bordman went out in a caterwheel truck, wearing a heatsuit, to watch it for all of twenty minutes. When he got back to the Project Engineer's office he gulped iced salt water and dug out the books he'd brought down from the ship. There was the spec-book for Xosa II, and the other volumes of definitions issued by the Colonial Survey. They were definitions of the exact meanings of terms used in briefer specifications, for items of equipment sometimes ordered by the Colony Office.

When Chuka came into the office presently, he carried the first crude pig of Xosa II iron in his gloved hand. He gloated. Bordman was then absent, and Ralph Redfeather worked feverishly at his desk.

"Where's Bordman?" demanded Chuka in that resonant bass voice of his. "I'm ready to report for degree-of-completion credit that the mining properties on Xosa II are prepared as of today to deliver pig iron, cobalt, zirconium and beryllium in commercial quantities. We require one day's notice to begin delivery of metal other than iron at the moment, because we're short of equipment, but we can furnish chromium and manganese on two days' notice—the deposits are farther away."

He dumped the pig of metal on the second desk, where Aletha sat with her perpetual loose-leaf volumes before her. The metal smoked and began to char the desktop. He picked it up again and tossed it from one gloved hand to the other.

"There y'are, Ralph!" he boasted. "You Indians go after your coups! Match this coup for me! Without fuel and minus all equipment except of our own making— I credit an assist on the mirror, but that's all—we're set to load the first ship that comes in for cargo! Now what are you going to do for the record? I think we've wiped your eye for you!"

Ralph hardly looked up. His eyes were very bright. Bordman had shown him and he was copying figures and formulae from a section of the definition book of the Colonial Survey. The book started with the specifications for antibiotic growth equipment for colonies with problems in local bacteria. It ended with definitions of the required strength of material and the designs stipulated for cages in zoos for motile fauna, sub-divided into flying, marine, and solid ground creatures: sub-sub-divided into carnivores, herbivores, and omnivores, with the special specifications for enclosures to contain abyssal creatures requiring extreme pressures, and the equipment for maintaining a healthfully re-poisoned atmosphere for creatures from methane planets.

Redfeather had the third volume open at, *"Landing Grids, Lightest Emergency, Commerce Refuges, For Use Of."* There were some dozens of non-colonized planets along the most traveled spaceways on which refuges for shipwrecked spacemen were maintained. Small forces of Patrol personnel manned them. Space lifeboats serviced them. They had the minimum installations which could draw on their planets' ionospheres for power, and they were not expected to handle anything bigger than a twenty-ton lifeboat. But the specifications for the equipment of such refuges was included in the reference

volumes for Bordman's use in making colonial sur-
veys. They were compiled for the information of
contractors who wanted to bid on Colonial Survey
installations, and for the guidance of people like
Bordman who checked up on the work. So they
contained all the data for the building of a landing-
grid, lightest emergency, commerce-refuge type, for
use of, in case of need. Redfeather copied feverishly.

Chuka ceased his boasting, but still he grinned.

"I know we're stuck, Ralph," he said, "but it's nice
stuff to go in the records. Too bad we don't keep coup-
records like you Indians."

Aletha's cousin—Project Engineer—said crisply:

"Go away! Who made your solar mirror? It was more
than an assist! You get set to cast beams for us. Girders!
I'm going to get a lifeboat aloft and away to Trent.
Build a minimum-size landing-grid! Build a fire under
somebody so they'll send us a colony-ship with supplies. If there's no new sandstorm to bury the radiation refrigerators Bordman brought to mind, we can
keep alive with hydroponics until a ship can arrive with
something useful!"

Chuka stared.

"You don't mean we might actually live through this!
Really?"

Aletha regarded the two of them with impartial
irony.

"Dr. Chuka," she said, "you accomplished the impossible. Ralph, here, is planning to attempt the preposterous. Does it occur to you that Mr. Bordman is
nagging himself to achieve the inconceivable? It is
inconceivable, even to him, but he's trying to do it."

"What's he trying to do?" demanded Chuka, wary
but amused.

"He's trying," said Aletha, "to prove to himself that
he's the best man on this planet. Because he's physically

least capable of living here. His vanity's hurt. Don't underestimate him!"

"He the best man here?" demanded Chuka blankly. "In his way he's all right. The refrigeration proves that. But he can't walk out-of-doors without a heat-suit!"

Ralph Redfeather, without ceasing his work, said:

"Nonsense, Aletha. He has courage. I give him that. But he couldn't walk a beam twelve hundred feet up. In his own way, yes. He's capable. But the best man—"

"I'm sure," agreed Aletha, "that he couldn't sing as well as the worst of your singing crew, Dr. Chuka, and any Amerind could outrun him. Even I could. But he's got something we haven't got, just as we have qualities he hasn't. We're secure in our competences. We know what we can do, and that we can do it better than any"—her eyes twinkled—"than any pale-face. But he doubts himself. All the time and in every way. And that's why he may be the best man on this planet. I'll bet he does prove it!"

Redfeather said scornfully:

"*You* suggested radiation refrigeration! What does it prove that he applied it?"

"That," said Aletha, "he couldn't face the disaster that was here without trying to do something about it— even when it was impossible. He couldn't face the deadly facts. He had to torment himself by seeing that they wouldn't be deadly if only this or that or the other were twisted a little. His vanity was hurt because nature had beaten men. His dignity was offended. And a man with easily-hurt dignity won't ever be happy, but he can be pretty good."

Chuka raised his ebony bulk from the chair in which he still shifted the iron pig from gloved hand to gloved hand.

"You're kind," he said, chuckling. "Too kind! I don't want to hurt his feelings. I wouldn't, for the world! But really—I've never heard a man praised for his vanity before, or admired for being touchy about his dignity. If you're right—why—it's been convenient. It might even mean hope. But—hm . . . would you want to marry a man like that?"

"Great Manitou forbid!" said Aletha firmly. She grimaced at the bare idea. "I'm an Amerind. I'll want my husband to be contented. I want to be contented along with him. Mr. Bordman will never be either happy or content. No paleface husband for me! But I don't think he's through here yet. Sending for help won't satisfy him. It's a further hurt to his vanity. He'll be miserable if he doesn't prove himself—to himself— a better man than that!"

Chuka shrugged his massive shoulders. Redfeather tracked down the last item he needed and fairly bounced to his feet.

"What tonnage of iron can you get out, Chuka?" he demanded. "What can you do in the way of castings? What's the elastic modulus—how much carbon in this iron? And when can you start making castings? Big ones?"

"Let's go talk to my foremen," said Chuka. "We'll see how fast my—ah—mineral spring is trickling metal down the cliff face. If you can really launch a lifeboat, we might get some help here in a year and a half instead of five. . . ."

They went out-of-doors together. There was a small sound in the next office. Aletha was suddenly very still. She sat motionless for a long half minute. Then she turned her head.

"I owe you an apology, Mr. Bordman," she said ruefully. "It won't take back the discourtesy, but—I'm very sorry."

Bordman came into the office from the next room. He was rather pale. He said wryly:

"Eavesdroppers never hear good of themselves, eh? Actually I was on the way in here when I heard— references to myself. It would embarrass Chuka and your cousin to know I heard. So I stopped. Not to listen, but to keep them from knowing I'd heard their private opinions of me. I'll be obliged if you don't tell them. They're entitled to their opinions of me. I've mine of them." He added, "Apparently I think more highly of them than they do of me!"

"It must have sounded horrible!" Aletha said. "But they—we—all of us think better of you than you do of yourself."

Bordman shrugged.

"You in particular. Would you marry someone like me? Great Manitou, no!"

"For an excellent reason," said Aletha. "When I get back from here—*if* I get back from here—I'm going to marry Bob Running Antelope. He's nice. I like the idea of marrying him. But I look forward not only to happiness but to contentment. To me—that's important. It isn't to you, or to the woman you ought to marry. And I—well—I simply don't envy either of you a bit."

"I see!" said Bordman with irony. He didn't. "I wish you all the contentment you look for." Then he snapped: "But what's this business about expecting more from me? What spectacular idea do you expect me to pull out of somebody's hat now? Because I'm frantically vain?"

"I haven't the least idea," said Aletha. "But I think you'll come up with something we couldn't possibly imagine. And I didn't say it was because you were vain, but because you are discontented with yourself. It's born in you. And there you are!"

"If you mean neurotic," snapped Bordman, "you're all wrong. I'm not neurotic. I'm hot, and I'm annoyed. I'll get hopelessly behind schedule because of this mess. But that's all!"

Aletha stood up and shrugged her shoulders ruefully.

"I repeat my apology," she told him, "and leave you the office. But I also repeat that I think you'll turn up something nobody else expects—and I've no idea what it will be. But you'll do it now to prove that I'm wrong about how your mind works."

She went out. Bordman clamped his jaws tightly. He felt that especially haunting discomfort which comes of suspecting that one has been told something about oneself which may be true.

"Idiotic!" he fumed, all alone. "Me neurotic? Me wanting to prove I'm the best man here out of vanity?" He made a scornful noise. He sat impatiently at the desk. "Absurd!" he muttered. "Why should I need to prove to myself I'm capable? What would I do if I felt such a need, anyhow?"

Scowling, he stared at the wall. It was a nagging sort of question. What would he do if she were right? If he did need constantly to prove to himself—

He stiffened, suddenly. A look of intense surprise came upon his face. He'd thought of what a self-doubtful, discontented man would try to do, here on Xosa II at this juncture.

The surprise was because he had also thought of how it could be done.

The *Warlock* came to life. Her skipper gloomily answered the emergency call from Xosa II. In a minute he clicked off the communicator and hastened to an exterior port, deeply darkened against those times when the blue-white sun Xosa shone upon this side of the hull. He moved the manual control to make it more transparent, and stared down at the monstrous, tawny, mottled surface of the planet five thousand miles away. He searched for the spot he knew was the colony's site.

He saw what he'd been told he'd see. It was an infinitely fine, threadlike projection from the surface of the planet. It rose at a slight angle—it leaned toward the planet's west—and it expanded and widened and formed an extraordinary sort of mushroom-shaped object that was completely impossible. It could not be. Humans do not create visible objects twenty miles high, which at their tops expand like toadstools on excessively slender stalks, and which drift westward, fray, and grow thin, and are constantly renewed.

But it was true. The skipper of the *Warlock* gazed until he was completely sure. It was no atomic bomb, because it continued to exist. It faded, but was constantly replenished. There was no such thing!

He went through the ship, bellowing, and faced mutinous snarlings. But when the *Warlock* was around on that side of the planet again, the members of the crew saw the strange appearance, too. They examined it with telescopes. They grew hysterical. They went frantically to work to clear away the signs of a month and a half of mutiny and despair.

It took them three days to get the ship to tidiness again, and during all that time the peculiar tawny jet remained. On the sixth day the jet was fainter. On the seventh it was larger than before. It continued larger. And telescopes at highest magnification verified what the emergency communication had said.

Then the crew began to experience frantic impatience. It was worse, waiting those last three or four days, than even all the hopeless time before. But there was no reason to hate anybody now. The skipper was very much relieved.

✦   ✦   ✦

Eighteen hundred feet of steel grid soared overhead. It made a criss-crossed, ring-shaped wall more than a quarter mile high and almost to the top of the surrounding mountains. But the valley was not exactly a normal one. It was a crater, now: a steeply sloping, conical pit whose walls descended smoothly to the outer girders of the red painted, glistening steel structure. More girders for the completion of the grid projected from the sand just outside its circle. And in the landing-grid there was now a smaller, elaborate, truss-braced object. It rested on the rocky ground, unpainted and quite small. A hundred feet high, perhaps, and no more than three hundred across. But it was visibly a miniature of the great, newly-uncovered, repainted landing-grid which was qualified to handle inter-stellar cargo ships and all the proper space-traffic of a minerals colony planet.

A caterwheel truck came lurching and rolling and rumbling down the side of the pit. It had a sunshade and ground reflector wings, and Bordman slouched on a hobby-horse saddle in its back cargo section. He wore a heat-suit.

The truck reached the pit's bottom and bumped up to a tool-shed and stopped. Bordman got out, visibly cramped by the jolting, rocking, exhausting ride.

"Do you want to go in the shed and cool off?" asked Chuka.

"I'm all right," said Bordman. "I'm quite comfortable, so long as you feed me that expanded air." It was plain that he resented needing even a special air-supply. "What's all this about? Bringing the *Warlock* in? Why the insistence on my being here?"

"Ralph has a problem," said Chuka blandly. "He's up there—See? He needs you. There's a hoist. You've got to check degree-of-completion anyhow. You might take a look around while you're up there. But he's anxious for you to see something. There where you see the little knot of people. The platform."

Bordman grimaced. When one was well started on a survey, one got used to heights and depths and all sorts of environments. But he hadn't been up on steel work in a good many months. Not since a survey on Kalka IV nearly a year ago. He would be dizzy at first.

He accompanied Chuka to the spot where a steel cable dangled from an almost invisibly thin beam high above. There was a strictly improvised cage to ascend in—planks and a hand rail forming an insecure platform that might hold four people. He got into it, and Dr. Chuka got in beside him. Chuka waved his hand. The cage started up.

Bordman winced as the ground dropped away below. It was ghastly to be dangling in emptiness like this. He wanted to close his eyes. The cage went up and up. It took many long minutes to reach the top.

There was a newly-made platform there. The sunlight was blindingly bright, the landscape an intolerable glare. Bordman adjusted his goggles to maximum darkness and stepped gingerly from the swaying cage to the hardly more solid-seeming area. Here he was in midair on a platform barely ten feet square. It was rather more than twice the height of a metropolitan skyscraper from the ground. The mountain-crests were only half a mile away and not much higher. Bordman was acutely uncomfortable. He would get used to it, but—

"Well?" he asked. "Chuka said you needed me here. What's the matter?"

Ralph Redfeather nodded formally. Aletha was here, too, and two of Chuka's foremen—one did not look happy—and four of the Amerind steel-workers. They grinned at Bordman.

"I wanted you to see," said Aletha's cousin, "before

we threw on the current. It doesn't look like that little grid could handle the sand it took care of. But Lewanika wants to report."

A dark man who worked under Chuka—and looked as if he belonged on solid ground—said:

"We cast the beams for the small landing-grid, Mr. Bordman. We melted the metal out of the cliffs and ran it into moulds as it flowed down."

He stopped. One of the Indians said:

"We made the girders into the small landing-grid. It bothered us because we built it on the sand that had buried the big grid. We didn't understand why you ordered it there. But we built it."

The second dark man said with a trace of swagger:

"We made the coils, Mr. Bordman. We made the small grid so it would work the same as the big one when it was finished. And then we made the big grid work, finished or not!

Bordman said impatiently: "All right. Very good. But what is this? A ceremony?"

"Just so," said Aletha, smiling. "Be patient, Mr. Bordman!"

Her cousin said:

"We built the small grid on the top of the sand. And it tapped the ionosphere for power. No lack of power then! And we'd set it to heave up sand instead of ships. Not to heave it out into space, but to give it up to a mile a second vertical velocity. Then we turned it on."

"And we rode it down, that little grid," said one of the remaining Indians, grinning. "What a party! Manitou!"

Redfeather frowned at him and took up the narrative.

"It hurled the sand up from its center, as you said it would. The sand swept air with it. It made a whirlwind, bringing more sand from outside the grid into its field. It was a whirlwind with fifteen mega-kilowatts of power to drive it. Some of the sand went twenty miles high. Then it made a mushroom head and the winds up yonder blew it to the west. It came down a long way off, Mr. Bordman. We've made a new dune area ten miles downwind. And the little grid sank as the sand went away from around it. We had to stop it three times, because it leaned. We had to dig under parts of it to get it straight up again. But it went down into the valley."

Bordman turned up the power to his heat-suit motors. He felt uncomfortably warm.

"In six days," said Ralph, almost ceremonially, "it had uncovered half the original grid we'd built. Then we were able to modify that to heave sand and to let it tap the ionosphere. We were able to use a good many times the power the little grid could apply to sand lifting. In two days more the landing-grid was clear. The valley bottom was clean. We shifted some hundreds of millions of tons of sand by landing-grid, and now it is possible to land the *Warlock*, and receive her supplies. The solar-power furnace is already turning out pigs for her loading. We wanted you to see what we have done. The colony is no longer in danger, and we shall have the grid completely finished for your inspection before the ship is ready to return."

Bordman said uncomfortably:

"That's very good. It's excellent. I'll put it in my survey report."

"But," said Ralph, more ceremonially still, "we have the right to count coup for the members of our tribe and clan. Now—"

Then there was confusion. Aletha's cousin was saying syllables that did not mean anything at all. The other Indians joined in at intervals, speaking gibberish.

Aletha's eyes were shining and she looked pleased and satisfied.

"What—what's this?" demanded Bordman when they stopped.

Aletha spoke proudly.

"Ralph just formally adopted you into the tribe, Mr. Bordman—and into his clan and mine! He gave you a name I'll have to write down for you, but it means, 'Man-who-believes-not-his-own-wisdom.' And now—"

Ralph Redfeather, licensed interstellar engineer, graduate of the stiffest technical university in this quarter of the galaxy, wearer of three eagle-pinion feathers and clad in a pair of insulated sandals and a breechclout—Ralph Redfeather whipped out a small paint-pot and a brush from somewhere and began carefully to paint on a section of girder ready for the next tier of steel. He painted a feather on the metal.

"It's a coup," he told Bordman over his shoulder. "Your coup. Placed where it was earned—up here. Aletha is authorized to certify it. And the head of the clan will add an eagle feather to the headdress he wears in Council in the Big Tepee on Algonka, and—your clan-brothers will be proud."

Then he straightened up and held out his hand.

Chuka said benignly:

"Being civilized men, Mr. Bordman, we Africans do not go in for uncivilized feathers. But we—ah—rather approve of you too. And we plan a corroboree at the colony after the *Warlock* is down, when there will be some excellently practiced singing. There is—ah—a song, a sort of choral calypso, about this adventure you have brought to so satisfying a conclusion. It is quite a good calypso. It's likely to be popular on a good many planets."

Bordman swallowed. He felt that he ought to say something, and he did not know what.

But just then there was a deep-toned humming in the air. It was a vibrant tone, resounding with limitless power. It was the eighteen-hundred-foot landing-grid, giving off that profoundly bass and vibrant note it uttered while operating. Bordman looked up.

The *Warlock* was coming down.

After Bordman made his report he found that the newest graduates of Space Survey training had been swallowed up by the needs of the service, and he was apparently needed as badly as before. But he protested vigorously, and went back to Lani III and enjoyed the society of Riki and his children for a full year and a half.

Then three Senior Officers died within one year, and the Survey's facilities were stretched to the breaking-point. Population-pressure required the opening of colonies. The safety of thousands and millions of human lives depended on the Survey's work. Worlds which had been biologically surveyed had also to be checked to make sure they were equipped to sustain the populations waiting impatiently to swarm upon them.

Reluctantly, to meet the emergency, Bordman agreed to return to the Service for one year only.

But he'd served seven, with only two brief visits to his children and his wife, when he was promised that after the checking of a single robot colony on Loren Two, his resignation would be accepted.

So he boarded a Crete Line Ship for his last active assignment in the Colonial Survey. . . .

COMBAT TEAM

The nearer moon went by overhead. It was jagged and irregular in shape, probably a captured asteroid. Huyghens had seen it often enough, so he did not go out of his quarters to watch it hurtle across the sky with seemingly the speed of an atmosphere-flier, occulting the stars as it went. Instead, he sweated over paperwork, which should have been odd because he was technically a felon and all his labors on Loren II felonious. It was odd, too, for a man to do paperwork in a room with steel shutters and a huge bald eagle—untethered—dozing on a three-inch perch set in the wall. But paperwork was not Huyghens' real task. His only assistant had tangled with a night-walker, and the furtive Kodius Company ships had taken him away to where Kodius Company ships came from. Huyghens had to do two men's work in loneliness. To his knowledge, he was the only man in this solar system.

Below him, there were snufflings. Sitka Pete got up heavily and padded to his water pan. He lapped the refrigerated water and sneezed. Sourdough Charley waked and complained in a rumbling growl. There were divers other rumblings and mutterings below. Huyghens called reassuringly, "Easy there!" and went on with his work. He finished a climate report, and fed figures to a computer. While it hummed over them he entered the inventory totals in the station log, showing what supplies remained. Then he began to write up the log proper.

"Sitka Peter," he wrote, "has apparently solved the problem of killing individual sphexes. He has learned that it doesn't do to hug them and that his claws can't penetrate their hide, not the top-hide, anyhow. Today Semper notified us that a pack of sphexes had found the scent-trail to the station. Sitka hid downwind until they arrived. Then he charged from the rear and brought his paws together on both sides of a sphex's head in a terrific pair of slaps. It must have been like two twelve-inch shells arriving from opposite directions at the same time. It must have scrambled the sphex's brains as if they were eggs. It dropped dead. He killed two more with such mighty pairs of wallops. Sourdough Charley watched, grunting, and when the sphexes turned on Sitka, he charged in his turn. I, of course, couldn't shoot too close to him, so he might have fared badly except that Faro Nell came pouring out of the bear-quarters to help. The diversion enabled Sitka Pete to resume the use of his new technique, towering on his hind legs and swinging his paws in the new and grizzly fashion. The fight ended promptly. Semper flew and screamed above the scrap, but as usual did not join in. Note: Nugget, the cub, tried to mix in but his mother cuffed him out of the way. Sourdough and Sitka ignored him as usual. Kodius Champion's genes are sound!"

The noises of the night went on outside. There were notes like organ-tones—song-lizards. There were the tittering, giggling cries of night-walkers. There were sounds like jack-hammers, and doors closing, and from every direction came noises like hiccoughs in various keys. These were made by the improbable small creatures which on Loren II took the place of insects.

Huyghens wrote out:

"Sitka seemed ruffled when the fight was over. He used his trick on the head of every dead or wounded sphex, except those he'd killed with it, lifting up their heads for his pile-driver-like blows from two directions at once, as if to show Sourdough how it was done. There was much grunting as they hauled the carcasses to the incinerator. It almost seemed—"

The arrival-bell clanged, and Huyghens jerked up his head to stare at it. Semper, the eagle, opened icy eyes. He blinked. Noises. There was a long, deep, contented snore from below. Something shrieked, out in the jungle. Hiccoughs, clatterings, and organ-notes. . . .

The bell clanged again. It was a notice that an unscheduled ship aloft somewhere had picked up the beacon-beam—which only Kodius Company ships should know about—and was communicating for a landing. But there shouldn't be any ships in this solar system just now! The Kodius Company's colony was completely illegal, and there were few graver crimes than unauthorized occupation of a new planet.

The bell clanged a third time. Huyghens swore. His hand went out to cut off the beacon, and then stopped. That would be useless. Radar would have fixed it and tied it in with physical features like the nearby sea and the Sere Plateau. The ship could find the place, anyhow, and descend by daylight.

"The devil!" said Huyghens. But he waited yet again for the bell to ring. A Kodius Company ship would double-ring to reassure him. But there shouldn't be a Kodius Company ship for months.

The bell clanged singly. The space-phone dial flickered and a voice came out of it, tinny from stratospheric distortion: *"Calling ground. Calling ground. Crete Line ship* Odysseus *calling ground on Loren II. Landing one passenger by boat. Put on your field lights."*

Huyghens' mouth dropped open. A Kodius Company ship would be welcome. A Colonial Survey ship would be extremely unwelcome, because it would destroy the colony and Sitka and Sourdough and Faro Nell and Nugget—and Semper—and carry Huyghens off to be tried for unauthorized colonization and all that it implied.

But a commercial ship, landing one passenger by boat . . . There were simply no circumstances under which that could happen. Not to an unknown, illegal colony. Not to a furtive station!

Huyghens flicked on the landing-field lights. He saw the glare over the field half a mile away. Then he stood up and prepared to take the measures required by discovery. He packed the paperwork he'd been doing into the disposal-safe. He gathered up all personal documents and tossed them in. Every record, every bit of evidence that the Kodius Company maintained this station went into the safe. He slammed the door. He moved his finger toward the disposal-button, which would destroy the contents and melt down even the ashes past their possible use for evidence in court.

Then he hesitated. If it were a Survey ship, the button had to be pressed and he must resign himself to a long term in prison. But a Crete Line ship—if the space-phone told the truth—was not threatening. It was simply unbelievable.

He shook his head. He got into travel garb, armed himself, and went down into the bear-quarters, turning on lights as he went. There were startled snufflings, and Sitka Pete reared himself to a sitting position to blink at him. Sourdough Charley lay on his back with his legs in the air. He'd found it cooler, sleeping that way. He rolled over with a thump, and made snorting sounds which somehow sounded cordial. Faro Nell padded to the door of her separate apartment, assigned her so that Nugget would not be underfoot to irritate the big males.

Huyghens, as the human population of Loren II, faced the work-force, fighting-force, and—with Nugget—four-fifths of the terrestrial non-human population of the planet. They were mutated Kodiak bears, descendants of that Kodius Champion for whom the Kodius Company was named. Sitka Pete was a good twenty-two hundred pounds of lumbering, intelligent carnivore, Sourdough Charley would weigh within a hundred pounds of that figure. Faro Nell was eighteen hundred pounds of female charm and ferocity. Then Nugget poked his muzzle around his mother's furry rump to see what was toward, and he was six hundred pounds of ursine infancy. The animals looked at Huyghens expectantly. If he'd had Semper riding on his shoulder they'd have known what was expected of them.

"Let's go," said Huyghens. "It's dark outside, but somebody's coming. And it may be bad!"

He unfastened the outer door of the bear-quarters. Sitka Pete went charging clumsily through it. A forthright charge was the best way to develop any situation—if one was an oversize male Kodiak bear. Sourdough went lumbering after him. There was nothing hostile immediately outside. Sitka stood up on his hind legs—he reared up a solid twelve feet—and sniffed the air. Sourdough methodically lumbered to one side and then the other, sniffing in his turn. Nell came out, nine-tenths of a ton of daintiness, and rumbled admonitorily at Nugget, who trailed her closely. Huyghens stood in the doorway, his night-sighted gun ready. He felt uncomfortable at sending the bears ahead into a Loren II jungle at night, but they were qualified to scent danger, and he was not.

The illumination of the jungle in a wide path toward the landing-field made for weirdness in the look of things. There were arching giant ferns and columnar trees which grew above them, and the extraordinary lanceolate underbrush of the jungle. The flood-lamps, set level with the ground, lighted everything from below. The foliage, then, was brightly lit against the black night-sky, brightly enough lit to dim the stars.

"On ahead!" commanded Huyghens, waving. "Hup!"

He swung the bear-quarters door shut, and moved toward the landing-field through the lane of lighted forest. The two giant male Kodiaks lumbered ahead. Sitka Pete dropped to all fours and prowled. Sourdough Charley followed closely, swinging from side to side. Huyghens came behind the two of them, and Faro Nell brought up the rear with Nugget nudging her.

It was an excellent military formation for progress through dangerous jungle. Sourdough and Sitka were advance guard and point, respectively, while Faro Nell guarded the rear. With Nugget to look after, she was especially alert against attack from behind. Huyghens was, of course, the striking force. His gun fired explosive bullets which would discourage even sphexes, and his night-sight—a cone of light which went on when he took up the trigger-slack—told exactly where they would strike. It was not a sportsmanlike weapon, but the creatures of Loren II were not sportsmanlike antagonists. The night-walkers, for example. But night-walkers feared light. They attacked only in a species of hysteria if it were too bright.

Huyghens moved toward the glare at the landing

field. His mental state was savage. The Kodius Company on Loren II was completely illegal. It happened to be necessary, from one point of view, but it was still illegal. The tinny voice on the space-phone was not convincing, in ignoring that illegality. But if a ship landed, Huyghens could get back to the station before men could follow, and he'd have the disposal-safe turned on in time to protect those who'd sent him here.

Then he heard the far-away and high harsh roar of a landing boat rocket—not a ship's bellowing tubes— as he made his way through the unreal-seeming brush. The roar grew louder as he pushed on, the three big Kodiaks padding here and there, sniffing for danger.

He reached the edge of the landing field, and it was blindingly bright, with the customary divergent beams slanting skyward so a ship could check its instrument-landing by sight. Landing fields like this had been standard, once upon a time. Nowadays all developed planets had landing-grids—monstrous structures which drew upon ionospheres for power and lifted and drew down star-ships with remarkable gentleness and unlimited force. This sort of landing field would now be found only where a survey-team was at work, or where some strictly temporary investigation of ecology or bacteriology was under way, or where a newly authorized colony had not yet been able to build its landing-grid. Of course, it was unthinkable that anybody would attempt a settlement in defiance of the law!

Already, as Huyghens reached the edge of the scorched open space, the night-creatures had rushed to the light, like moths on Earth. The air was misty with crazily gyrating, tiny flying things. They were innumerable and of every possible form and size, from the white midges of the night and multi-winged flying worms to those revoltingly naked-looking larger creatures which might have passed for plucked flying monkeys if they had not been carnivorous and worse. The flying things soared and whirred and danced and spun insanely in the glare, making peculiarly plaintive humming noises. They almost formed a lamp-lit ceiling over the cleared space, and actually did hide the stars. Staring upward, Huyghens could just barely make out the blue-white flame of the space-boat's rockets through the fog of wings and bodies.

The rocket-flame grew steadily in size. Once it tilted to adjust the boat's descending course. It went back to normal. A speck of incandescence at first, it grew until it was like a great star, then a more-than-brilliant moon, and then it was a pitiless glaring eye. Huyghens averted his gaze from it. Sitka Pete sat lumpily and blinked at the dark jungle away from the light. Sourdough ignored the deepening, increasing rocket-roar. He sniffed the air. Faro Nell held Nugget firmly under one huge paw and licked his head as if tidying him up to be seen by company. Nugget wriggled.

The roar became that of ten thousand thunders. A warm breeze blew outward from the landing field. The rocket-boat hurtled downward, and as its flame touched the mist of flying things, they shriveled and burned. Then there were churning clouds of dust everywhere, and the center of the field blazed terribly—and something slid down a shaft of fire—squeezed it flat, and sat on it—and the flame went out. The rocket-boat sat there, resting on its tail-fins, pointing toward the stars from which it came.

There was a terrible silence after the tumult. Then, very faintly, the noises of the night came again. There were sounds like those of organ-pipes, and very faint and apologetic noises like hiccoughs. All these sounds increased, and suddenly Huyghens could hear quite normally. As he watched, a side-port opened with a clattering, something unfolded from where it had been inset into the hull of the space-boat, and there was a metal passageway across the flame-heated space on which the boat stood.

A man came out of the port. He reached back in and shook hands. Then he climbed down the ladder-rungs to the walkway, and marched above the steam-ing baked area, carrying a traveling bag. At the end of the walk he stepped to the ground, and moved hastily to the edge of the clearing. He waved to the space-boat. The walk-way folded briskly back up to the hull and vanished in it, and almost at once a flame exploded into being under the tail-fins. There were fresh clouds of monstrous, choking dust, a brightness like that of a sun, and noise past the possibility of endurance. Then the light rose swiftly through the dust-cloud, sprang higher, and climbed more swiftly still. When Huyghens' ears again permitted him to hear anything, there was only a diminishing mutter in the heavens and a faint bright speck of light ascending to the sky, swinging eastward as it rose to intercept the ship from which it had descended.

The night-noises of the jungle went on, even though there was a spot of incandescence in the day-bright clearing, and steam rolled up in clouds at the edge of the hottest area. Beyond that edge, a man with a trav-eling bag in his hand looked about him.

Huyghens advanced toward him as the incandes-cence dimmed. Sourdough and Sitka preceded him. Faro Nell trailed faithfully, keeping a maternal eye on her offspring. The man in the clearing stared at the parade they made. It would be upsetting, even after preparation, to land at night on a strange planet, to have the ship's boat and all links with the rest of the cosmos depart, and then to find oneself approached—it might seem stalked—by two colossal male Kodiak bears, with a third bear and a cub behind them. A single human figure in such company might seem irrelevant.

The new arrival gazed blankly. He moved back a few steps. Then Huyghens called:

"Hello, there! Don't worry about the bears! They're friends!"

Sitka reached the newcomer. He went warily downwind from him and sniffed. The smell was satisfactory. Man-smell. Sitka sat down with the solid impact of more than a ton of bear meat landing on packed dirt, and regarded the man. Sourdough said *"Whoosh!"* and went on to sample the air beyond the clearing. Huyghens approached. The newcomer wore the uniform of the Colonial Survey. That was bad. It bore the insignia of a senior officer. Worse.

"Hah!" said the just-landed man. "Where are the robots? What in all the nineteen hells are these creatures? Why did you shift your station? I'm Bordman, here to make a progress report on your colony."

Huyghens said:

"What colony?"

"Loren II Robot Installation—" Then Bordman said indignantly, "Don't tell me that that idiot skipper can have dropped me at the wrong place! This is Loren II, isn't it? And this is the landing field. But where are your robots? You should have the beginning of a grid up! What the devil's happened here and what are these beasts?"

Huyghens grimaced.

"This," he said, "is an illegal, unlicensed settlement. I'm a criminal. These beasts are my confederates. If you don't want to associate with criminals you needn't, of course, but I doubt if you'll live till morning unless you accept my hospitality while I think over what to do about your landing. In reason, I ought to shoot you."

Faro Nell came to a halt behind Huyghens, which was her proper post in all out-door movement. Nugget, however, saw a new human. Nugget was a cub, and therefore friendly. He ambled forward. He wriggled bashfully as he approached Bordman. He sneezed, because he was embarrassed.

His mother overtook him and cuffed him to one side. He wailed. The wail of a six-hundred-pound Kodiak bear-cub is a remarkable sound. Bordman gave ground a pace.

"I think," he said carefully, "that we'd better talk things over. But if this is an illegal colony, of course you're under arrest and anything you say will be used against you."

Huyghens grimaced again.

"Right," he said. "But now if you'll walk close to me, we'll head back to the station. I'd have Sourdough carry your bag—he likes to carry things—but he may need his teeth. We've half a mile to travel." He turned to the animals. "Let's go!" he said commandingly. "Back to the station! Hup!"

Grunting, Sitka Peter arose and took up his duties as advanced point of a combat-team. Sourdough trailed, swinging widely to one side and another. Huyghens and Bordman moved together. Faro Nell and Nugget brought up the rear.

There was only one incident on the way back. It was a nightwalker, made hysterical by the lane of light. It poured through the underbrush, uttering cries like maniacal laughter.

Sourdough brought it down, a good ten yards from Huyghens. When it was all over, Nugget bristled up to the dead creature, uttering cub-growls. He feigned to attack it.

His mother whacked him soundly.

❖   ❖   ❖

There were comfortable, settling-down noises below, as the bears grunted and rumbled, and ultimately were still. The glare from the landing field was gone. The lighted lane through the jungle was dark again. Huyghens ushered the man from the space-boat up into his living quarters. There was a rustling stir, and Semper took his head from under his wing. He stared coldly at the two humans, spread monstrous, seven-foot wings, and fluttered them. He opened his beak and closed it with a snap.

"That's Semper," said Huyghens. "Semper Tyrannis. He's the rest of the terrestrial population here. Not being a fly-by-night sort of creature, he didn't come out to welcome you."

Bordman blinked at the huge bird, perched on a three-inch-thick perch set in the wall.

"An eagle?" he demanded. "Kodiak bears—mutated ones, but still bears—and now an eagle? You've a very nice fighting unit in the bears—"

"They're pack animals too," said Huyghens. "They can carry some hundreds of pounds without losing too much combat efficiency. And there's no problem of supply. They live off the jungle. Not sphexes, though. Nothing will eat a sphex."

He brought out glasses and a bottle and indicated a chair. Bordman put down his traveling bag, took a glass, and sat down.

"I'm curious," he observed. "Why Semper Tyrannis? I can understand Sitka Pete and Sourdough Charley as fighters. But why Semper?"

"He was bred for hawking," said Huyghens. "You sic a dog on something. You sic Semper Tyrannis. He's too big to ride on a hawking-glove, so the shoulders of my coats are padded to let him ride there. He's a flying scout. I've trained him to notify us of sphexes, and in flight he carries a tiny television camera. He's useful, but he hasn't the brains of the bears." Bordman sat down and sipped at his glass.

"Interesting, very interesting! Didn't you say something about shooting me?"

"I'm trying to think of a way out," Huyghens said. "Add up all the penalties for illegal colonization and I'd be in a very bad fix if you got away and reported this set-up. Shooting you would be logical."

"I see that," said Bordman reasonably. "But since the point has come up—I have a blaster trained on you from my pocket."

Huyghens shrugged.

"It's rather likely that my human confederates will be back here before your friends. You'd be in a very tight fix if my friends came back and found you more or less sitting on my corpse."

Bordman nodded.

"That's true, too. Also it's probable that your fellow-terrestrials wouldn't cooperate with me as they have with you. You seem to have the whip hand, even with my blaster trained on you. On the other hand, you could have killed me easily after the boat left, when I'd first landed. I'd have been quite unsuspicious. Therefore you may not really intend to murder me."

Huyghens shrugged again.

"So," said Bordman, "since the secret of getting along with people is that of postponing quarrels, suppose we postpone the question of who kills whom? Frankly, I'm going to send you to prison if I can. Unlawful colonization is very bad business. But I suppose you feel that you have to do something permanent about me. In your place I probably should, too. Shall we declare a truce?"

Huyghens indicated indifference.

"Then I do," Bordman said. "I have to! So—"

He pulled his hand out of his pocket and put a pocket blaster on the table. He leaned back.

"Keep it," said Huyghens. "Loren II isn't a place where you live long unarmed." He turned to a cupboard. "Hungry?"

"I could eat," admitted Bordman.

Huyghens pulled out two meal-packs from the cupboard and inserted them in the readier below. He set out plates.

"Now, what happened to the official, licensed, authorized colony here?" asked Bordman briskly. "License issued eighteen months ago. There was a landing of colonists with a drone-fleet of equipment and supplies. There've been four ship-contacts since. There should be several thousand robots being industrious under adequate human supervision. There should be a hundred-mile-square clearing, planted with food-plants for later human arrivals. There should be a landing-grid at least half-finished. Obviously there should be a space-beacon to guide ships to a landing. There isn't. There's no clearing visible from space. That Crete Line ship has been in orbit for three days, trying to find a place to drop me. Her skipper was fuming. Your beacon is the only one on the planet, and we found it by accident. What happened?"

Huyghens served the food. He said dryly:

"There could be a hundred colonies on this planet without any one knowing of any other. I can only guess about your robots, but I suspect they ran into sphexes."

Bordman paused, with his fork in his hand.

"I read up on this planet, since I was to report on its colony. A sphex is part of the inimical animal life here. Cold-blooded belligerent carnivore, not a lizard but a genus all its own. Hunts in packs. Seven to eight hundred pounds, when adult. Lethally dangerous and

simply too numerous to fight. They're why no license
was ever granted to human colonists. Only robots could
work here, because they're machines. What animal
attacks machines?"

Huyghens said:

"What machine attacks animals? The sphexes
wouldn't bother robots, of course, but would robots
bother the sphexes?" Bordman chewed and swallowed.

"Hold it! I'll agree that you can't make a hunting-
robot. A machine can discriminate, but it can't
decide. That's why there's no danger of a robot
revolt. They can't decide to do something for which
they have no instructions. But this colony was
planned with full knowledge of what robots can and
can't do. As ground was cleared, it was enclosed in
an electrified fence which no sphex could touch
without frying."

Huyghens thoughtfully cut his food. After a moment:

"The landing was in the winter time," he observed.
"It must have been, because the colony survived a
while. And at a guess, the last ship-landing was before
thaw. The years are eighteen months long here, you
know."

"It was in winter that the landing was made,"
Bordman admitted. "And the last ship-landing was before spring. The idea was to get mines in operation for
material, and to have ground cleared and enclosed—in
sphex-proof fence before the sphexes came back from
the tropics. They winter there, I understand."

"Did you ever see a sphex?" asked Huyghens. Then
he said, "No, of course not. But if you took a spitting
cobra and crossed it with a wild-cat, painted it tan-and-
blue and then gave it hydrophobia and homicidal mania
at once, you might have one sphex. But not the race
of sphexes. They can climb trees, by the way. A fence
wouldn't stop them."

"An electrified fence," said Bordman. "Nothing could climb that!"

"Not one animal," Huyghens told him. "But sphexes are a race. The smell of one dead sphex brings others running with blood in their eyes. Leave a dead sphex alone for six hours and you've got them around by dozens. Two days and there are hundreds. Longer, and you've got thousands of them! They gather to caterwaul over their dead pal and hunt for whoever or whatever killed him."

He returned to his meal. A moment later he said:

"No need to wonder what happened to your colony. During the winter the robots burned out a clearing and put up an electrified fence according to the book. Come spring, the sphexes come back. They're curious, among their other madnesses. A sphex would try to climb the fence just to see what was behind it. He'd be electrocuted. His carcass would bring others, raging because a sphex was dead. Some of them would try to climb the fence, and die. And their corpses would bring others. Presently the fence would break down from the bodies hanging on it, or a bridge of dead beasts' carcasses would be built across it—and from as far downwind as the scent carried there'd be loping, raging, scent-crazed sphexes racing to the spot. They'd pour into the clearing through or over the fence, squalling and screeching for something to kill. I think they'd find it."

Bordman ceased to eat. He looked sick.

"There were pictures of sphexes in the data I read. I suppose that would account for—everything."

He tried to lift his fork. He put it down again. "I can't eat," he said abruptly.

Huyghens made no comment. He finished his own meal, scowling. He rose and put the plates into the top of the cleaner. "Let me see those reports, eh?" he asked dourly. "I'd like to see what sort of a set-up they had, those robots."

Bordman hesitated and then opened his traveling bag. There was a microviewer and records. One entire record was labeled "Specifications for Construction, Colonial Survey," which would contain detailed plans and all requirements of material and workmanship for everything from desks, office, administrative personnel, for use of, to landing-grids, heavy-gravity planets, lift-capacity 100,000 earth-tons. But Huyghens found another. He inserted it and spun the control swiftly here and there, pausing only briefly at index-frames until he came to the section he wanted. He began to study the information with growing impatience.

"Robots, robots, robots!" he snapped. "Why don't they leave them where they belong—in cities to do the dirty work, and on airless planets where nothing unexpected ever happens? Robots don't belong in new colonies. Your colonists depended on them for defense. Dammit, let a man work with robots long enough and he thinks all nature is as limited as they are. This is a plan to set up a controlled environment—on Loren II! Controlled environment—" He swore. "Complacent, idiotic, desk-bound half-wits!"

"Robots are all right," said Bordman. "We couldn't run civilization without them."

"But you can't tame a wilderness with 'em," snapped Huyghens. "You had a dozen men landed, with fifty assembled robots to start with. There were parts for fifteen hundred more, and I'll bet anything I've got the ship-contacts landed more still."

"They did," admitted Bordman.

"I despise 'em," growled Huyghens. "I feel about 'em the way the old Greeks felt about slaves. They're for menial work—the sort of work a man will perform for himself, but that he won't do for another man for pay. Degrading work!"

"Quite aristocratic," said Bordman with a touch of irony. "I take it that robots clean out the bear-quarters downstairs."

"No!" snapped Huyghens. "I do. They're my friends. They fight for me. No robot would do the job right."

He growled, again. The noises of the night went on outside. Organ-tones and hiccoughings and the sound of tack-hammers and slamming doors. Somewhere there was a singularly exact replica of the discordant squeakings of a rusty pump.

"I'm looking," said Huyghens at the microviewer, "for the record of their mining operations. An open-pit operation would not mean a thing. But if they had driven a tunnel, and somebody was there supervising the robots when the colony was wiped out, there's an off-chance he survived a while."

Bordman regarded him with suddenly intent eyes. "And—"

"Dammit," snapped Bordman, "if so I'll go see! He'd—they'd have no chance at all, otherwise. Not that the chance is good in any case."

Bordman raised his eyebrows.

"I've told you I'll send you to prison if I can," he said. "You've risked the lives of millions of people, maintaining non-quarantined communication with an unlicensed planet. If you did rescue somebody from the ruins of the robot colony—does it occur to you that they'd be witnesses to your unauthorized presence here?"

Huyghens spun the viewer again. He stopped, switched back and forth, and found what he wanted. He muttered in satisfaction: "They *did* run a tunnel." Aloud he said, "I'll worry about witnesses when I have to."

He pushed aside another cupboard door. Inside it were the odds and ends a man makes use of to repair the things about his house that he never notices until they go wrong. There was an assortment of wires, transistors, bolts, and similar stray items.

"What now?" asked Bordman mildly.

"I'm going to try to find out if there's anybody left alive over there. I'd have checked before if I'd known the colony existed. I can't prove they're all dead, but I may prove that somebody's still alive. It's barely two weeks' journey away from here. Odd that two colonies picked spots so near!"

He picked over the oddments he'd selected:

"Confound it!" Bordman said. "How can you check if somebody's alive some hundreds of miles away?"

Huyghens threw a switch and took down a wall-panel, exposing electronic apparatus and circuits behind. He busied himself with it.

"Ever think about hunting for a castaway?" he asked over his shoulder. "Here's a planet with some tens of millions of square miles on it. You know there's a ship down. You've no idea where. You assume the survivors have power—no civilized man will be without power very long, so long as he can smelt metals—but making a space-beacon calls for high-precision measurements and workmanship. It's not to be improvised. So what will your shipwrecked civilized man do, to guide a rescue-ship to the one or two square miles he occupies among some tens of millions on the planet?"

"What?"

"He's had to go primitive, to begin with," Huyghens explained. "He cooks his meat over a fire, and so on. He has to make a strictly primitive signal. It's all he can do without gauges and micrometers and special tools. But he can fill all the planet's atmosphere with a signal that searchers for him can't miss. You see?"

Bordman thought irritably. He shook his head.

"He'll make," said Huyghens, "a spark transmitter. He'll fix its output at the shortest frequency he can contrive, somewhere in the five-to-fifty-meter waveband, but it will tune very broad—and it will be a plainly human signal. He'll start it broadcasting. Some of those frequencies will go all around the planet under the ionosphere. Any ship that comes in under the radio roof will pick up his signal, get a fix on it, move and get another fix, and then go straight to where the castaway is waiting placidly in a hand-braided hammock, sipping whatever sort of drink he's improvised out of the local vegetation."

Bordman said grudgingly:

"Now that you mention it, of course. . . ."

"My space-phone picks up microwaves," said Huyghens. "I'm shifting a few elements to make it listen for longer stuff. It won't be efficient, but it will catch a distress-signal if one's in the air. I don't expect it, though."

He worked. Bordman sat still a long time, watching him.

Down below, a rhythmic sort of sound arose. It was Sourdough Charley, snoring.

Sitka Pete grunted in his sleep. He was dreaming. In the general room of the station Semper blinked his eyes rapidly and then tucked his head under a gigantic wing and went to sleep. The noises of the Loren II jungle came through the steel-shuttered windows. The nearer moon—which had passed overhead not long before the ringing of the arrival-bell—again came soaring over the eastern horizon. It sped across the sky.

Inside the station, Bordman said angrily:

"See here, Huyghens! You've reason to kill me. Apparently you don't intend to. You've excellent reason to leave that robot colony strictly alone. But you're preparing to help, if there's anybody alive to need it. And yet you're a criminal, and I mean a criminal! There've been some ghastly bacteria exported from planets like Loren II. There've been plenty of lives lost in consequence, and you're risking more. Why the hell do you do it? Why do you do something that could produce monstrous results—to other human beings?"

Huyghens grunted.

"You're assuming there are no sanitary and quarantine precautions taken by my partners. As a matter of fact, there are. They're taken, all right! As for the rest, you wouldn't understand."

"I don't understand," snapped Bordman, "but that's no proof I can't! —Why are you a criminal?"

Huyghens painstakingly used a screwdriver inside the wall-panel. He lifted out a small electronic assembly, and began to fit in a spaghettied new assembly with larger units.

"I'm cutting my amplification here to hell-and-gone," he observed, "but I think it'll do. . . . I'm doing what I'm doing," he added calmly, "because it seems to me it fits what I think I am. Everybody acts according to his own real notion of himself. You're a conscientious citizen, a loyal official, a well-adjusted personality. You act that way. You consider yourself an intelligent rational animal. But you don't act that way! You're reminding me of my need to shoot you or something similar, which a merely rational animal would try to make me forget. You happen, Bordman, to be a man. So am I. But I'm aware of it. Therefore I deliberately do things a merely rational animal wouldn't, because they're my notion of what a man who's more than a rational animal should do."

He tightened one small screw after another.

Bordman said:

"Oh. Religion."

"Self-respect," corrected Huyghens. "I don't like robots. They're too much like rational animals. A robot will do whatever it can that its supervisor requires it to do. A merely rational animal will do whatever circumstances require it to do. I wouldn't like a robot unless it had some idea of what was fitting and would spit in my eye if I tried to make it do something else. The bears downstairs, now. . . . They're no robots! They are loyal and honorable beasts, but they'd turn and tear me to bits if I tried to make them do something against their nature. Faro Nell would fight me and all creation together, if we tried to harm Nugget. It would be unintelligent and unreasonable and irrational. She'd lose out and get killed. But I like her that way! And I'll fight you and all creation when you make me try to do something against my nature. I'll be stupid and unreasonable and irrational about it." Then he grinned over his shoulder. "So will you. Only you don't realize it."

He turned back to his task. After a moment he fitted a manual-control knob over a shaft in his haywire assembly. "What did somebody try to make you do?" asked Bordman shrewdly. "What was demanded of you that turned you into a criminal? What are you in revolt against?"

Huyghens threw a switch. He began to turn the knob which controlled his makeshift receiver.

"Why," he said, "when I was young the people around me tried to make me into a conscientious citizen and a loyal employee and a well-adjusted personality. They tried to make me into a highly intelligent rational animal and nothing more. The difference between us, Bordman, is that I found it out. Naturally, I rev—"

He stopped short. Faint, crackling, frying sounds came from the speaker of the space-phone now

modified to receive what once were called short
waves.

Huyghens listened. He cocked his head intently. He
turned the knob very, very slowly. Bordman made an
arrested gesture, to call attention to something in the
sibilant sound. Huyghens nodded. He turned the knob
again, with infinitesimal increments.

Out of the background noise came a patterned mutter. As Huyghens shifted the tuning, it grew louder.
It reached a volume where it was unmistakable. It was
a sequence of sounds like a discordant buzzing. There
were three half-second buzzings with half-second
pauses between. A two-second pause. Three full-second
buzzings with half-second pauses between. Another
two-second pause and three half-second buzzings, again.
Then silence for five seconds. Then the pattern
repeated.

"The devil!" said Huyghens. "That's a human signal! Mechanically made, too. In fact, it used to be
a standard distress call. It was termed an SOS,
though I've no idea what that meant. Anyhow, somebody must have read old-fashioned novels some time,
to know about it. And so someone is still alive over
at your licensed but now smashed-up robot colony.
And they're asking for help. I'd say they're likely to
need it."

He looked at Bordman.

"The intelligent thing to do is sit back and wait for
a ship, either my friends' or yours. A ship can help
survivors or castaways much better than we can. It
could even find them more easily. But maybe time is
important to the poor devils. So I'm going to take the
bears and see if I can reach him. You can wait here,
if you like. What say?"

Bordman snapped angrily:

"Don't be a fool! Of course I'm coming! What do

you take me for? And two of us should have four times
the chance of one!"

Huyghens grinned.

"Not quite. You forget Sitka Pete and Sourdough
Charley and Faro Nell. There'll be five of us if you
come, instead of four. And, of course, Nugget has to
come—and he'll be no help—but Semper may make
up for him. You won't quadruple our chances,
Bordman, but I'll be glad to have you if you want to
be stupid and unreasonable and not at all rational, and
come with me."

There was a jagged spur of stone looming precipi-
tously over a river-valley. A thousand feet below, a
broad stream ran westward to the sea. Twenty miles
to the east, a wall of mountains rose sheer against the
sky, its peaks seeming to blend to a remarkable even-
ness of height. Rolling, tumbled ground lay between
for as far as the eye could see.

A speck in the sky came swiftly downward. Great
pinions spread and flapped, and icy eyes surveyed the
rocky space. With more great flappings, Semper the
eagle came to ground. He folded his huge wings and
turned his head jerkily, his eyes unblinking. A tiny
harness held a miniature camera against his chest. He
strutted over the bare stone to the highest point and
stood there, a lonely and arrogant figure in the vastness.

Crashings and rustlings, and snuffling sounds, and
Sitka Pete came lumbering out into the clear space.
He wore a harness too, and a pack. The harness was
complex, because it had to hold a pack not only in
normal travel, but when he stood on his hind legs, and
it must not hamper the use of his forepaws in combat.

He went cagily all over the open area. He peered

over the edge of the spur's farthest tip, and prowled to the other side and looked down. Once he moved close to Semper and the eagle opened his great curved beak and uttered an indignant noise. Sitka paid no attention.

He relaxed, satisfied. He sat down untidily, his hind legs sprawling. He wore an air approaching benevolence as he surveyed the landscape about and below him.

More snufflings and crashings. Sourdough Charley came into view with Huyghens and Bordman behind him. Sourdough carried a pack, too. Then there was a squealing and Nugget scurried up from the rear, impelled by a whack from his mother. Faro Nell appeared, with the carcass of a stag-like animal lashed to her harness.

"I picked this place from a space-photo," said Huyghens, "to make a directional fix from you. I'll get set up."

He swung his pack from his shoulders to the ground, and extracted an obviously self-constructed device which he set on the ground. It had a whip aerial, which he extended. Then he plugged in a considerable length of flexible wire and unfolded a tiny, improvised directional aerial with an even tinier booster at its base. Bordman slipped his pack from his shoulders and watched. Huyghens put a pair of head-phones over his ears. He looked up and said sharply:

"Watch the bears, Bordman. The wind's blowing up the way we came. Anything that trails us will send its scent on before. The bears will tell us."

He busied himself with the instruments he'd brought. He heard the hissing, frying, background noise which could be anything at all except a human signal. He reached out and swung the small aerial around. Rasping, buzzing tones came in, faintly and then loudly.

This receiver, though, had been made for this particular wave-band. It was much more efficient than the modified space-phone had been. It picked up three short buzzes, three long ones, and three short ones again. Three dots, three dashes, and three dots. Over and over again. SOS. SOS. SOS.

Huyghens took a reading and moved the directional aerial a carefully measured distance. He took another reading, shifted it yet again and again, carefully marking and measuring each spot and taking notes of the instrument readings. When he finished, he had checked the direction of the signal not only by loudness but by phase, and had as accurate a fix as could possibly be made with portable apparatus.

Sourdough growled softly. Sitka Pete whiffed the air and arose from his sitting position. Faro Nell whacked Nugget, sending him whimpering to the farthest corner of the flat place. She stood bristling, facing downhill the way they'd come.

"Damn!" said Huyghens.

He got up and waved his arm at Semper, who had turned his head at the stirrings. Semper squawked and dived off the spur, and was immediately fighting the down-draught beyond it. As Huyghens readied his weapon, the eagle came back overhead. He went magnificently past, a hundred feet high, careening and flapping in the tricky currents. He screamed, abruptly, and screamed again. Huyghens swung a tiny vision-plate from its strap to where he could look into it. He saw, of course, what the tiny camera on Semper's chest could see—reeling, swaying terrain as Semper saw it, though of course without his breadth of field. There were moving objects to be seen through the shifting trees. Their coloring was unmistakable.

"Sphexes," said Huyghens dourly. "Eight of them. Don't look for them to follow our track, Bordman. They

run parallel to a trail on either side. That way they
attack in breadth and all at once when they catch up.
And listen! The bears can handle anything they tangle
with—it's our job to pick off the loose ones. And aim
for the body! The bullets explode."

He threw off the safety of his weapon. Faro Nell,
uttering thunderous growls, went padding to a place
between Sitka Pete and Sourdough. Sitka glanced at
her and made a whuffing noise, as if derisive of her
bloodcurdling sounds. Sourdough grunted. He and Sitka
moved farther away from Nell to either side. They
would cover a wider front.

There was no other sign of life than the shrillings
of the incredibly tiny creatures which on this planet
were birds, and Faro Nell's deep-bass, raging growls,
and then the click of Bordman's safety going off as he
got ready to use the weapon Huyghens had given him.

Semper screamed again, flapping low above the tree-
tops, following parti-colored, monstrous shapes beneath.

Eight blue-and-tan fiends came racing out of the
underbrush. They had spiny fringes, and horns, and
glaring eyes, and they looked as if they had come
straight out of hell. On the instant of their appearance
they leaped, emitting squalling, spitting squeals that
were like the cries of fighting tom-cats ten thousand
times magnified. Huyghens' rifle cracked, and its sound
was wiped out in the louder detonation of its bullet
in sphexian flesh. A tan-and-blue monster tumbled over,
shrieking. Faro Nell charged, the very impersonation
of white-hot fury. Bordman fired, and his bullet
exploded against a tree. Sitka Pete brought his massive forepaws in a clapping, monstrous ear-boxing
motion. A sphex died.

Then Bordman fired again. Sourdough Charley
whuffed. He fell forward upon a spitting bi-colored
fiend, rolled him over, and raked with his hind-claws.

The belly-hide of the sphex was tenderer than the rest. The creature rolled away, snapping at its own wounds. Another sphex found itself shaken loose from the tumult about Sitka Pete. It whirled to leap on him from behind, and Huyghens fired. Two plunged upon Faro Nell, and Bordman blasted one and Faro Nell disposed of the other in awesome fury. Then Sitka Pete heaved himself erect—seeming to drip sphexes—and Sourdough waddled over and pulled one off and killed it and went back for 4another. . . . Then both rifles cracked together and there was suddenly nothing left to fight.

The bears prowled from one to another of the corpses. Sitka Pete rumbled and lifted up a limp head. Crash! Then another. He went over the lot, whether or not they showed signs of life. When he had finished, they were wholly still.

Semper came flapping down out of the sky. He had screamed and fluttered overhead as the fight went on. Now he landed with a rush. Huyghens went soothingly from one bear to another, calming them with his voice. It took longest to calm Faro Nell, licking Nugget with impassioned solicitude and growling horribly as she licked.

"Come along, now," said Huyghens, when Sitka showed signs of intending to sit down again. "Heave these carcasses over a cliff. Come along! Sitka! Sourdough! Hup!"

He guided them as the two big males somewhat fastidiously lifted up the nightmarish creatures and carried them to the edge of the spur of stone. They let the beasts go bouncing and sliding down into the valley.

"That," said Huyghens, "is so their little pals will gather round them and caterwaul their woe where there's no trail of ours to give them ideas. If we'd been

near a river I'd have dumped them in to float downstream and gather mourners wherever they stranded.
Around the station I incinerate them. If I had to leave
them, I'd make tracks away. About fifty miles upwind
would be a good idea."

He opened the pack Sourdough carried and
extracted giant-sized swabs and some gallons of antiseptic. He tended the three Kodiaks in turn, swabbing
not only the cuts and scratches they'd received, but
deeply soaking their fur where there could be suspicion of spilled sphex-blood.

"This antiseptic deodorizes, too," he told Bordman.
"Or we'd be trailed by any sphex who passed to leeward of us. When we start off, I'll swab the bears' paws
for the same reason."

Bordman was very quiet. He'd missed his first shot,
but, the last few seconds of the fight he'd fired very
deliberately and every bullet hit. Now he said bitterly:

"If you're instructing me so I can carry on should
you be killed, I doubt that it's worth while!"

Huyghens felt in his pack and unfolded the enlarge-
ments he'd made of the space-photos of this part of
the planet. He carefully oriented the map with distant
landmarks, and drew a line across the photo.

"The SOS signal comes from somewhere close to
the robot colony," he reported. "I think a little to the
south of it. Probably from a mine they'd opened up,
on the far side of the Sere Plateau. See how I've
marked this map? Two fixes, one from the station and
one from here. I came away off-course to get a fix here
so we'd have two position-lines to the transmitter. The
signal could have come from the other side of the
planet. But it doesn't."

"The odds would be astronomical against other
castaways," protested Bordman.

"No," said Huyghens. "Ships have been coming here.

To the robot-colony. One could have crashed. And I have friends, too." He repacked his apparatus and gestured to the bears. He led them beyond the scene of combat and carefully swabbed off their paws, so they could not possibly leave a train of sphex-blood scent behind them. He waved Semper, the eagle, aloft.

"Let's go," he told the Kodiaks. "Yonder! Hup!"

The party headed downhill and into the jungle again. Now it was Sourdough's turn to take the lead, and Sitka Pete prowled more widely behind him. Faro Nell trailed the men, with Nugget. She kept a sharp eye upon the cub. He was a baby, still; he only weighed six hundred pounds. And of course she watched against danger from the rear.

Overhead, Semper fluttered and flew in giant circles and spirals, never going very far away. Huyghens referred constantly to the screen which showed what the air-borne camera saw. The image tilted and circled and banked and swayed. It was by no means the best air-reconnaissance that could be imagined, but it was the best that would work. Presently Huyghens said:

"We swing to the right, here. The going's bad straight ahead, and it looks like a pack of sphexes has killed and is feeding."

Bordman said:

"It's against reason for carnivores to be as thick as you say! There has to be a certain amount of other animal life for every meat-eating beast. Too many of them would eat all the game and starve."

"They're gone all winter," explained Huyghens, "which around here isn't as severe as you might think. And a good many animals seem to breed just after the sphexes go south. Also, the sphexes aren't around all the warm weather. There's a sort of peak, and then for a matter of weeks you won't see one of them, and suddenly the jungle swarms with them again. Then, presently, they head south. Apparently they're migratory in some fashion, but nobody knows." He said dryly: "There haven't been many naturalists around on this planet. The animal life's inimical."

Bordman fretted. He was accustomed to arrival at a partly or completely finished colonial set-up, and to pass upon the completion or non-completion of the installation as designed. Now he was in an intolerably hostile environment, depending upon an illegal colonist for his life, engaged upon a demoralizingly indefinite enterprise—because the mechanical spark-signal could be working long after its constructors were dead—and his ideas about a number of matters were shaken. He was alive, for example, because of three giant Kodiak bears and a bald eagle. He and Huyghens could have been surrounded by ten thousand robots, and they'd have been killed. Sphexes and robots would have ignored each other, and sphexes would have made straight for the men, who'd have had less than four seconds in which to discover for themselves that they were attacked, prepare to defend themselves, and kill the eight sphexes.

He found Nugget, the cub, ambling uneasily in his wake. The cub flattened his ears miserably when Bordman glanced at him. It occurred to the man that Nugget was receiving a lot of disciplinary thumpings from Faro Nell. He was knocked about psychologically. His lack of information and unfitness for independent survival in this environment was being hammered into him.

"Hi, Nugget," said Bordman ruefully. "I feel just about the way you do!"

Nugget brightened visibly. He frisked. He tended to gambol. He looked hopefully up into Bordman's face.

The man reached out and patted Nugget's head. It was the first time in all his life that he'd ever petted an animal.

He heard a snuffling sound behind him. Skin crawled at the back of his neck. He whirled.

Faro Nell regarded him—eighteen hundred pounds of she-bear only ten feet away and looking into his eyes. For one panicky instant Bordman went cold all over. Then he realized that Faro Nell's eyes were not burning. She was not snarling, nor did she emit those blood-curdling sounds which the bare prospect of danger to Nugget had produced up on the rocky spur. She looked at him blandly. In fact, after a moment she swung off on some independent investigation of a matter that had aroused her curiosity.

The traveling-party went on, Nugget frisking beside Bordman and tending to bump into him out of pure cub-clumsiness. Now and again he looked adoringly at Bordman, in the instant and overwhelming affection of the very young.

Bordman trudged on. Presently he glanced behind again. Faro Nell was now ranging more widely. She was well satisfied to have Nugget in the immediate care of a man. From time to time he got on her nerves.

A little while later, Bordman called ahead.

"Huyghens! Look here! I've been appointed nurse-maid to Nugget!"

Huyghens looked back.

"Oh, slap him a few times and he'll go back to his mother."

"The devil I will!" said Bordman querulously. "I like it!"

The traveling-party went on.

When night fell, they camped. There could be no fire, of course, because all the minute night-things about would come to dance in the glow. But there could not be darkness, equally, because night-walkers hunted in the dark. So Huyghens set out barrier-lamps which made a wall of twilight about their halting-place,

and the stag-like creature Faro Nell had carried became
their evening meal. Then they slept—at least the men
did—and the bears dozed and snorted and waked and
dozed again. Semper sat immobile with his head under
his wing on a tree-limb. Presently there was a glori-
ous cool hush and all the world glowed in morning-
light diffused through the jungle by a newly risen sun.
Then they arose and pushed on.

This day they stopped stock-still for two hours while
sphexes puzzled over the trail the bears had left.
Huyghens discoursed on the need of an anti-scent, to
be used on the boots of men and the paws of bears,
which would make the following of their trails unpopular with sphexes. Bordman seized upon the idea and
suggested that a sphex-repellant odor might be worked
out, which would make a human revolting to a sphex.
If that were done, humans could go freely about,
unmolested.

"Like stink-bugs," said Huyghens, sardonically. "A
very intelligent idea! Very rational! You can feel proud!"

And suddenly Bordman was not proud of the idea
at all. They camped again. On the third night they were
at the base of that remarkable formation, the Sere
Plateau, which from a distance looked like a mountain
range but was actually a desert table-land. It was not
reasonable for a desert to be raised high, while lowlands had rain, but on the fourth morning they found
out why. They saw, far, far away, a truly monstrous
mountain-mass at the end of the long expanse of the
plateau. It was like the prow of a ship. It lay, so
Huyghens observed, directly in line with the prevail-
ing winds, and divided them as a ship's prow divides
the waters. The moisture-bearing air-currents flowed
beside the plateau, not over it, and its interior was
desert in the unscreened sunshine of the high altitudes.

It took them a full day to get half-way up the slope.

And here, twice, as they climbed, Semper flew screaming over aggregations of sphexes to one side of them
or the other. These were much larger groups than
Huyghens had ever seen before, fifty to a hundred
monstrosities together, where a dozen was a large
hunting-pack elsewhere. He looked in the screen which
showed him what Semper saw, four to five miles away.
The sphexes padded uphill toward the Sere Plateau in
a long line. Fifty—sixty—seventy tan-and-azure beasts
out of hell.

"I'd hate to have that bunch jump us," he said
candidly to Bordman. "I don't think we'd stand a
chance."

"Here's where a robot tank would be useful,"
Bordman observed.

"Anything armored," conceded Huyghens. " 'One
man in an armored station like mine would be safe.
But if he killed a sphex he'd be besieged. He'd have
to stay holed up, breathing the smell of dead sphex,
until the odor'd gone away. And he mustn't kill any
others or he'd be besieged until winter came."

Bordman did not suggest the advantages of robots
in other directions. At that moment, for example, they
were working their way up a slope which averaged fifty
degrees. The bears climbed without effort despite their
burdens. For the men it was infinite toil. Semper, the
eagle, manifested impatience with bears and men alike,
who crawled so slowly up an incline over which he
soared.

He went ahead up the mountainside and teetered
in the air currents at the plateau's edge. Huyghens
looked in the vision-plate by which he reported.

"How the devil," panted Bordman, panting—they
had stopped for a breather, and the bears waited
patiently for them—"how do you train bears like these?
I can understand Semper."

"I don't train them," said Huyghens, staring into the plate. "They're mutations. In heredity the sex-linkage of physical characteristics is standard stuff. There's also been some sound work done on the gene-linkage of psychological factors. There was need, on my home planet, for an animal who could fight like a fiend, live off the land, carry a pack and get along with men at least as well as dogs do. In the old days they'd have tried to breed the desired physical properties in an animal who already had the personality they wanted. Something like a giant dog, say. But back home they went at it the other way about. They picked the wanted physical characteristics and bred for the personality, the psychology. The job got done over a century ago. The Kodiak bear named Kodius Champion was the first real success. He had everything that was wanted. These bears are his descendants."

"They look normal," commented Bordman.

"They are!" said Huyghens warmly. "Just as normal as an honest dog. They're not trained, like Semper. They train themselves." He looked back into the plate in his hands, which showed the ground six or seven thousand feet higher. "Semper, now, is a trained bird without too much brain. He's educated—a glorified hawk. But the bears want to get along with men. They're emotionally dependent on us. Like dogs. Semper's a servant, but they're companions and friends. He's trained, but they're loyal. He's conditioned. They love us. He'd abandon me if he ever realized he could; he thinks he can only eat what men feed him. But the bears wouldn't want to. They like us. I admit I like them. Maybe because they like me."

Bordman said deliberately:

"Aren't you a trifle loose-tongued, Huyghens? You've told me something that will locate and convict the people who set you up here. It shouldn't be hard to find where bears were bred for psychological mutations, and where a bear named Kodius Champion left descendants. I can find out where you came from now, Huyghens!"

Huyghens looked up from the plate with its tiny swaying television image.

"No harm done," he said amiably. "I'm a criminal there, too. It's officially on record that I kidnapped these bears and escaped with them. Which, on my home planet, is about as heinous a crime as a man can commit. It's worse than horse-theft back on Earth in the old days. The kin and cousins of my bears are highly thought of. I'm quite a criminal, back home." Bordman stared.

"Did you steal them?" he demanded.

"Confidentially," said Huyghens, "no. But prove it!" Then he said: "Take a look in this plate. See what Semper can see up at the plateau's edge."

Bordman squinted aloft, where the eagle flew in great sweeps and dashes. Somehow, by the experience of the past few days, Bordman knew that Semper was screaming fiercely as he flew. He made a dart toward the plateau's border.

Bordman looked at the transmitted picture. It was only four inches by six, but it was perfectly without grain and accurate in color. It moved and turned as the camera-bearing eagle swooped and circled. For an instant the screen showed the steeply sloping mountainside, and off at one edge the party of men and bears could be seen as dots. Then it swept away and showed the top of the plateau.

There were sphexes. A pack of two hundred trotted toward the desert interior. They moved at leisure, in the open. The viewing camera reeled, and there were more. As Bordman watched and as the bird flew higher, he could see still other sphexes moving up over the edge

of the plateau from a small erosion-defile here and
another one there. The Sere Plateau was alive with the
hellish creatures. It was inconceivable that there should
be game enough for them to live on. They were visible
as herds of cattle would be visible on grazing planets.

It was simply impossible.

"Migrating," observed Huyghens. "I said they did.
They're headed somewhere. Do you know, I doubt that
it would be healthy for us to try to cross the Plateau
through such a swarm of sphexes!"

Bordman swore, in abrupt change of mood.

"But the signal's still coming through. Somebody's
alive over at the robot colony. Must we wait till the
migration's over?"

"We don't know," Huyghens pointed out, "that they'll
stay alive. They may need help badly. We have to get
to them. But at the same time—"

He glanced at Sourdough Charley and Sitka Pete,
clinging patiently to the mountainside while the men
rested and talked. Sitka had managed to find a place
to sit down, one massive paw anchoring him in place.

Huyghens waved his arm, pointing in a new direction. "Let's go!" he called briskly. "Let's go! Yonder!
Hup!"

They followed the slopes of the Sere Plateau, neither ascending to its level top—where spheres
congregated—nor descending into the foothills where
spheres assembled. They moved along hillsides and
mountain-flanks which sloped anywhere from thirty to
sixty degrees, and they did not cover much territory.
They practically forgot what it was to walk on level
ground.

At the end of the sixth day, they camped on the top
of a massive boulder which projected from a moun-
tainous stony wall. There was barely room on the
boulder for all the party. Faro Nell fussily insisted that

Nugget should be in the safest part, which meant near
the mountain-flank. She would have crowded the men
outward, but Nugget whimpered for Bordman. Wherefore, when Bordman moved to comfort him, Faro Neil
drew back and snorted at Sitka and Sourdough and they
made room for her near the edge.

It was a hungry camp. They had come upon tiny rills
upon occasion, flowing down the mountainside. Here
the bears had drunk deeply and the men had filled
canteens. But this was the third night on the
mountainside, and there had been no game at all.
Huyghens made no move to bring out food for
Bordman or himself. Bordman made no comment. He
was beginning to participate in the relationship between
bears and men, which was not the slavery of the bears
but something more. It was two-way. He felt it.

"You'd think," he said, "that since the sphexes don't
seem to hunt on their way uphill, there should be some
game. They ignore everything as they file up."

This was true enough. The normal fighting formation of sphexes was line abreast, which automatically
surrounded anything which offered to flee and out-
flanked anything which offered fight. But here they
ascended the mountain in long files, one after the other,
apparently following long-established trails. The wind
blew along the slopes and carried scent sidewise. But
the sphexes were not diverted from their chosen paths.
The long processions of hideous blue-and-tawny
creatures—it was hard to think of them as natural
beasts, male and female and laying eggs like reptiles
on other planets—the long processions simply climbed.

"There've been other thousands of beasts before
them," said Huyghens. "They must have been crowding this way for days or even weeks. We've seen tens
of thousands in Semper's camera. They must be
uncountable, altogether. The first-comers ate all the

game there was, and the last-comers have something
else on whatever they use for minds."

Bordman protested:

"But so many carnivores in one place is impossible!
I know they are here, but they can't be!"

"They're cold-blooded," Huyghens pointed out.
"They don't burn food to sustain body-temperature.
After all, lots of creatures go for long periods without eating. Even bears hibernate. But this isn't
hibernation—or estivation, either."

He was setting up the radiation-wave receiver in the
darkness. There was no point in attempting a fix here.
The transmitter was on the other side of the sphex-
crowded Sere Plateau. The men and bears would
commit suicide by crossing here.

Even so, Huyghens turned on the receiver. There
came the whispering, scratchy sound of background-
noise, and then the signal. Three dots, three dashes,
three dots. Huyghens turned it off. Bordman said:

"Shouldn't we have answered that signal before we
left the station? To encourage them?"

"I doubt they have a receiver," said Huyghens. "They
won't expect an answer for months, anyhow. They'd
hardly listen all the time, and if they're living in a mine-
tunnel and trying to sneak out for food to stretch their
supplies, they'll be too busy to try to make complicated
recorders or relays."

Bordman was silent for a moment or two.

"We've got to get food for the bears," he said presently. "Nugget's weaned, and he's hungry."

"We will," Huyghens promised. "I may be wrong,
but it seems to me that the number of sphexes climbing
the mountain is less than yesterday and the day before.
We may have just about crossed the path of their
migration. They're thinning out. When we're past their
trail, we'll have to look out for nightwalkers and the

like again. But I think they wiped out all animal life on their migration-route."

He was not quite right. He was waked in darkness by the sound of slappings and the grunting of bears. Feather-light puffs of breeze beat upon his face. He struck his belt-lamp sharply and the world was hidden by a whitish film which snatched itself away. Something flapped. Then he saw the stars and the emptiness on the edge of which they camped. Then big white things flapped toward him.

Sitka Pete whuffed mightily and swatted. Faro Nell grunted and swung. She caught something in her claws.

"Watch this!" said Huyghens.

More things strangely-shaped and pallid like human skin reeled and flapped crazily toward him.

A huge hairy paw reached up into the light-beam and snatched a flying thing out of it. Another great paw. The three great Kodiaks were on their hind legs, swatting at creatures which flittered insanely, unable to resist the fascination of the glaring lamp. Because of their wild gyrations it was impossible to see them in detail, but they were those unpleasant night-creatures which looked like plucked flying monkeys but were actually something quite different.

The bears did not snarl or snap. They swatted, with a remarkable air of business-like competence and purpose. Small mounds of broken things built up about their feet.

Suddenly there were no more. Huyghens snapped off the light. The bears crunched and fed busily in the darkness.

"Those things are carnivores *and* blood-suckers, Bordman," said Huyghens calmly. "They drain their victims of blood like vampire-bats—they've some trick of not waking them—and when they're dead the whole tribe eats. But bears have thick fur, and they wake when they're touched. And they're omnivorous. They'll eat anything but sphexes, and like it. You might say that those night-creatures came to lunch. They are it, for the bears, who are living off the country as usual."

Bordman uttered a sudden exclamation. He made a tiny light, and blood flowed down his hand. Huyghens passed over his pocket kit of antiseptic and bandages. Bordman stanched the bleeding and bound up his hand. Then he realized that Nugget chewed on something. When he turned the light, Nugget swallowed convulsively. It appeared that he had caught and devoured the creature which had drawn blood from Bordman. But he'd lost none to speak of, at that.

In the morning they started along the sloping scarp of the plateau once more. After marching silently for awhile, Bordman said:

"Robots wouldn't have handled those vampire-things, Huyghens."

"Oh, they could be built to watch for them," said Huyghens, tolerantly. "But you'd have to swat for yourself. I prefer the bears."

He led the way on. Twice Huyghens halted to examine the ground about the mountains' bases through binoculars. He looked encouraged as they went on. The monstrous peak which was like the bow of a ship at the end of the Sere Plateau was visibly nearer. Toward midday, indeed, it loomed high above the horizon, no more than fifteen miles away. And at midday Huyghens called a final halt.

"No more congregations of sphexes down below," he said cheerfully, "and we haven't seen a climbing line of them in miles." The crossing of a sphex-trail had meant simply waiting until one party had passed; and then crossing before another came in view. "I've a hunch we've left their migration route behind. Let's see what Semper tells us!"

He waved the eagle aloft. Like all creatures other than men, the bird normally functioned only for the satisfaction of his appetite, and then tended to loaf or sleep. He had ridden the last few miles perched on Sitka Pete's pack. Now he soared upward and Huyghens watched in the small vision-plate.

Semper went soaring. The image on the plate swayed and turned, and in minutes was above the plateau's edge. Here there were some patches of brush and the ground rolled a little. But as Semper towered higher still, the inner desert appeared. Nearby, it was clear of beasts. Only once, when the eagle banked sharply and the camera looked along the long dimension of the plateau, did Huyghens see any sign of the blue-and-tan beasts. There he saw what looked like masses amounting to herds. Incredible, of course; carnivores do not gather in herds.

"We go straight up," said Huyghens in satisfaction. "We cross the Plateau here, and we can edge downwind a bit, even. I think we'll find something interesting on our way to your robot colony."

He waved to the bears to go ahead uphill.

They reached the top hours later, barely before sunset. And they saw game. Not much, but game at the grassy, brushy border of the desert. Huyghens brought down a shaggy ruminant which surely would not live on a desert. When night fell there was an abrupt chill in the air. It was much colder than night temperatures on the slopes. The air was thin. Bordman thought and presently guessed at the cause. In the lee of the prow-mountain the air was calm. There were no clouds. The ground radiated its heat to empty space. It could be bitterly cold in the night-time, here.

"And hot by day," Huyghens agreed when he mentioned it. "The sunshine's terrifically hot where the air is thin, but on most mountains there's wind. By day,

here, the ground will tend to heat up like the surface
of a planet without atmosphere. It may be a hundred
and forty or fifty degrees on the sand at midday. But
it should be cold at night."

It was. Before midnight Huyghens built a fire. There
could be no danger of night-walkers where the temperature dropped to freezing.

In the morning the men were stiff with cold, but the
bears snorted and moved about briskly. They seemed
to revel in the morning chill. Sitka and Sourdough
Charley, in fact, became festive and engaged in a mock
fight, whacking each other with blows that were only
feigned, but would have crushed the skull of any man.
Nugget sneezed with excitement as he watched them.
Faro Nell regarded them with female disapproval.

They started on. Semper seemed sluggish. After a
single brief flight he descended and rode on Sitka's
pack, as on the previous day. He perched there, sur-
veying the landscape as it changed from semi-arid to
pure desert in their progress. He would not fly. Soaring
birds do not like to fly when there are no winds to
make currents of which they can take advantage.

Once Huyghens stopped and pointed out to
Bordman exactly where they were on the enlarged
photograph taken from space, and the exact spot from
which the distress-signal seemed to come.

"You're doing it in case something happens to you,"
said Bordman. "I admit it's sense, but—what could I
do to help those survivors even if I got to them, without
you?"

"What you've learned about sphexes would help,"
said Huyghens. "The bears would help. And we left
a note back at my station. Whoever grounds at the
landing field back there—and the beacon's working—
will find instructions to come to the place we're trying to reach."

They started walking again. The narrow patch of non-desert border of the Sere Plateau was behind them, now, and they marched across powdery desert sand.

"See here," said Bordman. "I want to know something. You tell me you're listed as a bear-thief on your home planet. You tell me it's a lie, to protect your friends from prosecution by the Colonial Survey. You're on your own, risking your life every minute of every day. You took a risk in not shooting me. Now you're risking more in going to help men who'd have to be witnesses that you were a criminal. What are you doing it for?" Huyghens grinned.

"Because I don't like robots. I don't like the fact that they're subduing men, making men subordinate to them."

"Go on," insisted Bordman. "I don't see why disliking robots should make you a criminal! Nor men subordinating themselves to robots, either."

"But they are," said Huyghens mildly. "I'm a crank, of course. But—I live like a man on this planet. I go where I please and do what I please. My helpers are my friends. If the robot colony had been a success, would the humans in it have lived like men? Hardly. They'd have to live the way robots let them! They'd have to stay inside a fence the robots built. They'd have to eat foods that robots could raise, and no others. Why, a man couldn't move his bed near a window, because if he did the house-tending robots couldn't work! Robots would serve them—the way the robots determined—but all they'd get out of it would be jobs servicing the robots!"

Bordman shook his head.

"As long as men want robot service, they have to take the service that robots can give. If you don't want those services—"

"I want to decide what I want," said Huyghens, again mildly, "instead of being limited to choose what I'm offered. In my home planet we half-way tamed it with dogs and guns. Then we developed the bears, and we finished the job with them. Now there's population-pressure and the room for bears and dogs—and men!—is dwindling. More and more people are being deprived of the power of decision, and being allowed only the power of choice among the things robots allow. The more we depend on robots, the more limited those choices become. We don't want our children to limit themselves to wanting what robots can provide! We don't want them shriveling to where they abandon everything robots can't give, or won't. We want them to be men and women. Not damned automatons who live by pushing robot-controls so they can live to push robot-controls. If that's not subordination to robots—"

"It's an emotional argument," protested Bordman. "Not everybody feels that way."

"But I feel that way," said Huyghens. "And so do a lot of others. This is a damned big galaxy and it's apt to contain some surprises. The one sure thing about a robot and a man who depends on them is that they can't handle the unexpected. There's going to come a time when we need men who can. So on my home planet, some of us asked for Loren II, to colonize. It was refused—too dangerous. But men can colonize anywhere if they're men. So I came here to study the planet. Especially the sphexes. Eventually, we expected to ask for a license again, with proof that we could handle even those beasts. I'm already doing it in a mild way. But the Survey licensed a robot colony—and where is it?"

Bordman made a sour face.

"You took the wrong way to go about it, Huyghens.

It was illegal. It is. It was the pioneer spirit, which is admirable enough, but wrongly directed. After all, it was pioneers who left Earth for the stars. But—"

Sourdough raised up on his hind-legs and sniffed the air. Huyghens swung his rifle around to be handy. Bordman slipped off the safety-catch of his own. Nothing happened.

"In a way," said Bordman, "you're talking about liberty and freedom, which most people think is politics. You say it can be more. In principle, I'll concede it. But the way you put it, it sounds like a freak religion."

"It's self-respect," corrected Huyghens. "You may be—"

Faro Nell growled. She bumped Nugget with her nose, to drive him closer to Bordman. She snorted at him, and trotted swiftly to where Sitka and Sourdough faced toward the broader, sphex-filled expanse of the Sere Plateau. She took up her position between them.

Huyghens gazed sharply beyond them and then all about. "This could be bad!" he said softly. "But luckily there's no wind. Here's a sort of hill. Come along, Bordman!"

He ran ahead, Bordman following and Nugget plumping heavily with him. They reached the raised place, actually a mere hillock no more than five or six feet above the surrounding sand, with a distorted cactus-like growth protruding from the ground. Huyghens stared again. He used his binoculars.

"One sphex," he said curtly. "Just one! And it's out of all reason for a sphex to be alone. But it's not rational for them to gather in hundreds of thousands, either!" He whetted his finger and held it up. "No wind at all."

He used the binoculars again.

"It doesn't know we're here," he added. "It's

moving away. Not another one in sight. . . ." He hesitated, biting his lip. "Look here, Bordman! I'd like
to kill that one lone sphex and find out something.
There's a fifty per cent chance I could find out something really important. But—I might have to run. If
I'm right . . ." Then he said grimly, "It'll have to be
done quickly. I'm going to ride Faro Nell, for speed.
I doubt Sitka or Sourdough will stay behind. But
Nugget can't run fast enough. Will you stay here with
him?"

Bordman drew in his breath. Then he said calmly:
"You know what you're doing, I hope."

"Keep your eyes open. If you see anything, even at
a distance, shoot and we'll be back, fast! Don't wait
until something's close enough to hit. Shoot the instant
you see anything, if you do!"

Bordman nodded. He found it peculiarly difficult to
speak again. Huyghens went over to the embattled
bears and climbed up on Faro Nell's back, holding fast
by her shaggy fur.

"Let's go!" he snapped. "That way! Hup!"

The three Kodiaks plunged away at a dead run,
Huyghens lurching and swaying on Faro Nell's back.
The sudden rush dislodged Semper from his perch. He
flapped wildly and got aloft. Then he followed
effortfully, flying low.

It happened very quickly. A Kodiak bear can travel
as fast as a race-horse on occasion. These three plunged
arrow-straight for a spot perhaps half a mile distant,
where a blue-and-tawny shape whirled to face them.
There was the crash of Huyghens' weapon from where
he rode on Faro Nell's back; the explosion of the
weapon and the bullet was one sound. The monster
leaped and died.

Huyghens jumped down from Faro Nell. He became
feverishly busy at something on the ground. Semper

banked and whirled and landed. He watched, with his
head on one side.

Bordman stared. Huyghens was doing something to
the dead sphex. The two male bears prowled about,
while Faro Nell regarded Huyghens with intense curiosity. Back at the hillock, Nugget whimpered a little,
and Bordman patted him. Nugget whimpered more
loudly. In the distance, Huyghens straightened up and
mounted Faro Nell's back. Sitka looked back toward
Bordman. He reared upward. He made a noise,
apparently, because Sourdough ambled to his side. The
two great beasts began to trot back. Semper flapped
wildly and—lacking wind—lurched crazily in the air.
He landed on Huyghens' shoulder and clung there with
his talons.

Then Nugget howled hysterically and tried to swarm
up Bordman, as a cub tries to swarm up the nearest
tree in time of danger. Bordman collapsed, and the cub
upon him—and there was a flash of stinking scaly hide,
while the air was filled with the snarling, spitting
squeals of a sphex in full leap. The beast had over-
jumped, aiming at Bordman and the cub while both
were upright and arriving when they had fallen. It went
tumbling.

Bordman heard nothing but the fiendish squalling,
but in the distance Sitka and Sourdough were coming at rocket-ship speed. Faro Nell let out a roar that
fairly split the air. And then there was a furry streaking toward her, bawling, while Bordman rolled to his
feet and snatched up his gun. He raged through pure
instinct. The sphex crouched to pursue the cub and
Bordman swung his weapon as a club. He was literally too close to shoot—and perhaps the sphex had only
seen the fleeing bear-cub. But he swung furiously.

And the sphex whirled. Bordman was toppled from
his feet. An eight-hundred-pound monstrosity straight

out of hell—half wildcat and half spitting cobra with hydrophobia and homicidal mania added—such a monstrosity is not to be withstood when in whirling its body strikes one in the chest.

That was when Sitka arrived, bellowing. He stood on his hind legs, emitting roars like thunder, challenging the sphex to battle. He waddled forward. Huyghens approached, but he could not shoot with Bordman in the sphere of an explosive bullet's destructiveness. Faro Nell raged and snarled, torn between the urge to be sure that Nugget was unharmed, and the frenzied fury of a mother whose offspring has been endangered.

Mounted on Faro Nell, with Semper clinging idiotically to his shoulder, Huyghens watched helplessly as the sphex spat and squalled at Sitka, having only to reach out one claw to let out Bordman's life.

They got away from there, though Sitka seemed to want to lift the limp carcass of his victim in his teeth and dash it repeatedly to the ground. He seemed doubly raging because a man—with whom all Kodius Champion's descendants had an emotional relationship—had been mishandled. But Bordman was not grievously hurt. He bounced and swore as the bears raced for the horizon. Huyghens had flung him up on Sourdough's pack and snapped for him to hold on. He shouted:

"Damn it, Huyghens! This isn't right! Sitka got some deep scratches! That horror's claws may be poisonous!"

But Huyghens snapped "Hup! Hup!" to the bears, and they continued their race against time. They went on for a good two miles, when Nugget wailed despairingly of his exhaustion and Faro Nell halted firmly to nuzzle him.

"This may be good enough," said Huyghens. "Considering that there's no wind and the big mass of beasts is down the plateau and there were only those two around here. Maybe they're too busy to hold a wake, even. Anyhow—"

He slid to the ground and extracted the antiseptic and swabs. "Sitka first," snapped Bordman. "I'm all right!"

Huyghens swabbed the big bear's wounds. They were trivial, because Sitka Pete was an experienced sphex-fighter. Then Bordman grudgingly let the curiously-smelling stuff—it reeked of ozone—be applied to the slashes on his chest. He held his breath as it stung. Then he said:

"It was my fault, Huyghens. I watched you instead of the landscape. I couldn't imagine what you were doing."

"I was doing a quick dissection," Huyghens told him. "By luck, that first sphex was a female, as I hoped. And she was about to lay her eggs. Ugh! And now I know why the sphexes migrate, and where, and how it is that they don't need game up here."

He slapped a quick bandage on Bordman then led the way eastward, still putting distance between the dead sphexes and his party.

"I'd dissected them before," said Huyghens. "Not enough's been known about them. Some things needed to be found out if men were ever to be able to live here."

"With bears?" asked Bordman ironically.

"Oh, yes," said Huyghens. "But the point is that sphexes come to the desert here to breed, to mate and lay their eggs for the sun to hatch. It's a particular place. Seals return to a special place to mate—and the males, at least, don't eat for weeks on end. Salmon return to their native streams to spawn. They don't eat, and they die afterward. And eels—I'm using Earth examples, Bordman—travel some thousands of miles to the Sargasso to mate and die. Unfortunately, sphexes don't appear to die, but it's clear that they have an ancestral breeding-place and that they come to the Sere Plateau to deposit their eggs!"

Bordman plodded onward. He was angry; angry with himself because he hadn't taken elementary precautions; because he'd felt too safe, as a man in a robot-served civilization forms the habit of doing; because he hadn't used his brain when Nugget whimpered, with even a bear-cub's awareness that danger was near.

"And now," Huyghens added, "I need some equipment that the robot colony has. With it, I think we can make a start toward turning this into a planet that man can live like men on." Bordman blinked.

"What's that?"

"Equipment," said Huyghens impatiently. "It'll be at the robot colony. Robots were useless because they wouldn't pay attention to sphexes. They'd still be. But take out the robot controls and the machines will do. They shouldn't be ruined by a few months' exposure to weather."

Bordman marched on and on. Presently he said:

"I never thought you'd want anything that came from that colony, Huyghens!"

"Why not?" demanded Huyghens impatiently. "When men make machines do what they want, that's all right. Even robots, when they're where they belong. But men will have to handle flame-casters in the job I want them for. There have to be some, because there was a hundred-mile clearing to be burned off for the colony. And earth-sterilizers, intended to kill the seeds of any plants that robots couldn't handle. We'll come back up here, Bordman, and at the least we'll destroy the spawn of these infernal beasts! If we can't do more than that, just doing that every year will wipe out the race in time. There are probably other hordes than this, with other breeding-places. But we'll find them too. We'll make this planet into a place where men from my world can come and still be men!"

Bordman said sardonically:

"It was sphexes that beat the robots. Are you sure you aren't planning to make this world safe for robots?"

Huyghens laughed.

"You've only seen one night-walker," he said. "And how about those things on the mountain-slope, which would have drained you of blood? Would you care to wander about this planet with only a robot body-guard, Bordman? Hardly! Men can't live on this planet with only robots to help them. You'll see!"

They found the colony after only ten days' more travel and after many sphexes and more than a few stag-like creatures and shaggy ruminants had fallen to their weapons and the bears. And they found survivors.

There were three of them, hard-bitten and bearded and deeply embittered. When the electrified fence went down, two of them were away at a mine tunnel, installing a new control panel for the robots who worked in it. The third was in charge of the mining operation. They were alarmed by the stopping of communication with the colony and went back in a tank-truck to find out what had happened, and only the fact that they were unarmed saved them. They found sphexes prowling and caterwauling about the fallen colony, in numbers they still did not wholly believe. The sphexes smelled men inside the armored vehicle, but couldn't break in. In turn, the men couldn't kill them, or they'd have been trailed to the mine and besieged there for as long as they could kill an occasional monster.

The survivors stopped all mining, of course, and tried to use remote-controlled robots for revenge and to get

supplies for them. Their mining-robots were not
designed for either task. And they had no weapons.
They improvised miniature throwers of burning rocket-
fuel, and they sent occasional prowling sphexes away
screaming with scorched hides. But this was useful only
because it did not kill the beasts. And it cost fuel. In
the end they barricaded themselves and used the fuel
only to keep a spark-signal going against the day when
another ship came to seek the colony. They stayed in
the mine as in a prison, on short rations, without real
hope. For diversion they could only contemplate the
mining-robots they could not spare fuel to run and
which could not do anything but mine.

When Huyghens and Bordman reached them, they
wept. They hated robots and all things robotic only a
little less than they hated sphexes. But Huyghens
explained, and, armed with weapons from the packs
of the bears, they marched to the dead colony with the
male Kodiaks as point and advance-guard, and with
Faro Nell bringing up the rear. They killed sixteen
sphexes on the way. In the now overgrown clearing
there were four more. In the shelters of the colony they
found only foulness and the fragments of what had
been men. But there was some food—not much,
because the sphexes clawed at anything that smelled
of men, and had ruined the plastic packets of radiation-
sterilized food. But there were some supplies in metal
containers which were not destroyed.

And there was fuel, which men could use when they
got to the control-panels of the equipment. There were
robots everywhere, bright and shining and ready for
operation, but immobile, with plants growing up around
and over them.

They ignored those robots, and instead fueled
tracked flame-casters—after adapting them to human
rather than robot operation—and the giant soil-sterilizer

which had been built to destroy vegetation that robots could not be made to weed out or cultivate. Then they headed back for the Sere Plateau.

As time passed Nugget became a badly spoiled bear-cub, because the freed men approved passionately of anything that would even grow up to kill sphexes. They petted him to excess when they camped.

Finally they reached the plateau by a sphex-trail to the top and sphexes came squalling and spitting to destroy them. While Bordman and Huyghens fired steadily, the great machines swept up with their special weapons. The earth-sterilizer, it developed, was deadly against animal life as well as seeds, when its diathermic beam was raised and aimed.

Presently the bears were not needed, because the scorched corpses of sphexes drew live ones from all parts of the plateau even in the absence of noticeable breezes. The official business of the sphexes was presumably finished, but they came to caterwaul and seek vengeance—which they did not find. After a while the survivors of the robot colony drove the machines in great circles around the huge heap of slaughtered fiends, destroying new arrivals as they came. It was such a killing as men had never before made on any planet, and there would be very few left of the sphex-horde which had bred in this particular patch of desert.

Nor would more grow up, because the soil-sterilizer would go over the dug-up sand where the sphex-spawn lay hidden for the sun to hatch. And the sun would never hatch them.

Huyghens and Bordman, by that time, were camped on the edge of the plateau with the Kodiaks. Somehow it seemed more befitting for the men of the robot colony to conduct the slaughter. After all, it was those men whose companions had been killed.

There came an evening when Huyghens cuffed Nugget away from where he sniffed too urgently at a stagsteak cooking on the campfire. Nugget ambled dolefully behind the protecting form of Bordman and sniveled.

"Huyghens," said Bordman, "we've got to come to a settlement of our affairs. You're an illegal colonist, and it's my duty to arrest you."

Huyghens regarded him with interest.

"Will you offer me lenience if I tell on my confederates?" he asked, "or may I plead that I can't be forced to testify against myself?"

Bordman said:

"It's irritating! I've been an honest man all my life, but—I don't believe in robots as I did, except in their place. And their place isn't here! Not as the robot colony was planned, anyhow. The sphexes are nearly wiped out, but they won't be extinct and robots can't handle them. Bears and men will have to live here or else the people who do will have to spend their lives behind sphex-proof fences, accepting only what robots can give them. And there's much too much on this planet for people to miss it! To live in a robot-managed environment on a planet like Loren II wouldn't—it wouldn't be self-respecting!"

"You wouldn't be getting religious, would you?" asked Huyghens drily. "That was your term for self-respect before."

"You don't let me finish!" protested Bordman. "It's my job to pass on the work that's done on a planet before any but the first-landed colonists may come there to live. And of course to see that specifications are followed. Now, the robot colony I was sent to survey was practically destroyed. As designed, it wouldn't work. It couldn't survive."

Huyghens grunted. Night was falling. He turned the meat over the fire.

"In emergencies," said Bordman, "colonists have the right to call on any passing ship for aid. Naturally! So my report will be that the colony as designed was impractical, and that it was overwhelmed and destroyed except for three survivors who holed up and signaled for help. They did, you know!"

"Go on," grunted Huyghens.

"So," said Bordman, "it just happened—just happened, mind you—that a ship with you and the bears and the eagle on board picked up the distress-call. So you landed to help the colonists. That's the story. Therefore it isn't illegal for you to be here. It was only illegal for you to be here when you were needed. But we'll pretend you weren't."

Huyghens glanced over his shoulder in the deepening night. He said:

"I wouldn't believe that if I told it myself. Do you think the Survey will?"

"They're not fools," said Bordman tartly. "Of course they won't! But when my report says that because of this unlikely series of events it is practical to colonize the planet, whereas before it wasn't, and when my report proves that a robot colony alone is stark nonsense, but that with bears and men from your world added, so many thousand colonists can be received per year. . . . And when that much is true, anyhow. . . ."

Huyghens seemed to shake a little as a dark silhouette against the flames.

"My reports carry weight," insisted Bordman. "The deal will be offered, anyhow! The robot colony organizers will have to agree or they'll have to fold up. And your people can hold them up for nearly what terms they choose."

Huyghens' shaking became understandable. It was laughter. "You're a lousy liar, Bordman," he said. "Isn't it unintelligent and unreasonable to throw away a lifetime of honesty just to get me out of a jam? You're not acting like a rational animal, Bordman. But I thought you wouldn't, when it came to the point."

Bordman squirmed.

"That's the only solution I can think of," he said. "But it'll work." .

"I accept it," said Huyghens, grinning. "With thanks. If only because it means another few generations of men can live like men on a planet that is going to take a lot of taming. And—if you want to know—because it keeps Sourdough and Sitka and Nell and Nugget from being killed because I brought them here illegally."

Something pressed hard against Bordman: Nugget, the cub, pushed urgently against him in his desire to get closer to the fragrantly cooking meat. He edged forward. Bordman toppled from where he squatted on the ground. He sprawled. Nugget sniffed luxuriously.

"Slap him," said Huyghens. "He'll move back."

"I won't!" said Bordman indignantly from where he lay. "I won't do it. He's my friend!"

It was ironic that, after all, Bordman found that he couldn't afford to retire. His pay, of course, had been used to educate his children and maintain his home. And Lani III was an expensive world to live on. It was now occupied by a thriving, bustling population with keen business instincts, and the vapor-curtains about it were commonplaces, now, and few people remembered a time when they hadn't existed, when it was a world below habitability for anybody. So Bordman wasn't a hero. As a matter of history he had done such and such. As a matter of fact he was simply a citizen who could be interviewed for visicasts on holidays, but hadn't much that was new to say.

But he lived on Lani III for three years, and he was

restless. His children were grown and married, now, and they hadn't known him too well, anyhow. He'd been away so much! He didn't fit into the world whose green fields and oceans and rivers he was responsible for. But it was infinitely good to be with Riki again. There was so much that each remembered, to be shared with the other, that they had plenty to talk about.

Three years after his official retirement, he was asked to take on another Survey job for which there was no other qualified man. He talked to his wife. On retirement pay, life was not easy. In retirement, it wasn't satisfactory. And Riki was free too, now. Her children were safely on their own. Bordman would always need her. She advised him for both their sakes. And he went back to Survey duty with the stipulation that he should have quarters and facilities for his wife as well as himself on all assignments.

They had five wonderful years. Bordman was near the top of the ladder, then. His children wrote faithfully. He was busy on Kelmin IV, and his wife had a garden there, when he was summoned to Sector Headquarters with first priority urgency.

THE SWAMP WAS
UPSIDE DOWN

Bordman knew the Survey ship had turned end for end, because though there was artificial gravity, it does not affect the semicircular canals of the human ear. He knew he was turning head-over-heels, even though his feet stayed firmly on the floor. It was not a normal sensation, and he felt that queasy, instinctive tightening of the muscles with which one reacts to the abnormal, whether in things seen or felt.

But the reason for turning the ship end-for-end was obvious. It had arrived very near its destination, and was killing its Lawlor-drive momentum. Just as Bordman was assured that the turning motion was finished, young Barnes—the ship's lowest-ranking commissioned officer—came into the wardroom and beamed at him.

"The ship's not landing, sir," he said, like one explaining something to somebody under ten years old. "Our orders are changed. You're to go to ground by boat. This way, sir."

Bordman shrugged. He was a Senior Officer of the Colonial Survey, grown old in the Service, and this was a Survey ship that had been sent especially to get him from his last and still unfinished job. It was a top-urgency matter. This ship had had no other business for some months except to go after him and bring him to Sector Headquarters, down on Canna III, which must be somewhere near. But this young officer was patronizing him!

Bordman rather regretfully recognized that he didn't know how to be impressive. He was not a good sales-man of his own importance. He didn't even get the respect due his rank.

Now the young officer waited, brisk and alert. Bordman reflected verily that he could pin young Barnes' ears back easily enough. But he remembered when he'd been a junior Survey ship's officer. Then he'd felt a bland condescension toward all people of what-ever rank who did not spend their lives in the cramped, skimped quarters of a Survey patrol-ship. If this young Lieutenant Barnes were fortunate, he'd always feel that way. Bordman could not begrudge him the cockiness which made the tedium and hardships of the Service seem to him a privilege.

So he obediently followed Barnes through the ward-room door. He ducked his head under a ventilation-slot and sidled past a standpipe with bristling air-valve handles. It almost closed the way. There was the smell of oil and paint and ozone which all proper Survey ships maintain in their working sections.

"Here, sir," said Barnes. "This way."

He offered his arm for Bordman to steady himself. Bordman ignored it. He stepped over a complex of white-painted pipes, and arrived at an almost clear way to a boat-blister.

"And your luggage, sir," added the young man

reassuringly, "will follow you down immediately, sir. With, the mail."

Bordman nodded. He moved toward the blister door. He sidled past constrictions due to new equipment. The Survey ship had been designed a long time ago, and there were no funds for rebuilding when improved devices came along. So any Survey ship was apt to be cluttered up with afterthoughts in metal.

A speaker from the wall said sharply:

"Hear this! Hold fast! Gravity going off!"

Bordman caught at a nearby pipe, and snatched his hand away again—it was hot—and caught on to another and then put his other hand below. He applied a trifle of pressure. The young officer said kindly:

"Hold fast, sir. If I may suggest—"

The gravity did go off. Bordman grimaced. There'd been a time when he was used to such matters, but this time the sudden outward surge of his breath caught him unprepared. His diaphragm contracted as the weight of organs above it ceased to be. He choked for an instant. He said evenly:

"I am not likely to go head-over-heels, Lieutenant. I served four years as a junior swot on a ship exactly like this!"

He did not float about. He held onto a pipe in two places, and he applied expert pressure in a strictly professional manner, and his feet remained firmly on the floor. He startled young Barnes by the achievement, which only junior swots think only junior swots know about.

Barnes said, abashed: "Yes, sir." He held himself in the same fashion.

"I even know," said Bordman, "that the gravity had to be cut off because we're approaching another ship on Lawlor drive. Our gravity-coils would blow if we got into her field with our drive off, or if her field pressed ours inboard."

Young Barnes looked extremely uncomfortable. Bordman felt sorry for him. To be chewed, however delicately, for patronizing a senior officer could not be pleasant. So Bordman added:

"And I also remember that, when I was a junior swot I once tried to tell a Sector Chief how to top off his suit-tanks. So don't let it bother you."

The young officer was embarrassed. A Sector Chief was so high in the table of Survey organization that one of his idle thoughts was popularly supposed to be able to crack a junior officer's skull. If Bordman, as a young officer, had really tried to tell a Sector Chief how to top his suit-tanks . . . Why . . .

"Thank you, sir," said Barnes awkwardly. "I'll try not to be an ass again, sir."

"I suspect," said Bordman, "that you'll slip occasionally. I did! What the devil's another ship doing out here and why aren't we landing?"

"I wouldn't know, sir," said the young officer. His manner toward Bordman was quite changed. "I do know the Skipper came in expecting to land by the landing-grid, sir. He was told to stand off. He's as much surprised as you are, sir."

The wall-speaker said crisply:

"Hear this! Gravity returning! Gravity returning!"

And weight came back. Bordman was ready for it this time and took it casually. He looked at the speaker and it said nothing more. He nodded to the young man.

"I suppose I'd better get in the boat. No change in that arrangement, anyhow!"

He crawled through the blister door and wormed his way into the landing boat, one designed for a more modern ship, and excessively inconvenient in such an outmoded launching-device. Barnes crawled in after him.

He dogged the blister door from the inside, closed the boat-port and dogged it, and flipped a switch.

"Excuse me, sir. I'm to take you down."

"Ready for departure," he said into a microphone.

A dial on the instrument-board flicked half-way to zero. It stopped there. Seconds passed. A green light glowed. The young officer said:

"All tight!"

The needle darted a quarter-way further over, and then began to descend slowly. The blister was being pumped empty of air. Presently another light glowed.

"Ready for launching," said the young officer briskly.

The blister-seal broke with a clank, and the two halves of the boat-cover drew back. There were stars. To Bordman they were unfamiliarly arranged, but he could have picked out Seton and the Donis cluster in any case, and half a hundred more markers by taking thought of the position of the planet Canna III, on which Colonial Survey Sector Headquarters for this part of the galaxy were established.

The boat moved out of its place, and the ship's gravity-field ended as abruptly as such fields do.

The Survey ship floated away, as seen from the vision-ports of the boat. It apparently increased its drive, because the boat swirled and swayed as changing eddy-currents moved it. The ship grew small and vanished. The boat hung in emptiness, turning slowly. The sun Canna came into view. It was very large for a Sol-type sun, and its rim was almost devoid of the prominences and jet-streams of flaming gas that older suns of the type display. But even out at the third orbit it provided 0-1 climate—optimum: equivalent to Earth—for the planet below.

That planet now came swinging into view as the

ship's boat continued to turn. It was blue. More than ninety per cent of its surface was water, and much of the solid land was under the northern ice-cap. It had been chosen as Sector Headquarters because of its unsuitability for a large population, which might resent the considerable land-area needed for Survey storage and reserve facilities.

Bordman regarded it thoughtfully. The boat was, of course, roughly five planetary diameters out, the conventional distance to which a ship approached any planet on its own drive. Bordman could see the ice-cap clearly, and blue sea beyond it, and the twilight-line. There was one cyclonic storm just dissipating toward the night-side, and the edge of a similar cloud-system down toward the equator. Bordman searched for Headquarters. It was on an island at about forty-five degrees latitude, which ought to be near the center of the planet's surface as seen from where the ship's boat floated. But he could not make it out. There was only the one island of any importance and it was not large.

Nothing happened. The boat's rockets remained silent. The young officer sat quietly, looking at the instruments before him. He seemed to be waiting for something to happen.

A needle kicked and stayed just off the pin. It was an external-field indicator. Some field, somewhere, now included the space in which the ship's boat floated.

"Hm," said Bordman. "You're waiting for orders?"

"Yes, sir," said the young man. "I'm ordered not to land except under ground instructions, sir. I don't know why." Bordman observed:

"One of the worst wiggings I ever got was in a boat like this. I was waiting for orders and they didn't come. I acted very Service about it: stiff upper lip and all that. But I was getting in serious trouble when it occurred to me that it might be my fault I wasn't getting the orders."

The young officer glanced quickly at an instrument he had previously ignored. Then he said relievedly:

"Not this time, sir. The communicator's turned on all right."

Bordman said:

"Do you think they might be calling you without shifting from ship-frequency? They were talking to the ship, you know."

"I'll try, sir."

The young man leaned forward and switched to ship-band adjustment of the communicator. Different wave-bands, naturally, were used between a ship and shore, and a ship and its own boats. A booming carrier wave came in instantly. The young officer hastily turned down the volume and words became distinguishable.

" . . . *What the devil's the matter with you? Acknowledge!*"

The young officer gulped. Bordman said mildly:

"Since he ranks you, just say 'sorry, sir.'"

"S-sorry, sir," said Barnes into the microphone.

"*Sorry?*" snapped the voice from the ground. "*I've been calling for five minutes! Your skipper will hear about this! I shall—*"

Bordman pulled the microphone before him.

"My name is Bordman," he observed. "I am waiting for instructions to land. My pilot has been listening on boat-frequency, as was proper. You appear to be calling us on an improper channel. Really—"

There was stricken silence. Then babbled apologies from the speaker. Bordman smiled faintly at young Barnes.

"It's quite all right. Let's forget it now. But will you give my pilot his instructions?"

The voice said with strained formality:

"You're to be brought down by landing-grid, sir. Rocket-landings have been ruled non-permitted by the Sector Chief himself, sir. But we are already landing one boat, sir. Senior Officer Werner is being brought in now, sir. His boat is still two diameters out, sir, and it will take us nearly an hour to get him down without extreme discomfort, sir."

"Then we'll wait," said Bordman. "Hm. Call us again before you start hunting us with the landing-beam. My pilot has a rather promising idea. And will you call us on the proper frequency then, please?"

The voice aground said unhappily: *"Yes, sir. Certainly, sir."*

The carrier-wave hum stopped. Young Barnes said gratefully:

"Thank you, sir. Hell hath no fury like a ranking officer caught in a blunder! He'd have twisted my tail for his mistake, sir, and it could have been bad." Then he paused. He said uneasily, "But—beg pardon, sir. I haven't any promising ideas. Not that I know of."

"You have an hour to develop one," Bordman told him. Internally, Bordman was startled. There were few occasions on which even one Senior Officer was called in to Sector Headquarters. Interstellar distances being what they were, and thirty light-speeds being practically the best available, Senior Officers necessarily acted pretty much as independent authorities. To call one man in meant all his other work had to go by the board for a matter of months. But two! And Werner?

Werner was getting to ground first. If there was something serious ashore, Werner would make a great point of arriving first, even if only by hours. A keen sort of person in giving the right impression. He'd risen in the Service faster than Bordman. That other Lawlor field would have been his ship getting out of the way.

The young officer at his elbow fidgeted.

"Beg pardon, sir. What sort of idea should I develop, sir? I'm not sure I understand—"

"It's rather annoying to have to stay parked in free fall," said Bordman patiently. "And it's always a good practice to review annoying situations and see if they can be bettered."

Barnes' forehead wrinkled.

"We could land much quicker on rockets, sir. And even when the landing-grid reaches out for us, they'll have to handle us very cautiously or they'd break our necks, since we've no gravity coils."

Bordman nodded. Barnes was thinking straight enough, but it takes young officers a long time to think of thinking straight. They have to obey so many orders unquestioningly that they tend to stop doing anything else. Yet at each rise in grade some slight trace of increased capacity to think is required. In order to reach really high rank, an officer has to be capable of thinking which simply isn't possible unless he's kept in practice on the way up.

Young Barnes looked up, startled.

"Look here, sir!" he said, surprised. "If it takes them an hour to let down Senior Officer Werner from two planetary diameters, it'll take much longer to let us down from out here!"

"True," said Bordman.

"And you don't want to spend three hours descending, sir, after waiting an hour for him."

"I don't," admitted Bordman. He could have given orders, of course. But if a junior officer were spurred to the practice of thinking, it meant that some day he'd be a better senior officer. And Bordman knew how desperately few men were really adequate for high authority. Anything that could be done to increase the number.

Young Barnes blinked.

"But it doesn't matter to the landing-grid how far out we are!" he said in an astonished voice. "They could lock on to us at ten diameters, or at one. Once they lock the field-focus on us, when they move it they move us."

Bordman nodded again.

"So by the time they've got that other boat landed—why—I can use rockets and get down to one diameter myself, sir! And they can lock onto us there and let us down a few thousand miles only. So we can get to ground half an hour after the other boat's down instead of four hours from now."

"Just so," agreed Bordman. "At a cost of a little thought and a little fuel. You do have a promising idea after all, Lieutenant. Suppose you carry it out?"

Young Barnes glanced at Bordman's safety-strap. He threw over the fuel-ready lever and conscientiously waited the few seconds for the first molecules of fuel to be catalyzed cold. Once firing started, they'd be warmed to detonation-readiness in the last few millimeters of the injection-gap.

"Firing, sir," he said respectfully.

There was the curious sound of a rocket blasting in emptiness, when the sound is conveyed only by the rocket-tube's metal. There was the smooth, pushing sensation of acceleration. The tiny ship's boat swung and aimed down at the planet. Lieutenant Barnes leaned forward and punched the ship's computer.

"I hope you'll excuse me, sir," he said. "I should have thought that out myself without prompting. But problems like this don't turn up very often, sir. As a rule it's wisest to follow precedents as if they were orders."

Bordman said dryly:

"To be sure! But one reason for the existence of junior officers is the fact that some day there will have to be new senior ones."

Barnes considered. Then he said surprisedly:

"I never thought of it that way, sir. Thank you."

He continued to punch the computer keys, frowning. Bordman relaxed in his seat, held there by the gentle acceleration and the belt. He'd had nothing by which to judge the reason for his summoning to Headquarters. He had very little now. But there was trouble of some sort down below. Two senior officers dragged from their own work. Werner, now. . . . Bordman preferred not to estimate Werner. He disliked the man, and would be biased. But he was able, though definitely on the make. And there was himself. They'd been called to a headquarters where no ship was to be landed by landing-grid, nor any rocket to come to ground. A landing-grid could pluck a ship out of space ten planet-diameters out, and draw it with gentle violence shoreward, and land it lightly as a feather. A landing-grid could take the heaviest, loaded freighter and stop it in orbit and bring it down at eight gravities. But the one below wouldn't land even a tiny Survey ship! And a landing boat was forbidden to come down on its rockets!

Bordman arranged those items in his mind. He knew the planet below, of course. When he got his Senior rating he'd spent six months at Headquarters learning procedures and practices proper to his increased authority. There was one inhabitable island, two hundred miles long and possibly forty wide. There was no other usable ground outside the Arctic. The one occupied island had gigantic sheer cliffs on its windward side, where a great slab of bedrock had split along some submarine fault and tilted upward above the surface. Those cliffs were four thousand feet high, and from them the island sloped very gently and very gradually until its leeward shore slipped under the restless sea. Sector Headquarters had been placed here because it seemed that civilians would not want to colonize so limited a world. But there were civilians, because there was Headquarters. And now every inch of ground was cultivated, and there was irrigation and intensive farming and some hydroponic establishments. However, Sector Headquarters included a vast reserve area on which a space-fleet might be marshaled in case of need. The overcrowded civilians were bitter because of the great uncultivated area the Survey needed for storage and possible emergency use. Even when Bordman was here, years back, there was bitterness because the Survey crowded the civil economy which had been based on it.

Bordman considered all these items, and came to an uncomfortable conclusion. Presently he looked up. The planet loomed larger. Much larger.

"I think you'd better lose all planet-ward velocity before we hook on," he observed. "The landing-grid crew might have trouble focusing on us so close if we're moving."

"Yes, sir," said the young officer.

"There's some sort of merry hell below," said Bordman. "It looks bad that they won't let a ship come down by grid. It looks worse that they won't let this one land on its rockets." He paused. "I doubt they'll risk lifting us off again."

Young Barnes finished his computations. He looked satisfied. He glanced at the now-gigantic planet below, and deftly adjusted the course of the tiny boat. Then he jerked his head around.

"Excuse me, sir. Did you say we mightn't be able to lift off again?"

"I could almost predict that we won't," said Bordman.

"Would you—could you say why, sir?"

"They don't want landings. The trouble is here.

If they don't want landings, they won't want launchings. Werner and I were sent for, so presumably we're needed. But apparently there's uneasiness about even our landing. They won't send us off again. I suspect—"

The loud-speaker said tinnily:

"Calling boat from landing-grid! Calling boat from landing-grid!"

"Come in," said Barnes, looking uneasily at Bordman.

"Correct your course!" commanded the voice. *"You are not to land on rockets under any circumstances! This is an order from the Sector Chief himself. Stand off! We will be ready to lock on and land you gently in about fifteen minutes. But meanwhile stand off!"*

"Yes, sir," said young Barnes.

Bordman reached over and took the microphone. "Bordman speaking," he said. "I'd like information. What's the trouble down there that we can't use our rockets?"

"Rockets are noisy, sir. Even boat-rockets. We have orders to eliminate all physical vibration possible, sir. But I am ordered not to give details on a transmitter, sir."

"I sign off," said Bordman, dryly.

He pushed the microphone away. He deplored his own lack of aggressiveness. Werner, now, would have pulled his rank and insisted on being informed. But Bordman couldn't help believing that there was a reason for orders that overruled his own.

The young officer swung the rocket end-for-end. The sensation of pressure against the back of Bordman's seat increased.

Minutes later the speaker said:

"Grid to boat. Prepare for lock-on."

"Ready, sir," said Barnes.

The small boat shuddered and leaped crazily. It

spun. It oscillated violently through seconds-long arcs in emptiness. Very gradually the oscillations died. There was a momentary sensation of the faint tugging of planetary weight, which is somehow subtly different from the feel of artificial gravity. Then the cosmos turned upside down as the boat was drawn swiftly toward the watery planet below it.

Some minutes later, young Barnes spoke: "Beg pardon, sir," he said apologetically. "I must be stupid, sir, but I can't imagine any reason why vibrations or noises should make any difference on a planet. How could it do harm?"

"This is an ocean-planet," said Bordman. "It might make people drown."

The young officer flushed and turned his head away. And Bordman reflected that the young were always sensitive. But he did not speak again. When they landed in the spidery, half-mile-high landing-grid, Barnes would find out whether he was right or not.

He did. And Bordman was right. The people on Canna III were anxious to avoid vibrations because they were afraid of drowning.

Their fears seemed to be rather well-founded.

Three hours after landing, Bordman moved gingerly over grayish muddy rock, with a four-thousand-foot sheer drop some twenty yards away. The ragged edge of a cliff fell straight down for the better part of a mile. Far below, the sea rippled gently. Bordman saw a long, long line of boats moving slowly out to sea. They towed something between them which reached from boat to boat in exaggerated catenary curves. The boats moved in line abreast straight out from the cliffs, towing this floating, curved thing between them.

Bordman regarded them for a moment and then inspected the grayish mud underfoot. He lifted his eyes to the inland side of this peculiar stretch of mountainside muddiness. There was a mast on the rock not far away. It held up what looked like a vision camera.

Young Barnes said:

"Excuse me, sir. What are those boats doing?"

"They're towing an oil-slick out to sea," said Bordman absently, "by towing a floating line of some sort between them. There isn't enough oil to maintain the slick, and it's blown landward. So they tow it out to sea again. It holds down the seas. Every time, of course, they lose some of it."

"But—"

"There are trade-winds," said Bordman, not looking to seaward at all. "They always blow in the same direction, nearly. They blow three-quarters of the way around the planet, and they build up seas as they blow. Normally, the swells that pound against this cliff, here, will be a hundred feet and more from trough to crest. They'll throw spray ten times that high, of course, and once when I was here before, spray came over the cliff-top. The impacts of the waves are—heavy. In a storm, if you put your ear to the ground on the leeward shore, you can hear the waves smash against these cliffs. It's vibration."

Barnes looked uneasily at the cliff's edge and the line of boats pushing over an ocean whose waves seemed less than ripples from nearly a mile above them. But the line of boats was incredibly long. It was twenty miles in length at the least.

"The slick holds down the waves," Barnes guessed. "It works best in deep water, I believe. The ancients knew it. Oil on the waters." He considered. "Working hard to prevent vibrations! Are they really so dangerous, sir?"

Bordman nodded inland. A quarter mile from the

edge of the cliff there was a peculiar, broken, riven rampart of soil. It might have been forty feet high, once. Now it was shattered and cracked. It had the look of having been pulled away from where it was withdrawn. There were vertical breaks in its edges and broken-off masses left behind. At one place, a clump of perhaps a quarter-acre had not followed the rest, and trees leaned drunkenly from its top, and at the edge had fallen outward. All along the top of the stone cliff as far as the eye could see there was this singular retreat of soil and vegetation from the cliff's edge.

Bordman stooped and picked up a bit of the mud underfoot. He rubbed it between his fingers. It yielded like modeling clay. He dipped a finger into a gray, greasy-seeming puddle. He looked at the thick liquid on his finger and then rubbed it against his other palm. Young Barnes duplicated this last action.

"It feels soapy, sir!" he said blankly. "Like wet soap!"

"Yes," said Bordman. "That's the first problem here."

He turned to a ground-service Survey private, and jerked his head along the coast-line.

"How much have other places slipped?"

"Anywhere from this much, sir,' said the private, "to two miles and upward. There's one place where it's moving at a regular rate. Four inches an hour, sir. It was three-and-a-half yesterday."

Bordman nodded.

"Hm. We'll go back to Headquarters. Nasty business!"

He plodded over the messy footing toward the vehicle which had brought him here. It was not an ordinary ground-car. Instead of wires or caterwheels, it rolled upon flaccid, partly-inflated five-foot rollers. They would be completely unaffected by roughness or slipperiness of terrain and if the vehicle fell overboard it would float. It was thickly coated with the gray mud of this cliff-top.

As he moved along, Bordman was able to see the pattern of the rock underneath the mud. It was curiously contorted, like something that had curdled rather than cooled. And, as a matter of fact, it was believed to have solidified slowly under water at such monstrous pressure that even molten rock could not make it burst into steam. But it was above-water now.

Bordman climbed into the vehicle, and Barnes followed him. The bolster-truck turned and moved toward the broken barrier of earth. Its five-foot flabby rollers seemed rather to flow over than to surmount obstacles. Great lumps of drier dirt dented them and did not disintegrate. There were no stones.

Bordman frowned to himself. The bolster-truck more or less flowed up the crumbling, inexplicably drawing-back mass of soil. Atop it, things looked almost normal. Almost. There was a highway leading away from the cliff. At first glance it seemed perfect. But it was cracked down the middle for a hundred yards, and then the crack meandered off to the side and was gone. There was a great tree, which leaned drunkenly. A mile along the roadway its surface bucked as if something had pressed irresistibly upward from below. The truck rolled over the break.

It was notable that the motion of the truck was utterly smooth. It made no vibration at all. But even so it slowed before it moved through a place where buildings—houses and a shop or two—clustered closely together on each side of the road.

There were people in and about the house, but they were doing nothing at all. Some of them stared at the Survey truck with hostility. Some others deliberately turned their backs to it. There were vehicles out of shelter and ready to be used, but none was moving. All were pointed in the direction from which the bolster-truck had come.

The truck went on. Presently the extraordinary flatness of the landscape became apparent. It was possible to see a seemingly illimitable distance. The ocean forty miles away showed as a thread of blue beneath the horizon. The island was an almost perfectly plane tilted surface. There was no hill visible anywhere, nor any valleys save the extremely minor gullies worn by rain. Even they had been filled in, dammed, and tied in to irrigation systems.

There was a place where there was a row of trees along such a water-course. Half the row was fallen, and a part of the rest was tilted. The remainder stood upright and firm. All the vegetation was perfectly familiar. Most colonies have some vegetation, at least, directly descended from the mother planet Earth. But this island on Canna III had been above-water perhaps no more than three or four thousand years. There had been no time for local vegetation to develop. When the Survey took it over, there was nothing but tidal seaweed, only one variety of which had been able to extend itself in web-like fashion over the soil above water. Terrestrial plants had wiped it out, and everything was green and human-introduced.

But there was something wrong with the ground. At this place the top of the soil bulged, and tall corn-plants grew extravagantly in different directions. At another, there was a narrow, lipless gash in the ground's surface. An irrigation-ditch poured water into it. It was not filled.

Barnes said:

"Excuse me, sir, but how the devil did this happen?"

"There's been irrigation," said Bordman patiently. "The soil here was all ocean-bottom, once—it used to be what is called globigerinous ooze. There's no sand, and no stones. There's only bed-rock and formerly abyssal mud. And some of it underneath is no longer former. It's globigerinous ooze again."

He waved his hand at the landscape. It had been remarkably tidy, once. Every square foot of ground had been cultivated. The highways were of limited width, and the houses were neat and trim. It was, perhaps, the most completely civilized landscape in the galaxy. Bordman added:

"You said the stuff felt like soap. In a way, it's acting like soap. It lies on slightly slanting, effectively smooth rock, like a soap-cake on a sheet of metal that's tilted a bit. And that's the trouble. So long as a cake of soap is dry on the bottom it doesn't move. Even if you pour water on top, like rain, the top will wet, and the water will flow off, but the bottom won't wet until all the soap is dissolved away. While that was the process here, everything was all right. But they've been irrigating."

They passed a row of neat cottages facing the road. One had collapsed completely. The others looked absolutely normal. The bolster-truck went on.

Bordman said, frowning:

"They wanted the water to go into the soil, so they arranged it. A little of that did no harm. Plants growing dried it out again. One tree evaporates thousands of gallons a day in a good trade-wind. There were some landslides in the early days, especially when storm-swells pounded the cliffs, but on the whole the ground was more firmly anchored when first cultivated than it had been before the colonists came."

"But irrigation? The sea's not fresh, is it?"

"Water-freshening plants," said Bordman dryly. "Ion-exchange systems. They installed them and had all the fresh water they could wish for. And they wished for a lot. They deep-ploughed, so the water would sink in. They dammed the water-courses. What they did amounted to something like boring holes in that cake of soap I used for an illustration just now. Water vent right down to the bottom. What would happen then?"

Barnes said:

"Why the bottom would get wet—and the soap would slide! As if it were greased!"

"Not greased," corrected Bordman. "Soaped. Soap is viscous. That's different, and a lucky difference, too. But the least vibration would encourage movement. And it does. So the population is now walking on eggs. Worse, it's walking on the equivalent of a cake of soap which is getting wetter and wetter on the bottom. It's already sliding as a viscous substance does, reluctantly. But in spite of the oil-slick they're trying to keep in place upwind there's still some battering from the sea. There are still some vibrations in the bed-rock. And so there's a slow, gentle, gradual sliding."

"And they figure," said Barnes, "that locking onto a ship with the landing-grid might be like an earth-quake." He stopped. "An earth-quake, now—"

"Not much volcanism on this planet," Bordman told him. "But of course there are tectonic quakes occasionally. They made this island."

Barnes said uneasily:

"I don't think, sir, that I'd sleep well if I lived here."

"You are living here for the moment. But at your age I think you'll sleep."

The bolster-truck turned, following the highway. The road was very even, and the motion of the truck along it was infinitely smooth. Its lack of vibration explained why it was permitted to move when all other vehicles were stopped. But Bordman reflected uneasily that this did not account for the orders of the Sector Chief forbidding the rocket-landing of a ship's boat. It was true enough that the living-surface of the island rested upon slanting stone, and that if the bottom were wet enough that it could slide off into the sea. It already had moved. At least one place was moving at four inches per hour. But that was viscous flow. It would be enhanced by vibration, and assuredly the hammering of seas upon the windward cliff should be lessened by any possible means.

But it did not mean that the sound of a rocket-landing would be disastrous, nor the straining of a landing-grid as it stopped a spaceship in orbit and drew it to ground should produce a landslide. There was something else, though the situation for the island's civilian population was already serious enough. If any really massive movement of the ground did begin, viscous or any other, if any considerable part of the island's surface did begin to move, all of it would go. And the population would go with it. If there were survivors, they could be numbered in dozens.

The tall tamped-earth wall of the Headquarters reserve area loomed ahead. Sector Headquarters had been established here when there were no other inhabitants. Seeds had been broadcast and trees planted while the Survey buildings were under construction. Headquarters, in fact, had been built upon an uninhabited planet. But colonists followed in the wake of Survey personnel. Wives and children, and then storekeepers and agriculturists, and presently civilian technicians and ultimately even politicians arrived as the non-Service population grew. Now Sector Headquarters was resented because it occupied one-fourth of the island. It kept too much of the planet's useful surface out of civilian use. And the island was desperately overcrowded.

But it seemed also to be doomed.

As the bolster-truck moved silently toward Headquarters, a hundred-yard section of the wall collapsed. There was an upsurging of dust, and a rumbling of falling, hardened dirt. The truck's driver turned white. A civilian beside the road faced the wall and wrung his hands, and stood waiting to feel the ground under his feet begin to sweep smoothly toward the here-distant sea. A post held up a traffic signal some twenty yards from the gate. It leaned slowly. At a forty-five-degree tilt it checked and hung stationary. Fifty yards from the gate, a new crack appeared across the road.

But nothing more happened. Nothing. Yet one could not be sure that some critical point had not been passed, so that from now on there would be a gradual rise in the creeping of the soil toward the ocean.

Barnes caught his breath.

"That makes me feel—queer," he said unsteadily. "A shock like that wall falling could start everything off!"

Bordman said nothing at all. It had occurred to him that there was no irrigation of the Survey area. He frowned thoughtfully, even worriedly, as the truck went inside the Headquarters gate and rolled on over a winding road through park-like surroundings.

It stopped before the building which was the Sector Chief's own headquarters in Headquarters. A large brown dog dozed peacefully on the plastic-tiled landing at the top of half a dozen steps. When Bordman got out of the truck the dog got up with a leisurely air. And when Bordman ascended the steps, with Barnes following him, the dog came forward with a sort of a stately courtesy to do the honors. Bordman said:

"Nice dog, that."

He went inside. The dog followed. The interior of the building was empty, and there was a sort of resonant silence until somewhere a telewriter began to click.

"Come along," said Bordman. "The Sector Chief's office is over this way."

Young Barnes followed.

"It seems odd there's no one around," he said. "No secretaries, no sentries, nobody at all."

"Why should there be?" asked Bordman in surprise. "The guards at the gate keep civilians out. And nobody in the Service will bother the Chief without reason. At least, not more than once!"

But across the glistening, empty floor there ran an ominous crack.

They went down a corridor. Voices sounded, and Bordman tracked them, with the paws of the dog clicking on the floor behind him. He led the way into a spacious, comfortably nondescript room with high windows—doors, really—that opened on green lawns outside. The Sector Chief, Sandringham, leaned back in a chair, smoking. Werner, the other summoned Senior officer, sat bolt upright in a chair facing him. Sandringham waved a hand to Bordman.

"Back so soon? You're ahead of schedule on all counts! Here's Werner, back from looking at the fuel-store situation." Bordman suddenly looked as if he'd been jolted. But he nodded, and Werner tried to smile and failed. He was completely white.

"My pilot from the ship, who's kept aground," said Bordman. "Lieutenant Barnes. Very promising young officer. Cut my landing-time by hours. Lieutenant, this is Sector Chief Sandringham and Mr. Werner."

"Have a seat, Bordman," grunted the Chief. "You too, Lieutenant. How does it look up on the cliff, Bordman?"

"I suspect you know as well as I do," said Bordman. "I think I saw a vision-camera planted up there."

"True enough. But there's nothing like on-the-spot inspection. Now you're back, how does it look to you?"

"Inadequate," said Bordman. "Inadequate to explain some things I've noticed. But it's a very bad situation. Its degree of badness depends on the viscosity of the mud at bedrock all over the island. The left-behind mud's like pea soup. It looks really bad! But what's the viscosity at bedrock with soil pressing down, and I hope drier soil than at the bottom?"

Sandringham grunted. "Good question. I sent for you, Bordman, when it began to look bad, before the ground really started sliding. When I thought it might begin any time. The viscosity averages pretty closely at three times ten to the sixth. Which still gives us some leeway. But not enough."

"Not nearly enough!" said Bordman impatiently. "Irrigation should have been stopped a long while back!"

The Sector Chief grimaced.

"I've no authority over civilians. They've their own planetary government. And do you remember?" He quoted: "'Civilian establishments and governments may be advised by Colonial Survey officials, and may make requests of them, but in each case such advice or request is to be considered on its own merits only, and in no case may it be the subject of a *quid-pro-quo* agreement.'" He added grimly: "That means you can't threaten. It's been thrown at my head every time I've asked them to cut down their irrigation in the past fifteen years! I advised them not to irrigate at all, and they couldn't see it. It would increase the food-supply, and they needed more food. So they went ahead. They built two new sea-water freshening plants only last year!"

Werner licked his lips. He said in a voice that was higher-pitched than Bordman remembered:

"What's happening serves them right! It serves them right!"

Bordman waited.

"Now," said Sandringham, "they're demanding to be let into Sector Headquarters for safety. They say we haven't irrigated, so the ground we occupy isn't going to slide. They demand that we take them all in here to sit on their rumps until the rest of the island slides into the sea or doesn't. If it doesn't, they want to wait here until the soil becomes stable again because they've quit irrigating."

"It'd serve them right if we didn't let them in!" cried Werner in shrill anger. "It's their fault that they're in this fix!"

Sandringham waved his hand.

"Administering abstract justice isn't my job. I imagine it's handled in more competent quarters. I have only to meet the objective situation. Which is plenty! Bordman, you've handled swamp-planet situations. What can be done to stop the sliding of the island's soil before it all goes overboard?"

"Not much, offhand," said Bordman. "Give me time and I'll manage something. But a really bad storm, with high seas and plenty of rain, might wipe out the whole civilian colony. That viscosity figure is close to hopeless, if not quite."

The Sector Chief looked impassive.

"How much time does he have, Werner?"

"None!" said Werner shrilly. "The only possible thing is to try to move as many people as possible to the solid ground in the Arctic! The boats can be crowded— the situation demands it! And if the two space-craft in orbit are sent to collect a fleet, and as many people as possible are moved at once, there may be some survivors!"

Bordman spread out his hands.

"I'm wondering," he observed, "what the really serious problem is. There's more than sliding soil the matter! Else you would—I'm sure Lieutenant Barnes has thought of this—else you would let the civilian population into Headquarters to sit on its rump and wait for better times."

Sandringham glanced at young Barnes, who flushed hotly at being noticed.

"I'm sure you have good reasons, sir," he said, embarrassed.

"I have several," said the Sector Chief dryly. "For one thing, so long as we refuse to let them in, they're reassured. They can't imagine we'd let them drown. But if we invited them in they'd panic and fight to get in first. There'd be a full-scale slaughter right there! They'd be sure disaster was only minutes off. Which it would be!"

He paused and glanced from one to the other of the senior officers.

"When I sent for you," he said, "I meant you, Bordman, to take care of the possible sliding. I meant for Werner, here, to do the public-relations job of scaring the civilians just enough to make them let it be done. It's not so simple, now!"

He drew a deep breath.

"It's pure chance that this is a Sector Headquarters. Or else it's Providence. We'll find that out later! But ten days ago it was discovered that an instrument had gone wrong over in the ship-fuel storage area. It didn't register when a tank leaked. And a tank did leak. You know ship fuel is harmless when it's refrigerated. You know what it's like when it's not. Dissolved in soil-moisture, it's not only catalyzed to explosive condition, but it's a hell of a corrosive, and it's eaten holes in some other tanks—and can you imagine trying to do anything about that?"

Bordman felt a sensation of incredulous shock. Werner wrung his hands.

"If I could only find the man who made that faulty tank!" he said thickly. "He's killed all of us! Unless we get to solid ground in the Arctic!"

The Sector Chief said:

"That's why I won't let them in, Bordman. Our storage tanks go down to bedrock. The leaked fuel—warmed up, now—is seeping along bedrock and eating at other tanks, besides being absorbed generally by the soil and dissolving in the groundwater. We've pulled all personnel out of all the area it could have seeped down to."

Bordman felt slightly cold at the back of his neck.

"I suspect," he said, "that they came out on tip-toe, holding their breaths, and they were careful not to drop anything or scrape their chairs when they got up to leave. I would have! Anything could set it off. But it is bound to go anyhow! Of course! Now I see why we couldn't make a rocket-landing!"

The chilly feeling seemed to spread as he realized more fully. When ship-fuel is refrigerated during its manufacture, it is about as safe a substance as can be imagined, so long as it is kept refrigerated. It is an energy-chemical compound, of atoms bound together with forced-violence linkages. But enormous amounts of energy are required to force valences upon reluctant atoms. When ship-fuel warms up, or is catalyzed, it goes on one step beyond the process of its manufacture. It goes on to the modification the refrigeration prevented. It changes its molecular configuration. What was stable because it was cold becomes something which is hysterically unstable because of its structure. The touch of a feather can detonate it. A shout can set it off. It is, indeed, burned only molecule by molecule in a ship's engines, being catalyzed to the unstable state while cold at the very spot where it is to detonate. And since the energy yielded by detonation is that of the forced bonds, the energy-content of ship-fuel is much greater than a merely chemical compound can contain. Ship-fuel contains a measurable fraction of the power of atomic explosive. But it is much more practical for use on board ship.

The point now was, of course, that—leaked into the ground and warmed—practically any vibratory motion would detonate the fuel. Even dissolved, it can detonate because it is not a chemical but an energy-release action.

"A good, drumming, heavy rain," said Sandringham, "which falls on this end of the island, will undoubtedly set off some hundreds of tons of leaked ship-fuel. And that ought to scatter and catalyze and detonate the rest. The explosion should be equivalent to at least a megaton fusion bomb." He paused, and added with irony. "Pretty situation, isn't it? If the civilians hadn't irrigated, we could evacuate Headquarters and let it blow, as it will anyhow. If the fuel hadn't leaked, we could let in the civilians until the island's soil decides what it's going to do. Either would be a nasty situation, but the combination . . ."

Werner said shrilly:

"Evacuation to the Arctic is the only possible answer! Some people can be saved! Some! I'll take a boat and equipment and go on ahead and get some sort of refuge ready—"

There was dead silence. The brown dog who had followed Bordman from the outer terrace now yawned loudly. Bordman reached over and absent-mindedly scratched his ears. Young Barnes swallowed.

"Beg pardon, sir," he said. "What's the weather forecast?"

"Continued fair," said Sandringham, pleasantly. "That's why I had Bordman and Werner come down. Three heads are better than one. I've gambled their lives on their brains."

Bordman continued to scratch the brown dog's ears. Werner licked his lips. Young Barnes looked from one to another of them. Then he looked back at the Sector Chief.

"Sir," he said. "I—I think the odds are pretty good. Mr. Bordman, sir—he'll manage!"

Then he flushed hotly at his own presumption in saying something consoling to a Senior Chief. It was comparable to telling him how to top off his vacuum-suit tanks.

But the Sector Chief nodded in grave approval and turned to Bordman to hear what he had to say.

The leeward side of the island sloped gently into the water. From a boat offshore—say, a couple of miles out—the shoreline looked low and flat and peaceful. There were houses in view, and boats afloat. But they were much smaller than those that had been towing a twenty-mile-long oil-slick out to sea. These boats did not ply back and forth. Most of them seemed anchored. On some of them there was activity. Men went overboard, without splashing, and brought things up from the ocean bottom and dumped them inside the hulls. At long intervals men emerged from underwater and sat on the sides of the boats and smoked with an effect of leisure.

The sun shone, and the land was green, and a seeming of vast tranquility hung over the whole seascape. But the small Survey-personnel recreation-boat moved in toward the shore, and the look of things changed. At a mile, a mass of green that had seemed to be trees growing down to the water's edge became a thicket of tumbled trunks and overset branches where a tree-thicket had collapsed. At half a mile the water was opaque. There were things floating in it: the roof of a house, the leaves of an ornamental shrub, with nearby its roots showing at the surface, washed clean. A child's toy bobbed past the boat. It looked horribly pathetic.

There were the exotic planes and angles of three wooden steps, floating in the ripples of the great ocean.

"Ignoring the imminent explosion of the fuel-store," said Bordman, "we need to find out something about what has to be done to the soil to stop its creeping. I hope you remembered, Lieutenant, to ask a great many useless questions."

"Yes, sir," said Barnes. "I tried to. I asked everything I could think of."

"Those boats yonder?"

Bordman indicated a boat from which something like a wire basket splashed into the water as he gestured.

"A garden-boat, sir," said Barnes. "On this side of the island the sea-bottom slopes so gradually that there are sea-gardens on the bottom. Shellfish from Earth do not thrive, sir, but there are edible sea-plants. The gardeners cultivate them as on land."

Bordman reached overside and carefully took his twentieth sample of the sea-water. He squinted, and estimated the distance to shore.

"I shall try to imagine someone wearing a diving-mask and using a hoe," he said dryly. "What's the depth here?"

"We're half a mile out, sir," said Barnes. "It should be about sixty feet. The bottom seems to have about a three per cent grade, sir. That's the angle of repose of the mud. There's no sand to make a steeper slope possible."

"Three per cent's not bad!"

Bordman looked pleased. He picked up one of his earlier samples and tilted it, checking the angle at which the sediment came to rest. The bottom mud, here, was essentially the same as the soil of the land. But the soil of the land was definitely colloid. In sea-water, obviously, it sank because of the salinity which made suspension difficult.

"You see the point, eh?" he asked. When Barnes shook his head, Bordman explained, "Probably for my sins I've had a good deal to do with swamp-planets. The mud of a salt-swamp is quite different from a fresh-water swamp. The essential trouble with the people ashore is that by their irrigation they've contrived an island-wide swamp which happens to be upside down, the swamp at the bottom. So the question is, can it acquire the properties of a salt-swamp instead of a fresh-water swamp without killing all the vegetation on the surface? That's why I'm after these samples. As we go inshore the water should be fresher, on a shallowing shore like this with drainage in this direction."

He gestured to the Survey private at the stern of the boat.

"Closer in, please."

Barnes said:

"Sir, motorboats are forbidden inshore. The vibrations."

Bordman shrugged.

"We will obey the rule. I've probably samples enough. How far out do the mudflats run, at the surface?"

"About two hundred yards at the surface, sir. The mud's about the consistency of thick cream. You can see where the ripples stop, sir."

Bordman stared. He turned his eyes away.

"Er—sir," said Barnes unhappily. "May I ask—?"

Bordman said dryly:

"You may. But the answer's pure theory. This information will do no good at all unless all the rest of the problem we face is solved. However, solving the rest of the problem will do no good if this part remains unsolved. You see?"

"Yes, sir. But the other parts seem more urgent."

Bordman shrugged.

There was a shout from a nearby boat. Men were pointing ashore. Bordman jerked his eyes to the shoreline.

A section of seemingly solid ground moved slowly toward the water. Its forefront seemed to disintegrate, and a slow-moving swell moved out over the rippleless border of the sea, where mudbanks like thick cream reached the surface.

The moving mass was a good half-mile in width. Its outer edge dissolved in the sea, and the top tilted, and green vegetation leaned downwind and subsided into the water. It was remarkably like the way an ingot of non-ferrous metal slides into the pool made by its own melting.

But the aftermath was somehow horrifying. When the tumbled soil was all dissolved and the grass undulated like a floating meadow on the water, there remained a jagged shallow gap in the land-bank. There were irregularities: vertical striations and unevennesses in the exposed, broken soil.

Bordman snatched up glasses and put them to his eyes. The shore seemed to leap toward him. He saw the harsh outlines of the temporary cliff go soft. The bottom ceased to look like soil. It glistened. It moved outward in masses which grew rounder as they swelled. They flowed after the now-vanished fallen stuff, into the water. The top-soil was suddenly undercut. The wetter material under it flowed away, leaving a ledge which bore carefully tended flowering shrubs— Bordman could see specks of color which were their blossoms—and a brightly-colored, small, trim house in which some family had lived.

The flow-away of the deeper soil made a greater, more cavernous hollow beneath the surface. It began to collapse. The house teetered, fell, smashed. More soil dropped down, and more, and more.

Presently there was a depression, a sort of valley leading inland away from the sea, in what had been a rampart of green at the water's edge. It was still green, but through the glasses Bordman could see that trees had fallen, and a white-painted fence was splintered. And there was still movement.

The movement slowed and slowed, but it was not possible to say when it stopped. In reality, it did not stop. The island's soil was still flowing into the ocean.

Barnes drew a deep breath.

"I thought that was it, sir," he said shakily. "I mean—that the whole island would start sliding."

"The ground's a bit more water-soaked down here," Bordman said. "Inland the bottom-soil's not nearly as fluid as here. But I'd hate to have a really heavy rainfall right now!"

Barnes' mind jerked back to the Sector Chief's office.

"The drumming would set off the ship-fuel?"

"Among other things," said Bordman. "Yes." Then he said abruptly: "How good are you at precision measurements? I've messed around on swamp-planets. I know a bit too much about what I ought to find, which is not good for accuracy. Can you take these bottles and measure the rate of sedimentation and plot it against salinity?"

"Y—yes, sir. I'll try."

"If we had soil-coagulants enough," said Bordman, "we could handle that damned upside-down swamp the civilians have so carefully made here. But we haven't got it! The freshened sea-water they've been irrigating with is practically mineral-free! I want to know how much mineral content in the water would keep the swamp-mud from acting like wet soap. It's entirely possible that we'd have to make the soil too salty to grow anything, in order to anchor it. But I want to know!"

Barnes said uncomfortably:

"Wouldn't you—wouldn't you have to put the minerals in irrigation-water to get them down to the swamp?"

Bordman grinned, surprisingly.

"You've got promise, Barnes! Yes. I would. And it would increase the rate of slide before it stopped it. Which could be another problem. But it was good work to think of it! When we get back to Headquarters, you commandeer a laboratory and make those measurements for me."

"Yes, sir," said Barnes.

"We'll start back now," said Bordman.

The recreation-boat obediently turned. It went out to sea until the water flowing past its hull was crystal-clear. And Bordman seemed to relax. On the way they passed more small boats. Many of them were gardeners' boats, from which men dived with diving-masks to tend or harvest the cultivated garden-patches not too far down. But many were pleasure-boats, from double-hulled sailing craft intended purely for sport, to sturdy, though small, cabin cruisers which could venture far out to sea, or even around to the windward of the island for sport-fishing. All the pleasure-craft were crowded—there were usually some children—and it was noticeable that on each one there were always some faces turned toward the shore.

"That," said Bordman, "makes for emotional thinking. These people know their danger. So they've packed their children and their wives into these little cockle-shells to try to save them. They're waiting offshore here to find out if they're doomed regardless. I wouldn't say"—he nodded toward a delicately designed twin-hull sailer with more children than adults aboard—"I wouldn't call that a good substitute for an Ark!"

Young Barnes fidgeted. The boat turned again and

went parallel to the shore toward where Headquarters
land came down to the sea. The ground was firmer
there. There had been no irrigation. Lateral seepage had
done some damage at the edge of the reserve, but the
major part of the shoreline was unbroken, unchanged
solid ground, looming above the beach. There was, of
course, no sand at the edge of the water. There had been
no weathering of rock to produce it. When this island
was upraised, its coating of hardened ooze protected the
stone, the lee-side waves merely lapped upon bare,
curdled rock. The wharf for pleasure-boats went out on
metal pilings into deep water.

"Excuse me, sir," said young Barnes, "but—if the fuel
blows, it'll be pretty bad, won't it?"

"That's the understatement of the century," Bordman
commented. "Yes. It will. Why?"

"You've something in mind to try to save the rest
of the island. Nobody else seems to know what to do.
If—if I may say so, sir, your safety is pretty important.
And you could do your work on the cliffs, and—if I
could stay at Headquarters and—"

He stopped, appalled at his own presumption in
suggesting that he could substitute for a Senior Officer
even as a message-boy, and even for his convenience
or safety. He began to stammer:

"I m-mean, sir, n-not that I'm capable of it—"

"Stop stammering," grunted Bordman. "There aren't
two separate problems. There's one which is the compound of the two. I'm staying at Headquarters to try
something on the ship-fuel side, and Werner will spe-
cialize on the rest of the island since he hasn't come
up with anything but shifting people to the icepack.
And the situation isn't hopeless! If there's an earthquake
or a storm, of course, we'll be wiped out. But short
of one of those calamities, we can save part of the
island. I don't know how much, but some. You make

those measurements. If you're doubtful, get a Headquarters man to duplicate them. Then give me both
sets."

"Y-yes, sir," said young Barnes.

"And," said Bordman, "never try to push your ranking officer into a safe place, even if you're willing to
take his risk. Would you like it if a man under you tried
to put you in a safe place while he took the chance
that was yours?"

"N-no, sir!" admitted the very junior lieutenant.
"But—"

"Make those measurements!" snapped Bordman.

The boat came into the dock. Bordman got out and
went to Sandringham's office.

Sandringham was in the act of listening to somebody in the phone-screen, who apparently was on the
thin edge of hysteria. The brown dog was sprawled
asleep on the rug.

When the man in the vision-screen panted to a stop,
Sandringham said calmly:

"I am assured that before the soil of the island is
too far gone, measures now in preparation will be
applied to good effect. A Senior Survey Officer is now
preparing remedial measures. He is—ah—a specialist
in problems of exactly this nature."

"But we can't wait!" panted the civilian fiercely. "I'll
proclaim a planetary emergency! We'll take over the
reserve area by force! We have to—"

"If you try," Sandringham told him grimly, "I'll
mount paralysis-guns to stop you." He said with icy
precision: "I urged the planetary government to go easy
on this irrigation. You yourself denounced me in the
Planetary Council for trying to interfere in civilian
affairs. Now you want to interfere in Survey affairs!
I resent it as much as you did, and with much better
reason."

"Murderer!" panted the civilian. "Murderer!"

Sandringham snapped off the phone-screen. He swung his chair and nodded to Bordman.

"That was the planetary president," he said.

Bordman sat, down. The brown dog blinked his eyes open and then got up and shook himself.

"I'm holding off those idiots," said the Sector Chief in suppressed fury. "I daren't tell him it's more dangerous here than outside! If or when that fuel blows— do you realize that the falling of a single tree-limb might set off an explosion in the Reserve-area here that would— But you do know."

"Yes," admitted Bordman.

He did know. Some hundreds of tons of ship-fuel going off would destroy this entire end of the island. And almost certainly the concussion would produce violent movement of the rest of the island's surface. But he was uncomfortable about putting forward his own ideas. He was not a good salesman. He suspected his own opinions until he had proved them with painstaking care, for fear of having them adopted on his past record rather than because they were sound. And then, too, this plan involved junior ranks being informed about the proposal. If they accepted a dubious plan on high authority, and the plan miscarried, it made them share in the mistake. Which hurt their self-confidence. Young Barnes, now, would undoubtedly obey any order and accept any hint blindly, and Bordman honestly did not know why. But as a matter of the training of junior ranks—

"About the work to be done," said Bordman, "I imagine the seawater freshening plants have closed down?"

"They have!" said Sandringham. "They insisted on piling them up over my protests. Now if anybody proposed operating one, they'd scream to high Heaven!"

"What was done with the minerals taken out of the seawater?" Bordman asked.

"You know how the fresheners work," said Sandringham. "They pump seawater in at one end, and at the other one pipe yields fresh water, and the other heavy brine. They dump the heavy brine back overboard and the fresh water's pumped up and distributed through the irrigation systems."

"It's too bad some of the salts weren't stored," said Bordman. "Could a freshener be started up again?"

Sandringham stared. Then he said:

"Oh, the civilians would love that! No! If any man started up a water-freshener, the civilians would kill him and smash it!"

"But I think we'll need one. We'll want to irrigate some of the Reserve area."

"My God! What for?" demanded Sandringham. He paused. "No! Don't tell me! Let me try to work it out."

There was silence. The brown dog blinked at Bordman. He held out his hand. The dog came sedately to him and bent his head to be scratched.

After a considerable time, the Sector Chief growled: "I give up. Do you want to tell me?"

Bordman nodded. He said:

"In a sense, the trouble here is that there's a swamp underground, made by irrigation. It slides. It's really a swamp upside down. On Soris II we had a very odd problem, only the swamp was right-side-up there. We'd several hundred square miles of swamp that could be used if we could drain it. We built a soil-dam around it. You know the trick. You bore two rows of holes twenty feet apart and put soil-coagulant in them. It's an old, old device. They used it a couple of hundred years ago back on Earth. The coagulant seeps out in all directions and coagulates the dirt. Makes it watertight. It swells with water and fills the space between

the soil-particles. In a week or two there's a water-tight
barrier, made of soil, going down to bed-rock. You
might call it a coffer-dam. No water can seep through.
On Soris II we knew that if we could get the water
out of the mud inside this coffee-dam, we'd have
cultivable ground."

Sandringham said skeptically:

"But it called for ten years' pumping, eh? When mud
doesn't move, pumping isn't easy!"

"We wanted the soil," said Bordman. "And we didn't
have ten years. The Soris II colony was supposed to
relieve population-pressure on another planet. The
pressure was terrific. We had to be ready to receive
some colonists in eight months. We had to get the
water out quicker than it could be pumped. And there
was another problem mixed up with it. The swamp
vegetation was pretty deadly. It had to be gotten rid
of, too. So we made the dam and—well—took certain
measures, and then we irrigated it. With water from
a nearby river. It was very ticklish. But we had dry
ground in four months, with the swamp-vegetation
killed and turning back to humus."

"I ought to read your reports," said Sandringham
dourly. "I'm too busy, ordinarily. But I should read
them. How'd you get rid of the water?"

Bordman told him. The telling required eighteen
words. "Of course," he added, "we picked a day when
there was a strong wind from the right quarter."

Sandringham stared at him. Then he said:

"But how does that apply here? It was sound
enough, though I'd never have thought of it. But what's
it got to do with the situation here?"

"This swamp, you might say," said Bordman, "is
underground. But there's forty feet, on an average, of
soil on top." He explained what difference that made.
It took him three sentences to make the difference clear.

Sandringham leaned back in his chair. Bordman scratched the dog, somewhat embarrassed. Sandringham thought.

"I do not see any possible chance," said Sandringham distastefully, "of doing it any other way. I would never have thought of that! But I'm taking part of the job out of your hands, Bordman."

Bordman said nothing. He waited.

"Because," said Sandringham, "you're not the man to put over to the civilians what they must believe. You're not impressive. I know you, and I know you're a good man in a pinch. But this pinch needs a salesman. So I'm going to have Werner make the—er—pitch to the planetary government. Results are more important than justice, so Werner will front this affair."

Bordman winced a little. But Sandringham was right. He didn't know how to be impressive. He could not speak with pompous conviction, which is so much more convincing than reason to most people. He wasn't the man to get the cooperation of the non-Service population, because he could only explain what he knew and believed, and was not practiced in persuasion. But Werner was. He had the knack of making people believe anything, not because it was reasonable but because it was oratory.

"I suppose you're right," acknowledged Bordman. "We need civilian help and a lot of it. I'm not the man to get it. He is." He did not say anything about Werner being the man to get credit, whether he deserved it or not. He patted the dog's head and stood up. "I wish I had a good supply of soil-coagulant. I need to make a coffer-dam in the reserve area here. But I think I'll manage."

Sandringham regarded him soberly as he moved to the door. As he was about to pass out of it, Sandringham said. "Bordman—"

"What?"

"Take good care of yourself. Will you?"

Therefore Senior Officer Werner, of the Colonial Survey, received his instructions from Sandringham. Bordman never knew the details of the instructions Werner got. They were possibly persuasive, or they may have been menacing. But Werner ceased to argue for the movement of any fraction of the island's population to the arctic ice-cap, and instead made frequent eloquent addresses to the planetary population on the scientific means by which their lives were to be saved. Between the addresses, perhaps, he sweated cold sweat when a tree sedately tilted in what had seemed solid soil, or a building settled perceptibly while he looked at it, or when a section of the island's soil bulged upward.

Instead, he headed citizens' committees, and grandly gave instructions, and spoke in unintelligible and therefore extremely scientific terms when desperately earnest men asked for explanations. But he was perfectly clear in what he wanted them to do.

He wanted drill-holes in the arable soil down to the depth at which the holes began to close up of themselves. He wanted those holes not more than a hundred feet apart in lines which slanted at a little less than forty-five degrees to the gradient of the bed-rock.

Sandringham checked his speeches, at the rate of four a day. Once he had Bordman called away from where he supervised some improbable operations. Bordman was smeared with the island's grayish mud when he looked into the phone-plate to take the call.

"Bordman," said Sandringham curtly, "Werner's saying those holes you want are to be in lines exactly forty-five degrees to the gradient."

"That—I'd like a little less," said Bordman. "If they

slanted three miles across the grade for every two downhill, it would be better. I'd like to put a lot more lines of holes. But there's the element of time."

"I'll have him explain that he was misquoted," said Sandringham, grimly. "Three across to two down. How close do you really want those lines?"

"As close as possible," said Bordman. "But I've got to have them quickly. How does the barometer look?"

"Down a tenth," said Sandringham.

Bordman said:

"Damn! Has he got plenty of labor?"

"All the labor there is," said Sandringham. "And I'm having a road laid along the cliffs for speed with the trucks. If I dared—and if I had the pipe—I'd lay a pipe-line."

"Later," said Bordman tiredly. "If he's got labor to spare, set them to work turning the irrigation systems hind part before. Make them drainage systems. Use pumps. So if rain does come it won't be spread out on the land by all the pretty ditches. So it will be gathered instead and either flung back over the cliffs or else drained downhill without getting a chance to sink into the ground. For the time being, anyhow."

Sandringham said:

"Has it occurred to you what a good, pounding rain would do to Headquarters, and consequently to public confidence on this island, and therefore to the attempt of anybody to do anything but wring his hands because he was doomed?"

Bordman grimaced.

"I'm irrigating, here. I've got a small-sized lake made, and an ice coffer-dam, and the water-freshener is working around the clock. If there is labor, tell 'em to fix the irrigation systems into drainage layouts. That'd cheer them, anyhow."

He was very weary. There is a certain exhausting

quality in the need to tell other men to do work which may cause them to be killed. The fact that one would certainly be killed with them did not lessen the tension.

He went back to his work. And it definitely seemed to be as purposeless as any man's work could possibly be. Downgrade from the now thoroughly deserted area in which ship-fuel tanks had leaked—quite far down-grade—he had commandeered all the refrigeration equipment in the warehouses. Since refrigeration was necessary for fuel-storage, there was a great deal. He had planted iron pipes in the soil, and circulated refrigerant in it. Presently there was a wall of solidly frozen soil which was shaped like a shallow U. In the curved part of that U he'd siphoned out a lake. A peristaltic pump ran seawater from the island's lee out upon the ground—where it instantly turned to mud—and another peristaltic pump sucked the mud up again and delivered it down-grade beyond the line of freezing-pipes. It was in fact a system of hydraulic dredging such as is normally performed in rivers and harbors. But when top-soil is merely former abyssal mud it is an excellent way to move dirt. Also, it does not require anybody to strike blows into soil which may be explosive when one has gotten down near bedrock, and in particular there are no clanking machines.

But it was hair-raising.

In one day, though, he had a sizeable lake pumped out. And he pumped it out to emptiness, smelling the water as it went down to a greater depth below the previous ground surface. At the end of the day he shivered and ordered pumping ended for the time.

Then he had a brine-pipe laid around a great circuit, to the headquarters ground which was up-grade from the now-deserted square mile or so in which the fuel-tanks lay deep in the soil. And here, also, he performed excavation without the sound of hammer, shovel, or pick. He thrust pipes into the ground, and they had nozzles at the end which threw part of the water backward. So that when sea-water poured into them it thrust them deeper into the ground by the backward jet action. Again the fact that the soil was abyssal mud made it possible. The nozzles floated up much grayish mud, but they bored ahead down to bed-rock, and there they lay flat and tunneled to one side and the other, the tunnels they made being full of water at all times.

From those tunnels, as they extended, an astonishing amount of sea-water seeped out into the soil near bed-rock. But it was sea-water. It was heavily mineralized. It is a peculiarity of sea-water that it is an electrolyte, and it is a property of electrolytes that they coagulate colloids, and discourage the suspension of small solid particles which are on the borderline of being colloids. In fact, the water of the ocean of Canna III turned the ground-soil into good, honest mud which did not feel at all soapy, and through which it percolated with a surprising readiness.

Young Barnes supervised this part of the operation, once it was begun. He shamed the Survey personnel assigned to him into perhaps excessive self-confidence.

"He knows what he's doing," he said firmly. "Look here! I'll take that canteen. It's fresh water. Here's some soap. Wet it in fresh water and it lathers. See? It dissolves. Now try to dissolve it in seawater! Try it! See? They put salt in the boiled stuff to separate soap out, when they make it!" He'd picked up that item from Bordman. "Seawater won't soften the ground. It can't! Come on, now, let's get another pipe putting more salt water underground!"

His workmen did not understand what he was doing, but they labored willingly because it was for a purpose. . . . And downhill, in the hydraulic-dredged-out lake, water came seeping in, in the form of mud. And another pipe came up from the sea-shore. It was a rather small pipe, and the personnel who laid it were bewildered. Because there was a water-freshening plant down there and all the fresh water was poured back overboard, while the brine, saturated with salts from the ocean, unable to dissolve a single grain of anything, was being used to fill the small artificial lake.

The second day Sandringham called Bordman again, and again Bordman peered wearily into the phone-screen. "Yes," said Bordman. "The leaked fuel is turning up. In solution. I'm trying to measure the concentration by matching specific gravities of lake-water and brine, and then sticking electrodes in each. The fuel's corrosive as the devil. It gives a different EMF. Higher than brine of the same density. I think I've got it in hand."

"Do you want to start shipping it?" demanded Sandringham.

"You can begin pouring it down the holes," said Bordman. "How's the barometer?"

"Down three-tenths this morning. Steady now."

"Damn!" said Bordman. "I'll set up molds. Freeze it in plastic bags the size of the bore-holes so it will go down. While it's frozen they can even push it down deep."

Sandringham said grimly:

"There's been more damned technical work done with ship-fuel than any other substance since time began. But remember that the stuff can still be set off, even dissolved in water. Its sensitivity goes down, but it's not gone."

"If it were," said Bordman drearily, "you could invite in the civilian population to sit on its rump. I've got something like forty tons of ship-fuel in brine solution in this lake I pumped out! But it's in five thousand tons of brine. We don't speak above a whisper when we're around it. We walk in carpet-slippers and you never saw people so polite! We'll start freezing it."

"How can you handle it?" demanded Sandringham apprehensively.

"The brine freezes at minus thirty," said Bordman. "In one per cent solution it's only five per cent sensitive at minus nineteen. We're handling it at minus nineteen. I think I'll step up the brine and chill it a little more."

He waved a mud-smeared hand and went away.

That day, bolster-trucks began to roll out of Survey Headquarters. They rolled very smoothly, and they trailed a fog of chilled air behind them. And presently there were men with heavy gloves on their hands taking long things like sausages out of the bolster-trucks and untying the ends and lowering them down into holes bored in the top-soil until they reached places where wetness made the holes close up again. Then the men from Survey pushed those frozen sausages underground still further by long poles with carefully padded—and refrigerated—ends. And then they went on to other holes.

The first day there were five hundred such sausages thrust down into holes in the ground, which holes to all intents and purposes closed up behind them. The second day there were four thousand. The third day there were eight. On the fourth the solution of ship-fuel in brine in the lake was so thin that it did not give enough EMF in the little battery-cell to show how much corrosive substance there was in the brine. It was not mud any longer. Brine flowed at the top of bedrock, and it left the mud behind it, because salt water hindered the suspension of former globigerinous ooze particles. It was practically colloid. Salt water almost coagulated it.

The brine flowing from the salt-water tunnels upwind showed no more ship-fuel in it. Bordman called Sandringham and told him.

"I can call in the civilians," said Sandringham. "You've mopped up the leaked stuff! It couldn't have been done—"

"Not anywhere but here with bedrock handy just underneath and slanting," admitted Bordman. "Tell them they can come if they want to. They'll sort of drift in. I want to tap some more ship-fuel for the rest of those bore-holes."

Sandringham hesitated.

"Twenty thousand holes," said Bordman tiredly. "Each one had a six-hundred pound block of frozen saturated brine dumped in it with roughly one pound of ship-fuel in solution. We've gone that far. Might as well go the rest of the way. How's the barometer?"

"Up a tenth," said Sandringham. "Still rising."

Bordman blinked at him, because he had trouble keeping his eyes open.

"Let's ride it, Sandringham!"

Sandringham hesitated. Then he said:

"Go ahead."

Bordman waved his arms at his associates, whom he admired with great fervor in his then-foggy mind, because they were always ready to work when it was needed, and it had not stopped being needed for five days running. He explained that there were only three more miles of holes to be filled up, and therefore they would just draw so much of ship-fuel and blend it carefully with an appropriate amount of chilled brine and then freeze it in appropriate sausages. . . .

Young Lieutenant Barnes said:

"Yes, sir. I'll take care of it."

Bordman said:

"Barometer's up a tenth." His eyes did not quite focus. "All right, Lieutenant. Go ahead. Promising young officer. Excellent. I'll sit down here for jusht a moment."

When Barnes came back, Bordman was asleep. And a last one hundred and fifty frozen sausages of brine and ship-fuel went out of Headquarters within a matter of hours. Then a vast quietude settled down everywhere.

Young Barnes sat beside Bordman, menacing anybody who even thought of disturbing him. When Sandringham called for him Barnes went to the phone-plate.

"Sir," he said with vast formality. "Mr. Bordman went five days without sleep. His job's done. I won't wake him, sir!"

Sandringham raised his eyebrows.

"You won't?"

"I won't, sir!" said young Barnes.

Sandringham nodded.

"Fortunately," he observed, "nobody's listening. You are quite right."

He snapped the connection. And then young Barnes realized that he had defied a Sector Chief, which is something distinctly more improper in a junior officer than merely trying to instruct him in topping off his vacuum-suit tanks.

Twelve hours later, however, Sandringham called for him. "Barometer's dropping, Lieutenant. I'm concerned. I'm issuing a notice of the impending storm. Not everybody will crowd in on us, but a great many will. I'm explaining that the chemicals put into the bottom soil may not quite have finished their work. If Bordman wakens, tell him."

"Yes, sir," said Barnes.

But he did not intend to wake Bordman. Bordman, however, woke of himself at the end of twenty hours of sleep. He was stiff and sore and his mouth tasted as if something had kittened in it. Fatigue can produce a hangover, too.

"How's the barometer?" he asked when his eyes came open.

"Dropping, sir. Heavy winds. The Sector Chief has opened the Reserve Area to the civilians if they wish to come."

Bordman computed dizzily on his fingers. A more complex instrument was actually needed, of course. One does not calculate on one's fingers just how long a one per cent dilute solution of ship-fuel in frozen brine has taken to melt, and how completely it has diffused through an upside-down swamp with the pressure of forty feet of soil on top of it, and therefore its effective concentration and dispersal underground.

"I think," said Bordman, "it's all right. By the way, did they turn the irrigation systems hind end to?"

Young Barnes did not know what this was all about. He had to send for information. Meanwhile he solicitously plied Bordman with coffee and food. Bordman grew reflective.

"Queer," he said. "You think of the damage leaked ship-fuel can do. Setting off the rest of the store and all. Even by itself it rates some thousands of tons of TNT. I wonder what TNT was, before it became a ton-measure of energy? You think of it exploding in one place, and it's appalling! But think of all that same amount of energy applied to square miles of upside-down swamp. Hundreds or thousands of miles of upside-down swamp. D'you know, Lieutenant, on Soris II we pumped a ship-fuel solution onto a swamp we wanted to drain? Flooded it, and let it soak until a day came with a nice, strong, steady wind."

"Yes, sir," said Barnes respectfully.

"Then we detonated it. We didn't have a one per cent solution. It was more like a thousandth of one per cent solution. Nobody's ever measured the speed of propagation of an explosion in ship-fuel, dry. But it's been measured in dilute solution. It isn't the speed of sound. It's lower. It's purely a temperature-phenomenon. In water, at any dilution, ship-fuel goes off just barely below the boiling-point of water. It doesn't detonate from shock when it's diluted enough to be ionized, but that takes a hell of a lot of dilution. Have you got some more coffee?"

"Yes, sir," said Barnes. "Coming up."

"We floated ship-fuel solution over that swamp, Barnes, and let it stand. It has a high diffusion-rate. It went down into the mud. . . . And there came a day when the wind was right. I dumped a red-hot iron bar into the swamp-water that had ship-fuel in solution. It was the damnedest sight you ever saw!"

Barnes served him more coffee: Bordman sipped it, and it burned his tongue.

"It went up in steam," he said. "The swamp-water that had the ship-fuel dissolved in it. It didn't explode, as a mass. They told me later that it propagated at hundreds of feet per second only. They could see the wall of steam go marching across the swamp. Not even high-pressure steam. There was a woosh! and a cloud of steam half a mile high that the wind carried away. And all the surface-water in the swamp was gone, and all the poisonous swamp-vegetation parboiled and dead. So—" He yawned suddenly—"we had a ten-mile by fifty-mile stretch of arable ground ready for the coming colonists."

He tried the coffee again. He added reflectively:

"That trick, it didn't explode the ship-fuel, in a way. It burned it. In water. It applied the energy of the fuel to the boiling-away of water. Powerful stuff! We got rid of two feet of water on an average, counting what came out of the mud. It cost—hm—a fraction of a gram per square yard."

He gulped the coffee down. There were men looking at him solicitously. They seemed very glad to see him awake again. Outside a monstrous bank of cloud-stuff was visible piling up in the sky. He suddenly blinked at that.

"Hello! How long did I sleep, Barnes?"

Barnes told him. Bordman shook his head to clear it.

"We'll go see Sandringham," said Bordman. "I'd like to postpone firing as long as I can, short of having the stuff start draining into the sea to leeward."

Several mud-stained men were standing around the place where Bordman had slept. When he went, still groggy, out to the bolster-truck young Barnes had waiting, they regarded Bordman in a very respectful manner. Somebody grunted, "Good to have worked with you, sir," which is about as much of admiration as anybody would want to hear expressed. These associates of Bordman in the mopping-up of leaked ship's fuel would be able to brag of the job at all times and in all places hereafter.

Then the truck went trundling away in search of Sandringham. It found him on the cliffs to the windward side of the island. The sea was no longer a cerulean blue. It was slaty-color. There were occasional flecks of white foam on the water four thousand feet below. There were dark clouds, by then covering practically all the sky. Far out to sea, there were small craft heading for the ends of the island, to go around it and ride out the coming storm in its lee.

Sandringham greeted Bordman with relief. Werner stood close by, opening and closing his hands jerkily.

"Bordman!" said the Sector Chief cordially. "We're having a disagreement, Werner and I. He's confident that the turning of the irrigation systems hind end to—making them surface-draining systems, in effect—will take care of the whole situation. Adding the brine underground, he thinks, will have done a good deal more. He says it'll be bad, psychologically, for anything more to be done. He didn't speak of it, and it would injure public confidence in the Survey."

Bordman said curtly:

"The *only* thing that will make a permanent difference on this island is for the water-fresheners to be a little less efficient. Barnes has the figures. He computed them from some measurements I had him make. If the water-freshener plants don't take all the sea-minerals out; if they don't make the irrigation water so infernally soft and suitable for hair-washing and the like; if they turn out hard water for irrigation, this won't happen again. But there's too much water underground now. We've got to get it out, because a little more's going underground from this storm, surface-drainage systems or no surface-drainage systems."

Sandringham pointed to leeward, where a black, thick procession of human beings trooped toward the Survey area on foot and by every possible type of vehicle.

"I've ordered them turned into the ship-sheds and warehouses," said the Sector Chief. "But of course we haven't shelter for all of them. At a guess, when they feel safe they'll go back to their homes even through the storm."

The sky to windward grew blacker and blacker. There was no longer a steady flow of wind coming over the cliff's edge. It came in gusts, now, of extreme violence. They could make a man stagger on his feet. There were more flecks of white on the ocean's surface.

"The boats," added Sandringham, "were licked. There simply wasn't enough oil to maintain the slick. The radio reports were getting hysterical before I ordered them told that we had it beaten on shore. They're running for shelter now. I think they'd have stayed out there trying to hold the slick in place with their tow-line, if I hadn't said we had matters in hand."

Werner said, tight-lipped:

"I hope we have!"

Bordman shrugged.

"The wind's good and strong, now," he observed. "Let's find out. You've got the starting system all set?"

Sandringham waved his hand toward a high-voltage battery. It was of a type designed for blasting on air-less planets, but that did not matter. Its cables led snakily for a couple of hundred feet to a very small pile of grayish soil which had been taken out of a bore-hole, and went over that untidy heap and down into the ground. Bordman took hold of the firing-handle. He paused.

"How about the highways?" he asked. "There might be some steam out of this hole."

"All allowed for," said Sandringham. "Go ahead."

There was a gust of wind strong enough to knock a man down, and a humming sound in the air, as wind beat upon the four-thousand-foot cliff and poured over its top. There were gradually rising waves, below. The sky was gray, the sea slate-colored. Far, far to wind-ward, the white line of pouring rain upon the water came marching toward the island.

Bordman pumped the firing-handle.

There was a pause, while wind-gusts tore at his garments and staggered him where he stood. It was quite a long pause. Then a vapor came jetting out of

the bore-hole. It was perfectly white. It came out with
a sudden burst which was not in any sense explosive,
but was merely a vast rushing of vaporized water. Then,
a hundred yards away, there was a mistiness on the
grassy surface. Still farther, a crack in the surface-soil
let out a curtain of white vapor.

Here and there, everywhere, gouts of steam poured
into the air and tumbled into the storm-wind. It was
noticeable that the steam did not come out as an
invisible vapor and condense in mid-air. It poured out
of the ground in clouds, already condensed but thrust
out by more masses of vapor behind it. It was not
super-heated steam that came out. It was simply steam.
Harmless steam, like the steam out of the spouts of
tea-kettles. It rose from individual places everywhere.
It made a massive coating of vapor which the storm-
wind blew away. In seconds a half-mile of soil was
venting steam. In seconds more a mile. The thick fleecy
vapor swept across the landscape. The storm-wind
could only tumble it and sweep it away.

In minutes there was no part of the island to be seen
at all, save only the thin line of the cliffs reaching away
between dark water on the one hand and snow-white
clouds of vapor on the other.

"It can't scald anybody, can it?" asked Barnes
uneasily.

"Not," said Bordman, "when it's had to come up
through forty feet of soil. It's been pretty well cooled
off in taking up some extra moisture. It spreads pretty
well, doesn't it?"

The Sector Chief's office had tall windows—doors,
really—that looked out upon green lawn and many
trees. Now sheets of rain beat down outside. Wind
whipped at the trees. There was tumult and roaring
and the vibration of gusts of hurricane force. Even the

building in which the Sector Chief's office was vibrated slightly in the wind.

The Sector Chief beamed. The brown dog came in, looked around the room, and walked in leisurely fashion toward Bordman. He settled with a sigh beside Bordman's chair.

"What I want to know," said Werner, "is, won't this rain put back all the water the ship-fuel boiled away?"

Bordman said:

"Two inches of rain would be a heavy fall, Sandringham tells me. It's the lack of heavy rains that made the civilians start irrigating. When you figure the energy-content of ship-fuel, Werner, an appreciable fraction of the energy in atomic explosive, it's sort of deceptive. Turn it into thermal units and it gets to be enlightening. We turned loose, underground, enough heat to boil away two feet of soil-water under the island's whole surface."

Werner said sharply:

"What'll happen when the heat passes up through the soil? It'll kill the vegetation, won't it?"

"No," said Bordman mildly. "Because there was two feet of water to be turned to steam. The bottom layer of the soil was raised to the temperature of steam at a few pounds pressure. No more. The heat's already escaped. In the steam."

The phone-plate lighted. Sandringham snapped it on. A voice made a report in a highly official voice.

"Right!" said Sandringham. The highly official voice spoke again. "Right!" said Sandringham again. "You may tell the ships in orbit that they can come down now, if they don't mind getting wet." He turned. "Did you hear that, Bordman? They've bored new cores. There are a few soggy spots, but the ground's as firm, all over the island, as it was when the Survey first came here. A very good job, Bordman! A very good job!"

Bordman flushed. He reached down and patted the head of the brown dog.

"Look!" said the Sector Chief. "My dog, there, has taken a liking to you. Will you accept him as a present, Bordman?"

Bordman grinned.

Young Barnes made ready to rejoin his ship. He was very strictly Service, very stiffly at attention. Bordman shook hands with him.

"Nice to have had you around, Lieutenant," he said warmly. "You're a very promising young officer. Sandringham knows it and has made a note of the fact. Which I suspect is going to put you to a lot of trouble. There's a devilish shortage of promising young officers. He'll give you hellish jobs to do, because he has an idea you'll do them."

"I'll try, sir," said young Barnes formally. Then he said, "May I say something, sir? I'm very proud to have worked with you. But dammit, sir, it seems to me that something more than just saying thank you was due you! The Service ought to—"

Bordman regarded the young man approvingly.

"When I was your age," he said, "I'd the very same attitude. But I had the only reward the Service or anything else could give me. The job got done. It's the only reward you can expect in the Service, Barnes. You'll never get any other."

Young Barnes looked rebellious. He shook hands again.

"Besides," said Bordman, "there is no better."

Young Barnes marched back toward his ship in the great metal cross-cross of girders which was the landing-grid.

Bordman absently patted his dog as he headed back toward Sandringham's office for his orders to return to his own work.

❖   ❖   ❖

So Bordman went back to his wife Riki and the job he'd been working on. After that there was another job, and another. He received the high honor of being given the most impossible of the tasks the Survey was forced to do. Which was deeply satisfying. He regretted that he had to become relatively inactive when he became Sector Chief.

But his wife liked it very much. There was assurance, then, that they would be together for always, and Bordman still had his work and she could make—again—a home. When one of his daughters was widowed and came to live with them with her children, Bordman was beautifully contented. Then he had absolutely everything he wanted. As reward for a lifetime of work and separation, he had the satisfactions—in his family—that other men enjoyed as a matter of course.

But sometimes he was embarrassed when his juniors were too respectful. He didn't think he rated it.

ANTHROPOLOGICAL NOTE

The meeting of Miss Cummings and Ray Hale in a Krug village on Venus is one of those events for which there is no real explanation. Unless one believes that there was or is a Th'Tark, who arranged the matter, it simply doesn't make sense. But it did happen. Miss Cummings met Hale under quite preposterous circumstances in a female-Krug village. She had known him before, a good many years since and forty million miles away. Then she had passionately wished for sudden death to strike him. When, after years, she saw him again she knew the same wish and what followed very probably prevented the extermination of the Krug in the name of the prosperity of interplanetary commerce. This would amount to a proof of Th'Tark's interest if there ever was a Th'Tark. But it's all very complicated.

Th'Tark is or was the possibly mythical Law-giver of the Krug, who are the quasi-semi-humanoid inhabitants of the Krug Archipelago in the Summer Sea on Venus. They look more human than most earthly primates, probably because they aren't furry, and Th'Tark is said

411

to have set up their laws and customs and very dubious moral code some tens of thousands of Venusian years ago. It was Th'Tark who decreed that male Krug should live dispirited, gloomy lives in the jungles by the seashore while female Krug built villages, practiced agriculture and other useful arts, and raised children. Miss Cummings was the lady anthropologist who examined their culture and kept them from extermination.

She landed in their midst from a survey-ship offshore from an island which on the map is called Tanit. The morning of her arrival was quite ordinary. There was no sunrise, of course. There never is. There was blackness everywhere at first, and then the sky became ever-so-faintly gray, and the cloudbank overhead lightened by imperceptible degrees, and presently it was morning with leaping waves all about the ship and foaming surf on the beaches and at the foot of the cliffs of the island a mile away. She prepared to land alone, as a field expedition in anthropology with qualified assistants, in the base, which was the ship. Her purpose was pure science, but the reason was interplanetary trade.

Venus wasn't well-settled then, and the cost of transportation to Earth was so high that only very precious things indeed could stand the cost and show a profit. But in the Krug Archipelago such a product had been found. It was *crythli* pearls and pearl-shell. They were utterly beautiful and utterly past imitation. They were the most desirable gems that men had ever seen, and their value was fabulous. But the few—still extremely rare—specimens which had been found had been discovered in the possession of male Krug in the jungles. The Krug were not anxious to part with them. They mentioned Th'Tark and females—the latter very reluctantly—and shut up. Moreover, when a Krug began to gather *crythli* shell and pearls, it was a sign that shortly he would disappear. Permanently. So trade in *crythli* pearls and pearl-shell languished, and the economic status of the Venusian colony needed interplanetary exchange. Hence Miss Cummings.

On this particular morning a helicopter lifted heavily from the ship and droned toward the island. Miss Cummings was in a landing-basket slung below. At four thousand feet altitude she could see the whole island, ringed by foam, with high mountains and broad valleys in its interior. The copter skimmed sharp-edged mountain-peaks and then settled down and down into the valley where a chosen village lay. The village had been studied by telephotography from the air, and Miss Cummings already had a fascinating list of questions to be answered. Why, for example, were there only females and Krug-children in the village? No picture had showed any male older than what would be earliest teen-age in a human. Was it true that the larger, kraal-like thatched dwellings belonged to multiparous lady Krug, while the curiously incomplete circle of quite small houses belonged to hopeful maidens? And those small, rounded, flower-beds before the kraal-houses. Filter-photography insisted that they were tastefully bordered with *crythli* shell, used by the Krug as clamshells are sometimes used by the owners of beachcottages on Earth. If this were true, they were fabulously valuable and the prosperity of the human colony on Venus required that they be acquired—by peaceful means if possible, but acquired—for shipment back to Earth.

Miss Cummings knew the blissful anticipation of a lady anthropologist with a new culture to study and assurance of credit for the job. She was utterly happy as the copter droned on down to land her for the beginning of her research. Of all things and persons in the solar system, she thought least of Ray Hale. But he was of paramount importance to her job, actually.

As she watched the sprawling, thatched-roof village enlarge at her approach, Hale was doing some research, too. That very same morning, in fact. But his methods were his own.

He had quite a reputation, had Hale. The colonial government had learned of his arrival on Venus just too late to grab him before he vanished into unexplored territory. He wasn't welcome on a newly colonized planet. He'd caused the First Native War on Mars, by taking advantage of the fact that at that time human law had not defined the killing of Martians as murder. He was responsible for the B'setse Massacre on Titan, when a hundred and fifty human colonists died as the result of his treatment of the most ancient and therefore richest of the Titanian natives nearby. He got away with rich loot from Titan, as he had on Mars, but colonial government officials didn't want him around.

On this particular morning, not three hundred miles from where Miss Cummings landed, he was doing research in his own fashion. He'd caught a male Krug and was extracting information from him. Traders after *crythli* shell had developed a sort of pidgin-Krug with which limited communication was possible, and Hale used that as part of his process. The rest of it would not be nice to describe. But he was forcing his captive to try to tell him, by an inadequate means of communication, facts he probably didn't know about mysteries he almost certainly didn't understand and positively didn't like to think about.

It was an extremely revolting performance, and it lasted a long time, but Hale probably enjoyed it. He was still a fairly handsome man—his good looks had been important in the affair causing Miss Cummings' passionate desire for lightning to strike him—but he wasn't at all attractive as he worked on the Krug. The whole business was ghastly, but Th'Tark probably allowed it. After all, it bore upon the preservation of the Krug race and culture from extermination.

In any case, when Hale finally killed the Krug and washed the debris overboard from the deck of his stolen boat, he knew where *crythli* shells were found. But he didn't think of looking for them himself. Instead, he took other information the Krug had yielded, and rather zestfully worked out a pattern for action which should yield him all the *crythli* pearls a man could want. The shell itself was precious, as mother-of-pearl had been, but the pearls themselves were more precious a thousand times over.

Three hundred miles away, Miss Cummings arrived at the chosen village. The helicopter circled that straggling settlement and a small horde of Krug swarmed out to stare up at it. Maybe they thought Th'Tark had something to do with it. (Maybe Th'Tark had.) They stared up—almost exclusively female. The exceptions were children—boy-Krug. The copter settled gently until the landing-basket touched ground. Miss Cummings cast off. The copter rose to the cloud-bank over-head where Th'Tark was reputed to dwell, and remained handy to come back within two minutes if Miss Cummings called for it by communicator. She had a small, nearly invisible hand-weapon with which to hold Krug off that long if necessary.

She didn't need to. The villagers approached her warily. But they observed that she was female. She had adopted a costume which emphasized the Krugoid features of a human woman. She held up gifts. Beaming, she offered them.

In five minutes she informed the copter crew that she wouldn't need them, but they stayed overhead anyhow just in case.

The business of making friends went on swimmingly. Miss Cummings was beautifully equipped for field investigation of a female social system. Before coming to Venus she'd taught denatured anthropology to classes of human college girls. She knew her females. For example, the older matrons of the Krug village had exactly the authoritative and self-satisfied air of a committee of college alumnae. They were middle-aged or older and accustomed to having their own way under all circumstances. To them Miss Cummings was charmingly deferential. There was one awkward moment, but it soon passed over. Miss Cummings, trying to begin speech, pointed to some object and used the trade-Krug male language word for it. Her audience tittered. Miss Cummings knew instantly that male and female Krug spoke different languages—as in some primitive cultures on Earth—and it was indecorous for one sex to use a noun or verb appropriate to the other. But Miss Cummings made no other break. The younger females, she observed, wore the impatient expression of human college girls. She addressed them cheerfully. To the older matrons she distributed necklaces of fluorescent beads and to the younger she passed out bracelets and small mirrors. The young females thereupon treated her with the tolerant condescension the young give to the older in all races without exception.

She even dealt adequately with the children. Mature Krug wore crudely woven garments, but the Krug-children were as innocent of clothing as of guile. To them she distributed sweetmeats. Not candy, of course. Krug taste-buds are not like human ones. She passed out bonbons of almost pure quinine and the Krug-children went into ecstasies over the luxury. But Miss Cummings discovered that the community did not approve the wasting of such things upon boys. Only future Krug matrons were worthy of largesse.

By nightfall Miss Cummings had been accepted as a welcome visitor and assigned one of the smaller houses in the incomplete circle which from air-photos had been considered the maidens' houses. Next day she set to work to acquire a vocabulary.

Hale—a shade under three hundred miles away, now—caught a second Krug male. This time he chose one of the youngest of those dispirited creatures who loaf and lurk in the jungles of the Krug islands. This creature he treated gently, at intervals, plying him with quinine and alternate beatings and cajolings. He got from him—and recorded for study—the female-language words which the younger Krug remembered more fully than an older one would have done. It was a racking experience for the adolescent Krug. He'd been kicked out of his village and stridently told to go and associate with the other worthless males in the jungle. He was embittered. But Hale made him recall and repeat all his childhood experiences. In the end he kicked his second captive ashore and prepared to make use of the data he'd acquired. He had no faintest desire to perform any action for the preservation of the Krug race. It just happened that way—though only Th'Tark could possibly have thought of it in advance. *If* there is a Th'Tark.

At the end of a week in the village, Miss Cummings was in an anthropologist's idea of heaven. She was doing the first known research on an extensive race-culture, and she had skilled help on the steamer, and she would get all the credit. But the help was important. For example, the Krug language required careful analysis. Not only were there male and female versions which were wholly unlike, but there were honorific terms as in Japanese, which could have been pitfalls. Different forms of address were used to different Krug matrons according to whether they had one or two or more children up to a dozen, after which a super-honorific applied. This could have caused trouble.

With the research staff on the ship, however, she learned to speak with remarkable speed. Up to a certain point. At a definite place she ran into frustration. As a human being, Miss Cummings could never fully believe that the Krug language had no word meaning *why?* The lack of it was like a blank stone wall preventing progress. Her communicator sent all her gathered information to the ship, with her notes. The philologists labored over it. In long discussions between ship and village, Miss Cummings led in the discovery that the language had only one gender (female) but all personal pronouns had thirty-two forms, honorific or self-deprecatory. There was an incredibly complex system of verb-conjugations, and a fine and adequate vocabulary of nouns. But all the nouns were proper ones! The word which meant *tree* meant *this tree*. There was no word for the abstract notion of treeness which was common to all arborescent plants. Therefore there was no verbal machinery for the operations of logic.

On the face of it, the fact was impossible. The Krug were civilized in their fashion, and they definitely used speech to convey objective information. But they did not discuss. They did not argue. They were invincibly literal-minded, and therefore they were probably quite happy. But Miss Cummings was not pleased when she asked about this custom and that and the framing of a question was a tortuous process—and received the bland and irrelevant reply that she was this-unmarried-female. She couldn't ask why her status prevented her being told. There was no why. It was definitely a female culture.

She seethed. She almost resented her unmarried state, since it prevented the pursuance of anthropological research. With the peculiar jealousy of a woman scientific worker, she began to envision a married woman being hastily supplied with the data she'd compiled and then sent in to replace her. It could be said that she burned.

Th'Tark could have told her to be at ease, of course, if anybody could. If the Krug were to escape extermination by the march of progress, Miss Cummings had to be responsible. Because she knew Ray Hale.

He'd gathered quite a lot of information she didn't have, by the time the language difficulty had reached its most frustrating form for her. Before she'd been in the village more than two weeks, Hale had acquired close to a quart of *crythli* pearls—and no trader had ever before been able to gather as many as half a dozen in one trading-season from the Krug. Some of those that Hale acquired were rather crudely pierced for stringing, but he was well over a millionaire in *crythli* pearls, already, and they'd only cost him a couple of weeks of research and a few hair-raising moments and a crime most men would queasily prefer not to commit. But it wasn't murder, because Krug hadn't yet been ruled human—under the laws forbidding homicide.

In her third week in the village, Miss Cummings witnessed a partial parallel to Hale's enterprise, though she didn't know it.

It began at daybreak, when she was wakened by the morning-noises. There were snickering, giggling noises from the jungle, which was only a hundred yards from the incomplete circle of maidens'-huts. There were boomings deeper in the trees, and something honked discordantly, and something else made sounds as if of hysterical laughter. But Miss Cummings was used to such sounds now. They were commonplace. The noises that disturbed her were speech-sounds.

There were chitterings which were children—boys and females together. There were deeper, authoritative, firm notes which were those of matrons. There was a great congregation of the village near Miss Cummings' house.

She dressed herself and went out-of-doors. All the village was assembled in the center of the maidens'-huts ring. The unmarried-females were gathered together, and they fairly jittered with hopeful agitation. The Krug-children raced and scampered about a solemn group of the older females. Miss Cummings approached, with her communicator turned on and relaying everything to the tape-recorders on the ship. As she drew near, she saw that a *crythli* shell was being passed from hand to hand among the older matrons. They examined it with great care and extreme minuteness. They acted, indeed, like short-sighted alumnae caught without their eye-glasses and seeming rather to smell than to look at some interesting object.

The oldest, stoutest female—possessed of a preposterous number of offspring—seemed to debate a very long time. The maidens jittered more visibly than before. Then the oldest female solemnly handed the *crythli*-shell to one of them. The maiden clasped it to her breast with dramatic satisfaction. This particular young female stood out in Miss Cummings' mind because in a Kruggish way she resembled a frog-like undergraduate who'd infested one of Miss Cummings' classes at her woman's college on Earth. That undergraduate, with thick spectacles and buck teeth and an irritating personality, had been married the day after graduation to a millionaire. It had seemed injustice at the time. Now her Krug opposite number was plainly chosen for some splendid prize. The *crythli* shell, incidentally, would have fetched a good fifteen thousand credits in Venus City, and several times that on Earth.

A gabbling uproar rose, and the other maidens looked bitter over their contemporary's triumph. The matrons gathered about the chosen one, beaming at her. The Krug children burst into a run for the jungle. They vanished in its depths.

Miss Cummings fumed because all this was inexplicable and she couldn't ask the question, "Why?"

The morning passed. Miss Cummings, in her hut, conferred with her aides and superiors on the ship offshore. Whatever was coming, it was without precedent in this research. Therefore it must be important. She was urged not to miss any developments.

She went out as the village children returned from the jungle. They carried burdens. There were logs of the hollow, cane-like jungle-trees which broke off cleanly at their joints. They were of diverse lengths and thicknesses. Other children staggered under loads of jungle-leaves and vines and creepers. They marched to that part of the village where the kraal-like dwelling stood. They began to construct a new house.

This was as remarkable as anything else about the whole Krug culture. No adult supervised. No instructions were issued. The children swarmed about the enterprise like so many bees, and if Miss Cummings had not been engaged in getting barred from all the matrons and the frog-faced Krug girl, she would have gaped as the house went up. Because it was done perfectly. With a precision they could not possibly have learned, the Krug children heaved the feather-light logs into upright position without even a floor-plan scratched on the ground. They deftly flipped crosspieces into place and tied them with vines. They established a roofing framework in the same fashion and thatched it with absolute competence. Then they stuck limber saplings here and there and began matter-of-factly to thatch down the walls. In a matter of some four hours they had built a house indistinguishable from the kraal-like dwellings of the matrons, only with fewer rooms. But extra rooms could be added.

Having performed the work without instructions, they ceased it without being dismissed. Five minutes after it was done they were busy again with the normal and zestful and quite useless occupations of Krug childhood. And perhaps the most astonishing thing about the whole job was that there was neither anything lacking in the house nor any material left over. They'd brought back exactly enough.

It was too much for Miss Cummings to grasp. She was striving to gather information on what she considered more important matters. Barred from the society of the matrons, for today, she visited the other maidens in their huts. She found them occupied as usual. Some of them wove. Miss Cummings had shown them minor improvements in the process which improved their product, but they ignored her instructions. They used the cloth she'd partly woven, but they did not adopt her changes.

Miss Cummings chatted with them, subject to the limitations of the language. She could say "this-cloth-is-good" or "I-come-to-visit-you." And they could agree. She could observe "the-house-is-becoming," meaning that it was being built. Which was similarly true. She could even say, and did say, "the-maiden-with-the-*crythli*-shell-is-not-where-we-are." They agreed to that, also. But Miss Cummings, bursting with scientific curiosity, could not ask why a new house had been built or where the *crythli* shell had come from or why it was presented to the frog-like maiden and what it signified. The language blocked all efforts.

Roy Hale could have told her, though. He was only two hundred miles away, then, and he now had three quarts of *crythli* pearls and did not even bother to own more than a few shells—though practically any shell was worth ten thousand credits in Venus City. He was a multi-multi-millionaire in *crythli* pearls, and still he planned to grow richer. He considered it humorous that there was no law forbidding his enterprise. It had not been defined that Krug were human, and therefore there was no penalty for killing them.

But to Miss Cummings the matter was still mystery. A *crythli* shell in the center of the maidens'-hut ring. The gift of the shell to the especially repulsive Krug girl. The building of a house. The complete withdrawal into privacy of the Krug maiden and all the matrons. Miss Cummings made wild guesses and waited for something to happen to solve the mystery.

She had to wait until evening when the cloudbank overhead began faintly to dim, since there were no sunsets on Venus. The light was no more than half-way faded when the Krug girl came out of the newly built kraal-house. Miss Cummings saw her and fairly sputtered her excitement into the communicator.

The Krug girl sat down before the new house with an air of elaborate unconcern. Always, previously, she had worn the single crude cloth garment of her sister-maidens. Now she wore a quite special outfit of which Miss Cummings had had no inkling before. But being a woman she grasped its marvelousness and its meaning instantly. The Krug girl was dressed as a bride. But no human bride was ever arrayed in a headdress of *crythli* pearls which would have sold for millions on the Earth-market, nor wore necklaces of *crythli* pearls no mere millionaire could have hoped to buy, nor did any human bride ever wear armlets and belts and breast-plates of *crythli* shell, when a reasonably rich man's wife only hoped wistfully to own a single small shell disk.

Miss Cummings gasped the news into the communicator. She was about to witness, she said agitatedly, the marriage ceremony of the Krug. It must be! It was the more certain because there was no visible bridegroom!

The village gathered. Behind the gaudily decorated Krug girl the matrons of the village took their places. They were stout and bland and infinitely satisfied with themselves and all the world. They looked rather like an alumnae group posing for a photograph on their twentieth class reunion. As the cloudbank overhead became darker and darker and more nearly black, there was a hushed waiting atmosphere everywhere. The children appeared. They came filing out in a long line. The foremost—a Krug child barely toddling—carried a lighted torch with tremendous solicitude. The others carried things which might also be torches, but were unlighted. There was silence save for the noises of the nearby jungle. The cloudbank darkened and darkened, and presently it was truly night There was no light anywhere in the village except the one small torch in the hands of a toddling Krug child. And nothing happened for a very long time.

Then came crisp, grunting commands from the oldest of the matrons. The small child reached its light to the next. A second torch flamed. That torch swung to a third, and that to a fourth, and so on until fifty flaring, sparkling flames furnished a brighter light than Miss Cummings had ever seen in the village after nightfall.

Then, and only then, she saw the bridegroom. In the darkness, guided by the first and only burning torch, the male Krug had crept into the village and to the new house. He had doubtless been perceived, but Th'Tark had undoubtedly ordained that a pretense of invisibility should rule until he stood before his bride.

Now he seemed to shrivel in the torchlight. He appeared at once desperately to wish to be anywhere else on the planet—in which he was like many human bridegrooms—and despairingly to be resigned to his fate. In the torchlight, seeming numbed in some fashion, he unburdened himself of *crythli* shells. He laid them down, one by one, before the adorned but stonily unresponsive maiden. Shell after shell to a fabulous value was piled before her. He actually laid down a full two dozen of the gleaming things. Most human girls would have grown starry-eyed if presented with a single one.

He straightened up. The torchlight glistened on his body. Miss Cummings had an impression that he sweated like a man in absolute terror and despair.

The most ancient of the matrons grunted.

The seated, decorated Krug-bride looked scornfully upon the despised male. But, very, very condescendingly, she rose. She faced him. Then she reached out her hand and with a sort of infinite and conscious generosity she touched him. Which act of abandoning aversion appeared to be the official climax of the wedding.

There was a clamor. The children dashed their torches to the ground and stamped on them. The village reverted to darkness, Miss Cummings heard rustlings all about her as if the inhabitants of the village returned to their homes, the ceremony over.

She made her own way to her own maidens'-circle hut and settled down zestfully for a long conference over the communicator. She reported the wedding with the enthusiasm and rapturous sentimentality of a lady society reporter at the wedding of a human heiress to an Earth-Council member. She gloated over the bride's costume. Being a woman she considered the relative insignificance of the bridegroom and his total lack of male attendants a right and proper thing. She was even sentimental about the symbolism of the bride's formally excepting this one male from her abhorrence of masculine creation.

Presently she calmed down enough to talk proper anthropological shop. The absence of other males from the village population remained odd, but there were references to analogous social customs on Earth. There was a Himalayan culture in which after marriage there was a honeymoon lasting only three days, when the bride and bridegroom separated for most of a year before setting up housekeeping together. There was an Indo-Chinese culture in which females affected to ignore the existence of males for an almost indefinite period, remaining in their parental home until the bride's parents insisted that their daughter's husband take over the support of his by-then-numerous offspring. There were many human customs suggested by this Krug wedding. There was enthusiastic anthropological shop-talk on the ether-waves of Venus, that night.

Next morning Miss Cummings happily noted that the bride appeared in her usual costume—with only a little more cloth added to it in token of her matronly status—and joined the matrons in their activities. She was addressed by a new honorific, and all the personal pronouns appropriate to an unmarried girl were now changed in her speech and in speech to her. But her husband did not appear at all. Miss Cummings had almost expected it.

There was one other interesting item. Miss Cummings got up at the break of day, but not in time to see the ornamentation of the mounded, rounded flower-bed now existing before the home of the new matron. It had quite two dozen *crythli* shells disposed about it, but of course the flowers were not yet established. They had been planted, though.

Miss Cummings and her aides on the ship discussed the matter exhaustively. The *crythli*-shell gift of the bridegroom had its parallel in bride-prices paid on Earth. There had possibly been an additional gift of pearls which Miss Cummings had not observed. The use of precious shells to decorate a flower-bed was conspicuous waste like the potlatch festivals of Alaskan Indians. The fact that the bride-gift was without utility-value resembled the old Bornean custom, in which an aspiring lover had to present a new-taken human head to his inamorata, for her to think him a good catch.

The village settled down again. The bride faithfully watered the plants in her shell-bordered flower-garden. She preened herself on her new status. But her husband remained invisible.

Miss Cummings practically forgot about him during the week that followed. A disturbing change in her own status was beginning to appear. She was taking up, now, the distribution of authority in the village, and discovered that the oldest of the matrons had begun to regard her with a disturbing disapproval.

The status of this pompous dowager was approximately that of headwoman of the village, yet the authority she exercised was not quite that of command. From time to time she gave what could be considered signals for community activity—for cultivating the soil, for repairing the community huts. Everybody worked at whatever she indicated was to be the activity for the day. But she gave no orders. Nobody asked for instructions. Everyone down to the smallest Krug child seemed to know perfectly every duty that might be required. And conversation was strictly confined to observations of objective fact.

When Miss Cummings had been in the village for

five weeks, she received a special call from this strutting and authoritative female. The matron-Krug came
to Miss Cummings' maiden-hut and regarded her with
disapproval. Her air was something like the aloof
scorn with which an elderly married alumna, revis-
iting the college of her youth, looks upon a middle-
aged and unmarried professor who seems unlikely to
emulate the alumna's career. The stout lady Krug
made two statements to Miss Cummings. The first
one, the philologists on the ship decided, could be
translated as meaning, "you are-venerable-and-have-
no-children." The second would be translated variously
as finish, end, termination, or practically any word
meaning finality. The Krug matron then formally
handed Miss Cummings an odd pointed instrument
made out of the only really hard wood to grow in
the Krug Archipelago. And she waddled out of Miss
Cummings' hut.

Miss Cummings, disturbed, transmitted a picture of
the instrument to the survey-ship. The anthropological staff was able to determine that it was old, that it
was sharp, and that it was enigmatic. Miss Cummings,
however, had an intuition. She did not like it.

Here, Miss Cummings' instincts served her better
than Ray Hale's methods of research. She could guess
what it was for, and he could not. At this time he was
less than seventy miles from Miss Cummings' island.
He knew more about *crythli* pearls and shell than any
other human being. But he didn't know about that
instrument.

Miss Cummings guessed indignantly. The Krug were
absolutely practical creatures. The most ancient matron
had decided that Miss Cummings was too old to find
a husband So she had stated the fact and given Miss

Cummings the sharp and nasty instrument so Miss Cummings could take appropriate action.

Miss Cummings furiously determined to do nothing of the kind. They couldn't make her commit suicide! But if she didn't carry out the instructions—obey the signal—do whatever obedience to the head-woman's observations would be—why . . . they might do it for her!

Miss Cummings raged privately. She might have to be withdrawn from her field investigation! Another female anthropologist might have to take over! It could mean that the definitive anthropological report on the Krug race-culture would be written by somebody else, and contain merely a falsely warm acknowledgement of her contribution to the study in a preface nobody would ever read!

Miss Cummings began to wear a chip on her shoulder. It seemed to her that the villagers regarded her with mild reproof for being alive. The most authoritative matron stopped her in the street and repeated her two statements—the one that meant she was venerable without children—and the one meaning finality. A day or to later, two other matrons repeated them. A day later still, and Miss Cummings found herself ostracized. Even the Krug maidens said coldly to her that she was venerable and had no children and finality.

It was heart-breaking, and it was more than a little frightening. But also it was enraging. Miss Cummings felt that the Krug were her project! They belonged to her! She had learned their language! She had made complete evaluations of their technology and work-habits and the gradations of social prestige and had reported fully on their marriage-customs! She would not give them up!

She took to sleeping with the tiny, almost invisible hand-weapon under her head—so far as she managed

to sleep at all. But after two days in which she was
ignored by all the village, she slept from pure weari-
ness and then was awakened by the usual morning-
noises from the jungle. Only this morning she found
herself sitting bolt upright, and frightened.

She heard voices. Krug voices. Her heart skipped
beats. Perhaps this would be violence on the way. She'd
been given the signal to commit suicide and she hadn't done
it. Perhaps now she was to have forcible assistance . . .

She peered out of her doorway, ready to give an
emergency signal for rescue by helicopters from the
ship. There was a great congregation of the village in
the center of the maidens'-circle of huts. Krug-children
raced and scampered about.

The maidens of the village fairly jittered with hopeful
agitation. The congress of matrons examined a *crythli*
shell. As before, they examined it in the manner of
near-sighted alumnae caught without their glasses. As
if they were smelling it.

Then the most ancient matron, the headwoman of
the village, made grunting noises to the others. She
marched firmly to the hut occupied by Miss Cummings.
She presented the *crythli* shell. And Miss Cummings
took it.

She explained the matter crisply to her associates
on the survey-ship. She would expect, she said, to be
picked up shortly after nightfall. She would give a
suitable warning and advance estimate of the time. But
this was a perfect opportunity to record the initiatory
ceremonies preceding matrimony among the Krug. It
could not be expected that anybody else would have
the same chance. So, once the male Krug had
appeared, she would expect helicopters to drop smoke-
bombs, descend in their midst guided by aerial flares,
and carry her away with the absolutely invaluable

anthropological treasure of a Krug bridal outfit. In the meanwhile she was, of course, armed.

The children rushed into the jungle. They returned and began to build a house. Miss Cummings, herself, was taken in hand by the village matrons. She had her personal communicator turned on and during all the daylight hours it transmitted scientific anthropological data which sent the staff on the survey-ship into ecstasies. Much of it is still unintelligible, and nobody but another anthropologist would find any of it interesting. But it all got down on tape. For one thing, there was more detailed data about Th'Tark, than anybody had dreamed existed, and Miss Cummings' claim to be the authority on the Krug was settled for all time.

There was just one curious omission in the staff's and Miss Cummings' reaction. It did not occur to them that Th'Tark might have arranged their triumph, as part of the business of keeping the Krug from being exterminated.

Presently the cloudbank began to shade slightly toward a darker hue, and when it was distinctly gray Miss Cummings came out of the new kraal-type house that had been built for her prospective matronly estate. She wore the bridal costume of the village. And even Miss Cummings was almost overwhelmed by its richness. It was barbaric, of course. It was crude. But the luminous, changing colors of the pearl headdress and necklaces, and the incredible richness of the arm-bands and shell ornament gave her an extraordinary sensation.

The light faded still more, and the children disappeared, and presently the sky was black—and consequently all of the village—and then they returned, with the smallest child of all carrying a lighted torch while the others bore unlighted ones.

Miss Cummings sat in darkness, arrayed in wedding

garb of a richness such as no human daughter of a sultan ever wore. There were the night-noises of the jungle. She murmured into her communicator. A reassuring voice spoke in her invisible ear-receiver. The copter rescue-party was ready. Besides, she had her small hand-weapon in case of need. She was not even faintly timid, now. The data obtained today had made her scientific reputation permanent. From now on she would be secure in the fame of being the first truly great authority on the race-culture of the Krug of the Summer Sea on Venus. With that splendor in mind, she could not be afraid. And after five weeks and more in a Krug village she could assuredly not be frightened by any mere male!

There was a single, flickering torch some fifty yards away, solicitously held by the smallest ambulatory Krug child. There was a waiting, breathless silence for a very long time.

Then a voice panted words in Kruggish speech. A matron grunted. The child with the lighted torch passed the flame to another. The lighting spread. There were fifty flaming torches in the village night. And Miss Cummings looked with dazed, and shocked, and wholly incredulous eyes at Ray Hale.

He was smeared with pigments to enhance the Kruglikeness of the human race. He bore a burden of *crythli* shell. He looked at her, and his eyes widened with shock. Then sweat poured out on his skin in the torchlight. He knew her not only as a human woman, but as herself—and he was the one person she unfeignedly and by long habit hated past all considerations of charity.

He swallowed, and then panted:

"Play up! Or we'll both be killed!"

Miss Cummings caught her breath. He said more shrilly:

"Play up, I tell you!"

Miss Cummings said unsteadily, with her voice a mere whisper:

"There are copters overhead. I've only to call them—"

Hale glared at her like a trapped wild beast. His desperation was so evident that Miss Cummings sensed a deep approval among the female Krug about her.

"You married my little sister," said Miss Cummings in a strange, toneless monotone. "She loved you, and you broke her heart. You beat her! You were everything that was vile to her—and she died when you left her because she loved you. I've prayed that death would strike you down! Oh, you beast-beast-beast—"

A murmur of admiration from the Krug matrons. At least, it seemed so. Hale sweated in the torchlight. He gabbled:

"They'll kill me if you don't play up! You too!"

It was a lie. Miss Cummings did not know how she knew, but she was fully aware that her behavior accorded with the ideal of Kruggish female scorn of all masculinity. The most proper of previous Krug maidens had never displayed such magnificent scorn for their bridegrooms. Miss Cummings was abstractedly aware that she would be the pattern of bridal propriety from now on.

Ray Hale put down a *crythli* shell. He trembled with his terror, but he went through the routine of matrimony among the Krug. Shell after lustrous shell, coiled, iridescent, color changing beauty—he laid down the customary offering before Miss Cummings.

"I can let them kill you," she whispered, her throat taut. "They won't be punished. I can let them kill you as you should be killed—or I can call down the copters. . . ."

There was a voice in her ears. The rescue-party

overhead was ready to swoop down, but it was bewildered. They were waiting a summons for action. They heard highly improbable human speech where nothing of the sort should be. The voice asked anxious questions. Miss Cummings recovered herself.

"Something unexpected has developed," she said in a level voice for her communicator to send aloft. "I find that I am perfectly safe. I am confident that I will not need to be rescued. But make sure that all the recorders are ready for later data."

She flipped off the communicator-switch.

In the torchlight Ray Hale looked convincingly Kruglike and desperate and despairing as he ceased the putting-down of shell and stared at Miss Cummings with the air of a man who has heard his death sentence and waits for it to be carried out. He suddenly babbled:

"Here! Pearls! I'll give you all of them! Gallons of them! Anything—anything! But don't let them kill me. . . ."

He poured a double handful of *crythli* pearls into her lap. And Miss Cummings rose. She was ashenwhite, and she hated Ray Hale as she had never hated any other human being. But she was also an anthropologist. And Hale could not possibly have undertaken this enterprise if he hadn't gathered scientific information Miss Cummings still lacked.

Her lips twisted themselves into the most mirthless and seemingly most scornful of smiles. Actually, it was a grimace of anguish. She reached out and touched him—with the muzzle of her almost-invisible handweapon.

"If you try to escape in the darkness," said Miss Cummings, "I will pull the trigger when I feel no pressure on this gun."

A child dashed a torch to the ground. Instantly all

the spouting flames were rolling in the earth and small Krug children were stamping on them. Miss Cummings shepherded Hale into the kraal-house that had been built that day for her.

"I think," she said thinly, "you have information I lack. I shall turn on my communicator, now, and you will tell all you know about the Krug. It will be recorded for study. Then I will decide whether to kill you or not."

She stood beside him in the darkness. He gasped. She prodded him with questions—and with the weapon.

The weapon was part of Miss Cummings' equipment. It was very small, and it fired electronically, and when the slack on the trigger was taken up it necessarily emitted microwave radiation. The fact was very useful on Earth. It made the illicit use of weapons impractical, because armed officers arrived within minutes anywhere the trigger-slack of a weapon was taken up, and this worked out nicely for law-abiding citizens, but not so well for the lawless. On Venus the same fact kept non-terrestrials from making use of human weapons without permission. But for Miss Cummings, the important thing was that the emission of radiation from an electronic weapon was accompanied by a high-pitched humming sound.

Hale heard the thin drone of the pistol, and knew that Miss Cummings had only to tighten her finger ever so slightly to end his life. The sound meant that she was ready and willing to do it.

He whimpered. He was in a very great hurry to leave the bridal dwelling. He'd meant to remain there only minutes. But he did not dare to say why. When Miss Cummings asked him questions in a thinly level voice, he babbled an almost incoherent excuse for trying to go through the Krug marriage ceremony with a Krug female. But Miss Cummings wore the *crythli*-pearl headdress. She stopped him.

The thin whining sound of the ready-for-firing weapon drove him frantic, in combination with his other reasons for fear. He panted the truth. He'd made the ceremonial offering of a *crythli* shell to the center of the circle of maidens' cottages. He'd known that a bride would be chosen and a kraal-house built. The instant he entered the dwelling he meant—he panted it—to knock the female unconscious and escape with the costume worth millions of credits on earth.

"But," said Miss Cummings with the same thin steadiness, "you offered me gallons of pearls. How many times have you done this?"

He whimpered. He quivered with the need to flee. But she said as steadily and as deliberately as before:

"You would not risk only stunning the brides. You killed them, did you not? You strangled them?"

Hale babbled that the Krug were not human. It was not murder to kill them. And this was true—so far. Hale was mad to get away from the village now. Miss Cummings considered that he was fearful of a copter coming to pick him up as a criminal.

"Nobody will come from the ship unless I call them," she said with a sort of unearthly reasonableness. "It would spoil my research project for a copter to land in the village. But my sister died because she loved you. If you wish to live, you will tell me. . . ."

What followed was one of the most peculiar data-gathering interviews in the history of anthropology. With his own reasons for desperate and headlong flight urging him, and the whine of the taut triggered weapon holding him still, Hale tried—stumbling over his words in his haste—to answer all Miss Cummings chose to ask. He did not even try to lie. He gabbled in his effort to satisfy her scientific curiosity in the shortest possible time.

He trembled. He shook. Presently his breathing was only gasps. But she was inexorable. She held consultations with the ship to clarify what other questions she should ask. She reflected, and phrased her questions with precision. And all the time the weapon whined softly, ready to destroy Hale if he tried to flee.

It was an excellent interview, though. Miss Cummings got a full picture of the male side of the marriage-custom story, which no trader had been able to do. Male Krug were despised. But to marry they had to gather *crythli* shells. Preferably those bearing pearls. Tending to grow incoherent in his haste, Hale told her where the *crythli* shells were found and how they had to be acquired. Only a Krug would do it, and a Krug wouldn't do it for money. It had to be the stark necessity which drove a Krug to marriage. . . .

"I've got to get away from here!" panted Hale shrilly. "I can't stay here! I can't—I can't—"

Miss Cummings said thinly:

"I shall remain in the village a few days more to gather the data needed to complete what I know now. It would be inconvenient to have your body here. So I do not kill you. Go!"

She drew back the muzzle of the weapon, but it still whined faintly. She was aware of exhaustion, now. She'd remained standing and terribly tense for a length of time she didn't realize. Actually it was to be measured in hours. Only an anthropologist could have done it, and only then to gather information there would be no second chance to procure. Miss Cummings felt herself wilting as Hale sprang away from her and dived desperately into the blackness outside the kraal-house door.

But, weary as she was, she burst incontinently into sobs. She had been very, very fond of the sister whom Hale had married fifteen years before and who had died of her love for him. Miss Cummings wept exhaustedly. She was too exhausted even to try to muffle her sobbing.

But this, as it happened, was considered suitable behavior in a new matron. Among the Krug a new-wedded bride weeps loudly when her brand new husband makes his way back into the darkness from which he came. It is, in a way, a signal of his departure. Also, it covers any sounds that may be made outside.

As in this case.

When Miss Cummings appeared in public, next morning, she was saluted with the honorific pronouns she rated as a married lady Krug. She was regarded with complete approval, and in a matter of four days more she had gathered absolutely all the information the Krug female language could convey in the absence of a word for why. She felt only one minor disappointment as an anthropologist. It was that she did not take part in the making of the mound-like flower-bed she found before her kraal-house in the morning, nor in its decoration with the *crythli* shell that Hale had set out in the torchlight. Even the flowers were planted for her. But she watered them dutifully.

Before the week was out she went back to the ship, to the stark amazement of the Krug. In time she wrote a book about the Krug culture which brought her eminence among anthropologists and is still the standard work. Incidentally, her book prevented the extermination of the Krug by revealing where the *crythli* mollusks grow and how they have to be obtained. Humans do not attempt to gather them. They still leave that to the Krug. But it is now the custom to purchase the decorative shells from Krug villages when a kraal-house is torn down because of the demise of the lady

Krug who lived in it. Then the *crythli* shells have no more significance to the Krug, and they part with them readily for a fair price in quinine. Which, of course, means that the supply of *crythli* shell is steady but moderate and the price remains stable—which is good for interplanetary trade. Sometimes a few pearls are purchased, too.

And this may possibly have been the reason for the whole affair. Th'Tark could have arranged it. If there is a Th'Tark, this could be the explanation. But one has doubts.

The most recent editions of Miss Cummings' book have a three-page appendix added to them. The three pages add little of importance to the anthropological side of her work, but they do complete the biology. They report recent discoveries that once a Krug maiden becomes a matron, she produces offspring with a fine regularity for all the rest of her life, though she never sees her husband again. Biologists tend to speak of Krug males as "drones," nowadays, by analogy with honeybees and ants, whose males like the Krug are driven from the communities of working females, and who die after their mating. And philologists put a word in, too, arguing that since the Krug language is incapable of expressing the operations of logic, there is no evidence that the Krug think in concepts i.e., that they are reasoning beings. And the biologists join in zestfully to point out that the Krug technology and symbiosis with vegetation is certainly no more complex than that of the leaf-cutter ants. Other myrmidae and some kinds of bees and wasps approach it, too. Altogether, they make out quite a case.

The anthropologists consider that they have the last word, though. They point out triumphantly that the Krug must be considered human because there is no other case, among irrational animals, of social participation in a marriage rite. And especially, they point out, no other non-human creature engages in any sort of funerary activity. But the Krug do have a marriage ceremony. It is elaborate. They have a socially recognized honeymoon, during which the bride and her new husband are alone in the new home built for the bride, and during which for a matter of hours every other Krug returns to her own dwelling and the privacy of the wedding pair is absolute. Even the end of the honeymoon is no less officially recognized, because after a fixed interval—of as much as four hours—the Krug matrons gather about the hut again. When the new Krug bridegroom flees his new wife's hut he is met by this committee of mated females. And they dispatch him very dexterously with a sharp wooden instrument and bury him in a neat mound before his widow's door and ornament the mound with *crythli* shells. And afterward his widow dutifully waters the flowers that are planted there.

This, the anthropologists say, is human behavior.

It is not settled yet. Maybe Hale could throw some light upon the question. He knew a great deal about the Krug. Even in his frantic haste to tell all he knew, it took hours for Miss Cummings to exhaust her list of questions and the secondary questions suggested by his replies. Maybe he did know more than she learned from him, because she couldn't but be affected by his frantic anxiety to be gone. But nobody knows how much Hale had found out. He has never been seen since his Krug-wedding night, on Venus or elsewhere.

Maybe the only way to find out the facts would be to ask Th'Tark, who could, just possibly, have arranged the whole affair. It prevented the extermination of the Krug by the march of progress. Th'Tark would have wanted to bring that about, certainly.

If there is or was a Th'Tark.

SCRIMSHAW

Pop Young was the one known man who could stand life on the surface of the Moon's far side, and, therefore, he occupied the shack on the Big Crack's edge, above the mining colony there. Some people said that no normal man could do it, and mentioned the scar of a ghastly head-wound to explain his ability. One man partly guessed the secret, but only partly. His name was Sattell and he had reason not to talk. Pop Young alone knew the whole truth, and he kept his mouth shut, too. It wasn't anybody else's business.

The shack and the job he filled were located in the medieval notion of the physical appearance of hell. By day the environment was heat and torment. By night—lunar night, of course, and lunar day—it was frigidity and horror. Once in two weeks Earth-time a rocketship came around the horizon from Lunar City with stores for the colony deep underground. Pop received the stores and took care of them. He handed over the product of the mine, to be forwarded to Earth. The rocket went away again. Come nightfall Pop lowered the supplies down the long cable into the Big Crack to the colony far down inside, and freshened up the landing field marks with magnesium marking-powder if a rocket-blast had blurred them. That was fundamentally all he had to do. But without him the mine down in the Crack would have had to shut down.

The Crack, of course, was that gaping rocky fault which stretches nine hundred miles, jaggedly, over the side of the Moon that Earth never sees. There is one stretch where it is a yawning gulf a full half-mile wide and unguessably deep. Where Pop Young's shack stood it was only a hundred yards wide, but the colony was a full mile down, in one wall. There is nothing like it on Earth, of course. When it was first found, scientists descended into it to examine the exposed rock-strata and learn the history of the Moon before its craters were made. But they found more than history. They found the reason for the colony and the rocket landing field and the shack.

The reason for Pop was something else.

The shack stood a hundred feet from the Big Crack's edge. It looked like a dust-heap thirty feet high, and it was. The outside was surface moondust, piled over a tiny dome to be insulation against the cold of night and shadow and the furnace heat of day. Pop lived in it all alone, and in his spare time he worked industriously at recovering some missing portions of his life that Sattell had managed to take away from him.

He thought often of Sattell, down in the colony underground. There were galleries and tunnels and living-quarters down there. There were air-tight bulkheads for safety, and a hydroponic garden to keep the air fresh, and all sorts of things to make life possible for men under, if not on, the Moon.

But it wasn't fun, even underground. In the Moon's slight gravity, a man is really adjusted to existence when he has a well-developed case of agoraphobia. With such an aid, a man can get into a tiny, coffin-like cubby-hole, and feel solidity above and below and around him, and happily tell himself that it feels delicious. Some-times it does.

But Sattell couldn't comfort himself so easily. He knew about Pop, up on the surface. He'd shipped out, whimpering, to the Moon to get far away from Pop, and Pop was just about a mile overhead and there was no way to get around him. It was difficult to get away from the mine, anyhow. It doesn't take too long for the low gravity to tear a man's nerves to shreds. He has to develop kinks in his head to survive. And those kinks—

The first men to leave the colony had to be knocked cold and shipped out unconscious. They'd been underground—and in low gravity—long enough to be utterly unable to face the idea of open spaces. Even now there were some who had to be carried, but there were some tougher ones who were able to walk to the rocketship if Pop put a tarpaulin over their heads so they didn't have to see the sky. In any case Pop was essential, either for carrying or guidance.

Sattell got the shakes when he thought of Pop, and Pop rather probably knew it. Of course, by the time he took the job tending the shack, he was pretty cer-tain about Sattell. The facts spoke for themselves.

Pop had come back to consciousness in a hospi-tal with a great wound in his head and no memory of anything that had happened before that moment. It was not that his identity was in question. When he was stronger, the doctors told him who he was, and as gently as possible what had happened to his wife and children. They'd been murdered after he was seemingly killed defending them. But he didn't remember a thing. Not then. It was something of a blessing.

But when he was physically recovered he set about trying to pick up the threads of the life he could no longer remember. He met Sattell quite by accident. Sattell looked familiar. Pop eagerly tried to ask him questions. And Sattell turned gray and frantically denied that he'd ever seen Pop before.

All of which happened back on Earth and a long time ago. It seemed to Pop that the sight of Sattell had brought back some vague and cloudy memories. They were not sharp, though, and he hunted up Sattell again to find out if he was right. And Sattell went into panic when he returned.

Nowadays, by the Big Crack, Pop wasn't so insistent on seeing Sattell, but he was deeply concerned with the recovery of the memories that Sattell helped bring back. Pop was a highly conscientious man. He took good care of his job. There was a warning-bell in the shack, and when a rocketship from Lunar City got above the horizon and could send a tight beam, the gong clanged loudly, and Pop got into a vacuum-suit and went out the air lock. He usually reached the moondozer about the time the ship began to brake for landing, and he watched it come in.

He saw the silver needle in the sky fighting momentum above a line of jagged crater-walls. It slowed, and slowed, and curved down as it drew nearer. The pilot killed all forward motion just above the field and came steadily and smoothly down to land, between the silvery triangles that marked the landing place.

Instantly the rockets cut off, drums of fuel and air and food came out of the cargo-hatch and Pop swept forward with the dozer. It was a miniature tractor with a gigantic scoop in front. He pushed a great mound of talc-fine dust before him to cover up the cargo. It was necessary. With freight costing what it did, fuel and air and food came frozen solid, in containers barely thicker than foil. While they stayed at space-shadow temperature, the foil would hold anything. And a cover of insulating moon-dust with vacuum between the grains kept even air frozen solid, though in sunlight.

At such times Pop hardly thought of Sattell. He knew he had plenty of time for that. He'd started to follow Sattell knowing what had happened to his wife and children, but it was hearsay only. He had no memory of them at all. But Sattell stirred the lost memories. At first Pop followed absorbedly from city to city, to recover the years that had been wiped out by an axe-blow. He did recover a good deal. When Sattell fled to another continent, Pop followed because he had some distinct memories of his wife—and the way he'd felt about her—and some fugitive mental images of his children. When Sattell frenziedly tried to deny knowledge of the murder in Tangier, Pop had come to remember both his children and some of the happiness of his married life.

Even when Sattell—whimpering—signed up for Lunar City, Pop tracked him. By that time he was quite sure that Sattell was the man who'd killed his family. If so, Sattell had profited by less than two days' pay for wiping out everything that Pop possessed. But Pop wanted it back.

He couldn't prove Sattell's guilt. There was no evidence. In any case, he didn't really want Sattell to die. If he did, there'd be no way to recover more lost memories.

Sometimes, in the shack on the far side of the Moon, Pop Young had odd fancies about Sattell. There was the mine, for example. In each two Earth-weeks of working, the mine-colony nearly filled up a three-gallon canister with greasy-seeming white crystals shaped like two pyramids base to base. The filled canister would weigh a hundred pounds on Earth. Here it weighed eighteen. But on Earth its contents would be computed in carats, and a hundred pounds was worth millions. Yet here on the Moon Pop kept a waiting canister on a shelf in his tiny dome, behind the air-apparatus. It rattled if he shook it, and it was worth no more than so many pebbles. But sometimes Pop wondered if Sattell ever thought of the value of the mine's production. If he would kill a woman and two children and think he'd killed a man for no more than a hundred dollars, what enormity would he commit for a three-gallon quantity of uncut diamonds?

But he did not dwell on such speculation. The sun rose very, very slowly in what by convention was called the east. It took nearly two hours to urge its disk above the horizon, and it burned terribly in emptiness for fourteen times twenty-four hours before sunset. Then there was night, and for three hundred and thirty-six consecutive hours there were only stars overhead and the sky was a hole so terrible that a man who looked up into it—what with the nagging sensation of one-sixth gravity—tended to lose all confidence in the stability of things. Most men immediately found it hysterically necessary to seize hold of something solid to keep from falling upward. But nothing felt solid. Everything fell, too. Wherefore most men tended to scream.

But not Pop. He'd come to the Moon in the first place because Sattell was here. Near Sattell, he found memories of times when he was a young man with a young wife who loved him extravagantly. Then pictures of his children came out of emptiness and grew sharp and clear. He found that he loved them very dearly. And when he was near Sattell he literally recovered them—in the sense that he came to know new things about them and had new memories of them every day. He hadn't yet remembered the crime which lost them to him. Until he did—and the fact possessed a certain grisly humor—Pop didn't even hate Sattell. He simply wanted to be near him because it enabled him to recover new and vivid parts of his youth that had been lost.

Otherwise, he was wholly matter-of-fact—certainly so for the far side of the Moon. He was a rather fussy housekeeper. The shack above the Big Crack's rim was as tidy as any lighthouse or fur-trapper's cabin. He tended his air-apparatus with a fine precision. It was perfectly simple. In the shadow of the shack he had an unfailing source of extreme low temperature. Air from the shack flowed into a shadow-chilled pipe. Moisture condensed out of it here, and CO_2 froze solidly out of it there, and on beyond it collected as restless, transparent liquid air. At the same time, liquid air from another tank evaporated to maintain the proper air pressure in the shack. Every so often Pop tapped the pipe where the moisture froze, and lumps of water ice clattered out to be returned to the humidifier. Less often he took out the CO_2 snow, and measured it, and dumped an equivalent quantity of pale-blue liquid oxygen into the liquid air that had been purified by cold. The oxygen dissolved. Then the apparatus reversed itself and supplied fresh air from the now-enriched fluid, while the depleted other tank began to fill up with cold-purified liquid air.

Outside the shack, jagged stony pinnacles reared in the starlight, and craters complained of the bombardment from space that had made them. But, outside, nothing ever happened. Inside, it was quite different.

Working on his memories, one day Pop made a little sketch. It helped a great deal. He grew deeply interested. Writing-material was scarce, but he spent most of the time between two particular rocket-landings getting down on paper exactly how a child had looked while sleeping, some fifteen years before. He remembered with astonishment that the child had really looked exactly like that! Later he began a sketch of his partly-remembered wife. In time—he had plenty—it became a really truthful likeness.

The sun rose, and baked the abomination of desolation which was the moonscape. Pop Young meticulously touched up the glittering triangles which were landing guides for the Lunar City ships. They glittered from the thinnest conceivable layer of magnesium marking-powder. He checked over the moondozer. He tended the air apparatus. He did everything that his job and survival required. Ungrudgingly.

Then he made more sketches. The images to be drawn came back more clearly when he thought of Sattell, so by keeping Sattell in mind he recovered the memory of a chair that had been in his forgotten home. Then he drew his wife sitting in it, reading. It felt very good to see her again. And he speculated about whether Sattell ever thought of millions of dollars worth of new-mined diamonds knocking about unguarded in the shack, and he suddenly recollected clearly the way one of his children had looked while playing with her doll. He made a quick sketch to keep from forgetting that.

There was no purpose in the sketching, save that he'd lost all his young manhood through a senseless crime. He wanted his youth back. He was recovering it bit by bit. The occupation made it absurdly easy to live on the surface of the far side of the Moon, whether anybody else could do it or not.

Sattell had no such device for adjusting to the lunar state of things. Living on the Moon was bad enough anyhow, then, but living one mile underground from Pop

Young was much worse. Sattell clearly remembered the crime Pop Young hadn't yet recalled. He considered that Pop had made no overt attempt to revenge himself because he planned some retaliation so horrible and lingering that it was worth waiting for. He came to hate Pop with an insane ferocity. And fear. In his mind the need to escape became an obsession on top of the other psychotic states normal to a Moon-colonist.

But he was helpless. He couldn't leave. There was Pop. He couldn't kill Pop. He had no chance—and he was afraid. The one absurd, irrelevant thing he could do was write letters back to Earth. He did that. He wrote with the desperate, impassioned, frantic blend of persuasion and information and genius-like invention of a prisoner in a high-security prison, trying to induce someone to help him escape.

He had friends, of a sort, but for a long time his letters produced nothing. The Moon swung in vast circles about the Earth, and the Earth swung sedately about the Sun. The other planets danced their saraband. The rest of humanity went about its own affairs with fascinated attention. But then an event occurred which bore directly upon Pop Young and Sattell and Pop Young's missing years.

Somebody back on Earth promoted a luxury passenger-line of spaceships to ply between Earth and Moon. It looked like a perfect set-up. Three spacecraft capable of the journey came into being with attendant reams of publicity. They promised a thrill and a new distinction for the rich. Guided tours to Luna! The most expensive and most thrilling trip in history! One hundred thousand dollars for a twelve-day cruise through space, with views of the Moon's far side and trips through Lunar City and a landing in Aristarchus, plus sound-tapes of the journey and fame hitherto reserved for honest explorers!

It didn't seem to have anything to do with Pop or with Sattell. But it did.

There were just two passenger tours. The first was fully booked. But the passengers who paid so highly, expected to be pleasantly thrilled and shielded from all reasons for alarm. And they couldn't be. Something happens when a self-centered and complacent individual unsuspectingly looks out of a spaceship port and sees the cosmos unshielded by mists or clouds or other aids to blindness against reality. It is shattering.

A millionaire cut his throat when he saw Earth dwindled to a mere blue-green ball in vastness. He could not endure his own smallness in the face of immensity. Not one passenger disembarked even for Lunar City. Most of them cowered in their chairs, hiding their eyes. They were the simple cases of hysteria. But the richest girl on Earth, who'd had five husbands and believed that nothing could move her— she went into catatonic withdrawal and neither saw nor heard nor moved. Two other passengers sobbed in improvised strait jackets. The first shipload started home. Fast.

The second luxury liner took off with only four passengers and turned back before reaching the Moon. Space-pilots could take the strain of space-flight because they had work to do. Workers for the lunar mines could make the trip under heavy sedation. But it was too early in the development of space-travel for pleasure-passengers. They weren't prepared for the more humbling facts of life.

Pop heard of the quaint commercial enterprise through the micro-tapes put off at the shack for the men down in the mine. Sattell probably learned of it the same way. Pop didn't even think of it again. It seemed to have nothing to do with him. But Sattell undoubtedly dealt with it fully in his desperate writings back to Earth.

Pop matter-of-factly tended the shack and the landing field and the stores for the Big Crack mine. Between-times he made more drawings in pursuit of his own private objective. Quite accidentally, he developed a certain talent professional artists might have approved. But he was not trying to communicate, but to discover. Drawing—especially with his mind on Sattell—he found fresh incidents popping up in his recollection. Times when he was happy. One day he remembered the puppy his children had owned and loved. He drew it painstakingly—and it was his again. Thereafter he could remember it any time he chose. He did actually recover a completely vanished past.

He envisioned a way to increase that recovery. But there was a marked shortage of artists' materials on the Moon. All freight had to be hauled from Earth, on a voyage equal to rather more than a thousand times around the equator of the Earth. Artists' supplies were not often included. Pop didn't even ask.

He began to explore the area outside the shack for possible material no one would think of sending from Earth. He collected stones of various sorts, but when warmed up in the shack they were useless. He found no strictly lunar material which would serve for modeling or carving portraits. He found minerals which could be pulverized and used as pigments, but nothing suitable for this new adventure in the recovery of lost youth. He even considered blasting, to aid his search. He could. Down in the mine, blasting was done by soaking carbon black—from CO_2—in liquid oxygen, and then firing it with a spark. It exploded splendidly. And its fumes were merely more CO_2 which an air-apparatus handled easily.

He didn't do any blasting. He didn't find any signs

of the sort of mineral he required. Marble would have
been perfect, but there is no marble on the Moon.
Naturally! Yet Pop continued to search absorbedly for
material with which to capture memory. Sattell still
seemed necessary, but—

Early one lunar morning he was a good two miles
from his shack when he saw rocket-fumes in the sky.
It was most unlikely. He wasn't looking for anything
of the sort, but out of the corner of his eye he observed
that something moved. Which was impossible. He
turned his head, and there were rocket-fumes coming
over the horizon, not in the direction of Lunar City.
Which was more impossible still.

He stared. A tiny silver rocket to the westward
poured out monstrous masses of vapor. It decelerated
swiftly. It curved downward. The rockets checked for
an instant, and flamed again more violently, and
checked once more. This was not an expert approach.
It was a faulty one. Curving surface-ward in a sharply
changing parabola, the pilot over-corrected and had to
wait to gather down-speed, and then over-corrected
again. It was an altogether clumsy landing. The ship
was not even perfectly vertical when it settled not quite
in the landing-area marked by silvery triangles. One
of its tail-fins crumpled slightly. It tilted a little when
fully landed.

Then nothing happened.

Pop made his way toward it in the skittering, skat-
ing gait one uses in one-sixth gravity. When he was
within half a mile, an air-lock door opened in the ship's
side. But nothing came out of the lock. No space-suited
figure. No cargo came drifting down with the singular deliberation of falling objects on the Moon.

It was just barely past lunar sunrise on the far side
of the Moon. Incredibly long and utterly black shadows stretched across the plain, and half the rocketship

was dazzling white and half was blacker than blackness itself. The sun still hung low indeed in the black,
star-speckled sky. Pop waded through moondust, raising
a trail of slowly settling powder. He knew only that the
ship didn't come from Lunar City, but from Earth. He
couldn't imagine why. He did not even wildly connect
it with what—say—Sattell might have written with
desperate plausibility about greasy-seeming white crystals out of the mine, knocking about Pop Young's shack
in canisters containing a hundred Earth-pounds weight
of richness.

Pop reached the rocketship. He approached the big
tail-fins. On one of them there were welded ladder-
rungs going up to the opened air-lock door.

He climbed.

The air lock was perfectly normal when he reached
it. There was a glass port in the inner door, and he
saw eyes looking through it at him. He pulled the outer
door shut and felt the whining vibration of admitted
air. His vacuum suit went slack about him. The inner
door began to open, and Pop reached up and gave his
helmet the practiced twisting jerk which removed it.

Then he blinked. There was a red-headed man in
the opened door. He grinned savagely at Pop. He held
a very nasty hand-weapon trained on Pop's middle.

"Don't come in!" he said mockingly. "And I don't
give a damn about how you are. This isn't social. It's
business!"

Pop simply gaped. He couldn't quite take it in.

"This," snapped the red-headed man abruptly, "is a
stickup!"

Pop's eyes went through the inner lock-door. He
saw that the interior of the ship was stripped and
bare. But a spiral stairway descended from some
upper compartment. It had a handrail of pure, transparent, water-clear plastic. The walls were bare

insulation, but that trace of luxury remained. Pop gazed at the plastic, fascinated.

The red-headed man leaned forward, snarling. He slashed Pop across the face with the barrel of his weapon. It drew blood. It was wanton, savage brutality.

"Pay attention!" snarled the red-headed man. "A stickup, I said! Get it? You go get that can of stuff from the mine! The diamonds! Bring them here! Understand?"

Pop said numbly: "What the hell?"

The red-headed man hit him again. He was nerveracked, and, therefore, he wanted to hurt.

"Move!" he rasped. "I want the diamonds you've got for the ship from Lunar City! Bring 'em!" Pop licked blood from his lips and the man with the weapon raged at him. "Then phone down to the mine! Tell Sattell I'm here and he can come on up! Tell him to bring any more diamonds they've dug up since the stuff you've got!"

He leaned forward. His face was only inches from Pop Young's. It was seamed and hard-bitten and nerveracked. But any man would be quivering if he wasn't used to space or the feel of one-sixth gravity on the Moon. He panted:

"And get it straight! You try any tricks and we take off! We swing over your shack! The rocket-blast smashes it! We burn you down! Then we swing over the cable down to the mine and the rocket-flame melts it! You die and everybody in the mine besides! No tricks! We didn't come here for nothing!"

He twitched all over. Then he struck cruelly again at Pop Young's face. He seemed filled with fury, at least partly hysterical. It was the tension that space-travel—then, at its beginning—produced. It was meaningless savagery due to terror. But, of course, Pop was helpless to resist. There were no weapons on the Moon and the mention of Sattell's name showed the uselessness of bluff. Sattell would have depicted the complete set-up by the edge of the Big Crack. Pop could do nothing.

The red-headed man checked himself, panting. He drew back and slammed the inner lock-door. There was the sound of pumping.

Pop put his helmet back on and sealed it. The outer door opened. Outrushing air tugged at Pop. After a second or two he went out and climbed down the welded-on ladder-bars to the ground.

He headed back toward his shack. Somehow, the mention of Sattell had made his mind work better. It always did. He began painstakingly to put things together. The red-headed man knew the routine here in every detail. He knew Sattell. That part was simple. Sattell had planned this multi-million-dollar coup, as a man in prison might plan his break. The stripped interior of the ship identified it.

It was one of the unsuccessful luxury-liners sold for scrap. Or perhaps it was stolen for the journey here. Sattell's associates had had to steal or somehow get the fuel, and somehow find a pilot. But there were diamonds worth at least five million dollars waiting for them, and the whole job might not have called for more than two men—with Sattell as a third. According to the economics of crime, it was feasible. Anyhow it was being done.

Pop reached the dust-heap which was his shack and went in the air lock. Inside, he went to the vision-phone and called the mine-colony down in the Crack. He gave the message he'd been told to pass on. Sattell to come up, with what diamonds had been dug since the regular canister was sent up for the Lunar City ship that would be due presently. Otherwise the ship on the landing strip would destroy shack and Pop and the colony together.

"I'd guess," said Pop painstakingly, "that Sattell figured it out. He's probably got some sort of gun to keep
you from holding him down there. But he won't know
his friends are here—not right this minute he won't."

A shaking voice asked questions from the vision-
phone.

"No," said Pop, "they'll do it anyhow. If we were
able to tell about 'em, they'd be chased. But if I'm dead
and the shack's smashed and the cable burnt through,
they'll be back on Earth long before a new cable's been
got and let down to you. So they'll do all they can no
matter what I do." He added, "I wouldn't tell Sattell
a thing about it, if I were you. It'll save trouble. Just
let him keep on waiting for this to happen. It'll save
you trouble."

Another shaky question.

"Me?" asked Pop. "Oh, I'm going to raise what hell
I can. There's some stuff in that ship I want."

He switched off the phone. He went over to his air
apparatus. He took down the canisters of diamonds
which were worth five millions or more back on Earth.
He found a bucket. He dumped the diamonds casually into it. They floated downward with great deliberation and surged from side to side like a liquid when
they stopped. One-sixth gravity.

Pop regarded his drawings meditatively. A sketch of
his wife as he now remembered her. It was very good
to remember. A drawing of his two children, playing
together. He looked forward to remembering much
more about them. He grinned.

"That stair-rail," he said in deep satisfaction. "That'll
do it!"

He tore bed linen from his bunk and worked on the
emptied canister. It was a double-walled container with
a thermware interior lining. Even on Earth newly-
mined diamonds sometimes fly to pieces from internal

stress. On the Moon, it was not desirable that diamonds be exposed to repeated violent changes of temperature. So a thermware-lined canister kept them at mine-temperature once they were warmed to touchability.

Pop packed the cotton cloth in the container. He hurried a little, because the men in the rocket were shaky and might not practice patience. He took a small emergency-lamp from his spare spacesuit. He carefully cracked its bulb, exposing the filament within. He put the lamp on top of the cotton and sprinkled magnesium marking-powder over everything. Then he went to the air-apparatus and took out a flask of the liquid oxygen used to keep his breathing air in balance. He poured the frigid, pale-blue stuff into the cotton. He saturated it.

All the inside of the shack was foggy when he finished. Then he pushed the canister-top down. He breathed a sigh of relief when it was in place. He'd arranged for it to break a frozen-brittle switch as it descended. When it came off, the switch would light the lamp with its bare filament. There was powdered magnesium in contact with it and liquid oxygen all about.

He went out of the shack by the air lock. On the way, thinking about Sattell, he suddenly recovered a completely new memory. On their first wedding anniversary, so long ago, he and his wife had gone out to dinner to celebrate. He remembered how she looked: the almost-smug joy they shared that they would be together for always, with one complete year for proof.

Pop reflected hungrily that it was something else to be made permanent and inspected from time to time. But he wanted more than a drawing of this! He wanted to make the memory permanent and to extend it—

If it had not been for his vacuum suit and the canister he carried, Pop would have rubbed his hands.

❖   ❖   ❖

Tall, jagged crater-walls rose from the lunar plain. Monstrous, extended inky shadows stretched enormous distances, utterly black. The sun, like a glowing octopus, floated low at the edge of things and seemed to hate all creation.

Pop reached the rocket. He climbed the welded ladder-rungs to the air lock. He closed the door. Air whined. His suit sagged against his body. He took off his helmet.

When the red-headed man opened the inner door, the hand-weapon shook and trembled. Pop said calmly:

"Now I've got to go handle the hoist, if Sattell's coming up from the mine. If I don't do it, he don't come up."

The red-headed man snarled. But his eyes were on the canister whose contents should weigh a hundred pounds on Earth.

"Any tricks," he rasped, "and you know what happens!"

"Yeah," said Pop.

He stolidly put his helmet back on. But his eyes went past the red-headed man to the stair that wound down, inside the ship, from some compartment above. The stair-rail was pure, clear, water-white plastic, not less than three inches thick. There was a lot of it!

The inner door closed. Pop opened the outer. Air rushed out. He climbed painstakingly down to the ground. He started back toward the shack.

There was the most luridly bright of all possible flashes. There was no sound, of course. But something flamed very brightly, and the ground thumped under Pop Young's vacuum boots. He turned.

The rocketship was still in the act of flying apart. It had been a splendid explosion. Of course cotton sheeting in liquid oxygen is not quite as good an explosive as carbon-black, which they used down in the mine. Even with magnesium powder to start the flame when a bare light-filament ignited it, the canister-bomb hadn't equaled—say—TNT. But the ship had fuel on board for the trip back to Earth. And it blew, too. It would be minutes before all the fragments of the ship returned to the Moon's surface. On the Moon, things fall slowly.

Pop didn't wait. He searched hopefully. Once a mass of steel plating fell only yards from him, but it did not interrupt his search.

When he went into the shack, he grinned to himself. The call-light of the vision-phone flickered wildly. When he took off his helmet the bell clanged incessantly. He answered. A shaking voice from the mining-colony panted:

"We felt a shock! What happened? What do we do?"

"Don't do a thing," advised Pop. "It's all right. I blew up the ship and everything's all right. I wouldn't even mention it to Sattell if I were you."

He grinned happily down at a section of plastic stair-rail he'd found not too far from where the ship exploded. When the man down in the mine cut off, Pop got out of his vacuum suit in a hurry. He placed the plastic zestfully on the table where he'd been restricted to drawing pictures of his wife and children in order to recover memories of them.

He began to plan, gloatingly, the thing he would carve out of a four-inch section of the plastic. When it was carved, he'd paint it. While he worked, he'd think of Sattell, because that was the way to get back the missing portions of his life—the parts Sattell had managed to take away from him. He'd get back more than ever, now!

He didn't wonder what he'd do if he ever remembered the crime Sattell had committed. He felt, somehow, that he wouldn't get that back until he'd recovered all the rest.

Gloating, it was amusing to remember what people used to call such art-works as he planned, when carved by other lonely men in other faraway places. They called those sculptures scrimshaw.

But they were a lot more than that!

ASSIGNMENT ON PASIK

1: Crash Landing

The *Snark* hit atmosphere screaming, and Stannard grimly set himself to fight it out with the fins. A half hour since he'd used what jets remained in action, and the gyros too, past all sane risk. He had a good approach course now, though—it was a shallow, almost infinitesimal slant toward the planet's surface—but normal landing procedures were definitely out.

He saw seas and land and peninsulas below, so a random landing would be unwise. He had to depend on the fins and the *Snark*'s streamlining to gain some sort of control from the resistance of the air. He succeeded only in part.

The little ship bucked crazily. It jerked his head sidewise until he thought his neck would snap but he hung onto the levers. Then he realized that they were doing practically no good at all. The *Snark* bounced and the straps that held him in his chair dug into his flesh. Then the small space-car seemed to throw a fit.

It went spinning through some fleecy cirrus clouds a good four miles up, straightened out and skidded backwards, then spun and whirled at once and finally began to slow perceptibly and drop with obviously suicidal intent.

Then the tail went up and Stannard saw jungle below him, straight in front of the control room ports. The *Snark* seemed to decide that this was a good place to smash. It dived down with the evident purpose of splashing itself and Stannard over as much landscape as possible. At least, though, this was land. There was a sea not many miles away.

He let it dive to the last possible moment and then slammed in his jets. For one fleeting instant he wondered sardonically if all of them would fire again. The sabotage of his firing controls had been a thorough job.

But the *Snark* was consistent in its lunacy. The portside jets alone responded. The space-car made an erratic half-loop and for one instant pointed straight up. In that fraction of a second Stannard threw a full gyro-hold and kept her nose vertical despite the one-sided thrust.

The jets wouldn't hold her up. She sank, stern-first. Stannard almost relaxed. If the gyros seized now or the jets cut out—a trick they'd been doing for three days past—he was simply dead. He'd done everything there was to do.

He caught a fleeting glimpse of foliage rising past the side ports. Then jets sputtered erratically, he heard the beginning shriek of dry gyro-shafts, there was a crashing, then a violent bump, then a heaving, wrenching explosion. The control room split down the middle on either side of him, the whole scrap heap which was the *Snark* partly folded on itself like an accordion and partly billowed out like an expanding latex bubble— and there was a vast silence.

Stannard hung in the control seat with an expression of vast amazement on his face. The amazement was because he was alive. He didn't even seem to have any broken bones. But the *Snark* was not quite through. He heard a crackling, booming noise.

The fuel-store had caught. It might burn merely brightly or it might burn with the ravening ferocity of thermite or it might let go at any instant in a monstrous detonation which would blast everything up to half a mile away.

It was time to get away from there. Stannard broke loose the straps, pitched headlong and without dignity, scrambled through a gap in the plating and ran like the devil.

He dodged tree-trunks, panting, and came out on a patch of savannah just as the fuel blew. There was a sound like the end of all creation, a blast of air lifted him off his feet and hurtled him forward off the ground with his legs still making ridiculous running motions. He landed in a slough of mud. He fell hard. He went under. The mud tried enthusiastically to smother him.

He fought to the surface and cleared thick adhesive stuff from his mouth so that he could gasp in air. He cleared his eyes and nose. He floundered ashore to something solid, swept more mud from himself, saw squirming things wriggling frantically out of the stuff that still coated him—and began to swear.

Instants later he was out of his outer garments and ready for anything. But the squirming things were as anxious to get away from him as he was to avoid contact with them. They writhed and squirmed and inched themselves like measuring-worms, back toward the mud. They were two or three inches long and disgustingly naked flesh. They fled. He heard tiny sucking sounds as they regained their normal habitat and scrambled into clayey seclusion again.

Then there was stillness once more. He looked about and listened. In ancient days there had been tales of castaways. They were very glamorous exciting stories. But this was something else. In the act of estimating his own situation he grew angry all over again at the sabotage which had brought it to pass, for the ruining of the task on which he had been engaged.

He fumbled at the mud which was his outer clothing. He pulled loose and scraped off the belt, which contained a heat unit that, on occasion, could serve as a weapon. He slung the belt about himself and scraped further at his clothes.

He listened from time to time. The mud was infinitely adhesive. Presently he surveyed the mud-slough. There was a small, languid stream which flowed into it. There was a fallen tree-trunk which spanned it at its narrowest. He went out on the trunk and scrubbed off the mud with flowing water.

Four or five more squirming things came frantically out and dropped into the water. His garments became clean. He flapped them violently and the water-droplets flew away. He put his clothes on again, dry.

Somehow he felt better, though this was no enviable situation. Aside from the absolute failure of the job he'd been on he was in a bad fix. This was one of the planets of the Bornik star-cluster and he thought it was Pasik but he was not sure.

The whole group had been surveyed, a couple of centuries before and all the stars were yellow dwarfs, the planets were approximately solar-family types and vegetation on this one had been green as seen from space. Green vegetation plus seas meant breathable atmosphere and not too impossible a climate.

This could be Pasik, if he'd identified the local sun

correctly. But he wasn't sure even of that. This part of the galaxy wasn't much visited. Sometimes a hunting-party came through to land here and there and gather more or less improbable specimens.

There were races of low development on some of the planets and there was a vague commerce of sorts kept up by occasional traders. But the known facts about the planets were few. Men could live on them but few did. A castaway could survive but the odds against being picked up were so enormous that they were best expressed by zero.

A single castaway on a planet the size of Earth could escape notice even during a ninety-per-cent complete survey. When there was only one ship in years, which might touch only at one spot more or less at random, there was no chance at all.

So Stannard looked upon his life as a member of the human race as finished. Somebody else would have to take over his job.

In the stillness he heard the crackling of cooling metal sheets. There wouldn't be much to salvage from the *Snark* and what there was could wait. But still—

He moved back toward the site of the recent explosion. He came to trees bent outward from the blast. He went through them to stumps of trees snapped off by the explosion and piled in untidy windrows. He wormed through a passable place and saw the crater where the *Snark* had been.

There was literally nothing left but a hole in the ground. On one pile of shattered trees he saw a bit of torn plating. Caught among tree-stumps he saw a crumpled mass of metal. And that was all.

He managed to shrug. No stores, no tools, no food. Hopelessly isolated for all time—

Then he saw a movement across the clearing the explosion had made. Something glistened blackly among tree-branches. A thing came out of the tumbled, shattered trees. It carried a spear and it was about five feet high. It had a cylindrical body and glistening, jointed legs which looked mechanical.

It had two arms of nearly human size and two smaller, apparently specialized mandible-like upper arms and a head which was curiously humanoid without being in the least human. Another similar creature followed it, and another and another. There were thirty of them altogether. Some carried spears and others carried other weapons and several had bags containing mysterious objects slung over their shoulders.

They regarded the crater and made noises among themselves. Stannard froze. A man who stands motionless does not attract attention. This is true on all planets everywhere. Stannard stood still.

The sticklike men moved forward. Despite the angularity of their structure they moved gracefully. They peered into the crater where the fuel had blown a hole all of forty feet across. One of them pointed to the crumpled plating. More noises. One of them doubled up suddenly, and then was erect again. Others did the same.

They clustered around the crater and gesticulated to one another. Then, suddenly, they began to dance. It was a hilarious, unorganized, utterly gleeful dance. Stannard realized, blinking, that they knew exactly what the plating was.

They knew that a ship had crashed and blown itself to atoms and their doublings-up were laughter and the hopping and cavorting was the expression of exuberance that a creation of men had destroyed itself and—of course—apparently killed all the humans in it.

Then one of the stickmen saw Stannard. The dancing stopped instantly. All the stickmen—those with spears included—stared at him. They began to move toward him.

2: The Not-Quite-Humans

It was preposterous. It was absurd. Stannard felt his flesh crawl as the litter carried him swiftly through a narrow lane in the jungle which seemed to be unending. The litter which carried him had been hastily improvised but it was comfortable.

Stickmen carried him swiftly, some running with the flexible litter-poles on their shoulders, some running behind. At least one or two had gone racing on before to carry the news. From time to time the unburdened ones pelted up level with Stannard's bearers and deftly took their places while the relieved ones fell back. And the one who spoke English trotted alongside Stannard and babbled ecstatically whenever Stannard glanced in his direction.

"Pasiki have master!" he seemed to chortle. "Pasiki have man master to serve! All Pasiki love man master! All Pasiki glad to have master! Oh, master, we are happy to have master to serve!"

Stannard kept his face impassive. It did not make sense. That crazy zestful rejoicing dance about the scene of the Snark's explosion and now this babbling abasement—when the dancers first saw him they stopped short in their dance. They saw a man, alive, and a murmuring arose among them. Spears shifted.

Then a shrill voice called among the rest as they moved toward him. One came ahead. Twenty yards away he went down on hands and knees. The others stopped. The leader crawled to Stannard's very feet, and then abjectly lifted Stannard's foot and put it on his head. And he spoke—in English!

It was not speech from a throat somehow. It was actually the vibration of a diaphragm somewhere near where a man's throat would have been. But it formed English words. Now that same native babbled more English words, trotting swiftly beside the litter the others had made and brought for Stannard to ride in.

"Oh, master, such gladness! Pasiki do not know what to do without man master! Hundreds, thousands Pasiki serve with such gladness!"

Stannard said dryly, "How much farther do we go?"

"Not far, master," chortled the English speaking one. "We have sent for man-style servants, for man-style food, for man-things man master will want. Oh, such gladness!"

Stannard again had a crawling sensation in the back of his neck. If he'd ever seen triumphant hate in his life it had been the dancing about the crater where the *Snark* had struck.

And surely, if these sticklike, these antlike men— Pasiki, they called themselves, which would mean that this was the planet Pasik, barely mentioned in the Space Directory as an earth-type planet, friendly inhabitants of grade 2B, type exoskeletal tympanate—surely if these creatures had wanted to kill him they could have done so with their spears. Stannard reflected vaguely on tales of local deities to whom sacrifice was made. They did not fit, either.

"Where'd you learn man talk?" he asked abruptly.

"Man master, master," babbled the Pasiki, skipping in seeming glee as he kept pace with the litter. "Man master had many Pasiki to serve him. All Pasiki love man master! Our man master died, master. Some Pasiki went to serve woman master but they come more gladness to serve man master."

"Woman?" said Stannard. "There are men and woman masters here?"

"One woman master," said the Pasiki in seeming bliss. "Eight-nine-ten man master, master. You make 'leven man master for Pasiki!"

The trail widened ahead. There was a sort of glade with thick, leafy stuff for a carpet in the place of grass. There was a tent set up there. Stannard wanted to rub his eyes. It was not a tent but a pavilion—a shelter erected on poles, shimmering like silk.

There was a carpet on the ground. There was a table. There was a couch. There was a chair. The table was loaded with fruits and great platters heaped with foodstuffs. There were even bottles with colored contents. There was a stream of black glistening figures running out of the farther side of the glade where the trail reentered the jungle.

Each carried some object and every object was human. Stannard saw cushions, books, binoculars, pots and pans, silverware. He saw a sporting rifle being hustled out of the forest toward the pavilion. He saw clothing—all of a man's wardrobe carried piece by piece to be dumped at the back of the pavilion.

"Pasiki bring things for man master,'" chirruped the English speaking creature. "Everything our man master left, master. Not one thing lost! All for new man master."

Then Stannard stiffened. The things being brought out of the forest now were unbelievable. They looked like human bodies, except that they were carried with such lightness and such ease that they could not possibly be bodies. More, bodies would not be limp and boneless like that.

"Man-style servant suits, master," the skipping creature gloated. "Pasiki make master happy, master make Pasiki glad. You look! You see!"

✧   ✧   ✧

At sight of the litter the creatures carrying the limp objects stopped short. And then Stannard's eyes popped wide. The things that looked like human bodies were actually suits, of a sort. Like diving suits—but their look was utterly different.

The creatures who carried them put them hastily down. Then they struggled with them. They put them on. And suddenly, instead of glistening black articulated things that looked like ants or stick-insects, there were half a dozen startlingly human figures moving toward the pavilion.

When the litter stopped these oddities stood in amazing similitude of human servants to greet him. There was a figure which looked exactly like a butler out of an old book, complete with striped pants and vest. There was a valet. There were two footmen. There were two maids, similarly contrived.

They were incredibly convincing. Their flesh was lifelike. Their faces wore the reserved, detached expressions of perfect servants. Even their eyes moved and they had hands with fingers on them. The only thing that was not wholly lifelike was the fact that the garments on the figures had been molded on them.

The disguises—uniforms, servant suits—were made of some extraordinarily flexible plastic, on the order of foamflex, and each contained a hollow interior into which one of the insectile Pasiki fitted. With a stick creature inside the flexible creation stood erect and moved and looked human.

"Master," said the butler shape, "we have gladness! Welcome, master! You rest and eat, master?"

Stannard surreptitiously pinched himself. He got out of the litter. The food looked good and smelled good. The butler thing pulled back the chair. Stannard, his eyes a bit narrow, halted.

"Hm," he said suspiciously. "Did I see a rifle just now?"

An unintelligible sound. Then a glistening black creature darted from the back of the pavilion. It placed a rifle in the lifelike hands of a footman figure. The footman presented it to Stannard with an infinitely deferential bow. Stannard examined it closely. It seemed to be in perfect condition. He raised it and aimed at a tree-limb across the open space. He pulled the trigger. There were the normal violent surge of energy and the regulation flare of deep purple flame. The branch flew apart with a burst of steam.

Stannard lowered the rifle. It was a weapon all right, and in good working order. If these creatures had intended to kill him after some extraordinary hokus-pokus they wouldn't have given him a rifle with which he could kill scores of them.

"All right," he said grimly. "I guess this is straight. I'll have lunch. Then what?"

"Master's house waits," said the butler thing obsequiously. "If master wishes, he goes there. Or Pasiki make him new house here. Or anywhere. Anywhere master desires, Pasiki will do with gladness!"

Stannard sat down. The chair edged forward exactly right as he seated himself. A footman served him. There were two footmen and two maidservants and the butler. Their service was abjectly eager. It was such service as a sultan might have.

He could not reach for anything but it was instantly placed before him. He could hardly look at anything but it was offered him. And there were glasses filled and waiting. There were wines and Earth whiskey and a bubbling vintage of infinitely alluring aroma. He tasted one or two of the liquids cagily.

They were a bit too insidious. He had something

to think about. He began to have a queer so-far-unjustified hunch that this distinctly novel experience had something to do with the job he'd had on hand when he was shipwrecked.

"You wish music, master?" asked the butler, deferentially.

"Eh? Oh, surely," said Stannard, abstractedly.

His seat did not give him a view of the trail from which a file of black creatures still trotted, bringing burdens. Now he saw an orchestra file before him. It looked real. It had uniforms. He suddenly recognized it—a name band which had made visiphone records that, ten years before, had caught the fancy of half the galaxy.

Servant suits—plastic shapes into which the Pasiki slid themselves—reproduced the builds and faces of the original musicians. There were instruments. Music began. It was an excellent imitation of a visiphone record but after a moment Stannard noted that the movements of the instrumentalists did not match the music.

The sound did not come from the instruments then, but from that diaphragm each of the Pasiki possessed and which vibrated to make speech or sound. It was somehow shocking to realize it.

Then dancers appeared and Stannard almost started up. They were slim and graceful and shapely, and they had plainly studied visiphone records and learned the dances of human beings. But they were Pasiki, clothed in plastic suit-masks. Still, they were astonishingly like lissome human girls in a minimum of costume, dancing to sultry impassioned music.

But all this happened in bright sunshine and Stannard watched from a pavilion in a small clearing, surrounded by strange trees with lenticular leaves. And all about the clearing there were the black glistening bodies of the Pasiki, watching Stannard. It was oddly wrong.

Even the whirling, gracefully alluring figures of the dancers were foamflex, or something similar and inside each there was another glistening black body, faithfully making a marionette of itself for the diversion of the man who was—they said—their master.

Somehow, Stannard felt a little bit sick.

3: Lay That Blaster Down!

The days on Pasik were twenty-two hours long and it was on the third day that Stannard saw the girl. There were times in between when he doubted his sanity and the hunch that said all this connected some-how with the job he'd had on hand when *Snark* broke down.

There were other times when the temptation to complacent acceptance of his situation and the aban-donment of his task was very strong. And there were occasions on which he wanted to smash something out of pure perversity.

The Pasiki were irritating. There is something about abject submissiveness which revolts a normal man and anyhow Stannard could not forget the glee these same Pasiki had shown when they found a human ship had been destroyed—presumably with all its occupants.

The fact that now the Pasiki tended to greet Stannard's rising with songs and cheers and that they raptly assured him each lightest word was inspired and infinite wisdom and that they showed an enormous ingenuity in displaying the most passionate adoration—these things did not jibe. From time to time, at the most unlikely moments, he felt a crawling sensation at the back of his neck.

On the third morning, as he awoke, the butler form

hovered about his bed. The bed, like the palace to which he had been conducted, was shoddy and elaborate and falsely elegant. The building had plainly been constructed by the Pasiki under orders from a human being who considered that visiphone records portrayed the everyday life of aristocrats.

"Master," said the butler thing obsequiously, "man master comes to see you. In two hours."

Stannard rolled out of bed. The butler-masked Pasiki helped him to dress. Stannard wore the garments in which he had been wrecked including his belt. As he fastened it, the butler handed him another belt. It contained two hand-blasters in holsters.

"Why weapons?" asked Stannard. "If I'm to have a visitor—"

"Man masters, master," said the butler thing blandly, "always wear weapons to see each other."

He bowed to withdraw.

"But why?" demanded Stannard. "Custom or what?"

"Sometimes they kill," said the butler as if piously regretful. "It is not for Pasiki to understand, master. The master who was here before was killed by another master."

There was a mound, not far from this place, where a human grave was devotedly kept covered with blossoms of a lurid purple. Stannard had been told that it was the grave of his predecessor. But he had gathered an impression of the unknown—from his ideas of luxurious living—which had blunted his curiosity.

He had no morbid interest in the man who'd had all the foam suits of dancing-girl shapes made so that insectile Pasiki could dance for him in the appearance of scantily clad human girls.

Stannard said, "How'd the killing come about?"

"Who knows, master? They drank together and the

other master killed our master. You can ask, master, when he comes!"

"The same killer's to be my visitor, eh?" said Stannard. "And what happened after the killing?"

"He went away, master: He did not want our master's possessions."

"How about the law?"

The butler thing said blankly, "Law, master?"

"I see," said Stannard grimly: "Humans are above the law to Pasiki. And there are too few to make laws for themselves. But didn't you Pasiki do anything at all when your master was killed?"

"We asked what the other master wished to do, master," said the butler shape. "We wished to serve him. But he told us to go to the devil. Then he would not tell us how to do that thing and laughed as he went away."

"I see," said Stannard.

He buckled on the extra belt with two blasters. The Pasiki served men, apparently any man would do. There was no feeling of loyalty to an individual. One man killed another man and the Pasiki, who had been joyous slaves to the murdered man, promptly offered themselves as joyous slaves to the murderer.

It was somehow convincing. It looked quite a lot as if this fitted into Stannard's hunch about a connection between Pasik and his job. But there was no mention of a woman master yet. He'd almost forgotten the one mention of her that he'd heard.

He was at breakfast when, utterly without warning, she came into the room. Her entrance was partly hidden by the butler mask with its shiny-skinned occupant, who was serving Stannard his breakfast with elaborate ceremony.

Stannard saw the feminine form, but he had seen

enough foamflex servants. This one he had not seen before but he was not interested. He spooned out a morsel of a curious pink-fleshed fruit and put it to his lips. Then the butler thing moved obsequiously aside and bowed.

"Welcome!" said the butler thing profoundly. "Welcome to woman master! Pasiki have gladness!"

Stannard looked up blankly. The girl faced him across the table and she had a blaster in her hand. It pointed straight at Stannard.

"Good morning," said the girl in a taut voice. "I'd like to know something about you, please. Of course I'd better kill you out of hand, but I'd like to be fair."

Stannard blinked. His eyes went to the blaster, to her face. He suddenly noted that her costume was not a part of her body. It was not molded on. It had been donned.

"You—you're human!" he said blankly.

"Quite," said the girl. She was very pale. "And my Pasiki have let slip you were planning to pay me a visit, so I thought I'd visit first. Don't move, please! I'm going to take your blasters."

She moved around the table, keeping him covered. The human-seeming servants skipped agilely out of her way. She ignored them. Stannard sat still, his hands on the table.

"Don't move!" she repeated fiercely, "I've no reason not to shoot!"

She was behind him. The blaster muzzle touched the back of his neck. It pressed. Hard. She bent forward and reached around him to loosen the belt which held his weapons. He felt the warmth of her breath.

"Be still!" she commanded. But he caught the note of strain which was almost hysteria in her voice. "Keep still!"

The pressure of the blaster muzzle was almost

savage against his neck. Then he turned his head. Because of the pressure, the blaster muzzle slid off and past his cheek.

It flared as she desperately pulled the trigger.

A part of the opposite wall spurted intolerable flame. And then the girl was in his arms, fighting desperately, and he was twisting the blaster from her fingers. Flames roared from the ceiling as the blaster flashed again. The room filled with stinking smoke.

Then he had the weapon away from her. He stepped back, breathing fast. He released her.

"I'd rather not be killed this morning," he told her. "More especially, not for a Pasiki holiday!"

He gestured angrily about him. The foam figures—so incredibly convincing at any one glance—stared avidly at the picture of conflict between human beings. Other Pasiki—hordes of black, shining, inhuman shapes—pressed to look zestfully in through doors and windows.

"I've more than a hunch that they hate humans," he said wrathfully. "It would be only to be expected that they'd lie to you if it would make you try to kill me, perhaps to me to get me killed. But—is everybody here fooled by it? If my presence here's annoying I'll be delighted to leave! I didn't come here on purpose! These creatures aren't my idea of congenial society!"

He glowered at her. Then he turned and snarled at the Pasiki in servant suits and otherwise, who watched hopefully for a killing.

"Get the heck away from here!" he rasped.

Obsequiously the servants retired. The staring, inhuman faces outside vanished. Stannard tossed the girl's blaster contemptuously on the table.

"Sit down!" he said sourly. "I'll be glad to tell you anything you want to know, especially if you'll tell me a few things!"

The girl panted, staring at him as if she did not believe what she had seen and heard.

"You—let me go!" she said, as if stunned. "You really let me—go!"

Stannard went back to the pink-fleshed fruit.

"Why not? I've been here for—" he counted up. "This is my third day. I was in a space-car headed from Billem to Sooris. I was alone. I'd had some repairs made in Billem and they were badly done.

"Whether on purpose or not some fool soldered the firing control junctions instead of flash-welding them, and the vibration broke them loose. I landed here with four jets firing out of eighteen, all of them on one side. My gyros burned out too, trying to hold me on course. I hit out of control, jumped, and ran away before the fuel blew.

"I came back to find Pasiki dancing joyously about the crater my ship had made and then they fawned on me and said they loved me to death. They've been repeating that song ever since but I doubt their sincerity. I would like to get away from this planet. It isn't my idea of a sane or a wholesome atmosphere. Now, what else do you want to know?"

Her face worked suddenly.

"If—if that's true," she said unsteadily, "that's enough! If you were really shipwrecked and didn't come here like the others—"

He raised his eyebrows but his unreasonable hunch grew stronger. She was trembling. There was enormous relief in her voice.

"Sit down and have breakfast," he suggested. "By the way. I wasn't told you were coming. I guess that that was to give you an extra chance to kill me. I have been told that I'm to have a man visitor. Is he likely to have—ah—murderous intentions too?"

She looked scared.

"That would be Mr. Brent. He's the nearest. Y-yes. He'll probably kill you." And then she said desperately, "May I have my blaster back, please? Please! If he's coming I'll need it! But together we should be able to kill him instead."

4: The Pasik Story

Her name, she said, was Jan Casin, and she had been on Pasik for ten years—since she was a small child. The Hill Foundation had sent her father to the planet as a one-man scientific expedition. The Space Directory said that the local intelligent race was friendly to humans and there seemed to be no danger. But the Space Directory did not know of the later history of Pasik.

In the first century after its discovery it had been visited only twice, once by a survey ship which noted the essentials still printed in the Directory and once by one of the pioneer Bible reading merchant spacemen. He found no heavy metals or radioactives, reported the natives as friendly benighted and passed on to other scenes.

But a long while later—and this was *not* reported to the Space Patrol and hence never got into the Directory—the situation of the aborigines changed. A trader of a new sort landed. He was a typical trader of the later time, half merchant and two-thirds pirate when he dared.

The Pasiki, he discovered, had gemstones highly valued for technical uses. The trader bargained for them. But he and his crew were contemptuous of the sticklike, insectiform natives. The men were overbearing and rapacious. When the Pasiki grew resentful the traders seized a number of them and threatened to kill them unless they were ransomed for a full cargo of gemstones.

The Pasiki, in turn, managed to seize some members of the trader's crew for hostages. The trader's crew, enraged, blasted a Pasiki town. The Pasiki promptly killed the hostages. The trader departed, swearing vengeance.

Later the trader returned with five other trading ships. The Pasiki were furiously warned of wrath to come unless they made complete submission: They defied the six ships. And the ships set about a methodical, murderous slaughter.

Every town and every village was blasted. Pasiki by millions must have been killed. The gemstones wanted by the traders could be recovered from the ashes of blasted towns, and doubtless were.

And then the six ships set up fan beams—already illegal for any but Space Patrol ships to possess—and made gigantic round-ups of the survivors, driving them ahead of the curtains of agony until more thousands died of exhaustion and until the sobbing beaten remnant had lost all spirit and all hope.

When the six ships left the few survivors of the last enormity had been subdued as no race was ever subdued before. They had sworn terrible oaths for themselves and their descendants until the end of time.

They were the slaves of men. They were vermin under the feet of men. They would dig up the gemstones men craved and give them as tribute forever and ever and ever. And they were passionately resigned to it.

For thirty full years mine-slavery was their function. Then the gemstones lost their value because it became possible to crystallize carbon in any size and quantity wanted anywhere. There had never been many humans on Pasiki at any time and the Space Patrol had carefully been kept in ignorance of events there.

But when the gemstones lost value most humans left. Those who left, however, kept the secret of a planet to which any man could retire when troubles were close upon him and those who remained stayed on because they were wanted too badly by the Patrol to find safety anywhere else.

They turned the submissive Pasiki into domestic slaves. They built palaces and lived as kings over the scuttling little people. Before they died off they were joined by others, some their late comrades of the mining days and some badly wanted men who could pay slavishly for sanctuary.

Pasiki became an exclusive haven for the very cream of the aristocracy of crime. There was no law. There was no check upon anything any man chose to do. The Pasiki had lost the spirit to revolt. They abased themselves before any human, obeyed any order in blindly terrified haste.

Sometimes there were as many as forty or fifty retired criminals on the planet, living in infinite self-indulgence. But the death-rate was high. No man who was never crossed by any slave would submit to being crossed by his fellows. And the men were ruthless to begin with.

They killed each other in quarrels. They assassinated each other for fancied slights. They carried on insane, lethal, personal feuds. But none ever left the planet on the one seedy space-vessel which sometimes stopped by either to bring another fugitive or to bring second grade merchandise to exchange for the *dhassa* nuts and other produce still worth shipping, which the Pasiki gathered for their masters.

❖   ❖   ❖

The girl Jan Casin told this to Stannard, keeping her
hand close to the blaster he had returned to her after
she'd failed to kill him. She listened intently as she
talked, but she was not so much afraid of Stannard now.
Among the retired criminals on Pasik there was one
named Brent. He'd heard of her presence as a child
of course.

The Pasiki had an uncanny intelligence system akin
to telepathy, and everything that went on anywhere was
known everywhere at once. They told Brent of Jan,
then merely a child. He went to see her, playing with
dolls, and told her father amusedly that he would claim
her when she grew old enough.

"And he had Pasiki watching," said Jan, uneasily.
"When the Foundation ship came with supplies for us
he knew it first. He lured us away from home with a
message and he met the ship and told them that he
was a planter and that I'd died six months after landing
and Father a little later. So the ship went away and
never came back again."

She stopped and listened.

"I think someone's coming, judging by the way the
Pasiki sound talking to each other. Mr. Brent killed my
father when I was sixteen. He meant to take me but
I managed to get away. I made the Pasiki help me, of
course, but they wouldn't keep a secret from any
human who ordered them to talk."

"That made things difficult," commented Stannard.
He listened too.

"It did," said Jan briefly. She looked at Stannard with
level eyes. "But I managed! Pasiki are the slaves of any
human being who gives them commands. So I used
them. I had bearers. I had food. I even had watchmen
to warn me. And they'll never harm a human, so I was
safe from them.

"They wouldn't try to catch me for their masters, because I could always order them to let me go. I could only be caught by a human being in person and they—well, they get soft with slaves to wait on them all the time."

"I see," said Stannard.

"But I got tired of running away!" said the girl fiercely. "And I had no more books to read. I came back to my father's house to get books. Then my Pasiki warned me that you had come. They said a man master was coming after me. I decided to come to you first. I rather expected to kill you. I was tired of running away!"

"Natural enough," said Stannard. He cocked his ear, and thoughtfully drew one of two blasters. He made a fine adjustment at its muzzle. He put it on the table before him. The girl watched, and he went on in a natural voice, "I think I know something about a criminal named Brent. Quite a spectacular case, nine or ten years ago. Piracy."

They were quite alone in the dining hall. It was a huge space, thirty feet by sixty or more, with huge windows and decorative molded pilasters and an ornate ceiling. It would have made a good setting for a visiphone record production.

Outside there was the murmuring of Pasiki voices. They had an extraordinary range, as was to be expected from the fact that they were produced by vibrating diaphragms instead of vocal chords.

Jan said in a low tone, "He's here. I can tell by the Pasiki."

Stannard nodded. Without lowering his voice he said, "It seems to me that I remember the affair. He'd a trading ship and somehow he got arms for it. A tramp ship carried a colony to Verus and he laid aboard an hour after the landing. He beamed the men, carried

off the women and, as I recall it, sold the tramp ship
to a missionary society in the next star cluster. His
picture's on the refresher reel every spaceport guard
has to watch all over again every month."

Under his breath he said, "Talk naturally. If he hears
conversation—"

But that was unnecessary. A bulky swaggering figure stepped inside the far door. Behind it came a
smaller shape carrying a cloak. The manner of the
smaller form was abject, like that of all Pasiki servants
in foam suits.

Stannard nodded detachedly:

"Brent, eh? How do you do? You know Miss Casin?"

The bulky figure deliberately drew a blaster.

"I wish you wouldn't do that," said Stannard. "I've
something I'd like to say before the shooting starts.
After all, Miss Casin—"

The bulky figure raised the blaster. There was a
sudden spouting of steam from the heaped-up piles of
fruit on the table before Stannard. But there was no
corresponding purplish flare from the blaster the
bloated figure held. Instead, flame and smoke billowed
out from the cloak on the arm of the smaller figure.
There was a crackling explosion and the smaller figure cast down a smoking blaster and cursed horribly.

"You," said Stannard coldly to the bulky form, "drop
that blaster and get out of that servant-suit."

The huge form said obsequiously, "Much gladness,
master."

The larger figure split improbably down the back
and a skinny shining black shape came out of the limp-
ness which collapsed to the floor.

"Get out!" snapped Stannard. The insect-like
stickman fled. Stannard turned cold eyes upon the rows
of unhuman heads that again peered eagerly in the

window. They vanished a second time. He turned back to the cursing man who was nursing a scorched hand and arm.

"Amusing, eh?" said Stannard coldly. "You send a Pasiki on before you in a foam suit. He makes a threatening gesture. The man you intend to kill watches him and goes for his gun. And you blast him! Highly diverting! The trouble here was that I knew your name and something of what you looked like. Elementary, eh? Would you mind telling me why you intended to kill me?"

The swearing figure watched him with eyes that rage and pain made beastly.

"*Her!*" he snarled.

Stannard considered a moment. Small tendrils of steam still rose from the mound of fruit before him on the table. He'd adjusted his blaster to a pencil-beam for accuracy and fired through the fruit which had hidden his hand as he aimed the blaster and fired. Now he thoughtfully readjusted the muzzle to utility-size blast. It would lessen the range a little but fine shooting is not usually called for when a blaster comes into play.

"Hmmmm," said Stannard detachedly. "You've had her in your mind a long time. She's the only woman on the planet. But why the haste to murder me?" Then he nodded. "I see! Pasiki telepathy. Everybody else knows she came back to her father's house too. Are they making plans?"

"Blast 'em!" snarled the wizened figure of Brent. "They're all on the way here!"

"So you thought you'd get rid of me as a possible rival first," agreed Stannard. "Hm . . . There should be some interesting fighting if we stayed here. Rather messy though. I think I'll urge Miss Casin to return to a wandering life. But you—"

He turned his eyes to Jan.

"He murdered your father," he commented dryly, "and you more or less intended to kill me just because I was a man. Now's your chance. Why don't you blow his head off?"

5: The Long Flight

The picture of their progress was quite incredible. All about was darkness, the darkness of pure jungle. On either side were the slender tree-trunks, which were typical of the taller growths on Pasik. From time to time a thread of sky was visible overhead, thickly thronged with stars. Ahead there were torches.

Little glistening-bodied Pasiki ran on ahead, creating a shrill uproar to warn the carnivores of the jungle to draw aside. Behind them ran spear-bearing Pasiki, hating humans with all the passion a living creature can feel, yet prepared to battle to the death against— beasts only—in their defense.

Then came the litter. Pairs of thirty-foot, limber poles reached out before and behind, and fifty of the unhuman creatures trotted swiftly with their burden. Among so many the weight was not great and a minor horde of yet other Pasiki followed with various objects carried for the service of the humans. There were extra bearers to relieve the litter carriers from time to time.

The litter itself was like a rather wide easy chair in which two people—Stannard and Jan—fitted not uncomfortably, though a definite physical contact could not be avoided. Because of the springiness of the carrying poles the feeling of motion was rather soothing than otherwise. Stannard smoked reflectively.

"Somehow," he said, "I feel rather silly being carried like this. I don't like the idea of slaves or servants anyhow. And intelligent creatures shouldn't be beasts of burden!"

The girl, Jan, said restlessly, "I'm used to it. I certainly couldn't have kept away from Mr. Brent and the others on my own feet!"

The litter went on and on. Presently Jan spoke again, again restlessly. "I don't understand why I didn't kill Mr. Brent. Or why you didn't. My father, of course, wouldn't have killed anybody unless— Of course he'd have fought for me! But he didn't get a chance. Mr. Brent murdered him."

Stannard grinned in the darkness. "I wouldn't have let you actually kill Brent. But I wasn't sure you'd told me the truth about yourself. I thought you had, but I wasn't sure. Now I am."

She seemed to puzzle over it without result. Then she said, "What are you planning?"

"First, to get away from more fighting," said Stannard. "I've a rather good reason for wanting not to kill off all the other men on Pasik. It wouldn't make a tidy job."

He felt her turning in the seat beside him as if to try to see his face in the darkness.

"We'll get away," she assured him. "With the two of us to give orders and fresh Pasiki for bearers as often as we need them we can travel night and day."

"And," he agreed, "not trusting each other, the other men can't work together. I'd guess we're making ten miles an hour. That's two-forty—no, two hundred and twenty miles a Pasik day. I've a notion most of the others don't travel much. Right?"

"They've nothing to gain," said Jan. By her tone he knew she was frowning. "The Pasiki bring them everything they want. Of course if they knew I'd settled down somewhere and they thought I'd gotten careless—" He felt her stir uneasily.

"But I mean—you must have some idea of what you intend to do. I think that between us we could make— we could make ourselves safe. But of course, sooner or later the ship will come with other men or maybe just supplies the Pasiki can't make. If—other men come, m-maybe we could kill them too."

Stannard was silent.

"Not that I'd want to!" she added hastily. "I didn't even try to kill Mr. Brent. But they'd try to kill you because I'm with you!"

Stannard chuckled.

"I'm *not* bloodthirsty!" she insisted. "It's just that I— I want to be safe. I want—" she said desperately "—I want to know what you plan for always!"

He did not answer for a moment and suddenly she put her hands before her face in the darkness.

Then Stannard said gently, "You've been here ten years, since you were a child. You've never really talked to another woman. You've never seen a man you weren't afraid of—and with reason. Now you aren't afraid of me. So naturally you want to be sure you won't be left alone to be afraid again. That's it, isn't it?"

There was a long pause while the insect-like runners trotted swiftly through the darkness with a shrill and torchlit clamor going on before. The flamelight glittered on the chitinous forms of the Pasiki.

Jan gulped and said in a muffled, unsteady steady voice, "P-partly, that's it. But I—guess I don't know how to act like a girl." She sobbed suddenly. "I just don't know how! I've read books about men and girls and they were so different from here—I never could imagine myself acting that way."

"I assure you," said Stannard, amusedly, "you're

acting as femininely as any woman in the Galaxy could act. Anyhow, here's part of what you want to know. First, I'm going to stay right with you. Yes. Second, I'm going to contrive a way for us to be reasonably safe without having to kill off all the other men on Pasik. I've a reason for that. And third, I'm going to try to get the two of us away from Pasik."

"Leave Pasik?" she asked unbelievingly. "How could we? Only one ship ever comes here and it certainly wouldn't take us away. Why, if we got away and told about the men who hide here from the Space Patrol—"

"Maybe," said Stannard, "instead of having the ship take us, we'll take the ship. If—hm—if you can draw a map for me of a few hundred miles round about— the sea-coast especially—and if it looks all right and the Pasiki don't know much about boats and we have a little luck, I think we can get away."

"I've traveled more than anybody," said Jan quickly. "I can draw you a map. Surely! And the Pasiki don't make anything but rafts. They used to, but since they've been slaves they don't bother. I doubt if they remember how."

"Then I can almost promise you to get you away from Pasik," he told her. "I'd be pretty inefficient, with the training I've had, if I couldn't! And meanwhile, don't worry. I'll be right with you for just as long as you want me to be."

"That's—that will be for always," she said with a little, quick in-drawing of breath. "For *always!* You promise?"

He nodded but his thoughts were sardonic. He was the first man since her father had been murdered whom she hadn't feared. She had never talked to another woman. In the book sense she was educated but by ordinary standards she was utterly unsophisticated. She had full awareness of the bestiality of which men are capable. But her feeling of security was so new and so overwhelming that there could be no limit to her confidence in him.

It wouldn't be easy to justify that confidence. For a beginning he'd have to rouse the men to whom Pasik was paradise and make them desperate to destroy him. For another he'd have to take action the Pasiki could not know about nor understand.

He would need to create a complete surprise despite the Pasiki telepathy which spread news incredible distances in no time at all and at the end he'd have to risk his life and Jan's on a throw of pitch and toss.

It would be much easier to compromise and make a secure haven for Jan and himself and live out the rest of his life with multitudes of abject slaves to serve them. Jan would think that only natural.

But there was the job he had to do, the job which the wrecking of the *Snark* had interrupted.

The litter went swiftly along the trail. Something roared in the jungle to the right. Stannard had no faintest idea what it could be but the Pasiki trotted on. Then Jan stirred beside him.

"In—in books," she said rather breathlessly, "I've read about people who were going to—be with each other always and were very glad. M-may I ask you something?"

"Why not?" asked Stannard.

"W-would you say that we are—engaged?" asked Jan shakily.

He marveled at the ways of woman but he said gravely, "Why—we seem to be. If you wish. Yes."

"And it's for always?"

"Unless you want to break the engagement," he said, amused.

"I wouldn't do that!" she said quickly. "Oh, I

wouldn't do that! But in the b-books I've read—" She stammered a little. "S-sometimes they called each other—each other darling and they kissed each other. I wondered—"

He felt a little wrench at his heart. But he put his arm about her shoulders and bent over her upturned face. A moment later he said rather huskily, *"Darling!"*

The odd thing was that he meant it.

The litter raced on through the jungle. Insect-shaped Pasiki trotted swiftly. Torches raced ahead along with a high-pitched tumult which warned all the creatures of the wilderness to clear the way. A wavering thread of star-speckled sky wound overhead. Small articulated figures with shell-skins on which the starlight glittered ran up and relieved the bearers of the litter and it went on without a pause. A roaring in the dense forest fell behind. The two in the litter rode quietly, side by side.

A long time later Jan sighed a little, looking wide-eyed at the stars. "I like being engaged. It's nice!"

"And how many hours ago was it that you had a blaster at the back of my neck?" asked Stannard drily. "In fact, if you remember, you pulled the trigger."

Jan said ruefully, "Wasn't I silly, darling? I was too stupid for words!"

But Stannard reflected that he wasn't at all sure.

6: Counter Attack

They followed almost a ritual in their flight. The trails of the Pasiki were numerous and well traveled, with many branchings. But in three days and nights of journeying not one dwelling and certainly no village or city of the stickmen became visible. Before nightfall, each night, Stannard summoned the special Pasiki who invariably trotted beside the litter and as invariably was capable of human speech.

"We will want bearers to carry us through the night," he commanded. "Send messengers that they meet us."

"Yes, master!" chirruped the stickman as if in ecstasy. "Much gladness for Pasiki to serve man master!"

Then glistening-skinned figures darted on ahead and were lost to sight in the winding jungle trail. And presently there was a restless, glittering small horde of Pasiki waiting and the bearers who had brought the litter so far surrendered it and the new bearers went on.

When night fell there were torches flaring before, and the shrill clamor to drive away beasts. Stannard and Jan continued to move away from the neighborhood of the other humans present on the planet.

Then, when dawn showed greenish in the east, Stannard or Jan called again to the new runner beside the litter and commanded a message to be sent ahead to command yet other, fresher bearers for the litter. And presently there was another shifting mass of shiny insect-like creatures waiting to relieve this group.

Jan pointed out sagely that it was not only merciful but wise, because no bearers grew exhausted, and greater speed was possible. Three times already close pursuit by Brent or his fellows had failed because she commanded fresh bearers to carry her on while the men ceased to think of their slaves as requiring even the consideration of lower animals. Brent once had driven a party of worn-out Pasiki until half of them died of exhaustion. But they did not revolt.

"On the other hand," said Stannard grimly, "I doubt that they feel grateful to us for acting differently."

He did not like the Pasiki. Their abasement, their servility, their shrill cries of adulation—when he knew that they hated him and all his kind—alone would have made him dislike them. But he could not help despising them for the fact that they had kept their race alive, as slaves, rather than die as free creatures. It was that personal dislike which made him able to make use of them as he needed.

Riding in the litter was wearing. For the first twenty-four hours they went on without a pause. Their route was roughly due north. The second twenty-four they alighted from time to time to stretch their legs and to eat. They began to veer eastward.

In between they talked, and Stannard absorbed from Jan every item of information she possessed about the planet and its products and its people and its geography. At night, Jan dozed in the half-reclining seat with her head on Stannard's shoulder, while he watched.

And then he dozed as well as he could while she stayed awake. He made sure that they traveled close to the shore of a great bay she had sketched on a map she drew for him. Once he waked to find her holding his head tenderly in her arms while she smiled down at him.

He flushed and she said defensively, "We're engaged, aren't we?"

She had acquired an absolute unquestioning confidence in him. When his plans matured and he began to demand metal objects from the Pasiki, she phrased the commands for him so they would be best understood.

Once he took a copper pan and cut an elaborate form from it with the heat unit in his belt. He commanded that fifty duplicates of the arbitrary form be made and sent after them. Then he made other and smaller items—bits of some cryptic device that no Pasiki could understand but which they could make the separate parts for.

He demanded samples of Pasiki iron pots and chose

a special shape and size and commanded fifty specimens
to be sent after him. And Pasiki, in the hidden cities and
workshops which they prayed no human would ever
enter, labored to produce the parts required.

On the fourth day—they had passed around the
inland end of the bay they guided themselves by—he
demanded specific news of those who might have
pursued. The running leader beside the litter told him,
skipping as if with joy at the telling, that Brent had
returned to his own palace in great rage and that two
other men had essayed pursuit—not for revenge upon
Stannard but for possession of Jan—but had given up
the effort after one day's journey on learning that the
two fugitives traveled day and night.

On the fifth day Stannard called a halt to journeying. Their flight had been around the head of the great
bay and down its eastern shore until they were almost
opposite their starting point. But they were nearly a
thousand miles by land travel from anyone who could
wish to injure them, and the Pasiki would warn them
of any planned expedition against them.

Stannard chose a home site overlooking the waters
of the bay whose farther shore was below the horizon.
He commanded a cottage to be built. No palace but
a tiny place of two rooms, barely thirty feet from end
to end.

All this, he knew, the Pasiki would duly tell to the
other men a thousand miles away by land. But Stannard
was very particular about the roof of his house. It was
round and flat and pointed at both ends, and very
strongly built. The house had an awning before it,
under which he and Jan dined in state, and there was
a flagstaff on which a flag would doubtless be flown
at some future date.

When the house was finished—and he had had the

roof made completely strong and water-tight—he began the assembling of the devices whose component parts he had commanded to be made. He assembled them in secret with none of the Pasiki able to examine any one.

As he finished them, he welded their covers tight with the heat-unit from his belt. Jan gravely kept herself informed of all the telepathic information their Pasiki could give them of the doings of the men they had left behind.

Stannard had not expected action so soon but it was only twelve days after Jan's first encounter with Stannard, only fifteen after his arrival on Pasik, that important information arrived. Jan went wide-eyed to Stannard. A spaceship was expected.

The sheds in which *dhassa* nuts—a source of organic oils used in perfume synthesis—were stored against the coming of the trading ship were nearly full. The landing field which served as a spaceport had been ordered cleared of new growth. The one ship trading to Pasik was expected to land within days.

Ten men against Stannard—all warned and eager to burn him down for the seizure of Jan—would be only part of the odds. There would also be the crew of the trader, as definitely Stannard's enemies and Jan's pursuers as anybody else.

There was absolutely nothing that they could do without the Pasiki knowing about it and everything the Pasiki knew their enemies knew. They were plainly helpless.

But on the very day that—as it turned out—the trading ship landed, Stannard lined up fifty of the Pasiki in a row. He had them come one by one to the house with the curiously-shaped roof. He gave each one a single metal pot and specific instructions.

Each was to take the pot to a certain special place, dig a hole and bury it, leaving an attached cord out.

When he had concealed the burial place, so that even he would have trouble finding it again, he was to pull out the cord and bring it piously back to Stannard.

Each of the Pasiki had the same orders but each had a separate place to go to. They departed, running. They might hate Stannard utterly, and surely their tasks were meaningless, but they would obey.

Stannard waited. One day. Two days. Three and four and five. The trading-ship should be grounded for not less than ten days. Stannard waited out five of them. Then he smiled grimly at Jan. His task from before his shipwreck fitted in nicely with his immediate plans.

He summoned all the Pasiki within miles. He had them remove the roof inside and out in one piece— it was coated inside and out with foamflex—and turn it upside down. Jan, like the Pasiki, did not understand at all. They obeyed because Stannard commanded it. Jan watched absorbedly, blindly confident in Stannard's wisdom.

Hundreds of the black shiny articulated creatures struggled to carry the upturned roof down to the water. At Stannard's further command they brought the flag-staff and fitted it upright in holes which surprisingly seemed to have been made for it.

They brought the awning, and ropes which Stannard had ordered them to make and provisions and water. He shipped a rudder and they gazed in absolute incomprehension at a moderately seaworthy sailboat which was an artifact lost from their traditions. They did not even begin to grasp the idea until the boat was launched and Jan and Stannard were in it. Then they stared by the hundreds.

"I give commands," said Stannard sternly, regarding the horde of glistening black creatures on the shore. "We go to meet other man masters we shall summon from the sky.

"I have made machines, fifty of them, which send messages to other worlds.

"I made so many lest any one of them fail to reach its destined world with its message. I sent them away to be buried and to begin their message-sending. Even now the fifty machines send word through the skies to tell other man masters, to come and be served by the Pasiki, who wish no greater gladness than to serve man masters.

"I command that the machines be left untouched by all the Pasiki until the other man masters come. And now this woman master and myself go to meet the other man masters when they come down from the sky!"

He hoisted the sail. It had been an awning, but it filled. The boat pulled out from the shore. It heeled a little in the breeze but it made surprisingly little leeway. It was, in fact, a reasonably able small boat. The land fell rapidly behind. Jan looked at Stannard in marveling admiration.

"The Pasiki have telepathy," he told her drily, "but can they tell where we are when they do not know themselves? Or what we do?"

"N-no," said Jan. "But did you really send messages for other spaceships to come to Pasik? That is wonderful!"

"It's a lie," Stannard told her. "A space radio is a pretty delicate and complicated device. I couldn't make them out of stray parts manufactured by the Pasiki! But the Pasiki think I did. And how long before they send word by telepathy and our friends back there think all space is filling up with a howl for the cops?"

"Not long," said Jan. "It will be very quick! But why—"

"How will they take that?" asked Stannard dryly. "Brent, for one, is wanted for piracy, murder, and other assorted crimes. The others who came to Pasik by choice did it for similar reasons. They do not want the Space Patrol here. And there's nowhere else where they can be safe.

"The Pasiki don't want other men here either but they daren't touch those buried pots. How long before the men get busy finding those pots and digging them up to blast them before a message can be picked up from them? If they open one and find it a hoax that won't prove the others are! They have to find every one and smash it for safety's sake!"

Jan. blinked at him. "But still," she said plaintively, "I don't see why—"

He told her and she gasped in amazement. Then, with a curious grimness all her own, she checked over the blasters at her waist. Stannard grinned at her. She flushed.

"You can't tell," she said firmly. "Just because I didn't kill Mr. Brent when I had the chance doesn't mean I won't kill anybody who tries to kill you!"

"I was grinning," said Stannard, "because you once said you didn't know how to act like a woman."

But she did. She sat close beside him and shivered as the boat sailed toward the sunset.

The sky was barely paling to the east when the boat ran full-tilt aground. It had crossed the bay during the dark hours, and now Stannard was a little worried because he might be many miles out in his calculations. The map Jan had drawn him couldn't be expected to be too accurate.

But they forced their way through jungle and found a Pasiki trail and, within a mile, they came upon a little knot of three stickmen trotting along the path on their own private business. Stannard hailed them savagely and they knelt to him. Their regular master demanded extreme respect.

They led the way to the spaceport. Stannard walked boldly across the freshly jet-seared open space. The airlock door of the trader was open. He walked in with Jan crowding closely behind him. He closed the lock by manual control for silence.

"They've no discipline," he whispered in Jan's ear. "Trader!" There was scorn in the word. "Stay here. Blast anybody you see who isn't me. I'm going to see how many of the crew are on board."

But it was an anticlimax. Jan stood fiercely on guard until she heard his voice, very stern and very savage. Then there were scuffling footsteps and scared protestations. Two men only appeared, clad in the shapeless underwear of a space trader's forecastle.

"Sh-shall I shoot?" quavered Jan in a weak voice.

"No," said Stannard, behind them. "Only two men on board and they were fast asleep. All the others are out with parties of Pasiki, digging up the iron pots by telepathic instructions—which takes time—and blasting 'em to get them all destroyed as soon as possible. Stand aside, Jan."

He opened the airlock and drove the pair out.

He saw them running frantically for the edge of the field as the airlock closed again. He took Jan to the engine room and set the drive for control room handling. Gazing intently—she barely remembered the spaceship which had brought her to Pasik—she followed him to the pilot's cabin.

He strapped her in the co-pilot's seat and started the gyros, flashed the jets all around, then slowly and gently lifted the ancient trading ship off the ground. In fifteen minutes it was beyond atmosphere. In half an hour it was straightened out on a course for Sooris, which had been Stannard's destination in the *Snark*. In an hour he locked the automatic controls and turned to Jan.

She looked queer. Somehow upset and disappointed.

"What's the matter? Hate to leave Pasik?"

"Oh, no," she said uncomfortably. "Only—it seems as if something's missing. We got all ready for a fight. I thought you'd have to kill people and I was ready to kill anybody who tried to harm you and—and nothing happened."

"Except that we got away," said Stannard.

He watched her for a moment. Then he said amusedly, "Anticlimax, eh? But I'd have done a rather poor job of it if I'd let it end in smoking blasters and corpses all over the place. The Space Patrol doesn't work that way when it can be helped."

"Space Patrol?" said Jan, blankly.

"Me," said Stannard. "I'd been given an assignment that had me licked. There were rumors of a perfect asylum for criminals who could pay enough. I was set on the trail of it. I knew it was past Billem, and I thought it might be near Sooris. And I landed on Pasik by pure sabotage.

"But if I'd killed all the criminals who were supposed to be there and if I'd let the crew of this trader get away, why—I'd have fallen down on my job! And the Space Patrol doesn't like a man to try to guard too many prisoners. It's risky. So I—well—I locked them up on Pasik. Good rations and good care until a Patrol prison ship can come for them."

Jan's face cleared.

"Then—that's all right," she said relievedly. "You did exactly what you were supposed to do! I wanted to be able to boast, you know. Now I can!"

"Mmmmm," said Stannard, reflectively. "We've got

to do something about the Pasiki. They're all messed up for progress. Can't leave them to stew in their own fears and humans will have to keep off for a century or so.

"Maybe we can get some of those Miranians to take over and try to straighten them out. They aren't human but they're smart as whips. The Pasiki had a rotten deal."

He thought absorbedly. Jan stared at him. Presently she said diffidently, "Isn't the ship on automatic control now?"

"Eh? Surely!" said Stannard. "Why?"

"Darling," said Jan exasperatedly, "we're *engaged!*" They were.

REGULATIONS

It was only the dew-god making a monstrous noise off in the darkness, but Fahnes allowed his eyes to open and he halfway sat up. There was a shaded light over by Boles' bunk, and Boles was fussily arranging his kit for a journey to the trading-center in the Lamphian hills. Food, canteens, and the trading-stuff, these things would be left at the untended mart in exchange for a new lot of *llossa* fiber, which on Earth was equal in exchange pound for pound with platinum.

Fahnes made an apologetic noise as Boles whirled at his movement. Boles snorted indignantly.

"It's just one of them gods," he said scornfully. "They make a racket like that before dawn every mornin'."

Fahnes made himself grin sheepishly, as if half-awake. He knew about the dew-god. He had more brains than Boles, and he knew more than Boles about all the things that really mattered on Oryx, though he'd only been on the small planet five months. Because of his knowledge, he'd been awake for hours, fever-ishly debating with himself whether as a matter of common-sense he had not better murder Boles this morning. There were reasons for killing him, but it would be satisfying to let Boles come back from the Lamphian hills to find the trading-post in ashes, the Honkie village a mere black scar on the green surface of Oryx, and the supply-ship come and gone.

It would be amusing, too, to picture Boles trying to live on Oryx without supplies from Earth until another ship came to reestablish trade. Fahnes inclined not to do murder this morning, so Boles could learn what a fool he'd been. Meanwhile Boles regarded him in a superior fashion.

"I know," said Fahnes. He yawned, now. "But the racket does seem louder than usual this morning. I wonder—"

"Regulations say native customs an' religions ain't to be messed with," said Boles inflexibly. "You ain't paid to wonder. Quit it."

Boles checked off his equipment on a list. Then he glanced at the instrument-bank and laboriously began to copy the regulation before-dawn observations into the post's log book. Temperature. Humidity—always from 97 to 100 per cent in the day time, but sometimes dropping to a conservative 90 at night. Ionization-constant of the air. Fahnes watched with ironic zest. A lot of good these observations were!

He said impatiently, "I can fix the log, Boles. I'm going to do it while you're gone."

"While I'm here," said Boles dogmatically, "regulations say I got to do it. When I'm gone, regulations say you do it. You stick to regulations, Fahnes, an' you'll get along."

The unholy racket which was the dew-god off beyond the jungle seemed to grow louder yet. No man, it was said in the *Instructions for Oryx,* had ever yet seen a dew-god. But the native deities were of extreme importance to the Honkies, and the maintenance of trade-relations required that their religion should be undisturbed.

"Blister it!" said Fahnes, in private irony but seeming peevishness. "I wish regulations would let a man do something about that racket. It's tough to be waked up every morning by some kind of Honkie god with a voice like sixteen steam-whistles in different keys all going at once."

Boles struggled into his waterproof garments. On Oryx, where it never rains, one naturally wears waterproof clothing.

"Listen here!" said Boles firmly. "You get this! Before this post was set up, the Comp'ny had a survey-party on Oryx for months. You read the report. They studied the place, an' the natives, an' they made up regulations for this special planet. They're good regulations. You follow 'em an' you'll do all right. Same way with the Honkies.

"They found out, somehow, what hadda be done to get along. They didn't do it scientific, but like human people did back in the old days. They didn't call what they found out regulations. They called it religion. But it works. It's good regulations, for Honkies. You get the idea that Honkie religion is good regulations for them, an' ain't to be meddled with. Then you won't get into no trouble."

"I assure you," said Fahnes sarcastically, "I shan't try to make the Honkies atheists."

"Yeah," said Boles. "That's it. Don't."

Boles zipped his suit shut. He began to struggle into the various straps which would hold the articles of his equipment about him. Fahnes watched with concealed amusement. The Honkie religion was not to be meddled with?

The windows of the trading-post rattled from a sudden special uproar from the god. He, Fahnes, knew things about the Honkie religion that Boles didn't, that the survey party, apparently, hadn't found out. Gods which roared in the darkness could arouse the curiosity even of a man like Fahnes, who despised such stupidities as gods and regulations. Fahnes had taken satisfaction in breaking the regulations about Honkies under Boles' very nose. He'd set up a camera and flashbulb and trigger-string off where the dew-god roared even now and he, Fahnes, had a photograph of a dew-god.

The blinding flash of the flash-bulb had startled it. It had crashed into a jungle-tree in its flight. And at the scene of the accident—the crystal was in the pocket of Fahnes' sleeping-suit—he'd found a memento of Honkie religion. It had been torn from the headdress of the dew-god. The photograph of the dew-god told how many more such mementos the dew-god wore in his headdress. So Fahnes had planned murder for this morning, and was still in two minds about its necessity. The prospects before him were enough to make a man giddy.

But he wasn't giddy. His plan was carefully worked out. It was so brilliant that he'd honestly regretted that nobody would ever know how magnificent it had been. But there'd been two breaks—one a space-radio message and the other this decision of Boles' to make the trip. Fahnes could leave Boles alive to realize his situation, if he chose. When Boles came back, six days from now, he'd understand. Not completely, perhaps, but a memento—a small one, left on a stick where he'd be sure to see it—would enable him to piece out the story bit by bit as he tried hopelessly to live until another ship came to rebuild human trade on Oryx.

Boles was festooned with all the impedimenta that

regulations said should be carried on any journey on Oryx. It was still dead-dark outside. The dew-god still roared, though more faintly now.

"All right," said Boles curtly. "I'm off. Mind, you stick to regulations while I'm gone!"

"Just which ones do you think I'm planning to break?" asked Fahnes ironically. "The ones about leaving native women alone?"

Boles shook his head, unsmiling. Oryx females, with a greenish, semi-chitinous skin, were definitely not appealing to humans.

"Nope," said Boles heavily. "But you ain't got the right attitude. Regulations got sense behind 'em—even the Honkie regulations that they think are religion. Maybe I'd better—" He hesitated, and Fahnes knew coldly that Boles' life hung in the balance without his knowing anything at about it. "Oh, well," Boles said at last, and thereby removed the need for murder. "I guess you'll make out. So long."

He went out of the door and closed it behind him. Fahnes heard small splashings in between the dew-god's roarings. There was never any rain on Oryx. Never. So by dawn the jungle-trees were coated with dew in monstrous droplets. Boles, moving through the supple growths, marched sturdily under a constant waterfall from the trees his progress disturbed.

Then Fahnes laughed softly to himself. He took his hand from below the dry-blanket a man has to sleep under, on Oryx, if he isn't to wake in a pool of water. He had a bolt-pistol in his fingers. All the time Boles talked, there'd been that bolt-pistol ready to kill him. Perhaps—just possibly—it had been a mistake to let him live. But he'd gone off unarmed, anyhow. There was no need of weapons on Oryx. The Honkies didn't kill things. Their religion forbade it. And besides men had red blood like Honkies, and there was a religious prohibition against Honkies ever looking at anything which was red.

Fahnes got up and made an adjustment on the space-radio. It had been silent for four days—since he heard the first notice from the supply-ship that it was ten days ahead of schedule and would arrive before Boles expected it. He still didn't expect it, because Fahnes hadn't told him. And he'd gone off, now, and the ship would have come and gone and many things would have happened before his return. Now Fahnes readjusted the set for reception and dressed leisurely, smiling to himself.

Off through the jungle the noise of the dew-god died away. Fahnes glanced through the trading-post window. There was grayness to the east where the local sun rose. No coloring at all. Just light. As he watched, the white disk of the sun appeared. There was never any rain on Oryx, and the reason for that anomaly also prevented colorings in the sky at dawn and sunset.

Oryx was a magnesium planet. Magnesium was omnipresent on its surface, as sodium is everywhere on Earth. The chloride was the common compound. And just as on earth there is salt in some concentration everywhere, so on Oryx there was magnesium chloride in the body-fluids of the Honkies and the insects—there were no animals to speak of—and in the sap of the trees, and impregnated in every particle of the soil. The results were outstanding. A deliquescent substance is one which absorbs moisture from the air until it can dissolve in the water it has collected, and magnesium chloride is deliquescent to a high degree.

Everything on Oryx, therefore, attracted moisture to itself and held it. Everything on the planet was at least moist. If dust were formed by some extraordinary event, it could not remain dust on the ground. It would stick because of dampness.

So there was no dust on Oryx, and since there was no dust, there could be no sunset or sunrise coloring, no condensation of moisture on dust-particles to form clouds, and therefore no rain. And since there could be no rain there could be no brooks, ponds, pools, or lakes. The jungle covered everything, watered by dew which could only condense on solid substances because there was nothing else for it to condense on.

It was not a pleasant environment for men, but the Honkies lived in it contentedly with their soapstone implements and houses, and their elaborate religion with its ceremonies and taboos. Their culture was low. They had no fire, because there had never been lightning to show them that such a thing could be. They had no metals, because metals cannot be smelted without a fire. They lived a life of elaborate ritual.

Even the location of their villages was determined by a religious abhorrence of the color red. Cultivation of land with a red-clay under-soil was therefore impossible. But the local village was safe against accidental impiety. The fields in which the dew-god had roared were of a slaty-blue, sticky soil which Fahnes knew by experience was incredibly adhesive until the sun dried it.

He breakfasted comfortably. So far he had not done a single overt act save the muting of the space-radio, and that could not ever be proved. He had not murdered Boles. He could drop everything, make a formal report to the Company on what he had discovered, and undoubtedly receive a promotion and a few hundred credits a year more pay. He was enormously amused at the stupidity of which some men would be capable, when they could do as he was going to, and spend the rest of his life in the luxury and lavish enjoyment only unlimited riches could provide. But Fahnes, of course, was very clever. He approved of himself very much.

He finished his breakfast and looked out again. The sun was just two diameters high and the top of the jungle was a scintillating glory. Huge dew-drops covered every leaf. Each reflected all the rays of the sun. The landscape seemed covered with diamonds, save where Boles had marched. The jungle-trees he'd touched in passing were no longer jewel-studded. Their movements as he pushed them aside had made the dew coalesce and run down. His trail was clear. He had gone on to the Lamphian hills.

The restored space-radio muttered curtly:

"CHECK FOR ORYX TRADING-POST. COURSE AND SPEED HELD. WE WILL LAND AT YOUR POST IN THIRTY-TWO HOURS FIFTEEN MINUTES, EARTH MEASURE."

It was a repeat-notification from the supply-ship on the way.

That was the last thing Fahnes needed to be sure of. He buckled the pistol-belt about him. He went into the store-room and opened a soldered case in which a flame-rifle had remained in store since the post was opened. He cleaned it carefully. He loaded it from ammunition packed with it. He went to the store-room door and aimed at the jungle. He pulled the trigger.

There was a ten-yard circle of pure devastation. Smoke poured up. Then it stopped. Smoke-particles do not remain smoke in air which is super-saturated with moisture. Water condenses upon them. They become droplets of mist. The mist becomes rain. An appreciable shower fell upon the smoldering jungle-spot. The smoldering embers went out.

Fahnes grinned. He had not anticipated that, but it was amusing. Everything was amusing today. The sun rose higher and the glittering dew evaporated. It did not form a mist, but made the air actually thick to breathe. Fahnes remembered an authoritative lecture from Boles. Each dew-drop, said Boles, was a tiny burning-glass as long as it remained. Until it dried up it focused morning sunlight on the leaf under it, scorching its own support. So the roaring of the dew-god every morning, so loud that leaves vibrated near it, shook the dew-drops into flowing fluid which ran off. The Honkie crops, then, weren't scorched. But without the dew-god, the Honkies would starve.

Fahnes slung the flame-rifle over his shoulder, made sure the bolt-pistol was ready for action, and marched off toward the Honkie village. There were four or five hundred Honkies in the soapstone huts of the settlement. They were greenish in tint, and while their skin was not in actual plates like insects, it was thick and stiff and really flexible only at the joints. They were solemn-faced and quiet and lived their whole lives in impassioned absorption in their religion, as Boles lived his in devotion to regulations. Boles said that their religion was regulations, and that it made sense. But Fahnes had no religion, and he heeded no regulations save those he made himself.

The jungle dried about him as he walked. There was no longer the sensation of walking under a traveling shower-bath. It was—save for the wet thickness of the air—not uncomfortable. In half an hour he reached the slaty-blue soil on which the crops of the Honkie village were grown. He grinned excitedly and began to cross it toward the village. But he found himself slackening his pace to look at the soil absorbedly.

He realized, and chuckled to himself. He needn't look for mementos in the ground, here! The Honkies would have attended to that for him! He continued to grin as he pressed on. He was in open sunshine, now, with shoulder-high plants about him and the huddled soapstone huts of the village in clear view ahead. And he saw Honkies in the fields. They were working the crops. They used preposterously-shaped hoes and dug busily around the plants which formed their food-supply.

Out of the corner of his eye Fahnes saw them look at him, but he could never catch one actually in the act of staring. He'd expected protests, and the flame-rifle was ready, but whenever he jerked his head about, the Honkie he essayed to catch was absorbed in his agricultural labor.

This, of course, was unexpected. It was forbidden for humans to enter Honkie villages. The Company regulations by which Boles lived specifically forbade it under any and all conditions. It was a violation of basic principle. Men must not enter Honkie villages! It was forbidden by Honkie religion!

For a man to enter a Honkie village was sacrilege. It was blasphemy! It was crime! But the Honkies seemingly pretended not to notice. Fahnes grew irritated. He was ready to use the flame-gun to force his way in after what he knew was there. He was prepared to deal out murder wholesale. His intention to commit what the regulations called crime was obvious. But the Honkies feigned obliviousness.

They grew thicker as he neared the village. Male Honkies. Female Honkies. Smaller ones—male and female indiscriminately—scuttled about the taller figures who were adults. All eyed him furtively and knew that he committed sacrilege against their gods in approaching a village. None made any gesture, any actual sign, which really acknowledged his existence. Fahnes stopped short a bare ten feet from a male Honkie elaborately piling up dirt around the root-stock of a plant.

"My friend," said Fahnes ironically, knowing the Honkie would not understand. "I admire your industry. But isn't it a bit futile? Shouldn't you defend your gods and hearth and home? Don't you realize that I'm going into your village? Don't you even suspect I intend to rob your loudest-voiced god? In short, don't you think you ought to do something? Of course, if you do I will certainly kill you, but this pretense of not noticing me is silly."

The Honkie labored on, his leathery, expressionless face giving no sign that he heard the man's words. Fahnes grew jumpy, and his eyes turned ugly for no especial reason.

"What's the matter?" he asked, sneering. "You're afraid for that green skin of yours? Where's your piety? Here I am about to commit sacrilege against what I'm assured is almost important religion—and you pretend not to notice!"

The Honkie hoed on. Fahnes spat suddenly.

"To the devil with you!" he cried violently. He hated the green-skinned native of Oryx simply because he was about to commit a crime against the whole tribe. He needed resistance to assure himself of his courage and cleverness. He craved fear in his victims. He wanted to be able to live over, in his own mind, a scene of splendid derring-do as the source of the lavish luxury in which he would live for the rest of his life. "You're as big a fool as Boles! You and your gods! He and his regulations! To the devil with all of you!"

He glared at the lean, unhuman figure which

ploddingly moved on to the next plant and began to hoe there, having given no sign whatever that it knew that Fahnes was present.

Fahnes marched on, chewing upon rage. He passed other Honkies. Many of them. All pretended not to see him. He was definitely not afraid. The flame-gun could destroy all the Honkies on Oryx, if they tried to attack him. But he raged because he could not understand this embarrassed ignoring of his presence.

Then he reached the village. Every house was built of blocks of soapstone, carved to perfection and ornamented with elaborate designs for which Fahnes, at this moment, had no taste. The soapstone, Boles had said, had been brought on Honkie-back for fifty miles or more, just so the village could be built where there was no red clay under the soil to be turned up by an incautious hoe. It had stood here for generations. Perhaps for a thousand years.

It seemed to be deserted, but Fahnes knew better. The Honkies in the villages were not showing themselves, so that they might the more effectually pretend that he was not there. It was insult. It was stupidity. It denied the courage and the cunning and the cleverness of Fahnes, who had defied Honkie gods and Company regulations to go there and rob the god who roared hideously in the last hour before dawn.

He unslung the flame-rifle. He'd made his plans carefully, and more Honkies would not spoil them. White with tension and with unreasonable rage, he prepared to force the Honkies to play the part he had assigned them. The trick would be the swift and murderous use of destruction to clear the village of those who remained in it in hiding, and to force them to fury against him.

A brisk looting of the temple of the dew-god, facing him where he stood, would follow, and then a completely ruthless march back to the trading-post, using the flame-gun mercilessly to make his retreat secure, yet so sparingly that the maddened Honkies would yet have hopes of overwhelming him for his sacrilege and murder.

When the supply-ship dropped from the sky, the Honkies would be besieging the trading-post. His tale of a religious frenzy beginning with the murder of Boles—who was not murdered at all—would be convincing. Under regulations, there would be nothing for the supply-ship skipper to do but evacuate the trading-post, carrying Fahnes and the loot he'd have hidden, to the nearest civilized plant, where he would vanish utterly, with wealth incalculable.

And he'd demand that the skipper give the village a bath in take-off jet flame as the supply-ship rose skyward. With the tale he'd tell, that would be a certainty. It would prove his rage, because normally only a man in frenzy demands revenge, and Boles had an extraordinary popularity among the employees of the Consolidated Trading Company.

He fired. Coruscating flame enveloped the nearest house. There was the roar of suddenly-expanded air and of burning. A second blast of ravening destruction. A third—a fourth.

He saw a few, furtive, fugitive movements. The Honkies in the village had fled. They were still fleeing. His scheme was working as it would continue to work, and as Boles would some day figure it out with a single crystalline memento of the Honkie religion left behind for him, as an overwhelmingly lucid clue.

Fahnes now had the village utterly to himself. Swearing horribly for no cause, his throat dry and his eyes raging, he went into the temple of the dew-god to acquire the riches he knew were there. They had to be there. A brainy man like Fahnes had worked out, from a photograph of a dew-god from whose headdress a glittering crystal had dropped, from blue clay like the blue clay of Kimberley, on Earth, and from sheer logic, a brainy man like Fahnes had worked out an absolutely air-tight case proving that there was wealth incalculable in the temple.

The antiquity of the village only increased the estimate. Honkies had cultivated the blue-clay fields for probably a thousand years. Worshipping the dew-god, and finding bright crystals which looked like solidified dew-drops and reflected the sun as the dew did, surely they would make votive offerings of such crystals!

He wore strings of them upon his headdress! Fahnes had one in his pocket now, dropped by the god when frightened by a flash-bulb! Even the headdress would make Fahnes rich, but it was mathematically certain that for a thousand years every Honkie had devoutly turned over to the temple every rough diamond found in the growing fields. And a thousand years of such devoutness would mean untold wealth.

He fired the flame-gun again from sheer destructiveness, then went snarling into the temple, ready to deal out death to anyone who dared to dispute anything with him.

The tall Honkie squatted on the ground outside the trading-post and worriedly mouthed his few words of Terrestrial speech. Boles listened with an air of indignation.

"Your runner caught up to me an' brought me back," Boles said dogmatically. "Accordin' to regulations I got to help you out any way I can. But this is bad!"

The Honkie struggled again to convey his meaning in Earth language. Then he fell back upon his own tongue.

"Lord," he said with dignity. "It was the dew-god's doing. We do not understand. The man came through our fields, approaching our village. And this was against the Law, so all our people pretended not see, lest he be shamed. Yet he had no shame even in breaking the Law. He shouted at us in the fields. He went to the village, where again those who were present pretended not to see. Then he took an instrument we know not and struck houses with it, destroying everything."

"A flame-gun," said Boles, scowling. "This is goin' to make trouble. He busted regulations."

"He went into the temple of the dew-god," the worried Honkie chieftain went on with dignified emphasis, "and there are bright stones which look like the dew, save that they do not vanish in the sunlight. They are also hard, and we carve our bowls and houses with them. But often, because they are like the dew, we give them to the dew-god. The man seemed to desire them greatly. He tore them from the walls of the temple where they are set. And then he saw the inner part of the temple where the dew-god's holiness stays. We had put the most beautiful of the bright stones there, and the dew-god's holiness covered them. But the man desired the stones so greatly that he threw himself into the dew-god's holiness, and he could not endure it. So he died."

"The dew-god's holiness, eh?" said Boles skeptically.

"The dew-god," said the Honkie chief practically, "shakes the dew from our crops before dawn, so that they do not change color and grow uneatable like the wild things of the jungle. One of us, each morning, carries his headdress and blows his horn for him among the crops. As the dew falls from the leaves it hurries to the dew-god's temple. Each morning dew-drops by millions run into his temple and gather in a great, deep gathering which is the

holiness of the dew-god. And we place the brightest stones there to welcome them."

Boles blinked. Then he jumped.

"Holy?" he cried. "The dew's like a rainstorm,
shook off all at once, an' you got a drainage system.
Sure! You got a dewpond in the temple! A lake! A
swimmin'-pool full of shook-off dew. An' bright
stones were there?"

"Lord, the bright stones are covered by the holiness
for a large space," said the Honkie chieftain apologetically. "And the man seemed to desire them greatly. If
we had understood, we would have given them to him.
We bring them from a great distance, but it is our
religion freely to give one another the things that are
most desirable. If it is the custom of men to desire
those bright stones, we would surrender them."

Boles looked at the glittering handful of crystals he
had taken from the pockets of Fahnes, after the
Honkies had brought him back.

"It ain't worth while," he said vexedly. "They' what
man call zircons. They' pretty, but there ain't any value
to 'em for trade. They' just hard enough to use as tools
to cut soapstones. Fahnes thought they were diamonds,
I guess. When he saw a swimming-pool carpeted with
diamonds on the bottom he went outa his head. He
dived for 'em. An' the pool's prob'ly deeper than it
looks. He hopped in to grab zircons he thought was
diamonds, an' there wasn't any steps like a swimmin'-
pool should have, an' he couldn't get out again. So he
drowned—on Oryx, where it never rains. Good grief!"

"The dew-god destroyed him because he broke the
law," said the Honkie respectfully.

"He died because he was a fool who didn't keep to
regulations," said Boles caustically.

There was a booming noise overhead. It grew and

grew in volume. It became a monstrous roar. It was so loud that the leaves of the jungle-trees quivered.

The supply-ship descended smoothly, creating a tumult which seemed to shake the very ground. And Boles stood up and clenched his fists in the ultimate of exasperation.

"He musta known this!" Boles cried furiously. "He knew the ship was comin' in ahead of schedule. It was his job to listen on space-radio when news comes through. But he didn't tell me, an' me with no stuff packed for shipment an' due to catch tarnation for holdin' up the ship! Blast him! It's his fault. He shoulda kept to regulations."

THE SKIT-TREE PLANET

The communicator-phone set up a clamor when the sky was just beginning to gray in what, on this as yet unnamed planet, they called the east because the local sun rose there. The call-wave had turned on the set and Wentworth kicked off his blankets and stumbled from his bunk in the atmosphere-flier, and went sleepily forward to answer. He pushed the answer-stud and said wearily:

"Hello! What's the trouble? . . . Talk louder, there's some static. . . . Oh. . . . No, there's no trouble. Why should there be? . . . The devil I'm late reporting! Haynes and I obeyed orders and tried to find the end of a confounded skit-tree plantation. We chased our tails all day long, but we made so much westing that we gained a couple of hours light. So it isn't sunrise yet, where we are. . . ." He yawned. "Oh, we set down the flier on a sort of dam and went to sleep. . . . No, nothing happened. We're used to feeling creepy. We thrive on it. Haynes says he's going to do a sculpture group of a skit-tree planter which will be just

an eye peeking around a tree-trunk.... No! Dammit,
no! We photographed a couple of hundred thousand
square miles of skit-trees growing in neat rows, and
we photographed dams, and canals, and a whole irrigation system, but not a sign of a living creature....
No cities, no houses, no ruins, no nothing.... I've
got a theory, McRae, about what happened to the
skit-tree planters." He yawned again. "Yeah. I think
they built up a magnificent civilization and then found
a snark.... Snark! S-N-A-R-K.... Yes. And the snark
was a boojum." He paused. "So they silently faded
away."

He grinned at the profanity that came out of the
communicator speaker. Then McRae cut off, back at
the irreverently nicknamed *Galloping Cow,* which was
the base ship of the Extra-Solarian Research Institute
expedition to this star-cluster. Wentworth stretched, and
looked out of the atmosphere-flier's windows. He
absently noticed that the static on the communication-
set kept up, which was rather odd on an FM receiver.
But before the fact could have any meaning, he saw
something in motion in the pale gray light of dawn.
He squinted. Then he caught his breath.

He stood frozen until the moving object vanished.
It moved, somehow, as if it carried something. But it
was bigger than the *Galloping Cow*! Only after it
vanished did he breathe again, and then he licked his
lips and blinked.

Haynes' voice came sleepily from the bunk-space of
the flier.

"What's from the *Galloping Cow*? Planning to push
off for Earth?"

Wentworth took a deep breath and stared where the
moving thing had gone out of sight. Then he said very
quietly:

"No.... McRae was worried because we hadn't

reported. It's two hours after sunrise back where the ship is." He swallowed. "Want to get up now?"

"I could do with coffee," said Haynes, "pending a start for home."

Wentworth heard him drop his feet to the floor. And Wentworth pinched himself and winced, and swallowed again, and then twisted the opener of a beverage can labeled "Coffee" and it began to make bubbling noises. He put it aside to heat and brew itself, and pulled out two breakfast-rations. He put them in the readier. Then he stared again out the flier's window.

The light outside grew stronger. To the north—if where the sun rose was east—a low but steep range of mountains began just beyond the spot where the flier had landed for the night. It had settled down on a patently artificial embankment of earth, some fifty feet high, that ran out toward the skit-tree sea from one of the lower mountain spurs. The moving thing had gone into those mountains, as if it carried something.

Haynes came forward, yawning.

"I feel," he said, and yawned again, "as if this were going to be a good day. I wish I had some clay to mess with. I might even do a portrait bust of you, Wentworth, lacking a prettier model."

"Keep an eye out the window," said Wentworth, "and meanwhile you might set the table."

He went back to his bunk and dressed quickly. His expression was blank and incredulous. Again, once, he pinched himself. But he was awake. He went back to where steaming coffee and the breakfast-platters waited on the board normally used for navigation.

The communication-set still emitted static—curiously steady, scratchy noise that should not have come in on a frequency-modulation set at all, and especially should not have come in on a planet which had plainly once been inhabited, but whose every inhabitant and every

artifact had vanished utterly. Habitation was so evident,
and seemed to have been so recent, that most of the
members of the expedition felt a creepy sensation as
if eyes were watching them all the time. But that was
absurd, of course.

Haynes ate his chilled fruit. The readier had thawed
the frozen fruit, and not only thawed but cooked the
rest of breakfast. Wentworth drank a preliminary cup
of coffee.

"I've just had an unsettling experience, Haynes," he
said carefully. "Do I look unusually cracked, to you?"

"Not for you," said Haynes. "Not even for any man
who not only isn't married but isn't even engaged. I
attribute my splendid mental health to the fact that
I'm going to get married as soon as we get back to
Earth. Have I mentioned it before?"

Wentworth ignored the question.

"Something's turned up—with a reason back of it,"
he said in a queer tone. "Check me on this. We found
the first skit-trees on Cetis Alpha Three. They grew
in neat rows that stretched out for miles and miles.
They had patently been planted by somebody who
knew what he was doing, and why. We found dams,
and canals, and a complete irrigation system. We found
places where ground had been terraced and graded,
and where various trees and plants grew in what looked
like a cockeyed form of decorative planting. Those
clearings could have been sites for cities, only there
were no houses or ruins, or any sign that anything had
ever been built there. We hunted that planet with a
fine-toothed comb, and we'd every reason to believe
it had recently been inhabited by a highly civilized
race—but we never found so much as a chipped rock
or a brick or any shaped piece of metal or stone to
prove it. A civilization had existed, and it had vanished,
and when it vanished it took away everything it had

worked with—except that it didn't tear up its plantings or put back the dirt it had moved. Right?"

"Put dispassionately," said Haynes cheerfully, "you sound like you're crazy. But you're stating facts. Okay so far."

"McRae tore his hair," Wentworth went on, "because he couldn't take back anything but photographs. Oh, you did a very fine sculpture of a skit-tree fruit, but we froze some real ones for samples, anyhow. We went on to another solar system. And on a planet there we found skit-trees planted in neat rows reaching for miles and miles, and dams, and canals, and cleared places—and nothing else. McRae frothed at the mouth with frustration. Some not-human race had space-travel. Eh?"

Haynes took a cup of coffee.

"The inference," he agreed, "was made unanimously by all the personnel of the *Galloping Cow*."

Wentworth glanced nervously out the flier window.

"We kept on going. On nine planets in seven solar systems we found skit-tree plantations with rows up to six and seven hundred miles long—following great-circle courses, by the way—and dams and irrigation systems. Whoever planted those skit-trees had space-travel on an interstellar scale, because the two farthest of the planets were two hundred light-years apart. But we've never found a single artifact of the race that planted the skit-trees."

"True," said Haynes. "Too true! If we'd loaded up the ship with souvenirs of the first non-human civilized race ever to be discovered, we'd have headed for home and I'd be a married man now."

Wentworth said painfully:

"Listen! Could it be that we never found any artifacts because there weren't any? Could it be that a creature—a monstrous creature—could have developed instincts that led it to make dams and canals like beavers do, and plantings like some kinds of ants do, only with the sort of geometric precision that is characteristic of a spider's web? Could we have misread mere specialized instinct as intelligence?"

Haynes blinked.

"Could be— No. Seven solar systems. Two hundred light-years. A specific species, obviously originating on only one planet, spread out over two hundred light-years. Not unless your animal could do space-travel and carry skit-tree seeds with him. What gave you that idea?"

"I saw something," said Wentworth. He took another deep breath. "I'm not going to tell you what it was like, I don't really believe it myself. And I am scared green! But I wanted to clear that away before I mentioned— this. Listen!"

He waved his hand at the communicator-set. Static came out of its speaker in a clacking, monotonous, but continuous turned-down din.

Haynes listened.

"What the—? We shouldn't get that kind of stuff on a frequency-modulation set!"

"We shouldn't. Something's making it. Maybe what I saw was—domesticated. In any case, I'm going to go out and look for its tracks where I saw it moving."

"You? Not we? What's the matter with both of us?"

Wentworth shook his head.

"I'll take a flame-pistol—though running-shoes would be more practical. You can hover overhead, if you like. But don't try to be heroic, Haynes!"

Haynes whistled.

"How about air reconnaissance first?" he demanded. "We can look for tracks with a telescope. If we see a jabberwock or something on that order, we can skip for the blue. If we don't find anything from the air, all right. But a preliminary scout from aloft!"

Wentworth licked his lips.

"That might be sensible," he admitted, "but the damned thing scared me so that I've got to face it sooner or later. All right. Clear away this stuff and I'll take the ship up."

While Haynes slid the cups and platters into the refuse-disposal unit, he seated himself in the pilot's seat, turned off the watch-dog circuit that would have waked them if anything living had come within a hundred yards of the flier during the night-time, and gave the jets a warming-up flow of fuel. Thirty seconds later the flier lifted smoothly and leveled off to hover at four hundred feet. Wentworth took bearings on their landing-place. There were no other landmarks that would serve for keeping the flier stationary.

The skit-trees began where the ground grew fairly level, and they went on beyond the horizon. They were clumps of thin and brittle stalks which rose straight up for eighty feet and then branched out and bore copious quantities of a fruit for which no human being could imagine any possible use. Each clump of trees was a geometrically perfect circle sixty feet in diameter. There was always just ninety-two feet between clumps. They reached out in rows far beyond the limit of vision. Only the day before, the flier had covered fifteen hundred miles of westing without coming to the end of this particular planting.

With the flier hovering, Wentworth used a high-power telescope to search below. He hunted for long, long minutes, examining minutely every square foot of half a dozen between-clump aisles without result. There was no sign of the passage of any creature, much less of the apparition he would much rather not believe in.

"I think," he said reluctantly, "I'm going to have to go down and hunt on foot. Maybe there wasn't anything. Maybe I'm crazy."

Haynes said mildly:

"Speaking of craziness, is or isn't that city yonder a delusion?"

He pointed, and Wentworth jerked about. Many, many miles away, something reared upward beyond the horizon. It was indubitably a city—and they had searched nine planets over without finding a single scrap of chipped stone to prove the reality of the skit-tree planters. Wentworth could see separate pinnacles and what looked like skyways connecting them far above-ground. He snapped his camera to his binoculars and focused them—and of course the camera with them. He saw architectural details of bewildering complexity. He snapped the shutter of his camera.

"That," said Wentworth, "gets top priority. There's no doubt about this!"

The thing he had seen before sunrise was so completely incredible that it was easier to question his vision than to believe in it. He flung over the jet-controls so that the drive jets took the fuel from the supporting ones. The flier went roaring toward the far-away city.

"Take over," he told Haynes. "I'm going to call McRae back. He'll break down and cry with joy."

He pushed the call-button. Seconds later a voice came out of the communicator, muffled and made indistinct by the roar of the jets. Wentworth reported. He turned a tiny television scanner on the huge, lacy construction rising from a site still beyond the horizon. McRae's shout of satisfaction was louder than the jets. He bellowed and cut off instantly.

"The *Galloping Cow,*" said Wentworth, "is shoving off. McRae's giving this position and telling all mapping-parties to make for it. And he'll climb out of atmosphere to get here fast. He wants to see that city!"

The flier wobbled, as Haynes' hands on the controls wobbled.

"What city?" he asked in an odd voice.

Wentworth stared unbelievingly. There was nothing in sight but the lunatic rows of skit-trees, stretching out with absolutely mechanical exactitude to the limit of vision on the right, on the left, ahead, and behind to the very base of the mountains. There simply wasn't any city. Wentworth gaped.

"Pull that film out of the camera. Take a look at it. Were we seeing things?"

Haynes pulled out the already-developed film. The city showed plainly. It had gone on television to the *Galloping Cow*, too. It had not been an illusion. Wentworth pushed the call-button again as the flier went on toward a vanished destination. After a moment he swore.

"McRae lost no time! He's out of air already, and our set won't reach him. —Where'd that city go?"

He set the supersonic collision alarm in action, then the radar. They revealed nothing. The city simply no longer existed.

They searched incredulously for twenty minutes, at four hundred miles an hour. The radar picked up nothing. The collision-alarm picked up no echoes.

"It was here!" growled Wentworth. "We'll go back and start over!"

He sent the flier hurtling back toward the hills and the embankment where it had rested during the night. The communicator rasped a sudden furious burst of static. Wentworth, for no reason whatever, jerked his eyes behind. The city was there again.

Haynes photographed it feverishly as the flier banked and whirled back toward it. For a full minute it was in plain view, and the static was loud. Then the static cut off. Simultaneously, the city vanished once more.

Again a crazy circling. But the utterly monotonous landscape below showed no sign of a city-site, and it was impossible to be sure that the flier actually quartered the ground below, or whether it circled over the same spot again and again, or what.

"If McRae turns up in the *Galloping Cow*," said Haynes, "and doesn't find a damned thing, maybe he'll think we've all gone crazy and had better go home. And then—"

"Then you'll get married!" said Wentworth savagely. "Skip it! I've got an idea! Back to the mountains once more. . . ."

The flier whirled yet again and sped back toward its night's resting-place. Ten miles from it, and five thousand feet up, the static began still again. Wentworth kicked a smoke-bomb release and whirled the flier about so sharply that his head snapped forward from the sudden centrifugal force. There was the city. The flier roared straight for it. Static rattled out of the communicator. One minute. Two. He kicked the smoke-bomb release again. Already the first bomb had hit ground and ignited. A billowing mass of smoke welled up from its position. The second reached ground and made a second smoke-signal. Ten miles on, he dropped a third. The smoke-signals would burn for an hour, and gave him a perfect line on the vanishing city. This time it did not vanish. It grew larger and larger, and details appeared, and more details. . . .

It was a unit; a design of infinite complexity, but so perfectly integrated that it was a single design. Story upon story, with far-flung skyways connecting its turrets, it was a vision of completely alien beauty. It rose ten thousand feet from the skit-trees about its base. Its base was two miles square.

"They built high," said Wentworth grimly, "so they wouldn't use any extra ground they could plant their damned skit-trees on. I'm going to land short of it, Haynes."

The vertical jets took over smoothly as he cut the drive. The flier slowed, and two blasts forward stopped it dead, and then it descended smoothly. Wentworth had checked not more than a hundred yards from the outermost tower. It appeared to be made of completely seamless metal, incised with intricate decorative designs. Which was incredible. But the most impossible thing of all was that there was no movement anywhere. No stirring. No shifting. Not even furtive twinklings as of eyes peering from the strangely-shaped window-openings. And when the flier landed gently between two circular clumps of skit-trees and Wentworth cut off the jets and then turned off even the communicator—then there was silence.

The silence was absolute. Two miles high, there towered a city which could house millions of people. And it was utterly without noise and utterly without motion in any part.

"And then the prince went into the castle," said Wentworth savagely, "and he kissed the Sleeping Beauty on the lips, and she opened her eyes with a glad little cry, and they were married and lived happily ever after. Coming, Haynes?"

"I'll come," said Haynes. "But I don't kiss anybody. I'm engaged!"

Wentworth got out of the flier. Never yet had they found a single dangerous animal on any of the nine planets on which skit-trees grew—barring whatever it was he had seen that morning. Whoever planted skit-trees wiped out dangerous fauna. That had been one of the few seeming certainties. But all the same, Wentworth put a flame-pistol in his belt before he started for the city.

And then he stopped short. There was a flickering.

The city was blotted out. A blank metal wall stood before
him. It reared all around the flier and the men in it.
Between them and the city. Shining, seamless, gleaming metal, perfectly circular and a hundred feet high.
It neatly enclosed a circle two hundred yards across, and
hence some clumps of skit-trees with the men.

"Now—where the hell did that come from?" panted
Wentworth.

Then, abruptly, everything went black. There was
darkness. Absolute, opaque, blinding night.

For perhaps two seconds it was unbroken. Then
Haynes, still in the flier, pushed the button that turned
on the emergency landing-lights. Twin beams of some
hundreds of thousands candlepower lashed out, and
recoiled from polished metal, and spread about and
were reflected and re-reflected. There was a metal roof
atop the circular metal wall. Men and flier and clumps
of skit-trees were sealed up in a monstrous metal
cylinder.

Wentworth swore. Then he cried furiously:

"It isn't so! It simply can't be so!"

He marched angrily to the nearest of the metal
walls. Twin shadows of his figure were cast on before
him by the landing-light beams. Weird reflections of
the shadows and the lights—distorted crazily by the
polished surface—appeared on every hand.

He reached the metal wall. He pulled out his flame-
pistol and tapped at it. The wall was solid. He backed
off five paces and sent a flame-pistol beam at it. The
flame splashed from the metal in a coruscating shower.
But nothing happened. Absolutely nothing. When he
turned off the pistol the metal was utterly unmarred.
It was not even red-hot.

Haynes said absurdly:

"The sleeping beauty woke up, Wentworth. What's
the matter?"

He saw Wentworth gazing with stupefaction at a place where the metal cylinder touched ground. There was the beginning of a circular clump of skit-trees. And he saw a stalk at a slight angle. It came out of the metal wall. The skit-trees were in the wall. They came out of it. He saw another that went into it.

He went back to the flier and climbed in. He turned the communicator up to maximum power. The racket that came out of it was deafening. He punched the call-button. Again and again and again. Nothing happened. He turned the set off.

The dead stillness which followed was daunting.

"Well?" said Haynes.

"It's impossible," said Wentworth, "but I can explain everything. That wall isn't real."

"Then we ram through it?"

"We'd kill ourselves!" Wentworth told him exasperatedly. "It's solid!"

"Not real, but solid?" asked Haynes. "A bit unusual, that. When I get back to Earth and am a happily married man, I'll try to have a more plausible story than that to tell my wife if I ever come home late—not that I ever will."

Wentworth looked at him. And Haynes grinned. But there was sweat on his face. Wentworth grunted.

"I'm scared too," he said sourly, "but I don't make bad jokes to cover up. This can be licked. It's got to be!"

"What is it?"

"How do I know?" demanded Wentworth. "It makes sense, though. A city that vanishes and re-appears—apparently without anybody in it. That doesn't happen. This can—this tank we're in. There wasn't any machinery around to put up a wall like this. And the top wasn't heaved into place. It wasn't lowered down to seal us in. It didn't slide into position. One instant it wasn't there,

and the next instant it was. Like something that—hm—
had materialized out of nowhere. Maybe that's it! And
the city was the same sort of trick! Maybe that's the
secret of this whole civilization we're trying to trace."

His voice echoed weirdly against the metal ceiling
on every hand.

"What's the secret?"

"Materializing things! Making a—synthetic sort of
matter! Making—well—force-fields that look and act
like substance. Of course! If you can generate a building, why build one? We can make a magnetic field with
a coil of wire and an electric current. It's just as real
as a brick. It's simply different. We can make a picture on a screen. It's just as real as a painting. It's just
different. Suppose we could make something like a
magnetic field, with shape and coloring and solidity!
Why not solidity? Given the trick, it should be as easy
as shape or color. . . . If we had a trick like that and
wanted to stop some visitors from outer space, we'd
simply make the solid image of a can around them!
It would be made with energy, and all the energy
applied to it would flow to any threatened spot. It
would draw power to fight any stress that tried to
destroy it. Of course! And why should we build cities? We'd clear a place for them and generate them
and maintain them simply by supplying the power
needed to keep them in being! We'd make force-fields
in the shape of machines, to dig canals or pile up
dams. . . ."

He had raised his voice as he spoke. The solid walls
and roof made echoes which clanged. He stopped short.
Haynes said calmly:

"Then there wouldn't be any artifacts. When a city
was abandoned, it would be wiped out as completely
as the picture on a theatre-screen when the play is
done with. But Wentworth—"

"Eh?"

"If we had that trick, and we'd captured some meddle-some strangers from outer space by clapping a can over them, what would we do?" He paused. "In other words, what comes next for us?"

Wentworth clamped his teeth together.

"Get in the pilot's seat," he commanded, "and put your finger on the vertical flight button. When you see light, stab it down so we'll shoot straight up! If we trapped somebody, and if we lifted it, we'd have something worse than a trap to take care of them with. They'd do the same—and they've got what it should take!"

Silence. Haynes' voice:

"Such as?"

"I saw one Thing this morning," said Wentworth grimly. "I don't like to think about it. If they're bringing it over to snap us up when this can is lifted off of us . . . You keep your finger on the flight-button! That Thing was bigger than the *Galloping Cow*! I'll try to tip McRae what's happened."

He settled down by the communicator. Every ten minutes he tried to call the expedition's ship. Every time there came a monstrous roar of static as the set came on, and no other sound at all. Aside from that, nothing happened. Absolutely nothing. The flier lay on the ground with an unnatural assortment of reflected and re-reflected light beams from the twin landing-lamps. There were four clumps of skit-trees sharing the prison with the flier and the men.

Silence. Stillness. Nothing. . . . Every ten minutes Wentworth called the *Galloping Cow*.

It was an hour and a half before there came an answering when Wentworth made his call.

" . . . *llo!*" came McRae's voice through the crackling static. "*Down in. . . . gain. . . . no sign. . . . sort anywhere. . . .*"

"Get a directional on me!" snapped Wentworth. "Can you hear me above the static?"

"What stat. . . . oice perfectly clear. . . ." came McRae's booming. *"Keep. . . . talking. . . ."*

Wentworth blinked. No static at the *Galloping Cow*! When his ears were practically deafened? Then it made sense. All of it!

"I'll keep talking," he said fervently. "Use the directional and locate me. But don't try to help me direct. Take a bearing from where you find me to where a fifty-foot dirt embankment sticks out from a mountain-spur to the north. Get on that line and you'll hear the static, all right! It's in a beam coming right here at me! Follow that static back to the mountains, and when you find where it's being projected from, you'll find some skit-tree planters with all the artifacts your little heart desires! Only maybe you'll have to blast them. . . ."

He swallowed.

"It makes sense," he went on more calmly. "They built up a civilization based on generating instead of building the things they wanted to use. Our force-fields are globular, because the generator's inside. If you want a force-field to have a definite shape, you have to generate it differently. Their cities and their machines weren't substance, though they were solid enough. They were force-fields! The generators were off at a distance, throwing the force-field they wanted where they needed it. They projected solidities like we project pictures on a screen. They projected their cities. Their tools. Probably their spaceships too. That's why we never found artifacts! We looked where installations had been, instead of where they were generated and flung to the spot where they were wanted. There's a beam full of static coming from those mountains—"

Light! With all the blinding suddenness of an atomic explosion, there was light. Wentworth had a moment's awareness of sunshine on the brittle stalks of skit-trees, and then of upward acceleration so fierce that it was like a blow. The atmosphere-flier hurtled skyward with all its lift-jets firing full blast—and there was the *Galloping Cow* lumbering ungracefully through atmosphere at ten thousand feet, some twelve or more miles away.

And McRae's voice came out of a communicator which now picked up no static whatever.

"What the devil?" he boomed. "We saw something that looked like a big metal tank, and it vanished and you went skyward from where it'd been like a bat out of hell—"

"Suppose you follow me," said Wentworth grimly. "The skit-tree planters on this planet, anyhow, don't want us around. By pure accident, I got a line on where they were. They lured me away from their place by projecting a city. I went to look—and it vanished. I played hide and seek with it until they changed tactics and let it stay in existence. Maybe they thought we'd land on it, high up, and get out of the flier to explore. Then the city'd have vanished and we'd have dropped a mile or two—hard. But we landed on the ground instead, and they clapped a jail around us. I don't know what they intended, but you came along and they let the jail vanish to keep you from examining it. And now we'll go talk to them!"

The flier was streaking vengefully back to the embankment, to where only that morning, before sunrise, Wentworth had seen something he still didn't like to think about. The *Galloping Cow* veered around to follow, with all the elephantine grace of the animal for which she had been unofficially christened. She'd been an Earth-Pluto freighter before conversion for this expedition, and she was a staunch vessel, but not a handy one.

The flier dived for the hills. Wentworth's jaws were hard and angry. The *Galloping Cow* trailed, wallowing. The flier quartered back and forth across the hills, examining every square inch of ground. . . .

Nothing. Absolutely nothing. The search went on. The communicator boomed McRae's voice:

"They're playing possum. We'll land and make a camp and prepare to hunt on foot."

Wentworth growled angrily. He continued to search. Deeper and deeper into the hills. Going over and over every bit of terrain. Then, quite suddenly, the communicator emitted babbling sounds. Shouts. Incoherent outcries. From the ship, of course. There were sudden, whining crashes—electronic cannon going off at a panic-stricken rate. Then a ghastly crashing sound—and silence.

The flier zoomed until Haynes and Wentworth could see. They paled. Wentworth uttered a raging cry.

The *Galloping Cow* had landed. Her ports were open and men had emerged. But now a Thing had attacked the ship with a ruthless, irresistible ferocity. It was bigger than the *Galloping Cow*. It stood a hundred feet high at the shoulder. It was armored and possessed of prodigious jaws and incredible teeth. It was all the nightmares of mechanistic minds rolled into one and then magnified. It must have materialized from nothingness, because nothing so huge could have escaped Wentworth's search. But as Wentworth first looked at it the incredible jaws closed on the ship's frame and bit through the tough plates of beryllium steel as if they had been paper. It tore them away and flung them aside. A main-frame girder offered resistance. With an irresistible jerk, the Thing tore it free. And then it put its claws into the very vitals of the *Galloping Cow* and began to tear the old spaceship apart.

The crewmen spilled out and fled. The Thing snapped at one as he went by, but returned to its unbelievable destruction. Someone heaved a bomb into its very jaws, and it exploded—and the Thing seemed not to notice it.

Wentworth seized the controls of the flier from Haynes. He dived—not for the ship, but for the space between the ship and the mountains. He flung the small craft into crazy, careening gyrations in that space.

And then the communicator shrieked with clacking static. The flier passed through the beam, but Wentworth flung it back in. He plunged toward the mountains. He lost the beam, and found it again, and lost it, and found it. . . .

"There!" he said, choking with rage. "Down from the top of that cliff! There's a hole! A cave-mouth! The beam's coming from there!"

He plunged the flier for the opening, and braked with monstrous jettings that sent rocket-fumes blindingly and chokingly into the tunnel. The flier hit and Wentworth scrambled to the forepart of the little ship and leaped to the cliff-opening against which it bumped, and then ran into the opening, his flame-pistol flaring before him.

There was a blinding flash inside. The blue-white flame of a short-circuit making a gigantic arc. It died. The place was full of smoke, and something small ran feebly across the small space that Wentworth could see, and fell, and kicked feebly, and was still. A machine came to a jolting stop. And Wentworth, crouching fiercely, waited for more antagonists.

None came. The fumes drifted out the cave-mouth. Then he saw that the thing on the floor was a weirdly constructed space-suit, and that the thing in it was not human and looked very tired. It was dead. Then he saw an almost typical tight beam projector, linked with

heavy cables to a scanning device. He saw a model—
all of five feet high—of the city he and Haynes had
tried to reach. The model was of unbelievable delicacy
and perfection. But the scanning system now was
focused on a metal object which was a miniature Thing
with claws and jaws and armor. . . . It was two feet long,
and there was a cable control by which its movements
could be directed. A solidity which was controlled by
that ingenious mechanical toy could dig canals, or
gather the crop from the tops of skit-trees—when
enlarged in the projection to stand a hundred feet high
at the shoulder—or it could tear apart a spaceship as
a terrier rends a rat. . . .

There was more. Much more. But there was only
the one small inhabitant, who wore a space-suit on his
own planet. And he was dead.

Haynes called from the flier at the cave-mouth:
"Wentworth! What's happened? Are you alive?
What's up?"

Wentworth went savagely out. He wanted to see how
the *Galloping Cow* had withstood the attack. What he
had seen last looked bad.

It was bad. The *Galloping Cow* was a carcass. Her
engines were not too badly smashed, but her outer shell
was scrap-iron, her frame was twisted wreckage, and
there was no faintest hope that they could repair her
in the field.

"And—I'm engaged to be married when we get
back," said Haynes, white-faced. "We'll never get back
in that."

Less than a month later, though, the *Galloping Cow*
did head for home. Haynes, unwittingly, had made it
possible. Examination of the solidity-projector revealed
its principles, and Haynes—trying forlornly to make a
joke—suggested that he model a statuette of the last

inhabitant to be projected a mile or two high above the skit-tree plantations now forever useless. But he was commissioned to model something else entirely, and in his exuberance his fancy wandered afar. But McRae dourly permitted the model to stand, because he was in a hurry to start.

So that, some six weeks from the morning when Wentworth saw an impossible Thing moving in the gray dawn-light on an unnamed planet, the *Galloping Cow* was almost back in touch with humanity. Two weeks more, and the outposts of civilization on Rigel would be reached. A long, skeleton tower had been built out from the old ship's battered remnant. A scanner scanned, and a beam-type projector projected the image of Haynes' making to form a solid envelope of force-field about the ship. It was much larger than the original hull had been, there would be room and to spare on the voyage home. And Haynes was utterly happy.

"Think!" he said blissfully, in the scanning-room where the force-field envelope was maintained about the ship. "Two weeks and Rigel! Two months and home! Two months and one day and I'm a married man!"

Wentworth looked at the small moving object on which the scanners focused.

"You're a queer egg, Haynes," he said. "I don't believe you ever had a solemn thought in your head. Do you know what wiped out those people?"

"A boojum?" asked Haynes mildly. "Tell me."

"The biologists figured it out," said Haynes. "A plague. The last poor devil wore a space-suit to keep the germs out. It seems that some wrecked Earth ship drifted out to where one of their explorers found it. And they hauled it to ground. They learned a lot, but there were germs on board they weren't used to.

Coryza, for instance. In their bodies it had an incubation period of about six months, and was highly contagious all the time. Then it turned lethal. They didn't know about it in time to establish quarantines. No wonder the poor devil wanted to kill us. We'd wiped out his race!"

"Too bad!" said Haynes. But he looked down at the small moving thing he had modeled for a new hull for the *Galloping Cow*. "You know," he said blithely, "I like this model. I may not be the best sculptor in the world—as an amateur I wouldn't expect it. But for a while after we land on earth I'm surely going to be the most famous!"

And he beamed at the jerkily moving object which was the model for the hull of the *Galloping Cow*. It was twelve hundred feet long, as it was projected about the old ship's engine-room and remaining portions. It had a stiffly extended tail and an outstretched neck and curved horns. Its legs extended and kicked, and extended and kicked.

The *Galloping Cow*, in fact, exactly fitted her name by her outward appearance, as she galloped steadily earthward through emptiness.